Subterranean

BY JAMES ROLLINS

Altar of Eden

The Doomsday Key

The Last Oracle

The Judas Strain

Black Order

Map of Bones

Sandstorm

Ice Hunt

Amazonia

Deep Fathom

Excavation

Subterranean

Coming Soon in Hardcover

The Devil Colony

Subterranean

James Rollins

HARPER LUXE

An Imprint of HarperCollinsPublishers

SUBTERRANEAN. Copyright © 1999 by Jim Czajkowski. All rights reserved. Printed in the United States of America. No part of this book may be used or reproduced in any manner whatsoever without written permission except in the case of brief quotations embodied in critical articles and reviews. For information address HarperCollins Publishers, 10 East 53rd Street, New York, NY 10022.

HarperCollins books may be purchased for educational, business, or sales promotional use. For information please write: Special Markets Department, HarperCollins Publishers, 10 East 53rd Street, New York, NY 10022.

FIRST HARPERLUXE EDITION

HarperLuxe™ is a trademark of HarperCollins Publishers

ISBN: 978-0-06-206647-3

11 11 12 13 14 ID/OPM 10 9 8 7 6 5 4 3 2 1

For John Clemens

There are too many folks to thank for the production of this story. From Pesha Rubinstein, my literary agent, who saw some glimmer in the rough-cut draft; to Lyssa Keusch, my editor, who painstakingly polished this story into its current form; to my writing group, who arduously picked apart the plot and made it better (Chris Crowe, Dennis Grayson, Dave Meek, Jeffrey Moss, Jane O'Riva, Stephen and Judy Prey, Caroline Williams); and a special thanks to Carolyn McCray, for her support, criticism, love, and friendship.

And finally to two people for whom I must blame this all on: Thanks, Mom and Dad!

Great God! this is an awful place.

Found scrawled in the journal of the
failed South Pole explorer
Robert F. Scott

Subterranean

PROLOGUE

Mount Erebus, Antarctica

Blue ice encased the continent from horizon to horizon, scoured to a gritty shine by gale-force winds ripping shards across the frozen landscape. Nothing lived on the surface, except for grimy patches of yellow lichen, far older than any of the men stationed at McMurdo Base.

Two miles below Mount Erebus, through glacier, permafrost, and granite, Private Peter Wombley wiped sweat from his eyes. He dreamed of the fridge in his bunkroom stocked with a case of Coors. "This place is insane. Damned blizzard up top and hotter than a hooker's snatch down here."

"If you quit thinkin' about it, it wouldn't be so bad," Lieutenant Brian Flattery replied. He loosened his hand lantern from the transport motorcycle. "Let's go.

We've got three more relays to calibrate before the end of this shift."

Peter grabbed his lantern and clicked it on, spearing the cavern with a blade of light, and followed.

"Hey, watch your step there," Brian said, pointing his light at a crevice in the cavern floor.

Slipping past the black slit, Peter eyed it suspiciously. Since he'd arrived three months ago, he had learned a healthy respect for these honeycombed caverns. He leaned over the edge and pointed his light down the crevice. It seemed to go straight to the bottom of the world. He shivered, wondering if hell had a doorway. "Wait up!"

"I'm going to proceed to the relay," Brian said, pulling a transport sled into position at the lip of the tunnel. "You've got a five-minute break until I return."

Peter secretly sighed in relief. He hated those "wormholes," as the troop had nicknamed the smooth undulating passages, with diameters so small that a man could barely crawl through them. Only the motorized sleds made transport from cavern to cavern possible through the wormholes.

Like a boy on a toboggan, Brian sprawled belly down on the sled, head pointing toward the mouth of the tunnel. He engaged the throttle, the engine's roar echoing off the walls, doubling and tripling decibel levels. With a final thumbs-up, Brian shoved the throttle forward. The sled shot into the narrow tunnel.

Peter crouched down to watch Brian's departure. The lights faded as the sled roared around a distant curve. After a few moments more, even the sound of the sled whined down to nothing. Peter was alone in the cavern.

Using his lantern, he checked the time. Brian should be back in five minutes. He smiled. Maybe even twenty minutes if he needed to disassemble the communications relay and replace some parts. That gave him more than enough time. He slipped a joint from his vest pocket.

Peter set down his lantern and rotated it for wide dispersal to illuminate the area. Then he leaned back against the cavern wall, fished a match from his pocket, and struck a flame. He inhaled sharply on the narrow joint. Ahhh! Leaning his head back, he savored the smoke deep in his chest.

Suddenly, the sound of scraping rock echoed across the cavern.

"Shit!" Peter choked on the smoke and grabbed his light. He searched the open space, sweeping his lantern back and forth. No one. Just an empty cavern. He listened, straining, but heard nothing more. The shadows kept jumping in the lantern light.

All at once, it seemed a lot colder and a lot darker.

He glanced at his watch. Four minutes had passed. Brian should be heading back by now. He stamped the joint out. It was going to be a long wait.

Brian Flattery closed the panel on the side of the communications station. The unit checked out fine. Only two more relays to check. His support staff could have handled these routine tests, but this was his baby. The minor static was a personal affront to his expertise. Just a little fine tuning and everything would be perfect.

He crossed over to the idling sled and slipped into position. He twisted the throttle into gear and ducked his head a bit as he rode into the tube. Like being swallowed by a serpent, he thought. The smooth walls flew past his head, the headlamp guiding him forward. After a minute, the sled slipped from the tunnel into the cavern where he had left Peter.

Brian cut the engine. He glanced around. The cavern was empty, but a familiar scent lingered. Marijuana. "Goddamn it!" he exclaimed. Yanking himself from the sled, he raised his voice. "Private Wombley! Get your ass back here on the double!"

His words echoed off the walls. There was no answer from Peter. Searching the cavern with his lantern, Brian turned up nothing. The two motorcycles they had used to travel here were still in place across the cave. Where was that bastard?

He marched toward the cycles. His left boot slipped in a wet patch; he flailed for a handhold on the wall— and missed. With a squawk, he slammed hard on his backside. His lantern skittered across the cavern floor, finally coming to rest with the light pointed back toward him. Warm moisture seeped through the seat of his khakis. He ground his teeth together and swore.

Back on his feet, Brian wiped the seat of his pants, grimacing. A certain private was going to find a foot planted three feet up his butt. He went to tuck in his shirt when he noticed his dripping palms. He gasped and jumped back as if he could escape from his own hands.

Warm blood coated the palms.

BOOK ONE

Teamwork

ONE

Chaco Canyon, New Mexico

Damned rattlers.

Ashley Carter knocked trail dirt from her boots before climbing into her rusted Chevy pickup. She threw her dusty cowboy hat on the seat next to her and swiped a handkerchief across her brow. Leaning over the gearshift, she popped the glove compartment and removed the snakebite kit.

With a knuckle, she tapped the radio. Static rasped from the handheld receiver. Humming, she peeled back the wrapper from the syringe and drew the usual amount of venom antiserum. By now she could gauge it by sight. She shook the bottle. Almost empty. It was time to run into Albuquerque for more.

After cleaning her skin with an alcohol swab, she jabbed the needle into her arm and winced as she administered the amber fluid. Loosening her tourniquet a notch, she wiped iodine over the two punctures in her forearm, then applied a bandage.

Cinching her tourniquet a bit tighter, she glanced at the dashboard clock. Ten minutes, and she'd loosen the tourniquet again.

She picked up the radio handpiece and pressed the button on its side. "Randy, come in. Over." Static as she released the button.

"Randy, please pick up. Over." Her neighbor, Randy, was still on disability from a back injury at the mine. For the past ten weeks, he had earned a few extra bucks under the table by supplying day care for her son Jason.

She started the engine and pulled back onto the parallel ruts that constituted a road. The radio belched a garbled blast of noise, then she heard, ". . . up. Ashley, what's going on? We expected you back an hour ago."

She raised the handpiece. "Sorry, Randy. Found a new room in the Anasazi dig. Hidden by a rockfall. Had to check it out before the light went bad. But a diamondback had other ideas. I've got to check in with Doc Marshall now. Be back in about an hour. Could you pop the lasagna in the oven? Over." She hooked the receiver back on the radio.

A squelch of static. "A bite! Again! This is the fourth time since Christmas. You're pressing your luck, Ash.

This solo venturing is going to get you killed someday. But listen, after you get checked up by Doc Marshall, hurry home. There's some Marine types here waiting for you."

She furrowed her brow. Now what did she do? She groaned and grabbed the handpiece again. "What's up? Over."

"D'know. They're playing dumb," he said, then added in a lower voice, "and they're damned good at it. Real G.I. Joes. You'd hate 'em."

"Just what I need. How's Jason handling it? Over."

"He's fine. Eating it up. Talking the ear off of some corporal. I think he almost got the jarhead to give him his gun."

She smacked the steering wheel with the flat of her hand. "What are those bastards doing bringing guns into my home? Damn, I'll be there straightaway. Hold the fort! I'm out."

She never carried a gun. Not even into the badlands of New Mexico. Damned if she was going to allow some overgrown boys to bring weapons into her home. She slammed the truck in gear, her wheels clawing at loose rock.

Ashley jumped from the truck, arm tucked in a blue sling, and crossed through her cacti garden, hurrying toward a group of uniformed men huddled under the small green awning over her porch, which offered the only shade for a hundred yards.

As she stomped up the wooden steps, the men in front backed up. Except for one man, who sported bronze clusters on each shoulder and stood his ground.

She strode right up to him. "Who the hell do you think you are, barging in here with enough arsenal to blow away a small Vietnamese village? I have a boy in there."

The officer's mouth flattened to a thin line. He leaned back to remove his sunglasses, revealing a cold blue stare, void of any emotion. "Major Michaelson, ma'am. We are escorting Dr. Blakely."

She glared at him. "I don't know any Dr. Blakely."

"He knows of you, ma'am. He says you're one of the best paleoanthropologists in the country. Or so I've heard him tell the President."

"The president of what?"

He stared at her blankly. "The President of the United States."

A sandy-haired juggernaut plowing through the uniformed men covered her surprise. "Mom! You're home! You gotta come see." Her son eyed her sling, then grabbed the sleeve of her other arm. "C'mon."

Even though he stood only a little higher than their belt buckles, he ushered the military men aside.

Glaring, she allowed herself to be dragged through the door. As the screen door clapped shut behind her, she headed toward the family room and noticed a leather briefcase parked on the table. It wasn't hers.

The scent of garlic from a baking lasagna wafted toward her from the kitchen. Her stomach responded with a growl. She hadn't eaten since breakfast. Randy, armed with stained oven mittens, was attempting to extract the bubbling lasagna without spilling it. The sight of such a bear of a man, dressed in an apron, struggling with a pan of lasagna, brought a smile to her lips. He rolled his eyes at her.

As she opened her mouth to say hello, there was a sudden urgent tugging at her arm. "C'mon, Mom, see what Dr. Blakely has. It's bitchin'."

"Watch your tongue, mister," she warned. "You know we don't allow that sort of language here. Now show me what this is all about." She waved at Randy as she was tugged toward the family room.

Her son pointed to the briefcase and whispered, "It's in there."

The sound of rushing water from the hall bathroom drew her attention. The door opened and a tall black man, thin as a pole and dressed in a three-piece suit, entered the hallway. He was older, his close-cropped hair graying slightly. He pushed a pair of wire-rim spectacles farther up the bridge of his nose. Spotting Ashley, he broke out in a sudden smile of recognition. He stepped toward her quickly, hand proffered. "Professor Ashley Carter. Your picture in last year's *Archaeology* magazine failed to do you justice."

She knew a snow job when she heard one. Caked with trail dirt, arm in a sling, clad in mud-stained jeans, she was no beauty queen. "Can the crap, Doc. What are you doing here?"

He dropped his hand. His eyes widened a moment, and then he smiled even broader. He had more teeth than a shark. "I like your no-nonsense attitude," he said. "It's refreshing. I have a proposal to—"

"Not interested." She pointed to the door. "You and your entourage can hit the trail now. Thanks anyway."

"If you'll only lis—"

"Don't make me toss your butt outta here." She snapped her arm toward the screen door.

"It pays a hundred grand for two months' work."

"Just get your—" Her arm dropped to her side. Clearing her throat, she stared at Dr. Blakely, then raised an eyebrow. "*Now* I'm listening."

Since her divorce, she had been struggling to keep food on the table and a roof over their heads. An assistant professor's salary barely covered their living expenses, let alone her research projects.

"Wait," she started. "Wait a minute. Is it legal? It can't be legal."

"I assure you, Dr. Carter, this offer is legit. And that's only the beginning," Dr. Blakely continued. "Exclusive authorship of research garnered. Guaranteed tenure at the university of your choice."

She had dreams like this after too much sausage-and-onion pizza. "How can that be possible? There are university statutes . . . rules . . . seniority . . . How?"

"This is a project advocated by the highest people. I have been given free rein to hire whomever I want at whatever salary I desire." He sat down on the sofa and crossed his legs, arms spread the length of the sofa. "And I want you."

"Why?" Ashley questioned tentatively, still suspicious.

Leaning forward, he held up a hand, begging patience. He reached for his briefcase and clicked it open. Using both hands, he carefully lifted a crystal statuette from its interior. He turned it upright toward her.

It was a human figure—judging from the pendulous breasts and gravid belly, a female figure. The fading light caught the crystalline structure and reflected radiant bursts.

He nodded for her to take it. "What do you think?"

She hesitated, afraid to touch its fragile beauty. "Definitely primitive . . . Appears to be a type of fertility icon."

Dr. Blakely nodded his head vigorously. "Right, right . . . Here, look closer." He raised the heavy statue, arms shaking with the strain. "Please examine it."

She reached to take the statuette.

"It's sculpted out of a single diamond," he said. "Flawless."

Now she understood the armed escort. She withdrew her hands from such a priceless object as she pondered the implications. "Bitchin'," she whispered.

Across the kitchen table, Ashley Carter watched as Dr. Blakely flipped the cellular phone closed and returned it to his breast pocket. "Now, Professor Carter, where were we?"

"Is anything the matter?" Ashley asked, sopping up tomato sauce from her plate with a piece of garlic toast. The two of them sat at her green metal kitchen table.

The doctor shook his head. "Not at all. Just confirming the addition of one of your potential teammates. An Australian caving expert." He smiled reassuringly. "Now, where were we?"

She eyed him warily. "Who else will be joining the expedition?"

"I'm afraid those names are confidential. But I can tell you we're talking to a leading biologist in Canada and a geologist from Egypt. And a few . . . others."

Ashley could tell this line of questioning was futile. "Fine. Back to the diamond statue, then. You never told me where the artifact was discovered."

He pursed his lips. "That information is also confidential. Only for those involved with the research." He folded the gingham napkin on his lap.

"Doctor, I thought this was going to be a discussion. You're rather lean on your answers."

"Perhaps. But you still haven't given me a concrete answer yet either. Are you willing to join my research team?"

"I need more details. And more time to reorganize my work schedule."

"We'd take care of such minor concerns."

She thought of Jason, who was eating dinner from a rickety tray in front of the television. "I have my son. I can't just up and leave. And he's no *minor* concern."

"You have an ex-husband. A Scott Vandercleve, I believe."

"Jason's not staying with him. Forget it."

Blakely sighed loudly. "Then we do have a problem."

This point was going to be a stickler. Jason had been having trouble at school, and this summer Ashley had vowed to spend some time with him. "This is not up for debate," she said with as much conviction as she could muster. "Jason accompanies me, or I have no choice but to decline."

Blakely studied her silently.

She continued, "He's been on other digs with me. I know he can handle this."

"I don't think that would be prudent." He smiled wanly.

"He's a tough and resourceful kid."

Blakely grimaced. "If I agree to this point, then you'll join the team?" He paused, removing his glasses and rubbing at the indentations on the bridge of his nose. He seemed to be thinking aloud. "I suppose he could stay in Alpha Base. It's secure." Replacing his glasses, he reached across the table and held out an open palm. "Agreed."

Relieved, she let out her breath and shook his dry hand. "So why so much effort to get me on your team?"

"Your specialty. The anthropology of cliff-dwelling primitives. Your work on the Gila dwellings was brilliant."

"Still, why me? There are other paleoanthropologists with similar interests."

"Several reasons. One"—he began ticking off the points on his fingers—"you've demonstrated you can manage teams on other digs. Two, your nose for detail is superb. Three, your perseverance in solving mysteries is bone-hard obstinate. Four, you're in excellent physical shape. Five, you've earned my respect. Any other questions?"

Satisfied for now, she shook her head, slightly embarrassed. She fought back a blush. Rarely did one hear praise in her field. Uncomfortable, she changed the tack of the conversation.

"Now that we're partners, maybe you can tell me where you discovered this unique artifact." She rose to clear the dishes. "Somewhere in Africa, I'd guess."

He smiled. "No, in Antarctica, actually."

She glanced over her shoulder, trying to judge if he was testing her. "There are no primitive cultures on that continent. It's a barren glacier."

Blakely shrugged. "Who said on it?"

She rattled a dish in the sink. "So where, then?" She turned to him, leaned back against the sink, and dried her hands with a damp dish towel.

He just pointed a single finger toward the floor.

Down.

TWO

Black Rock, Australia

Benjamin Brust watched a brown cockroach skitter across the white lavatory sink. He crossed over to the bars, running a hand across the stubble that had grown over his cheeks since his incarceration. The stink of old urine in the cell was less intense by the door. A khaki-uniformed military guard glanced up from the *GQ* magazine on his lap. He nodded to the guard, who, without acknowledgment, returned to his reading.

At least Ben's client, Hans Biederman, was recuperating well. Thank god for that. He sure as hell didn't need an involuntary manslaughter charge on top of everything else. Mr. Biederman was due to fly back to Germany today, having received no more than a slap on the wrist for their little escapade—while Ben, as the planner of the expedition, had a long stint in a military prison ahead of him.

For the past five years, Ben had specialized in escorting those with the proper ticket price to exotic locales to see rare sights. Trips that required bending, even breaking a few rules to accomplish. He specialized in underground adventures: abandoned diamond mines in South Africa, monastic ruins buried under the Himalayas, undersea tunnels off the Caribbean coast—and now, here in Australia, a set of stunning caverns restricted by the military from human sight.

The caverns were on a remote section of the Black Rock military installation. These exquisite caves had been discovered and mapped by Ben himself four years ago when he had once been stationed here.

It had all been going perfectly until Herr Biederman, his pudgy German client, slipped and broke his leg. Ben should have just left him to rot for ignoring his warning, but instead Ben had tried to haul the bastard's sorry butt out of the caverns. Herr Biederman's bellows of pain drew the military police, and Ben got caught for his efforts.

He turned from the bars and dropped onto the moth-eaten cot, then leaned back, studying the stains on the ceiling. He heard hard-heeled boots tapping down the hall and something mumbled to the guard.

The heavy magazine slapped on the floor. "In there, sir. Fourth one down." He heard the fear in the guard's answer.

The tapping heels approached, then stopped. He pushed up onto his elbows to see who stood in front of the cell. He recognized the face of his old commander. Bald head, beak of a nose, gray eyes that drilled. "Colonel Matson?"

"Somehow I knew you would end up here. Always a troublemaker." But the smile playing at the corner of his lips softened the gruffness. "How have they been treating you?"

"Like it's the Hilton, sir. Room service is a bit slow, though."

"Isn't it always." The colonel gestured to the guard to open the cell. "Follow me, Sergeant Brust."

"It's Mr. Brust now, sir."

"Whatever," he said with a frown, turning away. "We've got to talk."

The guard interrupted. "Should I handcuff him, sir?"

Ben gave Colonel Matson his most innocent look.

"Yeah," Matson said. "You'd better. There's no trusting civilians."

"All right," Ben said, standing at mock attention. "You win. *Sergeant* Brust, reporting for duty."

Nodding, Colonel Matson waved the guard away. "C'mon, then, Sergeant. We're going to my office."

Ben followed him out of the prison, and after a short drive, they arrived at the Administration Building. The colonel's office had not changed. Same walnut desk with stained coffee mug circles; walls festooned with banners from the Old Guard; trophies lining the side wall. During the ride over, Ben could tell from the hesitancy in an otherwise ebullient man that something of importance was being withheld.

The colonel ushered Ben to sit, then Matson leaned on the edge of his desk and studied him. The colonel's face was stone. Ben tried not to squirm under his gaze. Finally his old commander spoke, his voice tired, "What the hell happened to you? The best of the best, and you just disappear."

"I had a better offer."

"What? Guiding yuppies with midlife crises on little thrill tours?"

"I prefer to call them 'Adventure Vacations.' Besides, I earn enough to help keep my dad's sheep station afloat."

"And earned yourself a bit of a reputation. Quite the cave hound. I read about that cavern rescue in the States. Big hero, huh?"

Ben shrugged.

"But that's not why you left here. It was Jack, wasn't it?"

Ben's face went cold at the mention of his friend's name. "I believed in the Guard. And honor. I believed in you."

Colonel Matson grimaced. "Sometimes political pressure bends rules. Distorts honor."

"Bullshit!" Ben shook his head. "The prime minister's son deserved every inch of the pummeling he got from Jack after the shit he tried with his girl."

"A prime minister has powerful friends. It couldn't go unpunished."

"Bloody hell!" Ben slammed his fist on the arm of his chair. "I'da done the same. His court-martial was a travesty." Ben stopped, swallowed hard, then continued in a quieter voice. "Jack was stripped of everything that made him a man. And you wonder why I left?"

Matson sighed, seemingly satisfied. "Then the balance of fate has shifted your way this time. Now the political pressures are aligned to help you."

Ben's brow furrowed. "What do you mean?"

"I should pretend I never received this letter. As much trouble as you caused, you sure as hell deserve a couple years behind bars."

"What letter?"

"A command from the Home Office. You're to be set free."

What joke was this? They were just going to let him walk? Ben watched a worried look pass over Matson's face. "What's up, Colonel?"

"There's a catch."

Of course, Ben thought. There always was.

"You must join an international expedition. A professor somewhere in the Americas has requested your expertise in cave exploration. Some hush-hush operation. No other details. They'll waive all charges and pay you for your services." He slid a sheet of paper toward Ben. "Here."

Ben quickly read the letter, and his eyes caught on the figure at the bottom of the page. He stared at all those zeros, daring them to change. This couldn't be right. After this, he could own his sheep station free and clear. No more shady tour operations.

"Almost too good to be true?" Matson leaned forward, his hands on Ben's shoulders. "But impossible to pass up."

He nodded, dazed.

"Something tells me you had better watch your ass, Ben." Matson strode to the chair behind his desk and sat. "The big boys are playing with you, and they have a tendency to roll over the little people. Remember your friend Jack."

Ben stared at the number at the bottom of the page, drawing a breath. Too good to be true.

Back in his cell, with an arm draped over his eyes, Ben drifted to sleep and was soon lost in a nightmare he hadn't had since childhood. He found himself, a boy again, threading his way through meter-wide columns of damp stone inside a huge cave. He knew this place. His grandfather had once brought him here to show him Aboriginal petroglyphs.

It was the same cave, but now the rock columns sprouted fruit-laden branches. Curious, he reached for a red pulpy gourd, but it was just beyond his reach. As he was pulling back his arm, he felt eyes drilling into the nape of his neck. He whipped around, but no one was there. Yet now those eyes were all around him. Just at the edge of his vision, he spotted motion from behind a large rock cylinder.

"Who's there?" he called, racing to peer behind the column. Just more empty space. "What do you want?"

The word "ghosts" came unbidden to his mind.

He started to run . . .

He felt something following him, calling him back. He ignored it and ran, searching for an exit. The pillars closed around him, slowing his progress. Then he sensed a soft touch at the back of his neck and heard garbled words whispered in his ear.

"You are one of us."

He screamed, bolting out of the dream.

He woke on his cot, his heart still racing, and rubbed at his temples. Bloody hell. What brought back that old nightmare? He closed his eyes, recalling that the nightmares had first started after an argument with his grandfather in an Aboriginal cave outside of Darwin.

"No, it's not true," the thirteen-year-old Ben had yelled, tears welling at the revelation.

"Yes, it is, young man. And I don't take to being called a liar." His grandfather's wrinkled leather face frowned at him. "This was once the ancestral home of my grandmother," he repeated, then poked him in the chest. "A direct relative of yours."

The implications that he could have Aboriginal blood running through his veins had horrified him. He and his friends had always made fun of the dark-skinned Aboriginal kids at school. And now, in a single heartbeat, he had been lumped in with them. He shook his head. "I am not a damned darkie!"

A stinging slap to his cheek. "You'll respect your ancestors."

Even now, he cringed at the memory. As a young-
ster, this heritage had shamed him. Aborigines, at
the time, were considered second-class citizens, only
slightly above animals. Luckily, diluted by generations of European blood, his blighted heritage was an
easily kept secret. Except from himself. It was then the
nightmares had started.

For countless nights, he'd awaken with his sheets
clinging to his sweating body, tears coursing down his
cheeks. Clenching handfuls of sheets, he would pray no
one would learn his secret.

Over time, he had matured, even come to respect
and appreciate his unique heritage, and the dreams had
eventually faded away, like old toys put in cardboard
boxes. Forgotten and no longer needed.

He shook his head. So why now? Why dredge up
this old childhood terror?

Must be this bloody cell, he concluded, and burrowed deeper under his ratty blanket. Well, thanks to
that timely letter, he would soon be rid of this damn
place.

Thirty days later, his mysterious benefactor telegraphed
Black Rock, and in twenty hours Ben found himself
upgraded from his cramped cell in Australia to a suite
of rooms at the Sheraton Buenos Aires in Argentina.

Ben tested the bathwater with his foot. He cringed at the heat, then smiled. Ahhh, perfect. After a month in the Black Rock prison, a month of tepid showers that barely penetrated the layer of grime caked into his pores, a full hot bath was just possibly orgasmic. He stepped into the tub and settled himself into the steaming water. He tapped the button for the jets. Tickling sprays massaged him from all sides, creating a gentle whirlpool. Definitely orgasmic.

He sighed, leaning back into the tub and allowing his body to relax and float in the jets.

There was a knock on the door.

Ignoring it, Ben slipped farther into the jets.

The knock came again, more persistently.

Using his elbows, he raised himself higher in the tub. "Who is it?"

A muffled voice replied, "Excuse me, sir, but Dr. Blakely requests your presence in the Pampas room on the main floor. The other guests are arriving now as well."

Ben rubbed his red eyes. "Gimme five minutes." He pushed out of the hot tub, the chill air raising goose-flesh on his bare legs. After dressing in an old brown tweed suit, Ben proceeded to the conference suite.

To his relief, the antechamber to the auditorium was set up with a mobile bar. A bartender hustling hooch paraded behind a shelf of bottles. Already a good number of men and women stood gathered in small groups.

He glanced around. No one looked his way. So much for the warm greeting. After searching the room one final time, he decided a whiskey would help his outlook on this "party." He stalked over to the bar.

"Your pleasure, sir?"

"Whiskey and a beer back." He leaned his elbow on the black Naugahyde padding that edged the bar and watched the room. It was not his kind of crowd. No loud laughs, no spilled drinks, no angry drunks. Boring. After dumping the whiskey straight into his stomach, he slapped down his shot glass, squeezing the burn, then settled in with his beer.

From behind him, he heard a woman's voice. "Whiskey. Neat, please."

He turned to see who had a similar taste in beverages. Whiskey-drinking women were as scarce as hen's teeth. He wasn't disappointed.

She toyed with the drink set before her, long fingers, short nails, polished. No rings. No wedding band—good. She stood as tall as him, surprising for a woman. Her skin was bronzed, a coppery rich hue that spoke of days under the sun. But what most caught the breath in his throat was her black hair, trailing in lazy curls to her waist.

"Can I buy you another?" he asked, stressing his Aussie accent. That always won a lady's attention.

She lifted her left eyebrow. "They're free," she said. "It's a hosted bar."

His roguish smile swelled. "In that case, how about two?"

She just stared at him with green eyes.

He thrust out a hand. "Ben Brust. From Sydney."

"I could've guessed from your accent," she said with a ghost of a smile. "But the drawl sounds more like western Australia than the New South Wales territory."

"Well," he said, lowering his arm and stumbling for cover, "I *actually* was raised on my daddy's sheep station outside Perth. Western Australia. But most people don't know Sydney from—"

"I thought so." Collecting her drink, she began to turn away. "The meeting should be starting soon."

Before she left, he begged for at least one bone. "And you are?"

"Ashley Carter." She slipped past him.

Ben watched her walk away. No professor's stroll, that. He swallowed the dregs of his beer while appreciating her exit.

THREE

Buenos Aires, Argentina

Ashley crossed to the young Spanish gentleman, who checked her identification. Nodding, he opened the door. The room was lined with some fifty seats, only a quarter occupied. An usher guided her to a reserved seat in the front row, then vanished. Shivering in the light skirt and jacket she wore, she wished they'd turn up the thermostat.

Now that she was seated, her mind began sifting over the events of the past weeks; her old anxieties wormed to the surface. One, especially.

Jason.

She hated leaving her son alone in the hotel room upstairs. He had seemed so quiet this evening, not his usual boisterous self. Her fingers tightened on her purse.

And this mission. A letter with airplane tickets had arrived in the mail with instructions to be prompt. "Everything else has been taken care of," the letter had stated. No other details.

A man sat down in the seat next to her. "Well, hi, there."

She glanced over. It was the Australian fellow again. Goddamn it. Couldn't she get a moment of peace? The empty canyons of her New Mexico home had never seemed so appealing.

"Let me try this again . . ." He held out a hand. "Benjamin Brust."

Not wanting to insult him, she gave his hand one shake. Now go away, she thought.

He smiled at her, white teeth against a ruddy background, his cheekbones hard, sun wrinkles at the corners of his eyes. Full lips. "So what do you know about all this?" he asked.

Ashley shrugged, trying to discourage conversation, and turned away.

"So many secrets," Ben mumbled.

She nodded. "Perhaps shortly we'll have a few answers."

He remained quiet. Still, she sensed his presence at her shoulder. His cologne was musky and rich; his breathing, deep and even.

She shifted. The auditorium was almost full. Now it was getting warm in here. She wished they would fix the thermostat.

"Do you trust him?" he asked in a whisper.

"No," she answered, looking straight ahead. She knew who he was talking about. "Not at all."

From a doorway, Blakely watched the auditorium fill. His team was gathered in the five front seats. He signaled his assistant, Roland, across the room.

Roland nodded and raised a microphone to his lips. "Ladies and gentlemen, please take your seats. We're ready to begin."

After a few more moments of bustling and last-minute arrivals, the doors to the auditorium were closed and the lights dimmed slightly. Blakely climbed the dais and stood behind the lighted podium. He dabbed his forehead with a handkerchief. He knew his speech by heart, words carefully crafted.

Blakely tapped the microphone, testing it. His tapping also signaled the murmuring crowd to hush. "First, thank you all for joining us." He paused. "I know it has been a hardship to leave your regular lives behind so abruptly. But in a few moments, I'm sure you will be convinced that the disruption was well worth it."

He picked up a remote control for the slide projector and pressed a button. A photograph of a snowcapped mountain with a plume of dirty smoke appeared on the screen. "Mount Erebus on Ross Island just off the coast of Antarctica. One of three volcanic cones on this continent. At the base of this volcano is the U.S. research station, McMurdo. My home for the past five years."

He clicked the button to zero in on a group of low metal buildings clinging to the surface of a gray glacier. A satellite array sprouted like a bizarre spider from the rooftops. "I have been conducting geothermal studies for the past ten years on some hot rifts still active deep under the cone and under the neighboring Ross Sea. NASA assisted with this research. Their third shuttle, six years ago, made radio scans of the earth's crust, looking for oil fields and other such pockets. I commissioned a scan of Mount Erebus and found some amazing things."

He tapped the button, and a cross-sectional diagram of the crust under the volcanic cone appeared on screen. A murmur arose from the crowd. "As you can see, an intricate cavern system was discovered below Erebus, spreading hundreds of miles."

He clicked to the next slide. "Closer investigation with sonar and radar revealed a huge cavern separated from the deepest rift by a mere six hundred meters of stone." He guided a pointer to show the network of rifts that led to the massive pocket. "We named this cave Alpha Cavern. Almost five miles in diameter, the cavern floor was plumbed at two miles below the surface of the continent. Almost three times deeper than man has ever stepped foot."

The next picture showed a group of smiling men, faces encrusted in dirt and dust, posing in front of a large raw-edged hole. "After three years of work, we blasted and mined our way into this chamber. It took another year to wire and set up a camp on this chamber's floor." A spotlighted set of Quonset huts and tents appeared next on the screen. A three-story wooden building protruded from the middle. A second, similar building, a mere skeleton of wooden framing and scaffolding, was under construction. "Alpha Base," he noted. "We worked in secret. Access restricted to those with the proper clearance."

The next slide caused his audience to gasp. Blakely smiled slightly. "Ladies and gentlemen, I present a mystery."

Ashley, who had been rubbing her eyes and yawning, wondering what all this talk of volcanic-activity and mining had to do with her, bolted out of her seat. It had to be a hoax. What she saw blew a mile-wide hole in accepted anthropologic theory.

The photograph projected on the screen revealed a spotlighted section of the cavern wall. Dug into the wall was a network of cliff-dwelling homes, rising several hundred feet up the wall. Unlike the organized Anasazi cliff dwellings she had studied in New Mexico, dwellings with distinct terraces and geometric conformations, these cavern dwellings were more rudimentary, crude, a haphazard series of rough caves.

Blakely continued after the audience's reaction had subsided to a quiet murmur. "Unfortunately, no one was home"—nervous laughter tickled across the room—"but we discovered a few scattered artifacts." He clicked through the next series of slides. One of the slides was the diamond fertility figurine.

Ashley was numb as she settled back into her seat. She raised her hand. "Excuse me, Dr. Blakely."

He acknowledged her with a wave, then paused to sip from a glass of water.

"Has the site been dated?" she asked.

He swallowed, nodding. "We did some cursory radiocarbon dating. As near as we can tell, about five-point-two million years."

"What!" Ashley jumped out of her seat a second time. "That's impossible."

"It's been repeated at several labs," he replied, his smile condescending.

The eyes of the auditorium were now upon her. Some lighting technician even highlighted her with a small spot. She shaded her eyes with a hand. "But the first hominids, the earliest ancestor of modern man, only appeared on the planet four million years ago. And these early hominids did not have the tools or social structure to build anything like this."

He shrugged. "That's why we're here." He clicked for the next slide: a photograph of a tunnel in the base of the wall. "These tunnels leave this colossal chamber in many different directions, connecting to other caverns and tunnels. We believe that down one of these passages lie the answers to the questions raised by Professor Carter. Who built the dwellings? Who made the carvings? Where are they now?"

The audience remained stunned, silent. Ashley sat back down, still in shock.

"I have put together a small team to begin that exploration. To venture deeper into the maze of tunnels and discover what else may lie below. The group will be led by Professor Ashley Carter, an expert in paleoanthropology and archaeology. The others on the team are leaders in their respective fields."

He pointed to a blond-haired woman seated several chairs over from Ashley. "Accompanying the team will be Professor Linda Furstenburg, a biology professor from the University of Vancouver, to study the unique biosphere we've discovered down there. Also a geologist, Khalid Najmon," he said with a nod toward an Arab gentleman seated with his legs crossed to Linda's left. "He, as many of you know, will be assisting us in mapping the riches below Antarctic ice. His findings may alter our view of this continent."

Blakely finished by pointing out the other two men seated in the front row. "All the way from Australia, Benjamin Brust, a world-renowned cave explorer, will be mapping the intricacies of this unique cavern system. And that smartly dressed man in the uniform is Major Michaelson of the U.S. Marines, who, with two other trained military men, will be accompanying the team to aid in logistics and protection."

He waved his arm to encompass the group before him. "Ladies and gentlemen, here is your team." A murmur of applause spattered across the crowd.

Ashley tried to sink deeper into her seat.

After some further details were explained and a handful of questions answered, the meeting ended. Satisfied, Blakely left the podium.

In the adjacent room, he sighed and loosened his tie. The first part was over. Roland, who had been his assistant for over fifteen years, entered with the slide tray. Blakely nodded to him.

"That went very well, sir," Roland said as he boxed the slides. "The government representatives and your other financial backers seemed very pleased."

"Yes," he said with a tired smile. "I think so too." He pulled off his jacket and let it drop on a nearby chair. He sat down in another.

Roland placed the slide carousel in a cardboard box. "No one even suspected there was a previous exploration team."

He shrugged. "They have no need for that information right now."

"But what if—"

"We're much better prepared this time. Don't worry. We won't lose this team."

FOUR

For the second time in as many months, Ashley stuck her nose in Major Michaelson's face. Even now, outfitted in his dress blues, she recognized the same blue-eyed plastic soldier boy who had escorted Dr. Blakely to her doorstep. "I don't care if you and your two goons come along with my team," she said, accosting him just outside the auditorium. "I want it made perfectly clear right now. This team is *mine*."

He stood straight, not pulling an inch from her face. "Ma'am, I have my orders."

She hated surprises like these. Blakely should have forewarned her that there would be armed escorts accompanying her team. "This is a scientific mission. Not a military one."

"As Dr. Blakely explained, we're merely going along for defensive reasons. For safety."

"Fine," she said, staring him square in the eyes. "But you remember, even though you may be carrying the guns, I give the orders. Understood?"

He did not blink, just nodded slightly. "I have my orders, ma'am."

She ground her molars, squelching an outburst. What could she do? She stepped back. "As long as we understand each other."

"Is there some trouble, ladies?" Ben had appeared at her elbow. He smiled, but there was a tightness to his lips as he eyed the major.

Ashley sensed Ben's edginess, nothing like his earlier casual attitude. Probably isn't too keen on the idea of being surrounded by guns either, she thought. "No," she said aloud. "We're just clearing up a few points."

"Good. We're going to be buried together for the summer in a hole two miles deep. Let's start out friends." Ben stuck out a hand toward the officer.

Major Michaelson ignored Ben's hand. "You do your job, and I'll do mine." With a nod toward Ashley, the major turned and strode away.

"Nice bloke," Ben said. "Real friendly." The sarcasm in his voice was tough to miss.

"I didn't need rescuing."

"Pardon me?"

"I can handle Major Michaelson without your intervention."

"I could see that." Ben looked hurt. Honestly hurt. "But that wasn't the reason I came over. I talked to Professor Furstenburg and Mr. Najmon. We're all going to the hotel bar. I just wanted to invite you along."

Ashley glanced down, embarrassed by her rude remark. It wasn't Ben who deserved her wrath. She had just needed someone to vent her frustrations upon, and unfortunately he was at hand. "Listen, I'm sorry. I didn't mean to—"

"Don't give it another thought." A smile had returned to his lips. "Us Aussies are a thick-skinned breed. So how about coming along?"

"I should be getting back to my room. My son. He's upstairs."

Ben raised his eyebrows. "You brought your son? How old is he?"

"Eleven," she said defensively. "He's been on digs with me before."

"Cool. Nothin' like getting your kids involved with your work." He pointed to a white hotel phone on the wall. "Why don't you check up on him? If he's fine, c'mon and join us."

She'd expected to be lambasted for dragging her son halfway across the globe, and his response eased her tension a bit. Maybe it *was* all right that Jason came along on this once-in-a-lifetime adventure. "You're right. Let me just call him."

A quick call from the lobby phone found Jason still hooked to his Nintendo Game Boy like an addict. She could hear the blips and dings of his portable video game in the background. "Can't talk, Mom. Almost to level twenty-three. I've never been this far. And I got three lives left."

"Sounds great, honey. Listen, I'll be up in about an hour. Is that all right?"

"Sure, sure. Whenever. I gotta go."

"Have fun, then." The line clicked off. She sighed and headed toward the bar.

After all, it would be good to get to know her teammates better before the trip tomorrow.

Maxi's, the hotel bar, was the designated watering hole. The decor was a Paris motif, with tiny café tables and intimate booths. A French flag hung over the bar. The tables were crowded now with the evening theater crowd. Espresso, café latté, and exotic drinks cluttered the tabletops. In contrast to the European trappings, the Latin music was loud, with a throbbing rhythm.

A booth in a distant corner had already been staked out by her team. She saw Ben ferrying drinks across the room. Balancing a beer and three cocktails between two hands, he maneuvered through the maze of elbows and feet, arriving with most of the drinks still in their respective glasses. Ashley slid into the booth just ahead of him.

Sliding in next to her, Ben passed her a glass. "If I remember, the lady likes whiskey."

She smiled. "Thanks."

"You two seem to know each other already," said the Egyptian geologist, Khalid Najmon, who sat across the booth next to Linda Furstenburg. His smile glowed against his desert tan, handsome in a dark way. "Have you known each other long?" he asked before taking a sip of his wine.

"No. We sat together at the meeting," Ashley explained. "Otherwise, we're complete strangers."

Ben feigned hurt feelings. " 'Strangers' is such a dirty word."

"Well," Khalid said, "while Mr. Brust was fetching drinks, I've been getting better acquainted with Professor Furstenburg."

"Please, call me Linda." She blushed a bit and kept pushing a loose strand of blond hair back over an ear. Her manner was outwardly relaxed, but she kept glancing around the room with glassy eyes.

He nodded. "Linda was just telling me about her doctorate research. Evolutionary biology. She's been studying the development of phosphorescent algae in cavern systems. Most fascinating."

"I've seen some of that glowing algae," Ben said. "In a cave in Madagascar. There were caverns so thick with the stuff that you almost wished you had sunglasses."

Linda nodded. "*Rinchari luminarus.* A beautiful species. Comes in a variety of colors too." She talked about how the individual species differed.

Ashley's attention drifted from the conversation. She studied Linda as she spoke. Her eyes were so blue that Ashley wondered if they were real. Her physique was ample, soft, with small hands, a child's delicate fingers. A direct contrast to Ashley's hard, lean body. No one would ever describe Ashley as soft.

Khalid never took his eyes from Linda, nodding every now and then as she continued her description. He was obviously entranced by more than just the genetic variations of glowing sludge. Even Ben had a perpetual smile on his lips as he listened.

Ashley felt like a piece of granite next to a rose. She swallowed her whiskey.

". . . and that's how I received my doctorate."

"I can see why Dr. Blakely wanted you," Ashley said. The two men seemed to come out of a trance.

"Your knowledge of unique evolutionary pathways will be helpful in documenting our exploration."

Ben cleared his throat. "Definitely an asset."

Khalid nodded. "Indeed."

Ben finally turned away from Linda. "So, Khalid, what's your angle? A geologist, huh?"

He sipped his drink, then spoke, "The Antarctic Treaty of 1959."

"Come again?" Ben asked.

"No one owns Antarctica. The 1959 treaty declared the continent to be used only for peaceful, scientific purposes. A world park."

"Yeah, I know about that. Australia has a few bases there."

"Yes, but did you know that because of the treaty's prohibition against mineral exploration, the extent of Antarctica's mineral wealth is still unknown? It's a big blank slate."

Khalid allowed that to sink in before continuing. "Well, the treaty ended in 1991. The continent is now open for mineral exploration, but with one critical stipulation: The land must be protected from damage."

It dawned on Ashley. The implications were enormous. "These subterranean tunnels will allow you to explore the continent's mineral wealth without harm to the surface."

"Yes," he said, nodding. "And any deposits—oil, minerals, precious stones—discovered are the property of the government who finds them."

"With the U.S. government's lust for future territorial claims," she said, "it's no wonder the National Science Foundation has been so generous with their funding. But who exactly are we in bed with here?"

"I imagine it's a combination of science, commerce, and politics," Khalid answered—and then with a grin, "I suppose much like your government's Manhattan Project."

Ashley scowled. "Great. And look how wonderful that turned out."

"So what do you think the likelihood of a significant find is?" Linda asked, drawing the Egyptian's attention.

"Considering that a researcher discovered Mount Erebus's volcanic plume emits gold dust—the only plume to do so on the planet—I think this research team's salary will be more than adequately covered."

"Gold in volcano smoke," Ben said. "Sounds pretty far-fetched."

Khalid scowled briefly at the interruption. "It's been widely written up."

The other team members remained silent. Dumbstruck.

Ashley bristled. Once again Blakely had failed to reveal the full extent of this mission. First the armed escort, and now this. "I don't know if I like this," she said. "Raping a continent. And for whose benefit?"

Linda nodded in agreement.

Everyone sat quietly, pondering the sobering news.

Then Ben, in a sudden outburst, destroyed the somber reverie. "To hell with it. Let's go dancing! It's the flipping birthplace of the tango. C'mon, Buenos Aires is just waking up."

Ashley frowned. This Australian sheepherder never stops, she thought. "I'll pass. I have a son to tuck into bed."

Khalid also shook his head. "We don't dance the tango in my country."

Linda brightened. "I'll go. I'd like to get out of this stuffy hotel."

"Superb!" Ben said. "I know of a bar in the San Telmo district. Quaint and authentic."

Ben scooted out of the booth and gave Linda his hand. "The night and the stars await us," he declared with a slight bow.

Bashfully, Linda smiled at Ben's drama.

As the two walked away, Ashley noticed Khalid's brows lower. He mumbled something in Arabic, then said his good-byes to her and slipped from the table also.

She watched as Ben escorted Linda across the bar. A small burst of her tinkling laughter could be heard as the two exited onto the street.

Ashley remained, nursing the rest of her drink. As if on cue, the plangent chords of a tango began wailing from the bar's speakers. The sultry music just made her feel that much lonelier.

BOOK TWO

Under the Ice

FIVE

I n a plane again, Ashley thought sourly, her nose
pressed to the window. Down below, glacier fought
granite from horizon to horizon.

This was the final leg of the two-day journey.
Yesterday, they had flown the eight hundred miles from
Buenos Aires to Esperanza, the Argentine army base
on the tip of an Antarctic Peninsula. There, Ashley had
her first taste of Antarctic air—like ice water poured
into her lungs. The team overnighted at the base's military barracks and the next morning were hauled once
again aboard the Argentine transport. By noon, Blakely
had promised, they would reach their final destination,
the U.S. naval base McMurdo.

Ashley longed to spend more than twenty-four
hours outside an airplane's cabin. She pushed herself

up a bit to see if Jason was behaving himself. He was seated across the rattling cabin next to Ben, talking animatedly, his hands expressive. The two had become fast friends since bunking together in the male dormitory of the barracks in Esperanza.

Ben noticed her stare and grinned over Jason's head at her. The Australian was demonstrating admirable patience. Jason's stories could get long-winded.

"He's fine," said Major Michaelson, seated next to her.

Startled, she snapped at him. "I didn't ask for your opinion."

"I just meant . . ." He shook his head with a frown. "Never mind."

Ashley bit her lower lip. He was obviously just trying to reassure her. "I'm sorry. That wasn't directed at you. I just have these nagging doubts about bringing Jason along."

The tension in his shoulders seemed to relax. "Your son has a lot of spunk. He'll do fine."

"Thanks. But what about Ben? He didn't come on this mission to be my babysitter."

The major smiled. "Maybe some of Jason's maturity will rub off on him."

She chuckled. "That man sure is a walking showboat."

"At least he knows his business." He nodded toward Ben. "I read his file. A celebrated search-and-rescue worker, specializing in cave reconnaissance. Two years ago, he rescued an experienced research crew in the Lechuguilla caves. The researchers had disappeared for eight days, and no one could find them. Ben went in alone and came out with a broken leg and the four crew members. He knows his caves. Almost a sixth sense."

"I didn't realize . . ." She glanced at Ben, who was now playing cards with Jason. She sat there pondering the revelation.

"Your file was just as impressive," the major said.

"My file?"

"You seem to have an amazing ability to ferret out new discoveries in otherwise heavily researched sites."

She just shrugged at his praise. The major seemed extraordinarily talkative. He'd otherwise been so close-lipped and stoic. She turned to him. "You sure as hell know a lot about us, but all I've received were tickets and a schedule. I don't even know your first name."

"It's Dennis," he said. "Dr. Blakely plans a full debriefing at Alpha Base."

Major *Dennis* Michaelson, she thought. With a first name, the major almost seemed human. She settled back in her seat. "Where are you from, Dennis?"

"Nebraska. Our family's farm is just outside North Platte."

"So why did you join the Marines?"

"My brother, Harry, and I joined together. He's a big motor buff—cars, bikes, drag racing, that sort of thing. He joined to get his hands dirty on even bigger engines. The guy was never happy unless his hands were filthy with oil. Always needing to tinker." An affectionate smile had appeared on Michaelson's face as he described his brother.

"And what about you? What drew you away from the farm?"

"Partly to keep an eye on Harry. But also, as I said, our family farm's just outside North Platte. And North Platte is just outside of nowhere."

"So you joined to see the world. And now here you are. Serving at the bottom of it."

"Yes," he said almost fiercely. "And right now North Platte never looked so good."

"So why not quit and go back to the farm?"

His face suddenly clouded over, black eyebrows pulling together. He shook his head but remained silent.

She tried to extract more from him. "How did you get hitched with such a dull assignment? Guarding a bunch of scientists."

"I volunteered," he mumbled.

She crinkled her nose. Not exactly the expected decision of a career military man. No prestige, no glory, stationed at the ass-end of the world. "Why?"

He shrugged his shoulders. "I have my reasons." He unbuckled his seat belt and climbed out of the seat, grumbling about using the restroom.

Alone, she went back to studying the landscape passing below the skis of the aircraft. Sun reflected off the ice. The more she got to know her teammates, the less she seemed to understand them. But what else was new? She never understood people. Look at her marriage. A honeymoon that lasted eight years until one day she came home early from a dig—nauseated by morning sickness—and discovered her husband in their bed with his secretary. No warning signs. No lipstick on a collar. No blond hair on his jacket. Nothing. A mystery to her.

Ashley placed a hand on her belly. Scott's infidelity was not the worst of it. She remembered the cramping pain and the rush of blood. The emotional overload from his betrayal had triggered a miscarriage. Losing the child had almost destroyed her. Only Jason, then seven years old, had kept her sane.

Even though years had passed, a part of her ached when she remembered how much she had lost. Not just the baby, but her faith in people. She refused to let herself be so gullible, so vulnerable again.

Slumping into her seat, she stared out the frosted window. Just at the edge of the horizon, a tower of smoke rose into the air, a dark signature against the blue sky. She sat up straighter. As the plane droned on, the source of the gray plume appeared, rising from the flat surface like some awakening giant. Mount Erebus.

The interior of the Dodge van reeked of cigarette smoke and bounced in rough sync with the bass beat of a Pearl Jam cassette. A tired midday sun protruded wanly over the summit of Mount Erebus. The driver, a young Navy ensign, bobbed his head to the music. "Almost home," he called over his shoulder. "Just around the next ridge of ice." The road from Williams Field to McMurdo Base was a rough-hewn stretch of carved ice. With a final molar-jarring bump as they circled the ridge, Ashley viewed their destination.

She swiped a glove over the steamed passenger window. The other team members were doing the same. Beside the blue ice shelf encasing the Ross Sea, McMurdo Base was a black smudge. An industrial complex of gray buildings dwarfed by a huge junkyard to the south. The van trundled past an ignited trash dump fuming oily smoke into the blue sky.

A Navy helicopter screamed over the van, the pressure and sound vibrating the windows. Jason covered his ears.

The base buzzed with other helicopters. Ashley tapped the driver on the shoulder. "Is it always this busy here?"

The driver gave her a thumbs-up sign. "This is a slow day," he yelled.

She leaned back into her seat. Great.

Blakely smiled. "We'll only be stopping here for a couple of hours, then we'll proceed directly to Alpha Base. It's much quieter down there." He glanced wistfully out the window. "Actually, after a year or so, you get accustomed to the commotion and smell up top here. I almost miss it."

"Seems like a lot of pollution for a scientific station," Linda said with a grimace. "These surrounding biocommunities are fragile."

Blakely shrugged. "We've been allocated a ten-million-dollar cleanup fund. It'll get better."

"I sure hope so," Linda said.

They were dropped off near a cement-block building. Ashley tightened her parka around her; the wind burned as it whipped across her cheeks. Frostbite could set in within mere minutes if unprotected. Her teammates dashed for the entryway. She made sure Jason was ahead of her. She didn't want him wandering off and getting lost.

Warmth. The interior was heated but felt humid and sticky, the pungent odor of sweat prevalent. Crinkling her nose, she noticed the hallway was lined with a rainbow of colored parkas hung on pegs.

Blakely directed them to hang up their parkas. "Don't worry about them being stolen. To steal someone's coat is a hanging offense here."

Ashley helped Jason off with his parka and hung it next to hers.

"We'll only be stopping for lunch, then proceeding directly to Alpha Base," Blakely continued. "The E-mess is at the end of this corridor. Help yourselves and unwind. We'll meet back here in two hours. There's also a recreation room with Ping-Pong and pool tables around the corner from E-mess. Enjoy yourselves."

"You won't be joining us?" Ashley asked.

"No, I'm meeting with the base captain to iron out the last few details."

After Blakely left, they proceeded to the mess hall. A few Navy personnel raised an eyebrow or two as they passed. One young gentleman stared at Ashley for longer than she liked, until a stern glare sent him scurrying. As a whole, though, the Navy crew seemed unfazed by the newcomers. She guessed that as a base of operation for the National Science Foundation, they had become accustomed to an influx of new faces.

Ashley balanced a tray laden with two apples, a thick sandwich of luncheon meats, and a pint of milk.

Jason had tried to fill his tray with pudding and cookies until she pointed for him to return the treats. "Lunch first. Then you can have a chocolate pudding and one cookie."

Jason moped his way to the table with the smallest sandwich he could find, his eye still straying to the dessert bar.

Ben joined them at their table. Major Michaelson, Khalid, and Linda took a neighboring table.

"We're almost there," Ben whispered in her ear as he sat. "At the threshold of a new world. How are you holding up, Captain?"

Whether from his words or his ticklish breath, a shiver traveled down her back. "Fine," she said. "Just wound up tight. Anxious to tackle the caves."

"Me too." With a big smile, he held out a hand, fingers trembling. "I get the shakes until I get started."

She couldn't tell if he was joking with her. He was so hard to read. "To be this close . . ." She shrugged. "It's nerve-wracking."

"I know how you feel," Ben said with a nod. "I've been caving for two decades. This is my first chance to scoop booty on a new system."

"Scoop booty? What's that?"

"Sheesh, Mom!" Jason said, seated beside her, appalled. He spoke around a mouthful of sandwich.

"It's a caving guy's word. It means to be the first to discover new stuff."

"Oh . . . I see," she said, smiling at her son's attempt to impress her.

"Ben and I talked. He's told me all about—what'd you call it again?—oh, yeah . . . the virgin's passage."

"What?" She turned to Ben. "What the hell have you been telling my son?"

"Virgin passages," Ben said, straining to hold back his laughter. "Passages never walked by man. That sort of thing."

"Oh," she said, suddenly chagrined. "I thought—"

He interrupted with a sloppy grin. "I know what you thought."

She bristled. "So you think you're the next Neil Armstrong?"

"Who?"

She shook her head at his ignorance. "The first man who stepped on the moon. 'One giant step for mankind.'"

Ben's eyes brightened. "Exactly! To be the first human to see something new. Like no other thrill."

She remembered the hidden Anasazi tomb she had discovered, pulse racing, breath shallow, as she tipped over the final stone to reveal the inner sanctum of the high priest. The musty smell of the ancient chamber.

The sun on her neck. To be the first to view a secret hidden for centuries. And now to do the same on a secret hidden for millennia. What would she find there? Her ears rang with her thudding heartbeat. Yes, she understood Ben's excitement.

"So are *you* ready to scoop some booty?" he asked.

She smiled into his laughing eyes. "Hell, yes. I hope there's still time later to explore those cliff dwellings. I'd even skip lunch for a chance to get at them today." Taking a hearty bite of her sandwich, she found the bread moist and the meat rubbery. "Especially *this* lunch."

Ben just kept smiling at her. "Don't like military fare?"

She smirked at him. "I'm going back for some pudding and a cookie."

"Mom!" Jason cried. "No fair!"

Jason's finger dabbed up every stray cookie crumb from his dessert plate. Then he sucked on his finger, savoring the hint of chocolate. "Can't I have one more cookie?" he begged his mother.

"You've already had two. That's enough. Why don't you go to the restroom and wash up?"

Jason mumbled something under his breath and shoved his chair back. "Fine."

Ben piped up as Jason passed, "How about a game of pool after you're done?"

Jason's tight features softened. He eyed his mother. "Can I?"

"Sure. Now scoot. We load up shortly."

"Be with you in a minute, Ben," Jason said, darting from the mess hall into the restroom across the hall. The bathroom was empty. Jason popped into the middle stall and fumbled with his belt.

As he sat down, he heard the door swing open, the noise from the hallway intruding until the door swung shut again. Someone whistled a tuneless melody as he approached the bank of toilet stalls and entered the cubicle on Jason's right. Still whistling, the man dropped his pack on the floor of the stall. Right beside Jason.

Jason watched, wide-eyed, as a black-haired hand reached down and released the pack's clasp, then fumbled within it. Jason heard a match strike . . . followed shortly by a long exhalation. He could smell a burning cigarette. Next he heard the unbuckling of a belt, and the whistling continued. As the whistler sat down, the man bumped his pack with his heel, sending it toppling over. A small pile of plastic-wrapped cubes of what looked like gray Play-Doh tumbled into Jason's stall.

A spat of foul foreign words flowed from the neighboring stall. He watched as the man reached to the floor of the stall to collect his pack and straighten it up. Jason raised his feet just in time as an arm swept into his stall and scooped up the cubes. More angry words. He could see the tip of a nose as the man checked to make sure he had all the cubes.

Just then, the door to the men's room swung open again. Another man crossed to the urinals. Jason heard a zipper whisk down, followed by a characteristic splashing. The man at the urinal sighed. Jason listened as his neighbor buckled his pants, then resecured his toppled pack.

His neighbor left the stall.

The man at the urinal spoke. Jason recognized Ben's accent. "Khalid, you're not supposed to smoke in here, mate."

"Ah, these Americans have too many rules. Who knows which to follow and which to ignore? Do you wish a cigarette?"

"Thanks for the offer," Ben retorted. "But right now I've a date to play pool."

The restroom door was shoved open, and Khalid tromped out.

Jason put his feet back on the floor and stood up. While fastening his belt, he looked down. The Egyptian man had missed one of those plastic-wrapped cubes. It had rolled to the far side of the toilet. Jason reached down and picked it up, wondering what to do. It squeezed like firm clay. He knew he should return it to Khalid, but then he would know Jason had been there eavesdropping. He was shoving it into his pocket when his stall door popped open.

"There you are!" Ben stood before him. "Your mom thought maybe you fell in."

Jason grinned. He pushed the cube the rest of the way into his pocket.

"What've you got there, mate? Did you pinch that third cookie?" Ben's smile took the heat from the accusation.

"No," Jason said, with a hiccup of laughter. "It's nothing."

"All right, then. Let's shoot some pool."

Blakely leaned into a gust of wind as he crossed the base. The CO's office was on the far side of the camp, away from the trash dump. If he didn't need this damned equipment so badly, he would have proceeded directly to Alpha Base. But communiqués and requests by Roland failed to sway the obstinate CO. He needed those damned circuit boards; they were essential to the communications net.

He strode up the steps to base headquarters, where a guard checked his identification. Blakely gave him a sour look while waiting. A red U.S. Navy helicopter buzzed them, spraying ice and debris into the guard's cubicle. Frowning, the guard glanced up.

"You're clear, Dr. Blakely."

"Thank you." He proceeded inside. Damned rules. He continued down the corridor after hanging up his parka. The CO's corner office was on the first floor. He strode up to the secretary, a yeoman with black-framed glasses and poor posture.

"I've come to speak to Commander Sung," Blakely said before the secretary could open his mouth.

"Do you have an appointment?"

"Just tell him it's Blakely. He'll see me."

"He's quite busy at the moment."

Blakely shook his head, recognizing bullshit when he smelled it. "Tell him I'm here."

"Just a moment." The secretary punched a button on a board of yellow lights. He turned away as he spoke, but Blakely could discern the words. "Excuse me, sir, but there's a Dr. Blakely wanting to speak to you." A pause as he listened to the phone, then, in an even quieter voice, "I tried that, sir. He's insistent." Another pause, his face reddening. It didn't take much to discern the secretary was on the receiving end of a good dressing-down. The conversation finished with a final, "Yes, sir."

The secretary, beads of sweat on his forehead, turned to face Blakely again. "The commander will see you now. Thank you for your patience."

Blakely felt sorry for the yeoman. He leaned down as he passed around the desk and whispered, "Don't worry, son, everyone knows Sung's an asshole."

The secretary grimaced. "Good luck."

You make your own luck, Blakely thought, as he pushed through the door to the inner office.

Commander Sung sat behind a wide mahogany desk so thickly lacquered it looked wet. Spread out before him were several open files. He pushed one file toward Blakely with a single finger as if repulsed by the touch. "I've read your request, Andrew."

Blakely hated when anyone called him by his first name. Especially a sanctimonious paper pusher like Sung. This was not the first time the two had locked horns. As the head researcher for the National Science Foundation, he was often in deadlock with Sung, the senior Navy officer. Oftentimes, science and the military were at odds on certain subjects—especially the scarce supplies stocked at this remote base.

Their animosity had intensified once Blakely had made his discovery of the diamond idol. He watched Sung turn green, coveting all the attention and money that had been flowing his way. Ever since, any cooperation with the military on the base was like pulling an impacted tooth.

Sung continued, a slight sneer at the corner of his lips, "I thought I already made myself perfectly clear. Those circuit boards are the last in stock. I cannot authorize their release until the backup supply arrives."

"That's bullshit, and you know it. I need those to repair a critical communications board."

Sung shrugged. "Damned unfortunate that your boards short-circuited."

"They wouldn't have if you'd supplied me with new boards instead of those ancient ones you scavenged off old equipment." He leaned his fists on the desk. "I want those *new* boards. I won't have you jeopardize this team."

"Then wait until the next shipment. It'll be here in three weeks."

"We've delayed long enough already."

"As CO of this camp, my decision is final." Sung rocked back in his chair.

Blakely had had enough of this bastard. He reached across the desk. Sung slid away, a look of shock on his face. Blakely suppressed a smile. The bastard thought he was being attacked. What a fool! He grabbed the phone on the desk and pulled it to him. What he was going to do was much worse.

Ignoring Sung's objections, he dialed a number and gave a password. He listened as he was connected through a series of operators. Finally, a familiar voice. Blakely answered, "Sir, I'm having trouble with the base commander." He paused. "Yes, sir. That's right. He's right here, sir."

Blakely smiled and passed the phone to Sung. "Your boss."

Sung slowly reached and took the phone. "Hello, this is Commander Sung."

Blakely watched the commander's face drain of color, then refill a bright red. Again Blakely could tell when someone's ass was getting chewed.

"Yes, I'll do it," Sung said, voice high. "Right away, Mr. Secretary. I understand the President's wishes."

The hel...

SIX

J ust a minute longer. Then it will be over.

Even though Ashley was strapped securely to her seat on the Navy helicopter, she gripped the handhold above her head. A sudden bump and turn of the craft caused her grip to tighten to a white-knuckled clamp. A dull throbbing behind her eyes warned of an impending headache. Just land this damned contraption, she thought. As if in answer, the helicopter dived downward.

Jason whooped as the helicopter tilted toward the icy wall of rock. The slopes of Mount Erebus filled the entire starboard view, seemingly an endless series of snowy cliffs and black chasms climbing to heaven.

Ashley closed her eyes, her stomach in her throat.

Jason tugged on her sleeve. "You gotta see this, Mom!"

She pushed his hand away. "Not right now, honey."

"But you can see the hole! It's freakin' weird."

She groaned, opening an eye. The world was a tilted plate, and the base of Erebus swung into view below them as they circled downward. The area below was festooned with orange tents, like boils on a white butt. A road of gouged mud and slush led out from the tent site to a black mouth in the cliff face of Erebus, large enough to drive a double-decker bus into. Snow blew from the opening as if the gaping mouth were exhaling.

The helicopter righted itself and descended like an elevator to the landing site, ice and snow billowing around them as they touched down.

Blakely yelled above the noise of the rotors inside the transport helicopter. "All right, folks! There's two Snow Cats just outside to transport us to the fissure."

Ben, seated across from her, grinned. "It's all downhill from here."

With her son begging for a window seat in the tight compartment of the wide-treaded Sno-Cat, Ashley had found herself squished between Jason and Ben. Linda, unencumbered by a son, had nabbed the seat next to the driver. The other members followed in a second vehicle.

The tunnel opening loomed ahead. It was originally a natural fissure that sliced deep into the side of Mount Erebus. Explosives and mining equipment had widened the fissure and smoothed a passageway into the volcanic mountain. She held her breath as their vehicle bounced over the lip into the cavernous tunnel, wide enough for two trucks. A regular two-lane highway into the heart of a volcano.

The walls, rough-hewn from blasting and drilling, were lighted by halogen lamps strung along the ceiling. As the Cat ground around a curve, daylight vanished; the lamps remained the only illumination. The driver clicked on the headlights, spearing the darkness ahead.

Though it seemed as if they were traveling on level ground, she knew from the briefing that they were heading at a downward angle; the tunnel, four miles long, would descend almost four thousand feet.

But it was slow progress. Even traveling at a snail's pace, the bumpy roadway kept jarring her into Ben's side. "Sorry," she said, pushing herself off his shoulder.

"No worries. I was sort of enjoying it."

She smirked at him. Did he ever stop?

Linda turned to face them. "Do you mind if I open my window a crack? I'd like to . . . well . . . it's kind of stuffy."

Ashley's eyebrows pulled together. Linda's complexion blanched, her lips dry and caked. Probably hadn't liked the helicopter ride either. She could definitely sympathize, but it was damned cold outside. "I don't know. I don't want Jason to catch a chill. Perhaps—"

"A little fresh air sounds good," Ben said. He reached and squeezed Ashley's hand. "Jason, do you mind?"

Ashley stared down at Ben's hand. He kept squeezing as though trying to communicate to her. She bit back a retort.

Her son, glued to the tunnel ahead, mouth open, waved a hand at them. "I don't mind."

"Fine," Ashley said, "go ahead, Linda. But Jason, you stay bundled up."

Linda grinned weakly and turned forward once more. A gush of icy wind swirled into the compartment as she lowered her window an inch. With her nose to the window, Linda inhaled deeply, visibly relaxing.

Ben released Ashley's hand. She burrowed deeper into her parka, clutching the hood around her face. She turned to question Ben, but he continued to study Linda, his brow tight with concern.

Resigned, Ashley leaned back and watched the overhead lamps wink by as they passed under them.

Down the white rabbit's hole went Alice.

· · ·

Blakely sat next to the driver, staring at the taillights of the Sno-Cat up ahead. He had been studying the passing tunnel walls, eyeing the electrical and communications cables. All was in order. As long as the base commander didn't try any last-minute sabotaging of his plans, everything was prepared.

Khalid leaned forward from where he sat in the rear of the Sno-Cat. "How much farther?" he asked.

Blakely glanced over his shoulder to face the geologist. "We'll reach the shaft elevators in about ten minutes. Be at Alpha Base by dinner. So relax. Enjoy the ride."

Khalid nodded, and Blakely watched the Egyptian return to studying the passing lamps and cables, his dark eyes taking in all the details.

Swinging back in his seat, Blakely understood the geologist's edginess. This waiting gnawed at one's nerves.

Ashley stretched muscles cramped by the ride. She glanced back as the second Sno-Cat trundled into the large cavern and discharged its passengers, then returned her attention to the massive elevator—a cage of iron bars.

Jason was exploring around the huge crates that filled the back half of the cave. He looked like a mouse scurrying among a child's spilled toy blocks. "Jason!" she called. "Stay close, hon."

Her son waved his acknowledgment.

Blakely, enlisting Ben's aid, waved toward the elevators. "Help me with these doors."

Ben and Major Michaelson hauled the doors aside so the crew could enter. Jason had wandered over. Ben tousled his hair. "Ready for this, mate?"

Jason grinned as he entered the garage-sized elevator, big enough to park both Sno-Cats. "Oh, yeah. This is so awesome."

Ashley eyed the interior of the elevator. The ceiling and floor were sheets of solid red iron, but the walls were just one-inch-thick iron bars. Like a gigantic birdcage.

"We'll travel about the equivalent of two hundred floors," Blakely said as the doors closed. "Took three years alone to mine out this six-hundred-meter shaft that separates the floor of this rift from the cavern below." He yanked a lever, and Ashley felt the familiar lurching as the elevator dropped with a rumble.

She held Jason's hand. How safe was this contraption? She voiced her concerns.

Blakely smiled. "We've hauled heavy machinery with this elevator. Even several trucks. It'll hold the group of us just fine." He tapped the metal wall of the cage. "This is the lifeline of Alpha Base. It's maintained like an expensive Swiss watch and guarded like the crown jewels."

Ashley noticed Khalid's smile. Amused at her feminine fears, she thought. Just another macho man, fearless in the face of reason. She watched him as he eyed the cage, studying it.

An uncomfortable silence took hold as the team continued their descent. The only illumination came from a single lamp in the ceiling of the cage. It felt like they were suspended in space.

Feeling the need to break the silence, Ashley turned to Blakely. "You know," she said, "something has been bothering me. And I imagine a few of the others too."

"Hmmm?" He seemed lost in reverie.

Ben perked up, pushing off the wall he had been leaning on. The others too were staring at them with interest.

"Let's be honest here," she said. "Are we here to investigate this continent or rape it?"

Blakely's eyebrows arched.

"We all know science doesn't pay"—she waved at the steel cage—"this *well*. More's at stake than just an archaeological investigation."

"True," Blakely said, taking off his glasses and rubbing at the bridge of his nose, "but let me assure you, first and foremost I *am* a scientist. To me, the mission has been and always will be a scientific one. That is one of the reasons I chose you to head this team, Professor Carter. I want this mission to remain a scientific venture. But we don't live in a vacuum. This mission does have some significant economic and political ramifications."

Blakely added, "Don't be so quick to judge. It gets the bills paid. Gets me my equipment." He pointed at the others, then at her. "And it gets me a prime team."

"Still," she said, "what's the final tradeoff for this exploration? If we end up with a strip-mined and blasted continent . . . that's too hefty a price tag. I can live without answering the mystery of the caverns."

He stared at her, a sad look on his face. "Can you really, Professor Carter?"

She opened her mouth to declare her convictions, but the lie would not come out. She had asked Blakely to be honest. Could she be any less? She remembered the diamond figurine, glowing in the last rays of the setting sun. She closed her mouth. Damn.

He nodded and pointed down. "Here it comes."

Just then a breeze rushed into the cage, blowing back her parka hood. A warm breeze! At the same time, light burst up from below. The elevator had just dropped into the cavern.

The ceiling of the cave, illuminated from below, dripped with damp stalactites, huge mountains hanging upside down. Several reached to the floor to form gigantic pillars. A natural colonnade. The elevator was descending beside a pillar twice the diameter of their own cage. Ashley noticed someone had scrawled graffiti on the column. An arrow pointing down with the rough-lettered words, "Hell . . . one mile!"

Ben frowned. "Defacing a cavern. That's not only poor taste, but among cavers it's considered bad luck."

Blakely scowled at his assistant Roland. "Let's get that removed—*today.*"

Ashley shook her head; droplets flew from the tip of her nose. She wiped her brow. Damp. The humidity must be close to a hundred percent. But the air! She inhaled deeply. It was so clean.

She squinted, but the far wall was blocked by the massive pillar. Damn. She had hoped to spy the dwellings.

"Mom! Look!" Jason pointed toward the cavern floor.

Sighing in exasperation, she stood on tiptoe, leaning her forehead against the cold bars. Below, buildings and tents dotted the floor, lit by searchlights and festooned with lamps. A deep chasm, like a black wound, cut the base in two. A lighted bridge crossed the gap, linking the two halves. It was their destination.

Alpha Base.

"Look over here," Linda exclaimed. "You can see fish!"

Ashley sidled behind Linda, placing a hand on her shoulder, peering over and down.

At the edge of Alpha Base, reflecting the lights of the camp, was a mammoth lake, covering several hundred acres, rippling gently. From above, a few glowing residents of the lake could be seen gliding and darting under the glassy surface. Strangely poetic.

"Cool," Jason exclaimed.

"And how, mate." Ben nudged Ashley with an elbow. "Amazing, ain't it?"

Ashley nodded, her mind numb. Anxious to explore, her qualms from a moment ago were a dim memory. "Am I remembering correctly? Did you say the cavern was five miles across?"

Blakely nodded, a smile playing about his lips. "Approximately."

Ben whistled.

Within minutes, the cage settled to the cavern floor, secure in its berth. A uniformed escort stood ready to guide them to their quarters. Blakely faced the group. "We're home!"

SEVEN

Alpha Base, Antarctica

Ashley watched with a smirk as Jason darted around his bedroom. Her own room in the two-bedroom suite was just as impressive. Hard to believe each member of the team had a separate suite in the main dormitory of the base. The perks of working on this mission were getting better and better. Lace curtains, walnut desks, thick upholstered chairs, designer wallpaper. Who would have thought they were two miles underground?

"Look, Mom." He pointed to a desk in the corner of his room. "A real Pentium II. Not one of those slowpoke clones."

She hated to burst his balloon, but he had to learn sometime. "That's for your homework."

Jason turned to her, his jaw hanging open. "It's the beginning of summer, Mom!"

"It's only a couple hours each day. While I'm gone, I want you to put this time to use. There's a library on the base. I want you to check out two books while I'm gone and write a book report on each."

He looked aghast, his eyes wide. "Some summer!"

"It'll be fun. Roland will be"—she dare not say "babysitting," or Jason would never forgive her—"watching you. He'll be staying here while I'm gone. I expect you to mind him."

He scrunched up his face, irate.

"If you mind your manners and do your homework . . . *without sulking* . . . there are some surprises in store for you."

"Yeah," he said, his voice thick with skepticism. "Like what?"

"First, I found a martial arts expert on the base who can continue your lessons here. If you want to get your yellow belt by year's end, you're gonna need to practice while I'm gone."

The black cloud over his face lifted just a bit.

"Plus, they have electric bikes and Jet Skis to ride."

Jason grimaced. "Why electric?"

"To help protect the ecosystem they limit the number of combustion engines down here. It's the military's small contribution to cavern preservation." Ashley remembered Ben's scowl as they traveled across the base, grumbling the entire way about the blatant abuse of the fragile ecology. Still, Jason's pout drew back her attention. She brushed some loose strands of hair away from her face. "But, Jason, that's not all they have planned. There's also fishing, basketball, you name it. Plenty to keep you entertained while I'm gone. *And* if you do well with your studies, Dr. Blakely has promised you can join him in the control room and help monitor our progress. You'll even be able to talk to me."

"Well, I guess that's okay," Jason said, still pouting a bit.

"Finally," she said, pointing back into the main room of the suite, "they have cable. A hundred and fifty channels, all decoded."

"Wow, I gotta check that out."

She caught him by the sleeve as he barreled past her. "Whoa, there, sonny. First, we have dinner in a half hour. Go get yourself cleaned up."

"Geez, Mom. Can't a guy have a little fun?" He stomped toward the bathroom.

She grinned. Just like home. Only two miles below the bottom of the earth's surface.

"So what do you think, kid?" Ben asked as he approached Linda's back.

She stood at the edge of the lake, nicknamed the "Bottomless Pit" by the grunts. Only a foot away, black water lapped at a rock from the waves created by a passing Navy pontoon boat.

He scratched at the stubble on his cheek.

She glanced over at him, the light of the camp dancing in her eyes. "It's wondrous." She pointed at the ceiling several hundred feet up. "It's like being outside."

He nodded, then shrugged in the direction of the water. "Thinkin' of skinny-dipping?"

She smiled. "No, but you could."

"Oh, no, you'd snatch up my skivvies and have the whole base laughing at me."

She grinned wider, more relaxed. "That's not what I meant. I meant you *could* actually swim in there. I've heard that some of the Marines do it. The water is quite warm. Eighty-two degrees. I tested it. Heated by volcanic vents."

"Seems strange," Ben said. "Up above, it's ice and freezing winds. Here, it's bathwater and tropical breezes."

"Not really so strange. I've heard that the seas around Deception Island off the coast of Antarctica sometimes heat to spa temperatures. The volcanic activity is so pronounced that often the water actually boils. Just meters away from a glacier."

"Uh-huh," he said, arching his eyebrows as if he doubted her.

She nudged him with her elbow. "It's true."

He smiled. "Actually, I believe you. I've been in other caverns warmed by subterranean rifts. Not really that rare. I was just testing you."

"Yeah, right," she said, rolling her eyes.

A glowing amber fish jumped a yard from shore, causing Linda to let out a quick gasp. Ben's eyebrows narrowed. "Listen, lass, there's something I want to talk to you about."

She wiped damp strands of hair from her face. "What?"

"I've been watching you, and I . . . well, I—"

She held up a hand. "I'm sorry, Ben. I know we went dancing in Buenos Aires, but that was only to let off a little steam. I want to keep this experience purely professional."

Ben grinned, realizing Linda thought he was making a pass at her. From her looks, she must get that a lot. "Whoa, there, lady. That's not why I'm here."

"Why, then?"

"Over the years, I've led bushels of tourists into caves, and . . . well, I can smell trouble. Since our night out dancing, I've been watching you. Both in that crowded bar and now here among the caves, you've been awfully edgy. Shallow breathing, sweaty palms, pale face." Ben saw her eyes sink to the stone floor with his words. "That's why I came out to talk to you alone. I thought maybe there was something you'd like to get off your chest."

She raised her face to him, her eyes rimmed with tears. "You're right, Ben. I have a problem with tight places."

"Claustrophobia?"

She rubbed at her forehead, eyes down again, and nodded.

"During the trip ahead, there are going to be *many* tight places. A panicked team member could jeopardize all of us."

"I know. But I'm on medication and have been through years of therapy. I can handle this."

"Even that tango bar in Buenos Aires shook you up."

"Because I didn't take my pills. Didn't think I would need them. The bar with its packed crowd and loud music just caught me off guard. I can handle this mission."

He reached over and held her shoulders. "You're sure?"

She looked at him. "I'll be fine. I can do this."

A fish jumped again. This time the splash failed to startle Linda. She continued to stare Ben straight in the eye.

Silent for several breaths, he weighed her resolve. "Did you pack a fishing pole?" he finally asked.

"Why?"

"You'll need it if you want to collect specimens during this trip."

"Right," she said with a smile. "So you won't mention this to anyone?" She wiped at her eyes.

Ben released her and picked up a flat stone. He skimmed it across the smooth lake surface. "Mention what?"

The more life changes, the more it stays the same, Ashley thought, staring at her plate. Before her, cheese bubbled and white pasta floated in a steaming marinara sauce. Waves of garlic assaulted her nose. Lasagna again. Ashley smiled, remembering the last lasagna dinner, when Blakely first proposed this mission. The food was the same, but not the surroundings. Linen, bone china, crystal chandelier, mahogany dining table. Not her trailer's kitchenette. She speared a forkful of the pasta.

"Professor Carter," Blakely said. "I've arranged a research associate, Dr. Harold Symski, to guide you on a tour of the north wall. He'll be calling on you around eight o'clock tomorrow morning."

With a hand held up, she swallowed her mouthful. "Since I only have the one day, I would rather start earlier. Say around six o'clock."

Blakely smiled. "I'll let Dr. Symski know."

Ben cleared his throat and wiped a dribble of cheese from his chin. "I'd like to go and check them out too."

"Fine with me," Blakely said. "Is that all right with you, Professor Carter?"

Ashley pictured Ben crawling beside her into a cramped cave, his body pressing against hers. "As long as he doesn't get in the way."

He raised his hands in feigned innocence. "Who, me?"

Blakely addressed the rest of the group. "Any others?"

Jason raised a tentative hand. "I'd like to go."

"I don't think that would be wise," Blakely said sternly. "There are many rockfalls and pits in that area. It's safer here."

Jason turned toward Ashley. "But Mom, I—"

Linda interrupted. "He can come with me to research the lake. The section I'll be surveying lies within the boundaries of the camp." She turned to the boy. "Would you mind helping me, Jason?"

Ashley looked down at her blushing son. "Is that okay with you, honey?"

He nodded, his voice squeaking a bit. "Sure. I'd like that."

Linda smiled. "Then it's settled. Jason and I will be doing research."

Ben, seated on Jason's far side, nudged him with an elbow. "Way to go, champ," he whispered, but purposefully loud enough for Ashley to hear. "Now we both have dates."

Jason covered a smile with a small hand.

Ashley rolled her eyes. Men.

Lights out. From his window, Khalid watched the lamps wink out as the camp was put to bed, fake sunset in the darkened cave. The importance of circadian rhythms in a darkened environment had been explained earlier by Blakely. Peak performance required tuning the environment to a regular diurnal pattern of darkness and light.

This worked well with his plans. Shadows wove a fine cloak.

Soon only a scattering of bulbs were still lit. Except for the searchlight by the elevator. Its shaft of light stabbed the ceiling, circling in slow ovals around the stalactites, black fingers pointing down.

He glanced at his watch. Ten o'clock. Time to go to work. He left his room and slipped out the dormitory's entrance. The "night" was still warm, almost balmy, moisture thick in the air. Nothing like the dry nights at home. Desert sands remained hot well into the chilly night. Stars spread across the sky like the fires of Allah's jihad.

Passing through the residential half of the camp, winding among an acre of khaki tents, Khalid seldom strayed from the shadows. Yet he kept his gait casual in case any eyes spied him. On the far side of the camp, across a deep gorge, were the research labs and military headquarters. His destination, the elevator, was located within that distant encampment.

His only obstacle: the bridge over the chasm. On the way from the elevator earlier today, he had noted it was guarded. That one guard was of no concern to him.

Khalid continued across the sleeping camp. After edging around a final Quonset hut, he spied the bridge, made of wood and metal, lighted with lamps on the corners. One corner's light had burned out. A single uniformed man leaned against a light pole, a rifle over his shoulder. A quick survey indicated the area was clear.

Checking his pocket, Khalid stepped into the island of light by the bridge and strolled toward the black gorge. The guard took note of his approach, pushed off the post, and unslung his rifle. Khalid crossed to the chasm's edge, a good yard from the bridge. Leaning over, he peered into the darkness, the chasm's bottom remaining a black mystery.

The guard, a young wheat-haired farm-boy type, called to him, "Careful, there. Those edges crumble away easily."

"I'll be careful. Just wanted a look." Khalid reached into his jacket's breast pocket, noting the guard didn't even raise an eyebrow at such a threatening move.

Good.

He pulled out a package of Winstons and tapped out a new cigarette. Popping it into his mouth, he returned the pack to his pocket and pulled a red Bic lighter out. He watched the guard from the corner of his eye as he lit up; the guard's attention was transfixed by the flame.

Khalid extinguished the lighter and dropped it into his side pocket, next to the knife. "Want a smoke?" he called over to the guard.

The guard shrugged. "Thanks, man." He left his post and crossed to where Khalid stood at the edge of the chasm.

Khalid fished out his pack of cigarettes and shook a few out for the guard. "Take a couple."

The guard slipped one to his lips and another into his uniform pocket. "Got a light?"

"Sure." Khalid reached into his pocket and wrapped his fingers around the stiletto, coughing to cover the *click* of the release as he pressed the button. "Have they ever searched the bottom of the chasm?"

"Nah." The guard glanced at the black crevice. "Too damn deep."

"Good." With the guard's attention diverted, Khalid whipped out the knife and slashed deeply into the Marine's neck, making sure to slice below the larynx to ensure a silent death. No scream, just a wet gurgle.

Stepping back to avoid the spurting arterial blood, he tipped the guard backward into the gorge. For a moment, the guard teetered, arms wheeling as he tried to regain balance, eyes stretched open in horror, a wash of blood flowing down his chest. Then he tumbled into the blackness.

Khalid listened. After a handful of seconds, he heard a distant thud.

Content, he crossed the bridge and slipped into shadows. From here he would need to move quickly and quietly. He proceeded across the base toward the elevator, avoiding pools of light. Thankfully, they were few and far between.

After four minutes, he was at the elevator. The area, well lighted but empty of eyes, was unguarded. The military, isolated so far from the world, was too damned confident with the security of their periphery.

After a minute of study, Khalid crouched and darted for the huge metal box that housed the elevator's motor assembly. He slipped a cube of plastique from his inner jacket pocket and secured it to the assembly in a darkened corner. He paused a moment. No time to be frugal. He took a second cube and positioned it next to the first. That was better. More than enough to leave a crater where the motors now stood. He carefully wired the bomb to ignite with the proper signal from his transceiver. He eyed his handiwork with a thin-lipped smile.

A security blanket. When the time was right, this should cover his escape, ensuring no one followed him back up.

After a final check, he fled into the dark.

EIGHT

S even o'clock in the morning? More like midnight.

Ashley shook her head, staring out the windshield as the electric vehicle bumped along. Due to the enclosed space of the caverns and the risk of fouling the air with carbon monoxide, internal-combustion engines had been prohibited, except for a few watercraft.

So the electric golf-cart-like transports, nicknamed "Mules" by the Navy personnel, were the only real means of travel around Alpha Cavern.

Ashley rubbed at the Mule's fogged window. Only the headlamps broke the darkness ahead. Beside her, with both hands firmly gripping the wheel, sat Dr. Symski, a young freckled researcher still new to his degree.

From the backseat, over the buzzing whine of the electric motor, Ben's snores erupted like shotgun blasts. She glanced over her shoulder at him. How could he just fall asleep like that? The trip was a one-hour excursion over rough terrain. An exceptionally large bump jarred her back into a forward position.

Dr. Symski turned one eye toward her. "I can't believe I'm sitting next to *the* Professor Carter," he said. "I've read your paper on the Gila dwellings. Amazing stuff. And now here you are."

"Thanks," she said. The young researcher had too much enthusiasm for so early in the morning. Her cup of coffee hadn't kicked in yet, and the stench of leaking ozone from the motor's batteries was making her queasy.

"I wish you were here with us from the start. I'm afraid there's nothing new left to explore. We've already searched, cataloged, diagrammed, and explored every square inch. It was all in the papers I sent you last night."

She rubbed at her red eyes. It had taken her until four in the morning to read the reams of data. Two hours of sleep did not make for a pleasant morning. "I wish someone had faxed me those earlier. I would have liked to have gone through them more thoroughly before viewing the site."

"Sorry, but all this is stamped confidential. We were ordered to restrict access until you arrived."

She watched the road ahead as the Mule crawled through the shadows. "More goddamn secrecy," she grumbled.

"I'll show you the main areas when we arrive. A guided tour, if you will."

Hell with that, she thought. "Listen, Dr. Symski, I'm sure your team was very precise, but I'd prefer to do a little exploring on my own. Get a feel for the place. The study of a site involves more than just numbering and cataloging."

"What do you mean?"

She drew a long breath. How to put this into words? The more you worked on a dig, the more each site developed its own character—or soul. For instance, the Gila dwellings "felt" different than the Chaco Canyon site. She found this perspective added a unique level of insight into the people and customs.

"Never mind," she said. "It's just what I do."

He shrugged. "I'll leave you on your own, then. I wanted to recheck some measurements anyhow."

She nodded. Good. He was starting to grate on her nerves.

Settling back into her seat, she allowed the road to lull her. Just as her eyes half closed, Dr. Symski stopped the Mule with a hard brake. "Here we are," he said.

She looked out. Nothing but darkness beyond the stretch of headlights. "Where?"

"Got to kick up the generator first." He opened his door, and the vehicle's interior lights flashed on. Ben awakened with a startled grunt.

"Are we there yet?" he asked huskily, rubbing a hand through his hair.

"Yes," she said, trying to drip as much disdain into her voice as possible. "You know, you could have caught up on your sleep back at camp."

"And miss this? No way."

She watched the young doctor, flashlight in hand, cross to the far wall where the generator sat. He bent over and began fiddling with the unit. Frowning, Ashley climbed from the truck, hoping the ham-fisted military researchers hadn't corrupted the dig. So many times in the past, key clues to an ancient society's history had been trampled on by the incompetent.

Within moments, the generator coughed, sputtered, then settled into an even rumbling sound. Floodlights ignited, blinding after the dark ride. The north wall lit up like a huge stage.

"Wow," Ben said as he climbed out next to her.

A scaffolding of metal frames and warped boards covered the honeycombed wall of the cavern. Dwellings extended up the wall in five distinct levels, she estimated a total of about forty yards in height. The levels connected to one another by either a series of handholds or sets of crude stairs. She squinted to the left; the excavated dwellings even extended over the lake, with plateaus of rock jutting over the water like porches.

"What do you think, Ashley?" Ben stood to her left.

"I could spend years here."

Ben nodded. "Who do you think built this place?"

She pointed at the wall. "One thing I know. This was not built by *Homo sapiens*."

"Then who did it?"

"An earlier species of man, I suspect. Look at the size of the caves. None over four feet in height. Too small for modern man. Perhaps *Homo erectus*, but I doubt even that." She found herself thinking out loud. "A Neanderthal tribe? I don't know. I've never seen evidence of a Neanderthal tribe building this extensively. And how did they get here?" She shrugged. "I've got to get a closer look."

"Shouldn't we wait for Dr. Symski?"

"I don't think that'll be necessary." She strode toward the wall, placing a mining helmet on her head.

She heard the scuff of Ben's boots as he followed her.

Dr. Symski called to her. "Careful where you step. There are many crevasses, some quite deep."

She waved at him in acknowledgment, but shook her head. What did he think, that she was some damned novice? She marched faster.

Suddenly something grabbed her from behind. Instinctively, she rammed her elbow backward.

"Ouch!" Ben said, releasing her and stepping back. "I was just trying to stop you from stepping in a hole." He pointed in front of her, rubbing at his solar plexus. "What do you do, sharpen that thing?"

She cupped her elbow, as if trying to hide it. "Sorry." Even pointed out, the black hole was barely discernible from the black rock. She stepped around it. "I didn't see it."

"You could have twisted an ankle."

"Thanks."

"You're welcome. But next time I touch you, try not to kill me."

Her face heated up. She cleared her throat, grateful that they had not reached the floodlit cliffs yet. The darkness hid her red face. "Let's check out the lower dwellings," she suggested, stepping away from him. She couldn't tell if she was more embarrassed by her near gaffe or mad at his action . . . or something else. He was so unlike her ex-husband. Where Scott, ever the accountant, was steady and often sullen, seldom sharing his intimate thoughts, Ben's easygoing manner and good humor were unsettling.

They arrived at one of the dwelling entrances. "Ladies first," Ben said.

Ashley avoided looking at him and crouched down, lighting up the interior with her helmet lamp. The chamber extended back about five yards. The walls, unadorned rock, were obviously carved from the stone and polished. She passed a hand over the smooth interior surface, impressed by the ingenuity and tenacity of early man. With crude tools, it must have taken years to excavate each one of the chambers.

The interior, devoid of any hints about its occupants, stood empty. Bending, she crawled inside. It never hurt to look.

Her helmet scraped across the ceiling as she wormed into the small opening. She noticed there was a small hollow in the floor near the entrance. Probably an ancient firepit. She proceeded to the back of the chamber. Nothing. She sat down for a moment, pondering who built these homes.

"Did you find anything?"

She looked back at Ben, helmeted and crouched on one knee by the entrance. He blocked the whole opening. "It's strange," she said.

"What?"

"Where did they all go?"

He shrugged. "Probably died off. Went extinct. Like the dinosaurs."

She shook her head. "No. That doesn't make sense with the state of this site."

"What do you mean?"

"The first researchers only discovered a handful of broken tools and crude stone bowls. Usually these primitive home sites are brimming with artifacts. But here . . . nothing."

"They must have moved on, taking their stuff with them."

"Exactly!" She nodded, impressed by Ben's intuitiveness. "But why leave? Why spend decades digging out this habitat only to abandon it? And what about the diamond statuette? Why leave it behind?"

Ben remained silent.

"If only I could spend more time here." She smacked the flat of her hand on the rock.

"Why? Sounds like they already went over everything with a fine-tooth comb."

She shook her head. "No. Clues are too often missed. Even after years of study. I need more time."

"But why bother? We might find a lot more answers during *our* exploration."

"I hope so." She crawled her way toward the entrance. Ben offered his hand to her as she exited. She took it, his hand hot in her cold palm. He pulled her toward him. She was surprised by his strength, and her left foot slipped in the damp hollow of the cave's firepit and she fell backward, landing her backside squarely into the firepit and dragging Ben down on top of her.

Ben's nose lay an inch from her breast. He looked up at her. "You're not going to hit me again, are you?"

"Sorry. I slipped." She blushed furiously, his body pressing hard on hers.

He cleared his throat. "No apology necessary," he said, grinning down at her. "A few more slips like this and we might have to get married."

She grimaced at him. "Just get off of me." She meant to be stern, but couldn't quite pull it off.

Suddenly, uncontrolled, she began laughing. She couldn't help it. And couldn't stop it. "I mean it . . ." she said between laughs. "Get off!"

Looking at her oddly, he crawled off her. "It's good to hear you laugh."

She wiped a tear from her eye, still wracked with occasional bursts of laughter. She dropped her head back on the floor, trying to catch her breath. She stared at the ceiling. And saw it. Up there on the ceiling, behind the lip of the entrance. "Goddamn!"

She squinted again at the ceiling. It wasn't her imagination. "Goddamn it!"

She sat up.

"What is it?" Ben asked, a concerned look on his face.

"Those amateurs said they had searched every square inch of this site. No artwork. No cave drawings." She pointed to the ceiling. "Then what the hell is that?"

Ben leaned over and twisted his head around. "What is what?"

"You have to lay down. I think that's why no one's found it." She moved to the side so he could lay down beside her. She pointed with the light of her headlamp. "Right there! Look!"

The crude carving stood in the circle of her light. Only a hand span wide, an oval was chiseled into the ceiling, bisected by a jagged line, like a lightning bolt.

Ben reached up and, with a long whistle, traced it with his finger. His next words were a whisper. "You know, this sort of looks familiar."

"What do you mean?" She expected some wise-crack.

"I've seen something like this. My granddaddy showed it to me."

"You're kidding."

"No, I'm serious." His voice sounded genuine. Almost amazed. "My great-grandmother was full Gagudja, an Aboriginal tribe in the Djuwarr region. Did I ever tell you that?"

"No."

He smiled an inch from her nose. "God's truth, my lady."

The man seemed to have more sides than the Pentagon. Either that or he was spinning a wild tale. She studied him and noted that his blue eyes were coldly serious. She swallowed and turned back to the design on the ceiling. "Does it remind you of anything specific?"

He shrugged, bumping her shoulder. "It's not exactly the same. But it looks sort of like the Gagudja symbol for one of their spirit peoples. One of their oldest, named Mimi."

She considered this information. Could there be some connection? Perhaps a lost Aboriginal tribe? But these dwellings were dated five million years ago. Aeons before the appearance of Aborigines on the Australian continent.

She frowned at the oval drawing. It was probably just a coincidence. She had seen the universality of some symbols across other cultures. Could this be the same case here? Hell, the symbol was rather basic. "This Mimi spirit," she began. "What type of spirit was it?"

"It's just nonsense. Stories."

"No, go on. Myths often have a kernel of truth. Tell me."

He patted the walls of the cave. "Mimis were spirits that lived in rocks."

She felt a chill crawl down her spine, noticing their stone enclosure.

"The Mimis taught the first Bushman to hunt and paint. They were greatly revered. And fear—"

Just then, Dr. Symski returned, standing at their feet. "What are you all doing?" His voice was both accusatory and embarrassed.

Conscious of their odd position, Ashley scrambled out. "I thought you searched this area."

"We did. Why?"

She pointed to the spot next to Ben. "Go look. Up on the roof."

The doctor crawled next to the Aussie. "My god!" he said when he looked where Ben pointed. "It's amazing. Jesus, what do you think it means?"

"I don't have a clue," she said, her hands on her hips, "but I mean to find out."

Linda, seated on a blanket, watched the crystal lake lap at the rocks along the shore a yard away. The water, clear as a window, teemed with small fish and other marine life. A luncheon basket, prepared by the mess hall cook, was open beside her. Two half-eaten sandwiches sat on a paper plate. Bologna and cheese.

"They look like little monsters," Jason said.

Smiling, Linda glanced over to the boy crouched over her portable Nikon microscope, viewing a water sample taken from the lake. "Those cone-shaped ones are called tintinnids," she said. "The squarish ones are diatoms."

"What are they? Some sort of bugs?"

"Not really. More like plants. They're in a family of organisms called phytoplankton. They take sunlight and convert it to energy the way a plant does."

"But if they need sunlight, like a plant"—Jason swiveled to face her, his face scrunched up with concentration—"how do they survive down here in the dark?"

She tousled his hair. "That's a very good question. I'm not really sure. But I believe there must be an underground current carrying the plankton from the surface waters to this underground lake. The water is very salty. Like diluted seawater."

"What's so important about . . . these . . ." He pointed at the microscope. "Bugs?"

As Linda considered the implication herself, she allowed her gaze to drift across the camp. She noticed a flurry of activity among the military personnel by the gorge that split the base. Probably some sort of training exercise.

"Well?" Jason asked, recalling her attention.

She turned back to the boy. "Do you want a science lesson?"

"Sure!" he replied enthusiastically.

"All right, you asked for it." She smiled at him, appreciating his inquisitiveness. "These *plankton* are the building blocks of life. On solid ground, grass turns sunlight into energy. Then a cow eats the grass. Then we eat the cow. This is the way the sun's energy is passed on to us. In the sea, it is the phytoplankton that turns sunlight into energy. The phytoplankton is then eaten by small creatures, such as jellyfish"—she pointed to the small fish just offshore—"which in turn get eaten by those tiny fish. Then even bigger fish eat the little fish. And so on. So even in the sea, sunlight's energy is passed along. Do you understand?"

"So these plankton thingies are like our grass."

"Exactly. They are the grassy fields from which this ecosystem sprouts."

He nodded. "Neat."

"So we've done step one and determined that the water is alive. Next, after we finish our sandwiches, we have to collect some of the creatures that live in the water. I saw some starfish close to the shore over there and some sponges. Wanna help me get a few?"

"You bet!"

"Later, one of the Marines promised to catch us one of those glowing fish too." She was curious about the phosphorescent properties of these large fish. Never having seen anything like them before, she grew excited by the prospect of classifying a new fish species.

"Why don't we start now?" Jason began to rise. "I saw some—"

"Hold it, young man." She pointed at the plate. "You finish your lunch first. You're my responsibility until your mother gets back."

He curled his lip and plopped back down on the blanket. "Oh, all right."

Passing him his sandwich, she took a bite of her own. "Let's hurry up, though. We've got fish to catch!"

"Big ones," he added with a small smile.

"The biggest. We could have them for dinner."

"Glowing fish? Yuck!"

"Hey, buddy, don't knock it. If the lights go out, you can still see what you're eating."

That started him laughing. She grinned, almost forgetting the miles of rock that hung over her head.

Ben watched Ashley bend over and study the altar site. Damn nice curves on that woman. He took off his helmet and wiped a red handkerchief across his damp forehead. It was getting late, and his stomach was growling. Thank god this was the last chamber to investigate.

He sighed as he watched Ashley pull out a measuring tape. "Not again," he cursed under his breath. Since this morning's discovery, he had felt like a third wheel, tagging along behind Ashley and Dr. Symski as they explored. Stopping in each chamber, measuring, scraping, sampling. Boring. He had hoped to spend more private time with Ashley, but with the discovery of the carving, both doctors were like bloodhounds on a scent. Nothing could distract them. Not a joke, not a quip. He was all but invisible.

"So this is where you found the diamond figurine?" Ashley knelt down beside the raised dais of stone. It mushroomed from the floor of one of the chambers. "The pedestal's carved from the base stone. Suggestive that the builders purposefully designed this chamber. All the other chambers have their firepits in this location." She pointed up to the ceiling. "Also this is the only room that doesn't have an oval symbol above the door."

Ben stood on the lip of rock that acted as a doorstep to the chamber. He glanced over the edge to the water far below. The chamber was on the highest level and was located on the section of cliff wall above the lake. Without the scaffolding, it would have been a difficult climb, even for him.

Ashley turned to Dr. Symski, who crouched in the back of the dwelling. "When your researchers found the statue," she asked, "was the figure facing out or in?"

"Well . . ." He shuffled his feet. "You see, there was this accident. The first man in here knocked it over. We don't know which way it was facing."

She slapped the altar stone. "What other key details did you botch?"

Dr. Symski flushed.

Ben, feeling irritable himself with all this nitpicking, intervened. "What difference does it make? Whether it was facing in or out or lying on its freakin' back?"

Ashley, with narrowed eyes, turned to him. "It makes all the difference in the world. This is the only significant artifact in the dig. It must have once had great importance to the culture here. If it was facing out when it was found, it was probably a warding charm, to keep evil spirits away. If it was facing in, then it probably was a worship tool, used in rituals."

Ben scratched behind his ear; a trickle of sweat ran down from under his helmet. "In the bigger scheme of things, what difference does it make if it was a charm or an idol? How is that going to solve the bigger mystery of where they went?"

She opened her mouth to answer, then shut it with an almost audible snap. "I give up," was all she mumbled as she shoved past him and began climbing down.

Ben immediately regretted his remark. He knew instinctively that he had blown any progress he'd made that day impressing and charming Ashley. "Wait up," he called, climbing down after her. Dr. Symski followed.

"To hell with both of you!" she called out, not even looking back.

It was a quiet ride back to Alpha Base.

NINE

"**M**om, you should have seen the fish we caught." Jason spread his arms as wide as he could reach, almost bumping Linda, who was seated next to him at the dinner table. "It was bigger than this."

"That's some fish," Ashley said.

"It was phosphorescent! That means it glowed."

Ashley noticed he had chosen to sit next to Linda at tonight's dinner table. The two of them must have had a great day together.

"It was blue. With huge teeth."

"Sounds bloody weird, mate," Ben said as he entered the dining room, his hair still damp from a shower. "A real dingoling."

"Hey, Ben!" Jason said, greeting him with a mile-wide smile. "You should have been there."

"Sorry, champ," Ben said. "Had to help your mother." He sat down—a couple seats away from Ashley.

She knew why he chose to sit so far away. She shifted her peas around her plate, admitting that she had been a real bitch this afternoon.

Perhaps she should apologize for her outburst earlier. She opened her mouth to speak when the dining room door swung open and Khalid entered.

"Good evening, everyone," he said as he crossed to sit on the other side of Linda. "Sorry I'm late, but I ran into Dr. Blakely, who asked me to mention he's going to be involved with last-minute arrangements and won't be joining us for dinner."

Ashley noticed someone else was missing. "Has anyone heard from Michaelson?"

"Yes," Linda said, holding up a hand. "Well, actually, not directly. A Marine who helped us fish today told me that Major Michaelson was housing in the military section of the base. Across that gorge."

"Why's he doing that?" Ashley said. "We've got plenty of room here. This building's practically empty."

"I guess he's getting those other two men ready for the trip," Linda said. "Our guards."

Great, she thought, two more gun-toting men along for the ride. But this was no time to grouse. It was the eve of their adventure. Besides, as leader, she should say something. Something dramatic. Something uplifting. Though her mind was blank, she set down her fork, determined to say something.

While she watched the others finish their dinners, she struggled to find the right words. By the time Ben had wiped the gravy off his plate with a slice of sourdough and patted his belly with a sigh, she still had no idea what to say. To hell with "proper" words.

Ashley cleared her throat. "I'd . . . like to . . . make a toast." She raised her water glass and stood up. The others looked at her expectantly. "Over the past few days, we've all had a lot thrown at us. And I think we're all feeling trampled on, but tomorrow we embark on a trip where the success of our mission will depend on our ability to work as a team. And as much as Blakely may get under my skin personally, I think he put a hell of a team together. So," she said, raising her glass higher, "here's to us. To the team."

"To the team!" the group echoed, hoisting their drinks.

"Yeah, to you guys!" Jason said, swigging from his cola.

Linda tousled his hair. "What about us girls?"

Jason blushed. "You know what I meant."

"I know." Linda leaned over and kissed him on the cheek. "Thanks."

Jason turned an uncomfortable shade of purple.

As Ashley smiled at her son's consternation, she felt a tap on her shoulder. Ben stood behind her. He leaned and whispered in her ear. "I'd like to talk to you. Would you mind a short walk after dinner?"

"Umm . . ." she hedged, caught off guard. This was the last thing she had expected. "I've got to put Jason to bed."

"Well, how about after that? I just need a few moments."

"Is it important? Can't it wait until morning?"

"Well, I'd rather get this off my chest tonight."

"Sure," she agreed reluctantly, "I guess I can see you in a bit. How's half an hour?"

"Fine. I'll meet you outside the entrance. I'm gonna fetch a jacket."

She nodded and watched him leave. "Jason, let's head back up to our room."

Her son, more his normal shade now that Linda's attention had turned to Khalid, pushed back his chair with a loud squeak. "Can I watch cable?"

"Sure, but only for a half hour, then to bed." She collected him under her arm, squeezing him, and waved to the other two. "See you in the morning."

Linda waved back, and Khalid nodded.

After settling Jason in front of a rerun of *Gilligan's Island*, Ashley pulled on a yellow sweater. "I'll be back in a little bit."

Jason waved to her as she left, his eyes never leaving the screen.

Ashley pushed through the door to the outside and spotted Ben talking to a guard. He waved to the Marine and crossed over to her. "Thanks for coming."

She wrapped her arms around her chest. "So?"

"How about we walk over to that gorge?" He pointed toward the opposite end of camp. "I've heard the area is a bonzer make-out spot."

She placed her fists on her hips. "If you think . . . That's not why I came out here."

Ben grinned at her. "I'm just teasing."

"Then *what* did you want to talk about?"

"C'mon. Let's walk. I really want to see this chasm. I barely caught sight of it when we crossed yesterday." He offered his arm. "C'mon."

She ignored the arm and walked past him. "I can't be away too long. Jason's waiting up."

He caught up and strode beside her. "About this afternoon—"

She held up a hand. "I know, I know. I overreacted."

"No, not at all, I was being a jackass."

She turned to him. "Is that what you think?"

"Sure do. I was butting my big nose where it doesn't belong."

She studied his serious eyes and determined jaw, limned in the lantern light of a nearby tent. "See," she said, a tightness in her throat thickening her words, "that's what's really bothering *me*."

"What?" He brushed a hand across hers, but she pulled away.

"I'm supposed to be the big leader here. Guiding and motivating the team. But a simple question sends me ballistic. Some leader I make." Her voice cracked a bit.

"Hey, don't beat yourself up." He reached out farther and clasped her hand, his touch igniting her like an electric shock. She made a weak attempt to pull away, but he held her too firmly. "Listen, Ash, you were pressed for time. Hell, you only had a single day to explore the ruins, and I had to distract you with stupid questions."

"Your questions weren't stupid. My response was." She tried to draw her hand free, but as she pulled, he stepped closer. "I . . ." How brightly his eyes reflected the lantern's light. "I . . . think we'd better continue with our walk." She finally freed her hand.

"Yeah . . ." He glanced away from her. "You're right."

They continued across the camp in silence.

The quiet soon became painful. "You know," she said, "now that I've had time to think about it . . . what really ticked me off this afternoon was that you were right."

"About what?"

"The statue. For now, it is not *that* vital to know in which direction the statue was facing. Sometimes I get so fixated on the details that I miss the bigger picture. And when you brought this to my attention, I lashed out. I'm sorry."

"Hey, you were under a lot of pressure. Besides, I like people who speak their mind."

She smiled.

"People like you," he said in a whisper.

"Thanks, Ben." They rounded a Quonset hut, and a black gash split the ground ahead. To the left, a lighted bridge crossed the gorge.

As soon as they stepped into the lighted area, a guard called to them from the bridge. "Stop right there." The gun pointed toward them punctuated his statement. "This area is restricted."

"My, my," Ben whispered in an aside to her as a second guard approached. "I can see why everyone thinks this is a romantic spot."

The stone-faced guard checked their identification cards. "You're clear." He turned to the other guard by the bridge and gave him a thumbs-up sign. "Sorry for the scare, but we're tightening security."

"Why?" she asked.

"Sorry, ma'am. That's classified information." He turned and proceeded toward the bridge.

Ashley turned to Ben. "What do you make of that?"

He shrugged. "Who can figure the military? Bunch of buffoons."

"I know. I wouldn't mind pushing the lot of them into that damned chasm."

"Hey, what do you know? We do have something in common." He spun on a heel, very militarylike, to head back to the dormitory. He offered his arm.

This time she took him up on his offer.

Blakely stretched, leaning away from the console. He glanced at a clock on the wall. A few minutes after midnight. Now, that was cutting it down to the wire. The team would be leaving in nine hours.

"All green lights," said a voice behind him. "Finally."

He turned to the head of communications, Lieutenant Brian Flattery. "I knew those new circuit boards would do the trick," the doctor said. "With the communications net intact, we'll be able to communicate to my team anywhere on the planet."

"That's good," said Flattery. "But still . . ."

"Don't fret. This time it'll be different."

Flattery glanced at the floor. "We never found Wombley's body. Only that splat of blood."

"I know, I know."

"And there's still no word from the other team. It's been four months. And what about the recent disappearance of the guard by the chasm?"

Blakely held up a hand. He had heard similar rumblings across the camp. "We're prepared this time. We'll be in regular communication."

"Shouldn't this group be forewarned of the risk they're taking?"

Blakely shrugged. "Major Michaelson and his two men know. That's what's important. I guess I'm going to have to give the rest of the team some details, but they don't need to know everything. This time we're proceeding with foreknowledge of the risks. We're properly armed."

"We don't really know that."

Blakely squinted at the line of green lights on the communications console. He tapped one light that fluttered. It stabilized to a steady green. "Nothing to worry about."

BOOK THREE

Chutes and Ladders

TEN

The pack was heavy, the cushioned straps cutting into Ashley's shoulders. She shrugged it off and set it down at her feet. Heavy, but manageable. She saw Linda grimace as she tried to adjust her own backpack over her shoulders. Ashley reached over and tugged the bag higher on Linda's back. "Carry it like that and it won't be so bad."

Linda smiled, but creases of worry still etched her brow. "Thanks. I just have to get accustomed to it."

Ashley nodded. We all do, she thought.

Ashley led Linda toward the group clustered near the team's radio. Blakely was explaining its operation to Ben, Khalid, and Major Michaelson. "Our web of receivers and transmitters operates at an ultra-low frequency. They're buried and spread out, so we will be able to communicate through hundreds of miles of rock in all directions."

Major Michaelson hefted the radio, testing its weight. "Sort of like the buried transmitters that guide our submarines."

"Exactly the same principle. Low-level reverberations. The system has been tested and checks out fine."

"How often do we establish contact?" Ashley asked as she stepped up.

"Three times a day. At the designated hours," Blakely responded. He pointed at the radio. "This is the most important piece of equipment you'll be carrying."

Major Michaelson tapped his pistol at his waist. "This is my most important piece of equipment."

Ben snorted. "You're both wrong. Shows your lack of caving experience." He pointed to his belt with its ring of batteries. "This is your most important piece of equipment. Without batteries, you have no light. Without light, you can't see what you're shooting at and no radio in the world is going to guide your ass out of a hole." He gripped his battery belt. "This is your lifeblood down here."

Everyone was staring now at Ben. "Of course," he said, pulling out a roll of toilet paper from his pack, "this is right bloody important too."

Ashley smiled, and Linda suppressed a giggle. Ben did have his moments; she had to give him that.

"What about water?" Khalid asked, standing up from where he had been hunched over the radio. "Dehydration is a major danger, isn't it?"

"Sort of. But most major cavern systems have abundant pools of potable water. Just conserve your canteen between watering holes."

Ashley gritted her teeth. Radios, guns, batteries, water. Lack of any of them could incapacitate the mission. Too many variables for her tastes.

The remainder of their pack contents was then explained. Freeze-dried food in tinfoil packets, electrolyte replacement fluid, collapsed air mattresses for sleeping, a first-aid kit, a small box of toiletries, and coiled on top of it all a thick spool of rope. Besides the backpack, each member had a lightweight climbing harness with a chalk bag to dry one's hands, and a helmet with a carbide lamp.

Ben's pack contained additional climbing equipment: carabiners, quick draws, and anchoring bolts. The need for this equipment was obvious to Ashley. Major Michaelson's pack, however, frightened her. It contained four more pistols, a collapsed rifle, and boxes and boxes of seal-cloth-wrapped ammunition.

If that wasn't enough, the team had finally been introduced to the two other members of their expedition—Major Skip Halloway and Major Pedro Villanueva. The insignia of an eagle gripping a trident on their shoulders advertised their expertise. Navy SEALs, the elite. They wore weapons at their waists, and each hefted a double pack. A heavy load, but they looked like muscled machines, workhorses with weapons.

Ben nudged her. "Bloody lot of firepower we're dragging with us."

She nodded. "I don't like it."

"I heard about those SEALs. Never go anywhere without a wicked arsenal."

Ashley chewed her lower lip. "Why do you think—"

Blakely interrupted, "From here, Professor Carter will be in charge. Her word is my word."

Ashley noticed a smirk from the redheaded SEAL, Skip Halloway. He elbowed his buddy, whose expression remained stoic. Black-haired and black-eyed, Pedro Villanueva was as difficult to read as a slab of marble.

She sighed. Great, two more macho men to keep under her thumb. She noticed she wasn't the only one checking out the newcomers. Khalid's face was clouded with an especially dour expression as he studied the

SEALs. His lips then curled up at the corners in an unpleasant manner. He turned away to whisper something in Linda's ear. She smiled, covering a laugh with a small hand.

"So," Ben said, "are you ready to lead this ragtag band of adventurers into the heart of the world?"

"Right now I'm just hoping there's no mutiny."

Ashley crossed toward the small opening in the south wall of the cavern. She eyed the tiny tunnel. Called a wormhole, it looked more like a sewer drain to her. The black entrance stood only two and a half feet high. She crouched and shined her hand lantern down the tube. With a backpack on, she estimated, it would be nearly impossible even to crawl through these holes.

To answer this riddle, the final piece of their equipment was introduced. Blakely handed her a wheeled plastic board.

"A skateboard?" Ashley spun a wheel across her palm.

"I prefer to call them transport sleds," Blakely said. "Specifically designed for these chutes. Here, let me show you." He picked up another of the seven fluorescent-colored boards. He slapped the surface of the board with the flat of his hand. "We already devised aluminum motorized sleds, but they are too bulky to carry. These, on the other hand, are high-impact plastic, both the board and the wheels. The ball bearings are composed of a corrosion-resistant titanium. Perfect for the terrain and the dampness. Just release this latch. Like so. And the board expands to the length of your upper torso, supporting chest and pelvis, and allowing the rider to ride belly down, using gloved hands and feet for propulsion and braking."

"Sort of like a surfboard," Ben said, "but on land."

"Well, yes, I guess that analogy is accurate. Once through a chute, the board can be collapsed back to its original size and stored in a pack. Each board has been fitted to the individual. Names are stenciled on the back of each. And each is a different color to make it easier to tell them apart."

Ashley practiced releasing and collapsing the board. Easy, and mercifully lightweight. All this preparation just to slide through these tubes.

"Dr. Blakely," asked Linda, "where did these wormholes come from? Are they lava tubes?"

"Yes and no," said Blakely. "True, this area is honeycombed with lava tubes, some no bigger than a fist and others as large as a man. Lava tubes are usually rough and irregular, as are most of the ordinary tubes around here. But tubes of this diameter"—he pointed at the wormhole—"are exceptions. They're uniform in size and polished to a remarkable smoothness. How and why?" He shrugged. "Yet another mystery to solve."

"How far have you explored up to now?" Ashley asked. Obviously many other chutes had already been studied.

"These wormholes extend from this central cavern like spokes on a wheel. Some just dead-end. But most, like this one, connect to a series of interconnecting caverns that extend deeper and deeper below the surface. Seismic readings suggest this system may extend several hundred miles."

"And you explored no farther?" Ashley raised her eyebrows. "But you've been down here for months."

Blakely just stared at her for several heartbeats, taking off his glasses. He pinched the bridge of his nose. The others stopped what they were doing and turned to them, attracted by the silence.

Ben put down one of the skateboards he had been examining and crossed over to Ashley's side.

Michaelson stepped up. "Tell them," he said, his eyes glued on Blakely. "They deserve to know more."

Blakely lifted a hand up, palm toward the major. "I was just getting to that."

Ashley had a sudden sinking feeling in her gut.

"Professor Carter," Blakely said, "I'm not proud of what I'm about to reveal. But certain expediencies

dictated this course. We've had to keep certain secrets."

"No kidding," Ben said.

Ashley hushed him with a glare, then turned an even
harsher eye on Blakely. "Go on. What secret?"

"You asked me if we've explored farther. Well, we
have." He pointed to the wormhole. "You're not the
first team to explore this route. A joint team of five researchers and one Marine entered this chute over four
months ago."

Ashley shook her head. "Then why drag all of us
here, if it's already been explored?"

"The other team has yet to return."

"What?" Ben said, stepping closer. "You mean
they're still down there?"

"Without radios, we had no means of tracking the
team. They were scheduled to return after two weeks
of exploring. Three weeks passed with no word from
them, so we sent in a search party. A cursory search revealed a massive maze of tunnels, shafts, and caverns.
No trace of the men was found."

"Why the hell didn't you expand the search?" Ben
was red-faced by now.

"Without adequate means of radio contact, the
search parties were at risk. They could meet the same
fate as the original team. So the search was called off.
The team was declared lost."

"Great," Ashley said. "What if we get in trouble? Do you just walk away from us too?"

"This is bullshit," added Ben. "Downright cowardice."

Blakely's fist clenched, a tightness narrowing his eyelids. "That team was under my supervision. I took their loss personally. I could not risk losing any others. We lost the first team because we were excited and proceeded without proper caution. I refused to allow any others to search farther until an adequate communications system could be installed." He shoved a finger toward the radio. "Now it is!"

Ben didn't back down. "Sorry, but I still think a small team—"

Michaelson interrupted. "It was my decision too."

Ashley turned toward the major, who stood by the packs. "Well, then why the hell didn't *you* do something?"

Michaelson met Ashley's stare squarely. "As head of the Marine contingent here, it was my call whether to proceed blindly or to take Dr. Blakely's advice and wait until he completed his radio net. I chose to proceed cautiously."

"Just like the military," Ben said sourly, a sneer frozen on his lips. "Personnel are just pawns, to be thrown away as needed. Who cares if this other team was comprised of real men with real lives? Just throw them to the wind."

Michaelson, his jaw clenched, spun away on a heel. Ben had an angry frown on his lips. An ugly expression for him, Ashley thought.

Ashley stepped after the major, meaning to confront him further, but Blakley reached and touched her elbow as she tried to pass by the doctor. He whispered in her ear, "The major's brother was on that other team."

Ashley stopped and watched Michaelson taking inventory of his pack, his motions hurried and jerky. "Harry?" she said softly, remembering the major's warm smile as he talked about his kid brother's fascination with vehicles and motors. Maybe she should say something . . .

But now Ben called to Michaelson's back, "Some camaraderie. Leaving those men to rot. If I were you—"

Ashley held a hand toward Ben. "Enough. It's done. Leave him be." She watched Michaelson pound his gear into his pack and walk away. She turned to Blakely. "Now what?"

Blakely cleared his throat. "The decisions of the past are moot. What we have to decide now is where we go from here. Regardless of what you all decide, the two SEALs and Major Michaelson will be proceeding today, searching for clues about the fate of the previous team. The rest of the team must make a decision. Knowing about the other group, how many of you want to continue with this team?"

Ben spoke up first. "If it weren't for those trapped men, I'd scrap this right now. But they've been waiting long enough. I'm going."

Eyes turned to Ashley. "This changes everything. I need time to think this through," she said. "We're now a rescue mission."

"No," Blakely said. "I consider it a *joint* mission. The first objective remains the same as the previous team's—to explore this system for clues to the origin of the cave dwellers. But since your team will be following in the footsteps of the first, I'm hoping both objectives can be achieved simultaneously."

Blakely pointed a finger at Ashley. "That's why I picked you to be the leader here. Do you still want to command this team?"

Ashley frowned. "You should have warned us earlier. I don't like being lied to."

"I never lied to you. It was merely a sin of omission. I too had no choice. I was under orders. The fate of the original team is still under tight wraps. Their families haven't even been told yet."

Ben snorted and mumbled under his breath.

Blakely ignored him. "Professor Carter?"

She found her thoughts drifting to Jason, who was safe back at the base under the care of Blakely's assistant, Roland. Should she take the risk? She had other responsibilities besides her career. She remained silent.

"I'll still go," Khalid said. "This is too important."

"Me too," said Linda. "We might need everyone's expertise to find the other team."

Ashley too could not stomach abandoning the other team. She turned to Blakely. "Fine. You still have a team! But if we don't have complete honesty from here—"

Blakely nodded, his voice serious. "You have my word." He stepped back and waved her forward. "Remember, we'll be in contact regularly to map your progress in case of any mishaps. Otherwise, the decisions from here are yours. Everything from how often to set up camp to the number of days you choose to explore before returning. Your word is law."

The eyes of the others fixed on her. The magnitude of the search threatened to overwhelm her. "Well," said Ashley, "we're never going to get anywhere just sitting here. Let's head out. Halloway, take the lead. Everyone else follow, and we'll meet up in the next cave."

The team checked their gear and collected their packs, strapping them over their shoulders. Ashley watched the others fumble with their transport sleds.

Halloway wasn't waiting around for any further discussion. He adjusted his helmet and dove down the chute on his board. The others waited in line to follow.

Satisfied that they were finally under way, Ashley pulled on her gloves and strapped the Velcro bands. She reached for her pack and slipped it over her shoulder. As Blakely stepped beside her, she faced the doctor as the others slipped into the wormhole. With ice in her voice, she said, "Take good care of my son."

"Of course. Roland will make sure the boy is at the radio each morning so you can check yourself."

She nodded, noting the others had by now all entered the wormhole. Kneeling down, she positioned the skateboard under her body. She lit her helmet's carbide lamp and grabbed the walls on either side to propel herself into the tube. Shoving off, she entered the chute.

Damn thing still looked like a sewer drain.

ELEVEN

Ashley pushed her board into her pack and crossed over to the group clustered by a grove of stalagmites. Beams of hand lanterns and helmet lamps crisscrossed the blackness like fireflies in a jar. The cavern was about the size of a football stadium, infinitely smaller than Alpha Cavern's Grand Canyon scale.

A firm breeze, balmy and moist, blew through the cavern. Linda held a handkerchief up, and it flapped like a flag in the breeze.

"Caverns breathe in and out," Ben was explaining to Linda as Ashley walked up. "A response to changes in barometric pressure. I've even flown a kite in a cavern in Belize."

Linda lowered her arm. "I love this wind. It's so . . . so refreshing."

"All right, team," Ashley said as she stepped next to Ben. "The next kilometer of this system has already been mapped, so we can proceed at a fast clip."

Ben raised a hand. "I'd like to make a suggestion."

Ashley nodded. "By all means, I want everyone to feel free to offer input and suggestions. We are a team."

"Before we get to the unexplored areas ahead, I think we should buddy up. Caving involves more climbing up and down than walking on flat surfaces. In pairs, we can assist each other over the rough spots."

"Sounds good," Ashley said. "I think—"

Ben continued, "Also, by buddying up, we can conserve our batteries by having each pair only keep a single lamp lit. In this darkness, even a single light casts a big spot." He grinned at her. "After a day down here, too much light hurts the eyes. Trust me."

She nodded. Turning to the rest of the team, she pointed a thumb at Ben. "Let's do it, then. Everyone pick a partner."

Ben stepped immediately toward her. "Howdy, partner."

"Whoa," Ashley said. "Did you happen to notice we have an odd number of people here? As leader, I'll join other pairs as the need arises."

By this time, Linda and Khalid had already matched up, and the two SEALs had their heads bowed together, whispering. The remaining teammates, Michaelson and Ben, stared at each other.

"Shit," the major mumbled.

"Me and my dumb ideas," Ben said with a shake of his head.

Ashley hid a grin as she adjusted her pack. "With that out of the way, let's head on. We've got a lot of ground to cover."

She nodded toward the pair of grumbling men. "Ben and Michaelson will take the point. Let's all pay strict attention to Ben for the next few miles. He's the most experienced in caving, and I want everyone to learn proper spelunking skills and safety precautions. Let's not end up like that other team."

The group shifted backpacks into place and excess hand lanterns were clicked off. The level of light, Ashley noted, did not diminish to any significant degree. She followed Ben and Michaelson. As she walked, she cast her lantern back and forth, the darkness sucking at her light.

Her mind turned to her mission—both missions. She imagined being stranded in this Stygian blackness, watching the last of her batteries drain away while the darkness enveloped her in a cold embrace. She shivered. And what about the cliff builders, those long-lost ancestors of man? How did they survive in this eternal darkness?

She shook herself from this reverie as the team arrived at the next wormhole entrance. She stepped to the front.

Ben had his notebook-sized compass open, a geopositional tool tuned to a radio transmitter at the base that allowed Ben to calibrate not only their precise position in relation to the points of the compass but also the team's depth.

"They call this a map?" Ben said. As guide, he was keeper of the sketchy diagram drawn by the previous searchers. "It's crap. Look." He shoved the paper toward her. "No compass points, no distinct cavern delineations, no depth markers . . . No wonder the other team got lost!"

"That's why you're here," Ashley said. "You just map our way back home. We're counting on you."

"Well . . ." he said, stumbling for words, the wind knocked out of his sails. "A child could have done a better job."

"Then that makes you right for the job."

He looked sharply at her, and she gave him her best innocent expression. Seemingly satisfied, he turned away, his compass in hand.

She shook her head. Sometimes he and Jason were frighteningly similar. "If everyone is ready," she said, "let's proceed. I want to be into the new territory by the time we set up camp tonight."

Ashley hesitated.

"Just a little farther," Ben called to her from below.

Sucking at her lower lip, she stared down the steep slope before her. It looked more like a mile. Greased with mud, the cliff was slick as ice. Her eyes snaked upward, following her rope. Michaelson was snugged into a crevice several yards above and secured in place with a safety rope. Above him, at the lip of the cliff, hung Villanueva, clinging to a spur of rock and secured with a safety line. It was these two men's jobs to ensure a safe descent for the other teammates.

Ashley took a deep breath and pushed away from the wall as she had been instructed, allowing the rope to brake in the carabiner bars to stop her descent. She scrabbled downward, the toe of her left boot balancing on a protruding stone. Just a little farther.

The stone that had been supporting her suddenly slipped loose and tumbled downward. She plummeted after it, the rope racing between her gloved hands. Ben had schooled them to yell, "Falling!" when this sort of thing happened, but with her breath caught in a fear-constricted grip, all she could do was let out a high-pitched whine.

After a heartbeat, the whistling rope snagged in her carabiner and her descent jerked to a halt. A grunt of protest echoed from above as Michaelson caught her weight.

"Hey, careful up there," Ben yelled. "You damn near gave me a rock facial."

"Sorry," she said to the muddy wall swinging inches from her nose, both hands clamped on the rope.

"C'mon, relax, kid," Ben said. "Just get those feet back on the wall and finish the descent. You're almost on solid ground."

It was the solidness of that ground that concerned her. She had pictured her head slamming into that solid ground as she was falling, but she wasn't about to remain hanging here. There was only one way out of this predicament. Pulling into a squatting position, she got her boots up on the wall and straightened her legs out, pushing from the wall. With a jump, she rappelled down two yards and caught the wall with her boots. Not hesitating this time, she shot outward again and dropped another couple of yards. After two more hops, she felt Ben's arms around her waist.

"There you go," he said in her ear. "Piece of cake."

She settled her legs on the rocky floor, her knees wobbling a bit. "Yeah, no problem."

"This is good practice. Luckily we came across this bunny slope the first day. I'm sure there's hairier cliffs ahead of us."

She craned her head back. Villanueva was just a blur of light at the edge of the cliff above. She suppressed a groan, leaning on a stalagmite. And this was only day one.

Ashley rubbed her back, lowering herself slowly onto her air mattress. She could hear Michaelson mumbling into the radio several yards away, giving his final report of the day. The team had discovered signs of the previous party's passage—discarded items, boot tracks in silt, scruffs on rock—and were sticking close to their trail.

She let out a long sigh, stretching. A sharp jab in her lower back protested the motion. Their progress today seemed more like a battle. Slippery mud covered most of the walkways; sharp gypsum crystals clung to her entire body like sand on a beach, and grew more abrasive with each step; steep slopes and sharp inclines impeded their forward movement, slowing them to a crawl.

Worst of all, though, was the heat. An omnipresent wet blanket that grew heavier as the day's journey wore on. She took off her headband and twisted it, wringing out a stream of sweat. She now understood how risky dehydration was in caving. She unscrewed the top of her canteen, almost empty now. Tipping it back, she swallowed the last warm drops.

"You'll have to watch your water," Ben warned. "We can't count on finding a water hole every day." He nodded toward the small lake pooled in the back half of the cavern, half hidden by an outcropping of rock.

"I knew about this water hole," she said. "It's on the map."

"True, but this is the last cavern marked on the map. From here, it's to points unknown."

"I know. I'll be more conservative tomorrow. We should remind everyone in the morning. Especially Linda. She ran out of water at lunch and has been borrowing from my canteen."

"Yours too, huh?" Ben said with a smile. "She finished the last of mine an hour ago."

"Clever girl," Ashley said. "By the way, where is she?"

"Over at the pond . . . getting a drink of water."

She shook her head. "Tomorrow we'll need to be more strict with rationing."

"Oh, just leave her be. I was just joking. She's over there doing a water analysis. Besides, she's having a tough time of it."

"We all are."

Ben gestured toward the two SEALs, who were setting up the campstove a handful of yards away. Light pooled around them from their lanterns. "They barely broke a sweat."

She watched as Villanueva stripped off a khaki T-shirt and wiped his face and armpits before slipping into a green vest. With a small pop, Halloway lit the butane for the campstove. Both appeared as refreshed as if today's journey were nothing more than a Sunday walk through the park, while everyone else dragged as if just completing the Bataan death march, haggard, bone-tired. Her stomach rumbled audibly.

Ben raised an eyebrow. "I'm hungry too. But there's nothing except freeze-dried beans and franks."

"Right now, that would fit the bill."

Ben grinned. "Though a beer to wash it all down . . . now, *that* would be heaven." As he sat down on his own mattress, he suddenly swatted at his arm. "Hey, something just bit me!"

"What?"

He shined a light on his arm.

She leaned over and looked at the spot. "Looks like a mosquito."

"Bloody large skeeter. Just 'bout took a chunk out of my arm."

"Quit exaggerating."

He poked her with a finger. "Wait until you get speared. Don't come crying to me."

"That's odd," she said, scratching behind an ear. "What's a mosquito doing in Antarctica? Way down here?"

Ben's expression became serious. "Good question. You don't often find insects down here. Crickets, a few spiders, centipedes, that sort of thing—but I don't think I've ever seen a mosquito."

Ashley wondered at the significance of such a discovery. "Maybe we'd better ask our biologist."

Thanks for sharing your water today, Khalid," said Linda. "I couldn't have made it without your help."

"Anytime," he said, breathing in the dank air. He sat on a rock, watching Linda scooping water into small glass vials. He appreciated the wide furrow of moisture down the middle of her back, pasting the cotton T-shirt to her body. The clasp of her bra was visible through the thin fabric. He bit his tongue to control his rising lust.

Smiling at him, Linda stood up and sat on the boulder beside him, shaking the vial in her hand. "That last ridge was brutal. I'm glad we're done for the day."

He could feel her body heat pulsing across the hand span of space between them. They sat in silence, Linda studying the crystal surface of the pond, Khalid studying her.

"My god!" she suddenly exclaimed, jumping to the edge of the black water. "Khalid, look over here." She crouched on her knees, waving him toward her.

He crossed to her, inhaling her scent, a hypnotic perfume in the moist air. "What is it?"

She lifted a curled shell, dripping and luminescent in the lamp's glow, that had been partially hidden by a rock in the shallows. Khalid cocked his head to the side. It looked similar to a snail's shell, but it was huge. Almost the size of a watermelon.

He asked again. "What is it?"

She rolled into a seated position, cradling the large shell in her lap. "If it's what I think it is . . ." She shook her head and placed a hand on his knee. "If it wasn't for your insistence that we stay a little longer, I may have missed it."

Her hand was a burning ember on his knee. He fought against pulling her into a hard embrace. A tightening in the crotch of his coveralls protested his restraint. "What's so special about an empty shell?" he asked in a strained voice.

Before she could answer, voices intruded.

"I'm telling you, the damned skeeter bit worse than a snake with broken fangs."

Ben spotted Khalid and Linda crouched by the shore of the pond. He noticed Linda slip her hand from the geologist's knee just as they rounded the rocky escarpment. Ben raised an eyebrow.

Ashley cleared her throat, announcing their presence. "Linda," she said as she approached, "Ben was just bitten by an insect that looks a lot like a mosquito. We wanted your opinion."

"Oh, sure, no problem. Did you catch one?"

"Well, kind of," he said, pointing to the smashed bug still smeared on his forearm.

She smiled, taking his forearm in her hands and rotating it into the light. "You didn't leave me much to go on." She leaned in closer. "I can't say for sure. There are hundreds of species of blood-hungry midges, flies, and mosquitoes. This could be anything." She released his arm.

"I was curious," Ashley said. "Ben told me there are seldom any biting insects in caves."

Linda scrunched up her eyebrows. "That makes sense. What *would* they feed on? No warm-blooded species down here." She shook her head. "They must gain sustenance in some other manner, but this individual was taking advantage of a new source for lunch." She shrugged. "These caverns just get more and more curious."

She clasped one arm around a large shell. "Look at this, for instance." She held up the shell for Ashley and Ben to examine. "Do you recognize this?"

Ashley took it from her and held it up, rotating it to view it from all angles and running a hand along its spiral loop. "Looks like a mollusk shell, but I'm unfamiliar with the species. Besides, you're the biologist."

"And you're the archaeologist. If it wasn't for my study of evolutionary biology, I wouldn't have recognized it."

"Well, what do you think it is?" Ben asked, lifting the shell into his hands, curious what all the commotion was about.

"It's the shell from an ammonite, a predatory squid," Linda said. "Species *Maorites densicostatus.*"

"What?" Ashley snatched the shell back from Ben. She examined it again with keener interest, now holding it like it was the finest porcelain. "That's impossible. This is an actual shell. Not a fossil."

Ben stared at his empty hands. "What's the big deal? What's so bloody exciting about it anyway?"

Both women ignored him. "Are you sure?" Ashley asked. "Paleobiology was not a specialty of mine."

"Yes," Linda said. "Look here, at these striations. No modern mollusk has this conformation. And look at the chambering inside. Only one species has this unique shell. Definitely an ammonite."

Ashley leaned in closer. "But what's it doing here? Ammonites died out with the dinosaurs at the end of the Cretaceous period. This is an old shell, but I don't believe it dates back sixty-five million years."

"Let me take a look," Ben said, lifting the shell. "Many caves have preserved fossils, protected from the weather. Maybe this shell is just well preserved."

Linda nodded. "Perhaps. But before the expedition, in preparation for the trip, I read up on Antarctica's wildlife. On Seymour Island not far from here, scientists discovered many ammonite fossils. Remains that dated *later* than the Cretaceous extinction."

"Cretaceous extinction?" Ben asked. "What're you talking about?"

Ashley answered, "About 65 million years ago, at the end of the Cretaceous period, a great cataclysm wiped out huge numbers of species, including the dinosaurs. Some researchers theorized a massive asteroid struck the earth at that time, blowing up clouds of dust that blocked the sun and chilled the planet."

"Right," Linda added. "And the paleontologists studying Antarctica now believe that Antarctica's polar vortex may have stirred the winds enough to keep the asteroid's sky-darkening particles clear of this area, sparing this continent the great extinction."

Ben interrupted. "That's all old history. So these snails survived longer than anyone thought. So what? I mean—"

"Linda!" Khalid called. He had wandered off and knelt by the edge of the pond. "Here's another shell." He reached into the water, immersing his arm almost to his shoulder. "I can't reach . . . wait, no . . . there . . . I got it." He pulled his drenched arm out, his hand clasped around a shell larger than the first one. He straightened up, holding the shell above his head like a trophy.

Ben shook his head. Showing off big-time, he thought. He opened his mouth to make a comment when suddenly, from the shell, a flurry of thrashing tentacles sprouted. Linda gasped.

The tentacles latched onto Khalid's arm.

Khalid tried to shove the squid off his arm, but it clung tenaciously. Tears welled at the corner of his eyes, and he grimaced with pain. "The damned thing is biting me." Rivulets of blood could be seen beginning to trail down his arm. Groaning, Khalid swung his arm, cracking the shell against the rock wall beside him—to no avail.

Ben pulled a knife from his belt. "Hold still!"

Khalid froze, then a spasm of agony contorted his face. "Just get the thing off," he said between clenched teeth.

Ben slipped the blade between tentacle and skin. It was a tight fit. The creature's appendages clamped tightly to the flesh of Khalid's arm. Ben sawed through the meat of one tentacle, and greenish black ooze spurted from the amputated end. The thing tightened its other appendages, eliciting a groan from Khalid.

The monster's strength was fierce. If it constricts much more, Ben thought, it'll crush bone. He cautiously worked the knife under a second tentacle and cut. This time the thing twitched and loosened. After slicing through two more appendages, the creature released Khalid's arm, dropped to the cave floor, wobbled, and sucked its remaining tentacles back into its shell.

Khalid dropped to his knees with a low moan, a hand clasped over the wound, blood seeping between his fingers.

Ben kept an eye on the shell, black ooze dripping from its opening. With a scowl, he swung a boot and kicked the shell in a high arc over the pond. With a splash, the creature sank from view.

Ashley yelled at him, "Why the hell did you do that? We could have studied it. My god, it's an extinct species."

Ben pointed to Khalid's bloody arm. "Extinct, my ass."

"He'll live," Major Villanueva said.

Ashley watched him apply the bandage to Khalid's arm with a piece of waterproof tape. The SEAL, with his advanced training as a field medic, had taken over as soon as they had arrived back at camp. After cleaning the wound, he treated Khalid with topical and systemic antibiotics.

"Can he continue on with us?" she asked.

Villanueva shrugged one shoulder. "Nothing more than a deep puncture to the muscle of the forearm and some bruising. He'll be fine."

She nodded and turned away. Good. She'd hate to lose a team member before they had reached uncharted territory. As she passed the campstove, Halloway offered her a bowl of lukewarm chili and beans in a tin pan. She accepted it with a curt word of thanks and settled onto her air mattress with the pan balanced in her lap.

Ben had already scraped his bowl clean and looked greedily toward her plate. "So how's Khalid's arm?" he asked.

"Fine. They shot him full of antibiotics and pain-killers."

Ben set down his plate. "That was one bloody weird creature."

She shrugged and spoke around a mouthful of beans. "I was talking to Linda. She said their main food source was a type of prehistoric lobster, and these waters are teeming with crustaceans of various types. So I suppose, in this isolated environment, the squid survived on similar food."

"Makes you wonder."

"About what?"

He nodded across the camp, where Michaelson had disassembled his rifle into small metal parts and inspected and cleaned each item. "What else has survived down here?"

That night, Ben had the dream again. He was walking through the cavern of his childhood nightmares, full of columns that sprouted fruit-bearing limbs. Light suffused from all directions, and as he wandered through the grove, something seemed to be drawing him forward, calling to him.

"Hello," he hollered into the empty cavern. "Who's there?"

Drawn toward the north side of the cavern, he tried to follow the song of the invisible sirens, but the trees crowded closer, blocking his passage. Unable to squeeze between the columns any farther, he could only peer past the trunks.

The north face of the cavern glowed with a soft light, except for a single black hole in the wall. A small cave, like the dwellings found near Alpha Base.

"Is anyone there?" he called, his face pressed between two trunks.

No answer. He waited, pushing against the trunks as if he could shift the rocky columns. As he watched, someone crawled from the small cave, on wrinkled hands and gnarled knees. The old man stood into the light, dark face painted with yellow and red stripes, dressed in a loincloth. The figure waved him forward.

Ben stretched out an arm, struggling to pass between the trunks of stone. "Grandfather!"

With a start, Ben jolted awake, bathed in sweat. He sat up on his air mattress. Only a single lantern illuminated the sleeping camp. Villanueva, who sat on a rock, raised a glance toward him. The SEALs had insisted on posting guards; after the squid incident, no one had argued.

Settling back into bed, Ben rolled over, his back to the light. The dream echoed in his mind, as if bouncing off the rock walls around him. He still felt a vague pull, a drive to continue deeper into the maze. He squeezed his eyelids closed.

TWELVE

"**C** 'mere," Ben called to Ashley. "Look at this."

Wiping her hands on the seat of her coveralls, she crossed over to Ben. "What did you find?" After three days on this trek into unmapped territory, she was getting used to Ben's continuous chatter. He was always pointing out unusual cave formations to her—dogtooth spars, box-work formations, cave pearls—often scowling when she didn't respond with the correct degree of awe. Coming up behind him, she leaned over his crouched form.

In his hands, he held a tin cup, dented on one side, the handle snapped off. It looked just like the ones they carried with their canteens.

"Yeah, so what?" she said.

"It's not ours."

She knelt at his side, taking the cup. "Are you sure? Maybe someone dropped—"

"No," he said. "It's caked in old silt. Half buried. It's got to be from the first team. I think they camped here for a night. This cavern has potable water." He pointed to a stream that crossed the center of the small cavern. "And look how this area of mud is trampled. I bet if we looked hard enough we would find other debris from their bivouac."

"I think you're right." She sighed. Since the last switchback yesterday, there'd been no signs of the previous explorers. "We should let Michaelson know. He's been nervous as a mare in heat since we lost track of the original team."

Ben snorted his agreement. "This should light a fire under him."

They crossed the cavern, hopping over a small stream that had dug a trough through the center of the cavern, and wove around the many stalagmites clustered across the floor. Ben proceeded ahead, Ashley's helmet light spotted on his backside. She watched as he climbed over a small outcropping, muscles bunching and relaxing, the damp and muddy coveralls clinging tight. She swallowed and pointed her lamp to the left, away from Ben. She wiped a hand across her brow. These damn caves were hot as hell.

Something moved to her left. Startled, she almost lost her grip on a muddy rock. Swinging her light in the direction of the movement, she searched but saw only the usual twisted stalagmites. Nothing was there.

Ben, noticing she had stopped, turned back to her. "Do you need a hand?"

"No. I just thought I saw something moving over there." She nodded across to the left. "But it was nothing. Just shadows moving with my lamp, I guess."

Ben feigned fear, eyes searching rapidly to his right and left. "Or perhaps it was that predatory snail looking for more of Khalid's blood. I can see it now: 'The vampire slugs of Antarctica.'"

She shoved him forward. "Get going."

Within moments, they arrived at the next wormhole, where the remaining team members clustered, slouching on rocks. Linda was examining Khalid's arm. Everyone looked exhausted, except, of course, the two SEALS. Perhaps the team should stop early, she thought, and camp for the night.

Searching for Michaelson, she noted he was missing. Great—did he start his own search already? She had told no one about Michaelson's brother being a member of the lost team. She figured if he wanted to keep it a secret, it was his business. But she had been watching as the lines of worry creasing his forehead had become deeper and more numerous. If he ran off . . . ? She called to Villanueva. "Where's Michaelson?"

He pointed down the chute ahead of him. "Recon."

Damn him, she thought. He couldn't sit still. He always had to be running ahead to check for clues about his brother. "I didn't authorize anyone to proceed ahead on his own."

Halloway shrugged. "You weren't around."

"Well, now I am. And I expect him back up here on the double."

Again she caught a condescending smirk on the soldier's face. "I'll tell him when he gets back."

She shoved a finger hard into Halloway's chest. "Find him now."

A dark cloud descended upon the SEAL's features. Halloway towered over her, like a lion before a mouse.

Ashley cut him off before he could open his mouth. "You have your orders, soldier." She drilled him with her eyes.

Halloway clenched his teeth, then suddenly smiled coldly. "Ready or not, Major Michaelson, here I come." He spun on a heel, and within a heartbeat, he vanished down the hole.

She quietly let out her pent-up breath.

Linda and Khalid stared at her. Villanueva, clearly unimpressed by the exchange, shrugged and went back to sharpening a knife.

Ben clapped her around the shoulders, causing her to jump. "Good job, Captain. Scary sorta bloke, isn't he?"

She couldn't stop herself from leaning into his arms, shaking just a little from the adrenaline surge of the altercation. He squeezed her tighter then guided her a few steps away from the others. In a quiet voice, he said, "You did good. But you didn't make a friend."

She nodded, then softly broke his embrace. "I have enough friends. But thanks, Ben."

"Anytime, Ash."

She looked away, resisting the urge to fall back into his embrace just for the momentary comfort. They just sat in silence, knees touching.

After a lengthy wait, Linda finally called, "Look, it's Major Michaelson."

Ashley glanced toward the wormhole and saw the major climbing to his feet by the entrance of the wormhole. From his dour expression, it was evident he was disappointed. "Michaelson," she said, "I thought we all agreed to congregate here for a rest break."

"I know, but I had to find out if the other team had come this way."

"If you hadn't been in such a flaming hurry to race ahead, and instead, like Ben, had searched this cavern more thoroughly, you would have found what you were looking for."

"What do you mean?" There was a hint of hope in his voice. "Did you find something?"

Ben stepped up. "Only this." He held up the dented cup. Not much of a trophy, but from Major Michaelson's response—his eyes lit up like Christmas tree bulbs, his slumped shoulders straightened—it could have been the Holy Grail.

As usual, though, he tempered his emotions. "Are you sure it's not one of ours?" he asked soberly.

Ben nodded.

"Good." He turned to settle his pack on a rock. "Then we're on the right path. After this rest break, we should push forward. It's still early."

"Whoa!" Ashley said. "It's been a long day. And with this discovery, perhaps we should start fresh in the morning."

Michaelson grimaced. "I hate to disagree. But my reconnaissance into the next cavern did reveal an obstacle we may want to cross today rather than tomorrow."

"And what's that?" Ashley asked, wondering if he was just trying to egg the team forward to keep them all racing after his brother.

"A river, about ten yards wide, fairly swift, cuts across the next cavern. We're going to have to cross it. I figured it would be better today. Get it over with. Rather than getting wet first thing tomorrow and being soaked all day."

Linda groaned, sliding past Khalid to join them. "Not today. I'd rather tackle that in the morning. Heck, we're wet all day anyway. What's a morning dip going to change?"

Khalid, of course, agreed. "It's late. I say we camp here too."

Ashley watched the lines on Michaelson's forehead deepen. Apparently the dented cup had made him even more anxious to search for his brother. She could tell he needed to push forward. "You're right. After the crossing, we can dry out our clothes overnight. Good plan, Major."

With much grumbling, they put their gear together and pulled out their skateboards. Ashley called across to Michaelson, "Is Halloway waiting down below?"

"Halloway?" Michaelson raised an eyebrow and glanced around.

Ashley's heart pounded. "I sent him down after you. I thought he was the one who sent you back up here."

Michaelson's features went cold. "I didn't see anyone."

THIRTEEN

A s Ashley scooted through the exit of the wormhole, she pushed quickly to her feet and stepped aside to allow Villanueva room to slide out. Good. He was the last team member. The rest scanned the new chamber with their flashlights. Ben bellowed Halloway's name. She stepped up to Michaelson. "Any sign?"

The Major shook his head. "No, and with all these damned obstacles it's going to be a long search."

Ashley grimaced. Time was precious. If Halloway was injured, any delay could mean his death. She waved her flashlight ahead and groaned at what she saw. This could take hours.

Huge spherical rocks, a yellowish ocher in color, dotted the floor, some as big as elephants, others the size of cottages. Several were clustered into nests like huge fossilized eggs. Others sat by themselves, brooding solitary behemoths. The boulders towered over the team.

She shook her head. The large rocks chopped up the view of the room, making a search with flashlights difficult. An injured Halloway could be sprawled behind any of those boulders.

"We'll split up into three teams," Ashley said, struggling to be heard above the echoing babble of the river that coursed in a deep trough through the middle of the cavern. She waved ahead. "We'll have to search behind each of these boulders."

Ben dragged a fingernail across the surface of one of the rocks. "Bloody hell! They're cave pearls!" He stepped back and scratched his head. "Never seen them anywhere near this big. Usually they're no bigger than grapefruits."

"Ben, we don't have time for that," Ashley said. "There are more important concerns. We need to—"

He held up a palm. "No, this is important."

"Why?" She sighed, praying he would be brief.

"You see, cave pearls are buildups of dissolved limestone layered around a pebble or piece of sand. They only form in eddies of flowing water, suggesting, at one time, this cavern had been flooded to the roof."

"Great," she said. "So what are you saying? Do you think this cavern might flood again? Cut off our return?"

He shook his head. "No. These pearls have been dry for aeons. The waterways must have shifted."

She sighed. "Ben, I appreciate your cavern lore, but right now we need to concentrate on finding Halloway."

"I know. That's just it. Even if he was behind one of these boulders, we'd know it." Ben clicked on his flashlight and placed it on the surface of the boulder. Suddenly the boulder lit up like a huge lamp, glowing a clear yellow color. "They're translucent. Even though they look opaque, light shines through the bloody things. If Halloway's here, he's without his lights."

Ashley sighed. Any chance of quickly finding Halloway was fading fast. "So he's either hurt or purposefully hiding."

Ben nodded.

Linda, who had walked over to the boulder, suddenly exclaimed, "My god! Look in the center of the rock!"

Ben was the next to spot it. He let out a long low whistle.

Ashley peered within the stone. "That's no pebble at the center of your pearl."

Ben pressed a palm flat on the rock. "Anything can seed a cave pearl." He waved Ashley over to his side. "We need more light to be certain."

Ashley crouched next to him and clicked on her flashlight, focusing into the heart of the stone. The stone glowed now with a clear white light. Even through the distortion of the crystalline layers, there was no mistaking the object at the core. "It's a skull. A human skull."

Linda spoke from a yard away, her voice wavering. "This one has a skull too. You don't think this could be the missing team, do you?"

Ashley shook her head, removing her flashlight from the stone. "No. From the extraordinary size of these rocks, they must have started forming a million years ago. I'd say these are our cave dwellers." She stepped away from the stone. God, she'd love to spend hours just studying this discovery, but this mystery would have to wait. Damn! After three bone-cracking days, they finally find a clue about the lost civilization, but have to ignore it, at least temporarily. Halloway's safety depended on an expedient search. She raised her voice. "Everybody regroup! We need to head out."

The other team members returned from their cursory check of the neighboring pearls. Michaelson arrived first. "I think we should proceed with a systematic search of this side of the river. Halloway may be injured or have fallen down a crevice."

Ashley nodded as Khalid and Villanueva stepped up to join them.

"Maybe he already crossed the river," Linda said doubtfully, glancing toward the remaining SEAL.

Villanueva shook his head, shifting his stubby-barreled CAR-1 assault rifle from one hand to the other. "He would not have abandoned the team," he said fiercely.

Ashley turned to face the group. "Then we search here. Linda and Khalid will stay by the wormhole in case Halloway comes back while we're out. Ben and Villanueva will head north, and Michaelson and I will curve south. That should allow us to canvass the entire area."

Ben interjected, "I think I should go with you."

"No. I want one armed personnel with each search team. We'll need to leave a weapon here with Khalid too." She turned away from Ben.

Since there were no further objections, the teams set out. Ashley called as she and Michaelson headed away. "Let's be careful out there. Keep your eyes open—and I want all lights on. Now's not the time to spare batteries."

She watched as other lights blossomed in the darkness. Good. She didn't want anyone else disappearing into the dark.

Michaelson helped her hop over a wide hole, yet another obstacle. So far their progress was impeded by the need to dodge around boulders, backtrack out of dead ends, and sidetrack dangerous crevices. It was no wonder Halloway was lost.

"This would've been a hell of a lot easier," Ashley said as she edged around a crevice, "if the team had been outfitted with walkie-talkies. We could have just radioed Halloway."

Michaelson grunted. "Too much rock. Wasn't feasible."

Ashley sighed and continued in silence for several yards, then asked for the third time, "So you saw and heard nothing while you were down here?"

"Wait until we reach the river. Its roar is deafening. A herd of buffalo could have stampeded through here and I wouldn't have heard it." He sounded exasperated. "I hate these delays. We should be over that river and on our way by now. Damn that Halloway!"

Ashley jumped slightly at the vehemence of his outburst. "It's not his fault."

"What do you mean?"

"You had orders. To stay by the wormhole. You took it upon yourself to venture ahead on your own. Because of that, I had to send someone after you. Now Halloway's lost."

Michaelson shook his head. "I was doing reconnaissance. Looking for ways to hasten our passage, avoid needless delays."

"That's bullshit, Dennis."

He stopped at her words, his back taut.

"Dennis," she said, "I know why you're down here. I know about your brother."

"So Blakely told you."

"It doesn't matter who told me," she said. "What matters is that your drive to find Harry is hurting this mission."

He tensed even more. "I don't see that."

"I know. That's why I'm bringing it up. Someone needs to tell you. You're thinking with your gut, not your head. You're racing past clues—like the dented cup, for instance. You're flying ahead of the rest of the team. Alone. Which is risky enough to yourself, but now you've put another team member in harm's way."

He tensed his shoulders and lowered his voice. "But I *have* to find my brother."

Ashley placed a consoling hand on his shoulder; he flinched from her touch. "We'll find him. But we work as a team."

He stood silently for several heartbeats, then took an awkward step forward, breaking the moment, clearing his throat. "We're almost to the river. It's just up ahead."

Shaking her head, Ashley followed Michaelson around the next boulder. The path became more difficult as they approached the roaring river. The last yards to the river were blocked by a cluster of cave pearls, forcing them to crawl.

Covered in mud, they finally reached the river's edge. Below, black water churned between steep banks. Its spray, rich with salt, stung their eyes.

Ashley wiped mud off her forehead with a damp handkerchief and leaned close to Michaelson, yelling directly in his ear, trying to outshout the river below. "He wouldn't have tried to cross this river alone."

Michaelson nodded. "Maybe Ben and Villanueva are having better luck," he hollered. "Why don't we—"

A scream pierced the roar of the river, echoing through the cavern.

Stunned, Michaelson and Ashley stared at each other.

"What the hell?" she hollered. "It sounded like it came from across the river!"

Michaelson tried to bore his light through the river's mist. "It could just be an echo."

"I don't like this. Let's get everybody back together." She turned to trace their route back when a second scream erupted. It cut off abruptly. "We'd better hurry."

Michaelson stood, his light fixed on the darkness beyond the river.

Ashley grit her teeth. She yanked on his arm. "Now, soldier. We're out of here."

Ben scratched behind his left ear. What was taking Ashley and Michaelson's team so long? He and Villanueva had completed their leg of the search fifteen minutes ago. The SEAL had set an intense pace. Ben had always considered himself to be in decent shape, but as he struggled to keep up with Villanueva, he felt like someone's arthritic grandmother. His contribution to the search consisted mostly of him yelling for the SEAL to slow down. Still, for all their effort, they found no sign of Halloway, arriving back at the wormhole with no new information for Linda and Khalid.

Ben glanced toward Villanueva. The SEAL paced back and forth, one hand on a holstered pistol. That man was wired as tight as a kangaroo in heat. It obviously tortured him to have to wait for the others to return.

Ben too was becoming concerned. They should have been back by now. He struck the rock he had been examining with his flashlight. He should have gone with her. He knew more about caves than Michaelson. What if she disappeared like Halloway?

Linda called from where she crouched by a cave pearl the size of a beachball. "Ben, come see this."

Ben crossed to her, squatted on his haunches beside her. "What?"

"Shine your light inside. The details are clearer here in this smaller stone."

"Linda, is this really the right time for this?" he grumbled, but did as she asked.

An escalating excitement hurried her words. "Look at the orbital ridges. They bulge too thickly. And the auditory orifices. They're too low on the skull." She turned to Ben, her eyes shining. "It's not *human*. Or I should say, not modern man. The size of the brain case does suggest an advanced hominid, but there's too much distortion for me to recognize the species. Ashley needs to see this. She'd know."

Linda suddenly looked around, voicing Ben's own concern. "What's taking them so long to get back?"

A sudden scream echoed through the cavern. Both Ben and Linda jumped up. Linda sidled closer to him.

Ben's heart had climbed into his throat and was caught there. Ashley!

Villanueva already had his pistol raised and stood frozen, his flashlight beam acting as a gunsight. Khalid crossed to Linda, and like a small moon pulled into a different orbit, Linda drifted from Ben into Khalid's shadow.

A second scream. Ben stepped over to Villanueva. "We need to go after them," Ben said. "They're in trouble."

"No," said Villanueva. "We stay here."

"Are you crazy? They're being attacked!"

The SEAL's face was stone. "No. The scream was far away. Beyond the river."

"How can you tell for sure? The acoustics in a cave are tricky."

Villanueva continued to study the darkness ahead. "I'm sure."

"I don't care. I'm heading out to check on them."

"If you try to leave, I'll shoot you in the leg." The casualness in which he said those words suggested he was not joking.

"Who the hell do you think you are?"

"I'm the senior ranking officer here. What I say goes."

"But—"

"This is the designated rendezvous location. If the others are in trouble, they will head here. We'll give them ten minutes."

"Then what? Go look for them?"

"No. We head back up."

"And leave them down here? Like hell I will!"

"Michaelson has the radio. Without him, we have no means of communicating topside. If he's not back in ten minutes, we evacuate."

Ben stared into the black curtain, beyond which he imagined horrible acts being played out. Ashley running, hiding, pursued by slavering creatures. Ashley mauled and bleeding. He held his breath for most of the ten minutes. To hell with the damned SEAL. If she didn't return . . . he knew how to take care of himself in caves.

Villanueva lowered his arm. The blackness quickly filled the void of his flashlight, greedily reclaiming its lost territory. "Pack up," he said over his shoulder. "We're heading out."

Ben shifted from foot to foot, straining to pierce the darkness.

"Let's go, Mr. Brust." The SEAL pointed with his gun. "Don't make this hard."

Ben had an idea. "Wait. Everyone turn out your lights."

"What?" said Linda, a tremor in her voice. "Are you nuts?"

"Just do it. If there's no sign of their lights, then we'll get the hell out."

Villanueva studied him, squinting warily. "One minute."

Linda snuggled closer to Khalid as they turned their lanterns off.

The camp was swallowed up by darkness.

It took a few seconds for Ben's eyes to adjust to the blindness, the vanquished camp lights still burning dull flares on his retinas. As these last traces faded, one area persisted, off to the left. His dilated pupils strained to focus. A glowing cave pearl. Then the glow shifted to another cave pearl. Closer. The lights were approaching. "Someone's coming," Ben said, his voice booming with relief. "They're on their way back."

Linda said, "Yes, I see it too!"

Villanueva called for lights. The darkness was beaten back by the flaring lanterns. Within minutes, bobbing flashlights could be seen approaching through the darkness. The SEAL still stood with his gun pointed forward. Once the lights were close enough, he yelled, "Stop there! Identify yourselves!"

Ashley's voice came back angrily, "Who the hell do you think it is?"

Then Michaelson's voice: "It's just us, Major. Relax."

Villanueva lowered his gun.

Ashley stomped into camp, followed by Michaelson, who kept glancing toward the river behind him. "Whose bright idea was it to turn your lights off like that?" Ashley asked sourly. "We were using them as a beacon back here. We thought something happened and started racing back. Almost ran myself right over a cliff."

Linda pointed a thumb at Ben.

"Just looking for you," he said, nodding his head toward the SEAL. "After we heard the scream, our mate here was planning on scrambling back topside with our tails between our legs if you didn't show."

Ashley bristled. "What the hell?"

Michaelson interrupted, a hand raised in the air. "He was correct. We had the radio. They didn't."

Ben swallowed. "But to leave you . . ."

Ashley rubbed her temples thoughtfully, then nodded. "He's right. Next time, listen to him, Ben." She brushed past him, scanning the camp. "Okay, under the circumstances, we need to make a decision whether to continue forward or go back."

Michaelson stepped forward. "I suggest Villanueva and I cross the river to take a closer look while the rest of the camp stays put."

Ashley shook her head. "No. We stick together. We've already seen what happens when we split up."

"Then we evacuate," Michaelson stated bluntly. "I won't risk any more civilians. Halloway knew the risks."

Ashley scowled. "And what if it was one of us out there *screaming*? Would you be so quick to leave?"

Michaelson remained silent.

"I thought so," she said. "I think Halloway deserves as much support as any of us."

Linda spoke up. "Besides, he might just be injured or unconscious. He's been silent since the first screams. We can't leave without at least looking thoroughly."

Michaelson began to object, but Ashley held up a hand. "Since it's our civilian butts on the line, it should be our decision to continue forward or not."

Ben and Linda nodded. Khalid merely stared.

"I say we go forward," Ashley said. "Any objections?"

The others remained silent.

"Fine," she said. "I want to be across that river in thirty minutes."

Ashley paced the river's edge. Villanueva had stripped to his underwear and cautiously waded into the oil-black water. A rope tied around his waist draped back to the team at the river's edge. Michaelson had anchored the rope around a stalagmite nearby.

"We could've all swum across by now," Ashley said. "All this jury-rigging is just wasting time."

"No," Michaelson said, looping a knot in the rope. "The current's too strong. If we tried to swim, someone could easily be swept away."

"Then just tie everyone together with rope." She didn't understand why he was being so obstinate. Didn't he realize every wasted second could mean Halloway's death?

Ben shook his head and tried to calm her with a smile. "Too easy to get tangled up, my dear. A good way to get someone drowned."

A loud splash drew her attention back to the river as Villanueva dove beneath the churning water, clearing half the stream before resurfacing. Strong arms cut the water in broad strokes, but still the current propelled the SEAL far downstream.

Linda grabbed Ashley's arm, pinching hard in panic. "Look!"

Ashley followed the biologist's outstretched arm back upstream from where they stood. A three-foot-tall dorsal fin, albino-white, crested the churning waters, then sank back from view.

Ben, openmouthed, had spotted it too. "Jesus Almighty Christ!"

Michaelson, with one hand tangled in the SEAL's anchoring rope, struggled to free himself, but the rope was cinched tight around his midsection. He freed his rifle and tossed it to Ben, who had the easier shot. "Use it. Before the thing reaches Villanueva."

Fumbling the rifle to his shoulder, Ben searched the water for his target. Then just below them a tip of white broke the surface, and a blast of rifle fire exploded. A small geyser of water erupted where the slug hit the water—a good several feet from the fin. Ben had missed.

"Shit," said Ben, pumping a second shell. Another miss.

Villanueva, having heard the shots over the noise of the river, had stopped and twisted around to stare at them, treading water. Linda and Ashley waved him toward the far shore. "Go! Get the hell out of there!" Ashley screamed.

The dorsal fin emerged again to its entire yard of height, now slicing the water halfway between the team and the SEAL. In an arcing dive the SEAL flung his body toward the far shore, the water churned white by his pumping arms and legs. But the current resisted his progress; he seemed to be wallowing, like a fly in amber. He won't make it to shore, Ashley thought, clenching her fists, willing him strength.

The fin turned smoothly toward the thrashing SEAL.

Ben had raised the gun once more, then lowered it. "Damn it. I don't have a clear shot. At this angle, if I miss I could hit Villanueva."

Ashley snatched the rifle and raised it to her shoulder. Her first shot tore a chunk out of the fin. She aimed lower for the second shot, below the fin. As she pulled the trigger, the recoil crashed into her shoulder. This time the geyser of water from the shell's impact spurted red.

The fin tilted to the side, then sank from view.

Ashley's teeth ground together; she expected the injured creature to suddenly lurch out of the water and grind up the SEAL. She watched, the rifle butt pressed tight to her shoulder, as Villanueva reached the riverbank and scrambled up the slippery rock. He acknowledged the team's cheers with a wave and marched back upstream.

Ben stepped next to her, taking the rifle from her shaking hands. "I thought you hated guns."

She rubbed at her hands. "You've got to know something to hate it."

Ben just nodded, seeming to sense she didn't want to continue this conversation.

She stared across the river. Villanueva had untied the rope from his waist and was rigging his end to a thick stalagmite. Michaelson tugged the slack up and secured his end of the rope to a rock on this side, creating a rope bridge slung between two stalagmites. The two worked as if nothing had happened. As if some creature of nightmare hadn't just tried to swallow up one of their teammates.

The major tested the security of the bridge by tugging at it. Satisfied, he turned to the team. "Now we can cross."

Taking a deep breath, Ashley steadied her still-pounding heart. Put it behind you, she told herself. There is still a team to lead and a teammate to find.

Using carabiner hooks to attach waist harnesses to the rope, the team scooted hand over hand across the bridge. Dangling from the rope, Ashley was careful not to look down. The drop was not far, but the thought of what else might be lurking under the black reflection of water was paralyzing.

Villanueva, now suited back into his coveralls, helped her unhook from the bridge. His hand shook a bit as he helped her stand. Whether from the cold of the water or from the aftershock of such a narrow escape, she couldn't tell.

"Thanks," he said quickly, an embarrassed look in his eyes. "I owe you."

She tried to answer, but he turned his back to her and returned his attention to Michaelson, the last in line, as he crossed over the river.

As soon as the major had set his boots on the rocky edge, Ashley called everyone together. "This section of the cavern is much smaller, so we'll explore this area as a group. Let's head out. Keep your eyes and ears open. Whatever caused those screams may still be out there."

This search is futile, Khalid thought. He dug black mud from under a fingernail with a small blade. Halloway had to be dead. When would these damned idiots realize it so they could move on?

He watched the SEAL examine the wormhole they had discovered. No trace of the missing teammate had been found. They had searched behind every pebble and down every black crack. Nothing.

"This is no use," Villanueva said as he shined his flashlight down the wormhole. "No one's been through this hole in years. Look at the layer of mud at the entrance. No footprints or sled marks."

Ashley crouched at his side and pushed a finger knuckle-deep into the mud. "You're right. If anyone had passed, there would be some sign." She pushed back up and faced the team. "There's got to be another exit we missed."

"Maybe," Khalid said, trying to wake the team up, to get them redirected to the mission at hand. He had an agenda to follow, whether Halloway was found or not. "Maybe he got caught in the river and was washed away."

Michaelson shook his head. "No. The scream was well beyond the river's edge. I agree with Ashley. There must be another exit."

Khalid hid a scowl.

"Before we leave here," Ashley said, "I think we should send someone down this wormhole. Just to make sure. Any volunteers?"

Villanueva pulled out his sled. "I'll go."

She nodded. "Be careful. Just check out where this exits and come right back. No solo venturing."

He nodded and slipped into the hole. Ashley checked her watch.

Rolling his eyes at another delay, Khalid walked over to where Linda sat on a rock. She had her arms wrapped tight around her chest as he sat down beside her.

"Do you think we'll find him?" she asked, her voice tiny.

"No. No matter what the major believes, I think he was washed away."

Linda shuddered. He could tell what she was thinking. The fin had been as white as the belly of a maggot. Like some ghost shark coming to claim their souls. Men and rock he could handle, but the creatures down here . . . first the squid trying to gnaw his arm off and now this monster . . . The sight of that fin had made his flesh crawl. As if Nature were showing them how small they were.

He remembered, as a boy, hearing about the sandstorm that had buried his mother's camp in Syria, killing everyone. The black hand of Allah, they had called it, but he knew better. It was just Nature, an indifferent god, oblivious to the plans of man. To her savagery, everyone was vulnerable. And Khalid hated feeling vulnerable.

Linda hugged herself and kept staring back at the river. "That albino shark. It was huge. To support such a predator, the aquatic ecosystem down here must be more extensive than anyone had imagined. If it weren't for Halloway, I wouldn't mind stopping and doing some tests."

Khalid scowled, rubbing at his arm where the ammonite had bit him. "I'd rather avoid that ecosystem myself and stick to dry land."

"I found something!" Ben called from several yards away.

Khalid craned his neck to stare over at Ben. He stood by the cavern wall with a match in his hand.

Ashley called to him. "What is it, Ben?"

"I found another passage out of here."

Who was he kidding? Ashley thought, eyeing the narrow crack, buried in the shadowed fold of the rock face? It extended from floor to ceiling, but gapped only a foot wide. Easy to miss. "Nobody could fit through there," she said. "It's too narrow."

"No, I measured it," Ben said.

"With what?"

"My boot."

She gave him a blank stare.

"It's a caver's rule of thumb. 'If it's wider than your boot, through there one can scoot.'"

"I don't think so. Especially Halloway. He's a big guy."

"It would be a tight squeeze, but I know he could've fit."

"Besides, who knows if there's anything on the other side?"

In answer, Ben held up a lighted match to the crack. The flame bent away from the opening. "Wind," he said. "There's a breeze blowing from beyond there."

Ashley watched the flame flicker. Perhaps . . .

A scraping from the wormhole behind her drew her attention away. A pair of legs slid backward out of the opening. It was Villanueva. He stood up, wiping his hands on his knees.

"It's blocked," he said, huffing a bit. "There's a rock-fall blocking the passage about thirty yards in. I had a hell of a time backing all the way up here."

Ashley swore. If it was blocked, then there was only one other way to proceed forward.

Linda stepped up and peeked into the narrow slit. "But would Halloway have gone this way?" She seemed to eye the crack with fear. "I mean, why would he even cross the river?"

Villanueva answered, "If something attacked him. Something he couldn't handle. He would try to lead it away. Keep it from surprising us like it did him."

"Why do you think that?" Ashley asked.

Villanueva met her eyes. "It's what I would have done."

Ashley chewed at her lip. "So what do you suggest we do?"

"He's trying to buy us time to escape. I say we use it."

She closed her eyes, hating the thought of abandoning him.

Ben called from where he had edged into the crack, exploring the passage. "Come see this!"

As Ashley approached Ben, he reached a hand toward her from the narrow slit. His palm was covered in blood. Fresh blood.

"He's been this way," Ashley muttered. "Just recently." She turned back to Villanueva. "So do you think we should still go back?"

His jaw muscles tightened. "You're the leader."

Ben climbed from the slit. "So who's going through first? We should hurry."

Ashley sighed. Obviously Ben had been deaf to their discussion. "It's more complicated than that."

"What? We're right behind him."

"Villanueva thinks Halloway might be trying to draw something away from us."

Ben's voice rose in anger. "Or maybe he's just bloody hurt! Seeking shelter." He grabbed her shoulder. "Ash, I swear he's just ahead of us. We can't leave him."

She rubbed at her tired eyes, then nodded. "Okay. Let's go."

Linda stood in her underwear, shivering by the wall. She had shed her backpack and even her coveralls. Less to snag and catch, Ben had said. Narrows the profile. She shuddered. How could she possibly wedge her body into that slit? The walls would squeeze the breath from her chest.

They waited for Ben to report on his reconnaissance of the crack. He had squished into the black rock over three minutes ago. Ashley and Michaelson stood as sentries to either side as he reported his progress.

"I'm through," he called, his voice echoing into their cavern. "The passage is only six feet long, then it abruptly widens into a decent-sized tunnel. It's a piece of cake. Only one doozy of a tight spot just near the end."

Ashley faced the group. "I'm gonna send Villanueva next. He's the widest of all of us. If he can make it through, then we all can."

No one argued.

Linda held her breath, hoping the SEAL would fail; then she wouldn't have to face the crush of those walls. Her heart sank when she heard Ben's cheer.

"He's through! Scraped his chest a bit, but no harm done."

Ashley rubbed her hands together. "All right! Let's move!"

Khalid went next. Before he left her side, he gave Linda's hand a squeeze. She hardly felt it. Linda watched as he disappeared, a rope trailing from his waist. Once through, the rope would be used to ferry the packs through the slit.

"All clear!" Ben called. "Send the packs next!"

It took ten long minutes to hook and drag the packs of supplies and weapons to the far side.

"That's the last of them," Ashley yelled. She turned to Linda. "You're next."

Linda didn't move, staring at the black crack. She willed her legs forward, but they refused. It was getting hard to hear the others over her pounding heart, her wheezing breath.

"Linda?"

"I . . . I . . . can't do it."

"Sure you can. Villanueva is twice as big as you."

She shook her head, swallowing hard, pushing the words through her constricted throat. "No. I can't. It's too tight."

Ashley came over and put an arm around her. Linda shivered uncontrollably. "We can't leave you behind." Ashley tightened the arm around Linda's shoulder. "I tell you what. I'll go with you. Be right behind you. You can do this, Linda."

Ashley stepped forward, forcing her to follow.

"I . . . I'll try," Linda said dragging her leaden feet. "But please hold my hand. Don't let go." Her voice cracked at the end.

"I won't. We'll do this together."

Linda attempted a smile, but failed miserably. Led by the hand, she was coaxed forward. Her mouth felt as if someone had poured a bucket of sand down her throat.

"Just keep your helmet light pointing forward," Ashley said. "Lean your back on the left wall. According to Ben, it's the smoothest. Then just slide."

Linda maneuvered her left shoulder into the crack, her toes pointing forward and backward. Inching into the crack, she tried to halt the panicked flutter of her heart and just concentrate on going forward. Up ahead, light diffused around the curve of the narrow crack. Just steps away, the others waited for her.

The crack swallowed her up. The walls pressed, too tight even to turn her head to see Ashley behind her. All she could do was slide one leg forward and drag her body along behind it. She counted the steps, trying to divert her mind. A trick from therapy.

"You're doing fine," Ashley said behind her, squeezing her hand. "Just a little farther."

. . . Five . . . six . . . seven . . . Her breathing had steadied to a regular rhythm. One breath with each step. She could now see the end of the passageway, a face peering back at her.

"Good girl," Ben said. "You are one amazing piece of work. Three more steps and you're through."

A ghost of a smile played about her lips. She was doing it! eight . . . nine . . . te . . . Her left foot moved forward, but when she tried to wiggle her body to follow, her chest jammed snug in the crack. A squeak escaped her throat. In panic, she tried to force herself ahead, only pinning herself tighter. She squirmed backward, trying to free herself, but failed.

Please, not this way! she prayed. Don't let me die this way. By now she was beginning to hyperventilate, pinpoints of light began swirling before her eyes, her knees began to give way.

"Linda," Ashley said. "Don't stop now. You're just about through."

"I'm stuck," she squeaked, a panicked pitch to her voice.

"Ben," Ashley called ahead. "Linda's caught."

"Bloody hell," he said. "Give me more lights here!"

In a heartbeat, the crack blazed with light.

"I see," Ben said. "Listen to me, Linda. Reach a hand forward. Stretch it to me. There. I've got your hand. Now, on the count of three, I want you to blow out all the air from your lungs, shrink your chest, and I'm going to yank you through."

"No," she whispered, closing her eyes. She could hardly expand her chest now. "I'll get stuck again. Then I won't be able to breathe at all."

Silence. A standoff. Then Linda felt Ben release her hand and someone else take it. She recognized the grip.

It had supported her over many obstacles. Khalid, her caving partner.

The Egyptian spoke in a calm, reassuring voice, almost as if trying to hypnotize her. "Linda, you know I won't fail you. You know the strength of my arms. Do as Ben says. I will pull you to me. Trust me."

Linda's heart pounded. She opened her eyes again; the pinpoints of light had multiplied to small constellations. She knew she was close to passing out. She nodded her head. "I trust you."

"On the count of three," Ben said from behind Khalid. "One . . . two . . . three!"

Linda pushed all the air from her chest, her lungs protesting. Her arm was pulled forward, dragging her body ten inches farther until she jammed again. Tears now coursed her cheek. This was how she would die.

Sudden pain shot through her shoulder. Her arm was yanked again, almost separating her shoulder joint. She screamed the last ebb of air from her lungs. It was enough. She popped out of the crack, like a cork from a shaken champagne bottle. Free.

"Is she all right?" Ashley asked as she slipped from the treacherous crack, noticing that Linda was supported in Khalid's arms.

Ben nodded. "I think so. Mostly shaken up. Her shoulder's going to ache like a son of a bitch, but she'll be fine."

She nodded. "That leaves only Michaelson. I want everybody ready to continue once he arrives."

Villanueva, who was crouched several yards down the tunnel, called to them. "Halloway's been this way." The SEAL shone a light on his upraised finger. It was red with blood. He then turned the light down the passageway. "It trails that way."

Ashley didn't say a word. Halloway was still running. "I want everyone armed," she said in a small voice. "Now!"

At the sound of scraping behind her, she turned to see Michaelson scrambling from the crack, his T-shirt torn. Ashley waved the group together. "Let's gear up. We leave in two minutes. I want a pistol or rifle in everyone's hand."

"Maybe we should just leave," Linda said, her cheeks still wet with tears, her voice trembling.

Ashley rested a hand on Linda's shoulder. "We've come too far. We've all got to stick together."

Linda took a deep breath, seeming to gird herself. When she spoke, her voice was steadier. "You're right."

Ashley squeezed Linda's shoulder, then faced the team. "Let's get moving."

No one else argued. Within moments, the group was hiking down the tunnel. Villanueva and Ben took the point, scouting several yards ahead.

"Stay within sight," she called when Ben drifted too far ahead. "Let's keep a tight group."

The tunnel split at a fork. Which way? Ashley looked questioningly at her scouts. Villanueva pointed with his light. "Blood trail goes this way," he said.

Ashley waved with her pistol for them to proceed ahead, expecting to find Halloway's collapsed body behind every turn of the tunnel. As each step drew them farther down the tunnel, their pace became more furious. Ashley's group now dogged the more cautious point men.

"You're on my back, woman!" Ben hissed at Ashley. "It won't help Halloway if we run over a cliff."

"Sorry, but there's so much blood."

"We're going as quickly as safety will allow."

Villanueva halted their discussion with a firm motion of his arm. He pointed around the next corner. Ashley crept next to him and peered past the curve. Up ahead, the tunnel dumped into a large cavern. "I think I should proceed alone," the SEAL said. "Check out the area."

"No. Not this time," Ashley said firmly. "I want the team together. More eyes to watch backs, and more trigger fingers to protect those backs."

Villanueva shrugged.

The team proceeded as a group into the cavern, flashlights flared out like the spokes of a wheel. The chamber was similar to the others they had crossed in their journey here. Stalagmites littered the floor; stalactites stabbed downward. Except there was one new feature. Ashley rubbed a snowflake from her eyelash. "Damn. It's snowing in here."

A small flurry of soft flakes fluttered through their light beams.

Linda held a hand out and flakes settled on her palm. "They're not cold or wet."

Ben shouldered his way to Ashley's side, brushing at the sifting of flakes. "This is bad."

"Why?"

"It's not snow. It's gypsum crystals." He pointed his flashlight to the branches of gypsum crystals festooning the ceiling of the chamber like twenty-foot white chandeliers. "They're fragile, delicate structures. Body heat can cause them to weaken and flake away."

Ashley brushed flakes from her shoulders, like dandruff. "I still don't see the danger."

"For this snowfall to be happening now, a lot of body heat had to recently pass through here. More than one injured SEAL."

Ashley's eyes widened with the implication. "We're not alone down here."

. . .

The drifting of gypsum crystals thickened as the team crossed the cavern. Lights jittered in every direction, shadows jumping and lunging. Ashley adjusted the handkerchief she had tied over her nose and mouth to keep from inhaling the flakes. She glanced at the others, masked like a bunch of bandits sneaking up on an unsuspecting victim.

Villanueva still had the point, crouching low and darting from cover to cover, before waving them forward with an all-clear sign. No one spoke much, fearful of just what else might be lurking in the next shadow.

Ben marched beside her, pointing his gun forward. He shifted his light to the cavern floor. "Blood trail is thinning," he whispered.

Their evening report to Alpha Base was now an hour past due, but they couldn't halt their search now. It would take half an hour to unwrap the radio's components from their waterproof plastic, assemble the parts, and make their report. Time, like the SEAL's blood trail, was running out.

A frantic hissing from Villanueva drew her attention away from the red trail. The others had frozen in crouched positions. She was the only one still standing.

Ben pulled her down beside him. He kept a hold on her hand.

The SEAL, crouched at the base of a huge boulder, held a finger to his lips and motioned her to come forward . . . quietly. Ashley crept to the point position.

Villanueva pressed his lips to her ear. He spoke in a hurry. "We've reached the other side of this cave. There're two exit points. A large tunnel and small wormhole."

"So? Let's go. Which way does the blood trail go?"

He shook his head. "I can't say for sure. The mud is too chewed up out there to get a clear trail."

"So we just check both," she said, leaning away.

"Wait. That's not why I called you over." He pointed beyond the boulder. "Poke your head around the corner and listen."

Raising an eyebrow, Ashley craned her neck around the boulder. In the rock face before her, she spotted another rough-walled tunnel, like the one that had led them to this cavern. At first she didn't hear anything above her own panting breath. Perhaps her ears weren't as sharp as the SEAL's. As she was turning to ask Villanueva for elaboration, she heard it too. A cracking and crunching, like dry sticks underfoot. And a throaty slurping. A shiver passed through her. It was coming from the tunnel ahead.

She raised her light to flash it into the heart of the tunnel when Villanueva swatted her arm back down.

"No," he hissed. "Whatever's in there doesn't know we're here."

"Maybe it's Halloway," she said earnestly, but even she didn't believe her words.

"Bullshit," the SEAL said.

"Well, what do we do? Just sit here and wait?"

A sharp sneeze retorted from behind them. Ashley whipped around. Khalid shrugged apologetically and pointed to the drifting flakes, his other hand restraining a second outburst.

Turning back to Villanueva, Ashley held her breath. "I can't hear it anymore," she whispered.

The SEAL nodded. He had his eyes closed. "Neither can I."

Shit! Whatever was in that tunnel now knew they were here. There was no further use hiding. She stood up, now holding her pistol in both hands. "Ben, Villanueva. You're both with me. Michaelson, you stay under cover behind the boulder with the others."

Michaelson stepped forward. "This is a military matter. You should remain here. It's safer. I'll go with Ben and Villanueva."

"No," she said, checking her pistol. "I want you here. Guarding our, rear. And protecting the others. We may need a fast retreat."

She watched the major chew over her decision. Apparently unable to find fault, he nodded. "Be careful."

She cocked her pistol. "Let's go."

Her group crossed to the front of the boulder, gun barrels pointing toward the tunnel opening.

"I say we open fire," the SEAL said quietly. "Blast the tunnel and ask questions later."

"No," Ashley hissed. "There's still a chance Halloway may be in there."

Villanueva raised his assault rifle. "We take the advantage while we've got it."

She shoved his rifle with her shoulder and stepped forward. "Halloway!" she called. "If you're in there, give us some signal!"

The tunnel just stared blankly back at them.

"Satisfied?" The SEAL's contempt dripped from the word as he repositioned. He lowered his head closer to his rifle sights. The cavern exploded with rifle fire as he blasted blindly into the dark eye of the tunnel. The reverberations rocked through the cavern.

Her ears still rang after the SEAL ceased firing. A cloud of rock dust and smoke rolled from the assaulted opening.

Ben narrowed his light beam, trying to dig deeper into the inky blackness, but failed. "Damn."

From the mouth of the tunnel erupted a ululating cry, like a keening hawk, but more guttural and rasping. Ashley winced at the noise. A primordial part of her responded, wanting to cower and flee, but she dropped to one knee and raised her pistol higher.

Then something small bounced out into the main cavern.

"Jesuschristgoddamnmotherfu . . ." Villanueva swore a stream, backing a step away.

It was Halloway. His head. The decapitated head of the former SEAL bumped to a stop a yard away, eyes staring up, snowflakes settling softly on the eyelashes.

FOURTEEN

Jason plopped into his chair in the office, expelling a sigh loud enough to draw his "babysitter's" attention. He had been waiting for five minutes already. Five minutes! He was going to be late for his karate practice.

Roland looked up from his papers; his glasses drooped to the tip of his long nose. "Oh, Jason. Are you still here? I thought you had already left for the gym."

"You know I can't." He stressed each syllable.

"Why?"

Jason rolled his eyes. "Dr. Blakely said I was not to leave any of the buildings without a stupid baby-sitter." He scrunched up his face and imitated the nasal quality of Blakely's voice. "It's for my own protection."

"Well, that's just silly. The gym is right next door. Be a good boy and scoot on over there. I've still a huge pile of reports to log and index."

Jason's face brightened. All right! He shoved his chair back with a loud squeak and bolted away. He ran down the hall and out the door, his gym bag bumping against his leg. He sprinted the ten yards to the next building. Lieutenant Brusserman was probably already waiting. Once through the door, Jason was assaulted by the familiar smells of a gymnasium. Sweaty cotton jerseys, varnish on the basketball court's floor, and the tang of disinfectant.

He searched the aerobics area for Lieutenant Brusserman, but saw no sign of him. Jason crossed the gym, heading for the locker room. He stopped to watch a game of one-on-one being played on the basketball court. Jason recognized Major Chan, with whom he had gone boating yesterday.

Signaling a time out, Major Chan crossed over to where Jason stood. He was winded and spoke between gulps of air. "Hi, kid. Listen, the lieutenant called. He won't be able to make it today, but he said to say sorry. He'll see you tomorrow." The major faked a punch at him playfully and then returned to his game.

Jason's heart sank. "But what am I supposed to . . ." The major was already back in the game, defending a drive to the basket.

Darn it! Now what? He didn't want to go back to Roland's office. He'd be stuck thumbing through those boring magazines about Navy life.

He nudged open the door and slipped outside. A group of white-smocked researchers milled past him, heading toward the dormitories, joking and laughing.

Jason sat on the steps and searched in his gym bag for something to do. His Nintendo Game Boy? He crinkled his nose. No—boring. His hand curled around a Spider-Man comic book, but he'd read it.

Sighing, he juggled the contents. A few coins jingled, and a pack of gum fell out of his bag. Frowning, he picked up the package of Juicy Fruit and shoved it into the side compartment of his bag. While doing so, his hand fell upon a hard, round object hidden in the pocket.

He fished it out. Oh, yeah! He fingered the old red firecracker. A cherry bomb. He smiled, remembering how he had traded for it with Billy Sanderson for an X-Men comic book. Almost forgot about this little baby. Glancing around him with a mischievous gleam in his eye, he pondered sneaking off and trying it out.

Just then a white-smocked scientist turned a corner nearby and walked in his direction. He quickly returned the firecracker to its hiding place. Maybe he'd better wait until he returned to the States. If his Mom found out about his little treasure . . . no, he'd better play it cool.

He zipped up his bag, still unsure what to do with his free time.

Standing, he moved from the steps, shifting his gym bag to his other hand. Just then, angling around the corner of the hut, a group of officers passed by, one of whom was decked out with enough medals to choke an elephant.

The decorated man took off his hat and wiped his brow. "Is it always this damned hot down here?"

One of his companions spoke up. "It's not the heat, it's the humidity."

"It's the *heat*, Lieutenant," the man said with authority.

"Yes, sir, yes, Admiral."

Jason, impressed by the fear this man could generate, stood transfixed.

"Now, where is that Blakely fellow?" the admiral asked, replacing his hat.

"This way, sir." The lieutenant bumbled his way around the corner.

Wow! Something big must be happening. Jason peered around the corner. The men disappeared into one of the concrete-block buildings.

Jason knew that building. It was the communications center. He had been in it three times, when he was allowed his two minutes of morning air time to talk to his mother. Usually the conversation consisted of his mother questioning if he was obeying his "baby-sitters." Still, he thought with a sigh, it had been good to hear her voice over that static.

Scratching behind an ear, Jason wondered what all that brass wanted with Dr. Blakely. He pursed his lips. Maybe he could find out. He knew his mother hated his eavesdropping, but he couldn't resist a good scoop. Besides, it might be information about his mother.

He slinked around the corner and crept to the door. No one was around. The secretary, Sandy, was not at her desk. What luck! He slipped inside. As he reached for the door to the main hallway, the doorknob turned and the door swung open.

Sandy stood in front of him, a half-empty coffeepot in her hand.

"Oh, Jason!" she said with a big smile, pushing a stray lock of blond hair back over an ear. "I didn't know you were coming by."

Jason bit his lip and backed a step, ready to bolt. He cleared his throat. "I . . . I just wanted to tell something to Dr. Blakely."

She placed the coffeepot down and fingered out a new filter. "I'm sorry, hon, but the doctor is busy. Why don't I tell him for you?"

"No! . . . You see," he stammered, wide-eyed, "it's something personal . . . private."

She pursed her lips, then smiled. "I see. Well, then why don't you have a seat, and we can wait until Dr. Blakely is free?"

He nodded. This was getting him nowhere. Perhaps he should just leave and say he'd talk to Blakely later. That would be the smart thing to do. His mouth had other ideas. "I have to use the restroom."

"Well, dear. It's just through the door on the left."

Of course, he already knew that. More importantly, it was also next to the main communications room. He crossed to the door. "Thanks."

Sandy smiled up from her computer keyboard and winked at him.

Holding his breath, Jason passed into the hallway. His sneakers squeaked on the waxed linoleum. No one was in the hall, but he could hear the buzz of voices from the various offices. Rising on tiptoe, he crept down the hall, trying to move as silently as possible. He reached the door that led to the main communications room.

Freezing in midstep, he listened. Blakely's voice was clear and curt. "Why the hell do you think I wanted this communications net? You damned well know from my reports that there is an undetermined danger down here. We need to—"

The admiral's voice interrupted. "Be that as it may, your team's evening report is only an hour late. I think calling this red alert was premature."

"If able, Michaelson would not be a second late with his reports."

"The major's too close to this mission. It's too personal for him. You should never have allowed him to go."

"We've had this argument before. It's done. Now I want to know what you're going to do about this."

"Nothing."

A large crash. "Listen here, I have motion sensors going crazy. Yesterday, another man was lost in Sector Four. And now my team is late with their report. And you're going to do what? Sit on your ass and wait for more of my people to disappear?"

The next words were so cold that Jason shivered. "No. Washington sent me to do only one thing: upon my judgment, to decide if you are fit to continue command. You've made my decision easy. As of this moment, you're relieved of duty."

Silence, then words spat with vehemence: "You jackasses planned this all along, didn't you? You never had any intention of keeping this a civilian project. When did the brass decide to snag this facility from me? Was it when the last team was lost? Or since the very beginning?"

Dead silence followed.

Before Jason could react, the door burst open. Blakely, wild-eyed, bowled into the boy, knocking him down. "Jason!"

"I . . . I . . . I . . ."

"What are you doing here?"

"I was going to . . . I mean . . ."

"Never mind." Blakely bent down, helping Jason up. "C'mon."

Pushed toward the door, Jason stumbled ahead. "What's going on? Is my mom okay?"

The old man ignored him. "I need to get you somewhere safe. I should never have allowed you to come down here."

The admiral stepped out into the hall. "If that is Jason Carter, leave him be. He is my responsibility now."

"Go to fucking hell!" Blakely yelled, pushing Jason through the hallway door.

Half shoved, Jason tumbled into the reception area. Too frightened to think, focused on trying to keep one step ahead of the raving doctor, he bumped into the door.

Sandy, her mouth hanging open in surprise, stood up from her typing. "What's happening?"

No one gave her an answer. Jason was brushed through the door, Blakely's arm around his shoulder.

By now, tears started to flow down Jason's cheek; he clutched his gym bag to his chest.

In the open air, Blakely seemed to be calming down. "I'm sorry, Jason. I didn't mean to scare you. But you should know—"

A siren blasted through the cavern, its scream so piercing that Jason cringed, covering his ears. "What is it?" he yelled.

"Periphery sensors. The base is under attack. Hurry." Blakely yanked Jason's arm.

FIFTEEN

Silence now. Ten long heartbeats had passed since the scream had blasted from the tunnel. The dark entrance was beginning to clear of smoke from Villanueva's assault. Was it killed? Swallowing hard, Ashley stared down the length of her pistol's barrel. From the corner of her eye, she could see Halloway's head; it still lay a yard from her toe, staring at her as if asking why she let this happen.

She risked a quick glance toward Ben on her right. He caught her look and shrugged. Maybe whatever killed the SEAL *was* dead. Maybe they had lucked—

With a bellow, it burst from the tunnel.

A flash of teeth, needle-sharp and serrated.

"Christ!" Ashley yelled. In shock, she stumbled backward, losing her shot.

Ben knocked her to the side, out of the way of the lunging jaws, then hauled her behind a jumble of boulders.

Somewhere far off she heard Linda screaming.

"What the hell—" Ashley began, but Ben silenced her with a hand over her mouth.

A foul carrion scent flooded their hiding place as a massive snouted head, reptilian, like a crocodile, swung over the lip of a boulder, weaving on a scaled neck; its nostrils, open wide, snorted the air, searching. Oily black skin stretched over skull and jaw. Then its snout swept toward them, rolling a lidless black eye, like a chunk of polished obsidian, in her direction.

Beside her, Ben struggled to free his rifle, to swing it around, but the narrow space behind the boulder was too small.

Ashley went to raise her pistol, but her hand was empty, the gun lost in the fall. Shit!

Villanueva stood his ground, silent, fearing movement would distract the beast and ruin his shot. He studied his target, searching for a weakness.

What the hell was it?

Villanueva squinted through his rifle sight. It stood ten feet tall, pitch-black, towering on two heavily muscled hind limbs, balanced with a thick tail. Its arms, spindly when compared to the muscled hind limbs, ended in articulated claws like some feral cat. He could see the claws, razor-edged, extending and retracting as it scrabbled at the boulder's surface.

Villanueva continued to watch as it stalked back and forth, its head out of sight behind the boulder. The hooked scimitars of its hind limbs gouged the cavern floor.

How to kill it? The creature was thick across the chest, layered in mud and scales that looked iron-hard. Could a rifle blast to the chest penetrate to the heart? Maybe. But it was risky. He would get only one shot. He swung his rifle sight forward. It would have to be the head.

The creature still probed behind the pile of boulders where Ben and Ashley had fled, keeping Villanueva's target out of sight. Suddenly its body tensed; its tail stopped twitching. It had discovered something behind that boulder . . . and he could guess what that was—either Ben or Ashley.

A loud hiss arose from it. Like a rabid dog raising a hackle, a ridge of spiked bristles sprouted in a crest along the back of its snaking neck, tracing down the length of its body.

Show me your head, you fuckin' monster, Villanueva thought. Gimme one clean shot.

He ground his molars. A nonfatal shot would just enrage the beast, making a second shot impossible. He tried to will it to move. Helpless, he watched the beast's muscles bunch up as it prepared to spring on its quarry.

He had to distract it!

Villanueva's knuckles whitened as he gripped his rifle.

Retreat, thought Michaelson. Linda and Khalid were his responsibility.

He huddled behind the sheltering boulder. He hated to abandon the others, but he was in no real position to offer any help. He glanced over at Linda, who still shook in Khalid's arms. They needed to retreat to a more defensible position.

He pushed off the boulder and scrambled next to them. "Grab your packs. We're heading out."

Linda raised a white face from Khalid's shoulder. "But the others?"

"Now!" he said hoarsely, shoving her pack toward her.

Khalid tossed his pack over a shoulder and helped Linda pull hers on. "He's right. We can't help them."

Michaelson, with his rifle in hand, herded his two wards forward. As they passed around the first boulder, a panoramic view of the bowl-shaped cavern opened up before them. Here at the lip, Michaelson had a view of the sloping valley they had crossed just an hour ago.

"Shit!" he said, stopping.

Khalid stood at his elbow. "What is it?"

"Over there. Just past the next ridge of rock."

Khalid looked where he pointed, then said something foul in his native tongue. Linda crushed her face into his shoulder.

Michaelson studied the view. Four reptilian heads swayed above the boulder-strewn floor, long necks stretched upward, looking in their direction. Like malignant prairie dogs. As he watched, one of the heads lowered out of sight.

There was no telling how many of them were out there, but one thing was sure: An attempt to cross would be suicide. Their retreat was cut off. Jaw tight, he wound his hand tighter into the rifle's strap.

A sudden motion caught the corner of his eye.

He swung his light to the left. Ten yards away stood a stocky stalagmite, like thousands they had passed to get here. Nothing moved there now. He clenched his jaws, tightening his grip on his rifle. Was there something behind it? Suddenly the stalagmite sprouted a snaking tail and a snouted head, perfectly camouflaged against the oily rock. Even lit up, it was hard to say where the rock began and beast ended.

The black eyes swung in his direction. Its mouth opened, revealing row after row of teeth.

Ashley cringed as the snout turned in her direction. It hissed, its breath reeking of carnage. Reaching blindly for any weapon, her hand fell upon the flashlight attached to her belt. Maybe she could club it away. Grabbing the thick handle, she swung the flashlight forward.

Ben stopped his struggle to dislodge his rifle. "Turn it on!" he yelled. "High beam!"

Reacting spontaneously to his command, she clicked the lever all the way up. A spear of light lanced out of their hiding place, stabbing the beast squarely in the eye.

Roaring, the creature snapped its head away.

As it retreated beyond the ridge of the boulder, an explosion of rifle fire erupted. Villanueva, she thought. He's still out there. She pushed onto her knees. A second round of rifle fire, this time from behind them. Ashley turned a questioning eye on Ben.

"Go!" he yelled.

She sprang to her feet, jumping a few steps away, clearing room for Ben, just as another blast of rifle fire exploded from ahead.

A scream of hissing rage echoed through the cavern, followed by a loud crash into the boulders.

"Watch out!" Ben shoved her from behind.

Falling forward, she rolled onto her side and saw the cascade of boulders tumble between her and Ben, filling the space where she just stood. "Ben!"

From behind the wall of rock: "I'm okay! . . . But I don't see a way to get to you!"

"Then try for Michaelson!"

"Bloody hell, I'm not leaving you!"

"Go!"

Not waiting any longer, fearing for Villanueva, she cautiously crept to the front of the boulders and peeked beyond its edge.

Her eyes widened in terror.

Villanueva's shot went sour, missing the head and glancing harmlessly off the beast's neck, but it was enough to draw its attention.

It struck at him, like a riled snake.

The mouth snapped at where the SEAL had been standing, but he had already hopped several yards back. It opened its mouth and bellowed, its eyes reflected red. He backed up another faltering step. The beast's head lowered closer to the ground, its body bunched close behind, taut with quivering muscles.

It was going to lunge.

Aiming from the waist, Villanueva pulled the rifle's trigger as the beast burst toward him. The shot hit home, striking the beast in the shoulder, a spout of blood flying.

Unfazed, it barreled forward.

He dodged to the right.

This time he was too slow.

As he tried to turn away, his arm was yanked back, toppling him onto the hard rock. Suddenly his whole body was jerked into the air and dangled by an arm from the jaws of the beast. Searing pain threatened to swallow him into darkness.

Clenching his teeth, he struggled for his rifle, the leather strap still wrapped around his forearm. But it dangled just out of reach. He pulled it up to his chest, trying to grip it one-handed.

Just as his fingers slipped in place, the beast shook him like a dog with a rag doll. His shoulder popped from its socket.

A bone snapped.

A tidal wave of blackness washed over him, drowning him.

The rifle slipped from his limp fingers.

Michaelson shoved Linda behind him. "Get back." He dodged behind yet another boulder, his rifle raised to cover their retreat. It was stalking them, backing them toward the wall. From the sound of gunfire, they were being forced in the direction of the group battling the other monster.

A clever move, he thought. It was trying to corral him back into the jaws of the other beast. "Khalid, get your butt up front here," he yelled. "I want your gun on this trail. I need to reload."

No answer.

"Khalid!"

He glanced over his shoulder.

No Khalid. No Linda. Where were they?

He turned forward to face the trail again. Two yards away, a head the size of a bull's snaked around a boulder. Small nostril flaps, spread like Chinese fans, tested the air as it hunted. It shied from his light, then stepped into view. It walked upright on two thickly muscled legs. Its mouth gaped open, almost like it was grinning. It lowered its head close to the rock floor, searching for scent. With its back bent, Michaelson noted the ridge of raised quills running down its back.

Fuckin' monster. He raised his rifle and zeroed his sights on its butt-ugly face. Smiling grimly, he pulled the trigger.

—snick—

The firing pin snapped on an empty chamber.

Ashley crawled forward. Please . . . still be alive.

Villanueva hung limp in the jaws of the beast. The creature jerked the SEAL's body back and forth a final time, then dropped him to the rocky floor.

Cringing, Ashley held her breath. Blood soaked his entire torso. Shit! He wasn't moving.

The beast cocked its head from side to side, studying its catch, like a bird with a worm. Focused on its prey, it was unaware of her.

Careful, she thought. Don't draw its attention. She crouched and placed each step cautiously. Her pistol was three yards away. She swallowed and took another step forward.

Almost there.

Clenching her teeth, she slipped to the gun.

The beast still toyed with Villanueva. Using a daggered claw, it flipped the SEAL's sprawled body over. She could hear it sniffing at his blood.

Ashley reached for her pistol. As her fingers wrapped around the gun, she froze.

Voices rose behind her.

"It's just over here." She recognized Khalid's thick accent.

"Are you sure?" Linda's strained voice.

The beast whipped its head around, right toward Ashley. She froze, afraid to move, praying the creature's vision was poor.

"We'll be safe in the wormhole. Too narrow for them to get to us." The voices were approaching her location. "We'll make a dash for it."

The beast's neck strained forward, head cocked. Still as stone, it listened to the voices and sounds of movement approaching. Perhaps . . .

She raised her gun, moving with agonizing slowness. No sudden motions to distract it.

Focusing down the barrel, she tried to target its obsidian eye, but a huge bridge of bone protected it. She didn't have a shot, unless it tilted its head just slightly.

From behind her, Linda cried, "It's Ashley!"

Shut up, she silently willed the woman. Linda obviously hadn't rounded the boulder far enough to see what else was out here.

Ashley heard Linda's boot heel scrape loose shale. "Khalid, Ashley must have had the same idea as— Oh! God!"

The beast twitched its head in Linda's direction, an eye rolling into view. Ignoring Linda's scream, Ashley pulled the trigger twice in rapid succession, the recoil dumping her backward.

Unsure if she had hit her mark, she struggled back up into a crouched position, expecting to see a maw of teeth snapping down on her.

She cringed as the beast's head, which had been thrown back by the impact of the bullets, swung once again in her direction, one eye now a cratered ruin.

It took a step toward her, hissing a piercing note. Ashley scrambled backward, tumbling into Linda.

"Get back!" Ashley screamed, fumbling to raise her gun again. Before she could take aim, it lunged at her. Ashley dodged to the side.

Linda, however, didn't.

It snagged the biologist's backpack as she twisted to flee. It dragged her past Ashley, a scream frozen on her features.

Ashley pointed her pistol, but Linda's flailing body blocked her shot.

Khalid ran forward. "Do something!"

She pressed the gun forward with both fists. No clean shot. Linda's eyes met hers, pleading and terrified. Still no shot.

A loud explosion rent the air. Everyone froze. Then, like a marionette with its strings cut, the beast crashed to the floor. Ashley, trembling now, continued to point the gun at the monster. It lay still.

Beyond the bulk of the beast, she saw Villanueva, bloody as hell, sitting up with his rifle propped in his good arm. Smoke trailed from its muzzle. He fell backward with a moan.

She rushed to where the SEAL lay sprawled. He struggled to push himself up, but Ashley held him down.

"Don't move," she said, wincing. It was difficult to look at him. A fragment of bone poked from his upper arm. Blood flowed thickly from ragged wounds.

"He saved my life," Linda whispered, coming up behind Ashley to kneel beside him, taking his scraped hand in hers.

He tried to grin. Twin trails of blood seeped out of his broken nose. "I feel like I got hit head-on by a locomotive." His eyes were glassy with pending shock. He coughed thickly.

"Don't try to talk," Ashley said, then turned to Khalid. "Go get the packs. I need the medical kit."

Khalid, who still stood a few feet away, glanced at the wormhole opening, then back at her. "We don't have time . . ."

Linda stood up. "We can't leave him here, Khalid. If you won't get the packs, I will." She stepped away.

Scowling, he followed.

Ashley turned her attention back to Villanueva, as another volley of rifle fire erupted from across the cavern. The SEAL's eyes closed. "Others are coming," he mumbled. "Khalid's right. You need to get out of here. Just leave my rifle."

"Shut up. We're all getting out of this fucking cavern. Every one of us." She turned back to search the darkened cave.

Did you hear that, Ben? she thought. That means you too.

Michaelson yanked the trigger again. Another empty chamber. No time to slap in another magazine.

With an angry hiss, the creature lunged at him.

Using his rifle like a baseball bat, he slammed the wooden butt into the soft sinus tissue as the snout snapped at him. The creature grunted, taking a step back. It pawed at its nose with a tiny forearm.

Not waiting, Michaelson bolted away, thanking the gods for his years of Little League back in Nebraska.

While sprinting down the trail, Michaelson pawed for the extra magazine in his breast pocket. Distracted, his foot slipped in a hole. He stumbled but managed to stay upright, but his ankle shot a bolt of pain up his leg. He hopped a few steps. Twisted or broken, he couldn't tell.

He hobbled farther. After several painful yards, he realized he would lose this race. He stopped and glanced back. All clear still. He'd have to make a stand.

As he kept his eyes fixed on the trail, he struggled to force the rifle's magazine into place but had it upside down. Damn it all.

Flipping the magazine the right way, he slammed it home as he shouldered his way around a boulder and aimed down his back trail. Now come to me, you ugly fucker.

He heard something approaching, cautiously.

A shadow suddenly popped between two boulders just a few feet in front of him. Startled, Michaelson jerked his trigger finger. The round blasted past the figure.

"What the hell do you think you're doing?" Ben said, covering his singed ear.

"Sorry. I thought—"

"A simple 'Please move' will do fine next time."

Just beyond Ben's right shoulder, Michaelson noted a familiar bruised snout edging around the trail's bend. He raised his rifle again. "Move!"

Not hesitating, Ben scrambled next to Michaelson, swinging around with his own rifle.

As the head edged completely into view, Michaelson aimed and pulled the trigger. The head bounced backward, and blood fountained from its mouth. Its body flopped into the trail, its tail beating convulsively several times before finally ceasing.

"Jesus Christ! How many of them are there?" Ben said, winded.

"I spotted at least four."

"We need to hurry," Ben urged. "Ashley and Villanueva are still struggling with the other one."

As if on cue, a pistol shot rang clear as a bell, followed by a second. "Let's go," Ben said. His eyes shined with worry.

"My ankle's screwed up. I can't move very fast."

Ben bit his lower lip. "Then you go first. I'll cover the trail behind us. We'll work our way back as best we can."

"No, you go on alone. I'll get there when I can."

"Forget it," Ben said. "I'm not leaving you out here injured. Now move it. We're wasting time."

The stubborn stiffness of the Aussie's shoulders told Michaelson it was useless to argue. He pushed off the rock and winced when his ankle touched the ground. He hopped two steps on his good leg for every one on his bad.

Ben's next words sped up his hopping. "We've got company."

Lying on her sled and peering out from the opening of the wormhole, Ashley winced with each rifle blast. For the past fifteen minutes, shots rang out sporadically.

Five shots in a row, then nothing for a minute, then an explosion of gunfire again. But for the past two minutes, the cave was silent. Not a sound. The quiet was agony.

C'mon, Ben, just get back here.

From far down the wormhole, she heard Villanueva mumble something. The morphine had made him incoherent. His arm was bandaged and wrapped to his chest. It took a good dose of painkiller and a sharp pull to his arm to get his shoulder in place. Afterward, he had slipped into a fitful slumber. Damn, he was one strong son of a bitch.

Still, he needed more help than a glorified first-aid kit could supply. As soon as they were somewhere safe, they would radio for assistance in the form of huge guns. Bazookas, preferably.

Linda and Khalid had moved the packs and helped haul the SEAL deeper down the shaft. Ashley waited at the entrance, watching the cavern. Where are you, Ben? She strained her eyes in an attempt to pierce the wall of blackness.

From behind her, she heard wheels scraping rock. "Do you see anything?" Linda asked.

Ashley glanced over her shoulder. Underneath the helmet, Linda's face was pale, her breathing raspy. "No," she answered, "and it's too damned quiet out there."

"Ashley, I need to get into the open."

"It's safer in the wormhole."

"No . . . I can't breathe. I need air."

Ashley finally realized. Hell, there'd been enough signs. "You're claustrophobic, aren't you?"

Linda remained silent, then a timid, "Please."

"Okay. I'll go with you."

Ashley slid out first, releasing a hand lantern and flashing the immediate area. She turned to wave Linda out, but the biologist was already standing up, slightly wobbly on her legs.

Linda took a few steps, breathing deeply.

Ashley studied the cave. Still no sign of anyone or anything.

Linda spoke behind her, her voice trembling slightly. "So . . . what do you make of . . . this creature?"

Ashley turned to her. The small woman stood by the collapsed bulk of the beast, the back of its head a bloody mass. The biologist nudged it with a toe.

Ashley shrugged, not in the mood to discuss it, not with Ben still out there. "I don't know."

Linda knelt down by the huge creature, her nose crinkling in disgust at the odor. She ran a finger over the ridge above the good eye. "The orbit of the eye is strange for a reptile. The zygomatic arch is wrong. More mammalian. And the pelvic structure is odd.

Look how it moved: upright, with birdlike joints and legs." She talked as if in a dream, half aware of what she was saying. "I've never seen anything like it."

Ashley shrugged, sweeping her light across the boulder face. "Hell, it's been isolated here for centuries. No telling what evolutionary pressures created this monstrosity," she mumbled, distracted. Only one thought occupied her full attention: Where are you, Ben?

Linda continued to examine the creature's carcass, moving down its sprawled length. "Hmm, come look at this."

Ashley turned to Linda, pointing her light.

The biologist was raising and lowering a few of the bristled spines that composed the creature's ridged crest. "This isn't scale. It's bunched hair."

Intrigued, Ashley stepped closer.

"Careful," Linda warned. "I think the bristles may be poisoned. See the glistening sheen at the tip of each and the pulpy gland at the base of the bristles. Be cautious." Linda moved aside, sliding farther down the carcass, continuing her examination.

Ashley knelt beside the damaged skull and carefully lifted one of the bristles with a gloved finger. Then she sat on her haunches. "Maybe it's some unknown species of dinosaur. I can see several primordial reptilian traits. Even its scales are similar to the scales of the plesiosaurs, a species of dinosaur, but what about the rest of it? The temporamandibular joint is too low on the skull, hinging its jaw like a snake, allowing its mouth to open wide enough to swallow a small pig in one gulp. And I know of no dinosaurs sprouting hair."

"Ashley, come see this."

Ashley crouched next to the biologist. "What did you find?"

"It's not a dinosaur. Or a reptile. Or a mammal." Linda reached to the exposed belly of the beast. Pulling back a flap of skin, she revealed a pouch in its abdomen. "It's a monotreme."

Her mind fuzzy and distracted, Ashley recognized the term, but couldn't quite recall its exact meaning. "A what?"

"An egg-laying marsupial. Like the Australian platypus. The species shared characteristics of both reptiles and mammals. Supposedly an evolutionary dead end."

The injured SEAL moaned stuporously from the tunnel behind Ashley.

"Hell of a dead end," Ashley said.

Big Bertha was still behind him. From several yards away, Ben watched the largest of the trio of beasts that stalked his trail. She leaned down, reaching with a claw, and picked up one of the expelled shells from his rifle. She snorted at it, then threw it away. The other two crowded behind her until she hissed them away.

Ben rolled back around the boulder. Three against one. Not good odds. Maybe he shouldn't have been so hasty to send Michaelson on ahead. His plan to lead the trio away to buy the major some time now seemed bloody daft.

Rifle fire had drawn the group after him, but the buggers were getting smart, skulking behind boulders, making difficult targets. And no matter how fast he ran, they matched his pace. Just minutes ago, one had almost outflanked him, catching him by surprise. A lucky shot that ricocheted off a rock and struck it in the tail had delayed it long enough for him to slip past.

He pushed off the rock and ran. He needed something to distract them, buy himself some time to slip away. He heard the characteristic snuffling as the hunters pursued.

Think, damn you! You're smarter than a freakin' cave monster.

Then it came to him in a flash. Maybe, just maybe . . .

He sped up, searching for a perfect spot. Luck, for once, was with him. He came upon a clearing in a grove of boulders. He mapped out the plan in his brain.

If he stood over there, hidden by that rockfall . . . hell, this just might work.

He reached for his belt to set the trap.

Once finished, he crammed his body into the narrow space between two jagged slabs of broken rock, careful not to entrap his rifle arm. From this vantage point, he had a view of the entire open area. His hand lantern rested in a crevice nearby, illuminating the area ahead but leaving him in shadow.

He raised his rifle and waited, counting each heartbeat. The cavern was quiet as a tomb. Then a soft snuffling arose, followed by a blast of angry hissing. Big Bertha stepped into the circle of light, cautious, head low. She darted forward. Damn, she moved fast. Within a single twitch of an eye, she had jumped to the center of the clearing, drawn by the shiny object. The two others, younger it seemed, slinked in behind her. She picked up the bundle of rifle shells Ben had taped together.

Ben rested his cheek against his rifle butt, eyeing his sight lines. He allowed a small smile to come to his lips. Curiosity kills.

Bertha raised the shells to her nose, sniffing at them. Ben targeted the bundle and pulled the trigger. Upon impact, a thunderous explosion rocked the cavern.

Where Bertha's right arm had once been, now only a bloody stump remained, waving plumes of black blood. Her snout was now a ruin of bone and gristle. She teetered, then crashed to the floor, thrashing in death throes.

Panicked, the others jumped away, one leaping atop a high boulder. They screamed at each other, whipping their tails angrily. Taking advantage of their confusion, Ben slipped from his hiding place, grabbed his flashlight, and ran.

That should keep them distracted for a while . . . he hoped. He pounded away at a dead sprint. He needed five minutes. Then he would be far enough ahead. After ten yards, he spared one look over his shoulder. Two reptilian heads stared in his direction. No longer hissing at each other. They had figured out his ruse and knew who to blame.

Turning forward, he willed his legs to move faster. A quick glance backward showed the heads had vanished.

The chase was on.

Ashley stared at the pouch of the beast. "So it's some sort of marsupial? How could that be?"

Linda shrugged. "All manner of marsupial species existed. At one time, they filled every environmental niche: predator, prey, et cetera. I'd say this is an early prototype. Something that eventually died on the evolutionary vine. Even if—"

Suddenly the sound of approaching movement intruded.

Ashley snapped her head around. Several yards away, a single lantern, bobbing erratically, appeared around a boulder. Ashley flashed her light in its direction.

Michaelson, limping with a pained expression, hobbled up to them.

Ashley kept staring over his shoulder. "Where's Ben?"

"He was behind me, covering the rear." Michaelson turned a worried eye to the black cavern. "But I haven't seen him or heard any rifle fire in a while. Just that loud explosion."

"So you just left him there? On his own?"

"He insisted that—"

She stopped him with a raised palm. "Later. Right now I want you two in the wormhole. We're too exposed sitting out here."

Michaelson shook his head. "I'll stay and cover the entrance until Ben gets here."

"No," Ashley said, eyeing his ankle. "With your injury—I'll stand guard."

Frowning, he obeyed her orders.

Soon Ashley stood alone with a pistol in one hand and a flashlight in the other, her heartbeat so loud she was sure it could be heard across the cavern. C'mon, Ben. Don't stand me up.

From a distance down the wormhole, Michaelson called, "Any sign of Ben?"

Ashley stood at the entrance. "No. Just keep moving. I'll tell you when I see something." By now her palms were sweaty, her pistol slick in her grip. Ten minutes had already elapsed since Michaelson had arrived. Surely Ben should have been back by now. Her mind conjured up all kinds of horrors befalling Ben. Just get back, here, she willed to him.

Then, from across the open space, another lantern appeared, bouncing wildly. Thank god, she thought, raising her own light. Ben was running at a full gallop toward her. He threw his rifle over his shoulder and waved her away.

"Run!" he yelled.

From behind him, two huge bulks stalked into the open area, necks twisting back and forth as they spied their escaping prey.

"Get inside!" he hollered to her.

Panicked, she turned to obey, then stopped. How would Ben . . . ? Whipping back around, she shoved her pistol into her belt, picked up his sled and yelled to him, "Catch!"

She flung his board toward him and watched him snag the board in midair. Then she did the hardest thing in her life. She turned her back on Ben and dove headfirst into the wormhole.

Holding her breath, she scooted down the shaft. Once she was a safe distance away, she braked to a stop and looked over her shoulder. From this angle, she could see Ben racing toward the entrance, a reptilian snout just over his shoulder. Hurry!

He sprang for the hole, sled clutched to his chest. She cringed. He was going to miss the entrance and hit the wall.

But instead he landed with a loud "Ooof" and dove smoothly into the tunnel.

He made it! Unclenching her fists, she let out a long sigh.

Bumping into her, Ben smiled, his expression both strained and relieved. "Now, isn't this cozy."

His rough hands held her legs. She wished those hands would wrap her up, hold her. Reaching back to him, she squeezed his hand.

Suddenly the shaft was drowned in a scream of anger. One of the pursuers plunged its head down the hole toward them, its jaws open wide.

Ben shoved her forward. "Time to go!"

She started to sweep her hands forward, pulling farther away, when she heard a yelp from Ben. She twisted around.

He was sliding away from her, back toward the entrance. The creature had snagged his boot and was hauling him back out. Ben kept kicking at its snout with his other heel.

She flipped onto her back, sacrificing her sled, hearing it skitter down the shaft away from her, then snatched her pistol. "Lay flat, Ben! Down!"

Eyeing the muzzle, Ben slammed flat, covering his head.

Her hands clutched her gun, stone-steady. Over the hump of Ben's back, she spotted the eye within her sights, then pulled the trigger, the blast deafening within the tunnel.

An echoing screech of pain instantly followed. Within a moment, Ben was rolling toward her again. Before she could react, his mouth was against hers. Their lips crushed together. He suddenly withdrew as if shocked himself. She blinked at him, her mouth still slightly parted.

"Damn," he said.

"Ouch!" Ben shifted his hips beneath her. "You're crushing me."

Riding on Ben's back, she felt his muscles flexing beneath her as he drove their sled forward. Emotions warred within her: giddy relief at their close escape, trepidation for what lay ahead, and a rising lust for the man beneath her. "Sorry," she said, scooting farther back, resting her head on his left shoulder, her hands at his waist. The heat from his body was like that of a furnace, steady and hot. She closed her eyes, allowing her cheek to brush against the nape of his neck.

Ben said, "I see lights up ahead."

She raised her chin to look forward. "It's the others. I told them to stay in the tunnel."

They slid forward. Michaelson was last in line. He contorted his large bulk in the shaft as he turned toward them. He had a look of genuine relief on his face that was oddly touching.

"Jesus Christ," Michaelson said. "You had us worried. First that scream and gunfire, then your empty sled slides down."

"We decided to carpool." Ben smiled. "Saves gas and is good for the environment."

Ashley pinched his waist, eliciting a pained expression from him. She craned her neck to look over Michaelson's head. "How's Villanueva?"

"Groggy still, but stable. Breathing evenly now. Strong pulse."

"Good. Then let's pause here. Try to contact Alpha Base. Can you reach the radio?"

Michaelson nodded. "I already tried."

"And?"

"Only static."

She wrinkled her brow. If they couldn't contact someone, get some help . . . "Maybe we're too confined here. All this rock."

"No, it shouldn't make any difference. Down here, we're always surrounded by rock."

"Then what's the matter? Is the radio damaged?"

"No, it checked out fine, and the communications center at the base is staffed around the clock. For them not to have responded . . ." His words stumbled to a stop.

"What?"

"Something damned serious must be going down."

SIXTEEN

"Run," Blakely said, pushing Jason from behind. "To my office."

"But—"

"Hurry!"

Blakely raced for his office, passing the boy and dragging him by the arm. Thankfully, Jason, still shocked by the commotion, allowed himself to be towed.

Sirens wailed in Blakely's ears, making it difficult to think. Men and women raced about them. A thousand floodlights swung in wild arcs across the rooftop. From the sounds of gunfire, the assault was striking the base periphery from all sides.

Blakely pounded up the steps of the administration building. Jason stumbled after him, his gym bag strap tangling around his feet. Once through the door and down the hall, they burst into Blakely's private office.

Roland was stuffing papers into a briefcase by the handful. He didn't look up as he spoke. "I heard. Almost ready."

"Good. Make sure you get the research documents in my desk drawer too. Those military assholes might take my base, but I'll be damned if they're going to get my work."

"Why the alarms?" Roland asked. "What's going on?"

He ran a hand through his thinning hair. "It's a full base alert. I have a feeling—"

A huge explosion rocked the building. Jason hugged his gym bag tighter to his chest. Tears started to well.

Roland began shoving papers faster. "That sounded like the munitions dump on the south side."

Blakely nodded. "Leave the rest. We evacuate now."

He opened a drawer and pulled out a .45 Colt automatic. He checked to make sure it was loaded and handed it to Roland along with a spare clip. "Take it."

Roland looked as if he had just been offered a venomous snake. He shook his head.

Another explosion caused the building to shake and ceiling dust to sift downward.

Roland snatched the pistol.

With a tiny key, Blakely opened a locked drawer and pulled out a sawed-off shotgun. He cracked it open; two red shells sat in the firing chamber. He snapped it closed.

Turning, he stumbled into Jason. Their collision loosened the boy's quaking control. "My . . . mom . . ." he sobbed between tearful breaths.

Blakely knelt and held the boy's shoulders. "Jason, I need you to be strong right now. We're going to make a run for the elevator. Try to get you topside."

Machine gun fire rattled from only a handful of yards away.

"Time to go," Roland said, holding the briefcase in one hand and the Colt in his other. "Out the back way. It's a shorter route to the elevator."

"Good," Blakely said, standing and keeping one hand on the boy's shoulder. "Lead the way. I'll cover the back."

Roland swung around and headed out the door. They followed on his heels, Blakely clutching the shotgun with both hands.

Outside, the sirens had cut off, but islands of gunfire flared around them. Armed men ran in every direction. Two men running with a stretcher darted past them toward the small hospital, a draped figure writhing on the canvas. A bloody arm slipped free of the sheet, and fingers dragged on the ground.

Blakely searched around the milling men. He needed information. A wild-eyed private backed around a corner into their group. His helmet was gone, and his gun shook in his hand. Blakely recognized the red hair, the freckles.

"Private Johnson," Blakely said, pushing as much authority into his voice as possible. "Give me a report."

Johnson swung around, a look of panic frozen on his face. Blood dribbled from a wound on his forehead. He stumbled back to some semblance of military decorum, coming to shaky attention. "Sir, the base has been breached. They came from everywhere. Popping out of holes, pouring out of tunnels. My . . . my platoon was overrun. Wiped out." As he reported, his eyes became wider and more glazed, and his shivering worsened.

"Who, Private? Who's attacking?"

With a wildness in his eyes, Johnson blurted, "They . . . they're coming this way. We have to get out of here."

"Who?" Blakely tried to grip the man's shoulder, but the private whirled from reach, afraid to be touched, then darted away.

Roland stepped next to Blakely. "The elevator's south of us. If it's been lost, then . . ."

"It's the only way out of here," Blakely mumbled. "We'll have to try and avoid the worst of the fighting."

Roland nodded. Jason stuck close to the aide's side.

They proceeded cautiously, zigzagging away from areas of gunfire. Slipping around a darkened Quonset, Blakely bumped into Roland, who had suddenly stopped. Blakely followed Roland's gestures and carefully peeked around the corner.

The space between the next two buildings was crowded with four torn bodies, limbs shredded from torsos, intestines strewn like party streamers. Suddenly one of the torsos jerked into the darkened alley beyond, dragged by something hidden in shadow.

Blakely suppressed a scream as he too was jerked backward. But it was only his assistant's hand, pulling him out of sight. A howl erupted from only yards away, something wild, inhuman. An answering scream bellowed from behind them. Close.

Roland tested the door to the Quonset hut; the hinges squealed with rust as he swung the door open. They hurried inside, fearful of what the noise might attract. Blakely coaxed the door closed as silently as the hinges would allow, then flipped the deadbolt. Darkness swallowed the group.

Blakely snapped on a small penlight attached to a key chain; it cast no more than a weak glow. In the dimness, rows of stacked boxes stretched the length of the long building. The tight columns went from floor to ceiling. No clutter, no cover to hide behind. But there should be an exit on the far side of the Quonset.

Blakely pointed with his light. "Down the rows! To the other door—"

A large crash boomed as something heavy hit the door. A bellow of protest followed. Again something crashed into the door. This time the frame buckled, metal groaned, but the deadbolt held.

"It won't take another hit!" Blakely yelled above the din. "Run!"

Roland sprinted forward. Blakely grabbed Jason's hand and hauled the boy with him, racing between the walls of boxes.

A third crash echoed through the supply hut. A screech of metal, then light flooded the room. Blakely's breath caught in his chest as something large pushed into the building, blocking the outside lamplight for a moment, plunging the room in darkness.

The smell hit Blakely first. The rot of a charnel house. Then the sound. Scraping and scrabbling. It certainly didn't sound like any footsteps he'd ever heard. In a heartbeat, it crashed into the neighboring row, hissing as it paralleled their course down the building.

In near panic, he jerked Jason forward, causing the boy to yelp and stumble. Before Jason hit the floor,

Blakely grabbed a fistful of shirt and pulled the child back up. But it was too late . . .

The pile of boxes just behind his heels tumbled down as a scream of anger erupted. The boxes were being tossed aside like toy blocks. In moments it would be on them. Searching in front of him, he could see Roland nearing the door. Scooping up Jason, Blakely tried to race forward, but his old knees couldn't manage with the boy's weight. His breath burned in his chest.

Jason seemed to sense this and squirmed. "Put me down. I can run."

Not having the breath to argue, he dropped the boy and willed him speed. The boy was a rabbit, off and running as soon as his sneakers touched the ground.

Blakely took a step in pursuit when a tumbling crate knocked him forward, pinning his legs. He let out a loud cry as he slammed into the floor. Struggling with his arms, he pulled frantically at his legs. Jason had stopped several yards ahead and turned. The boy took a step toward him.

"No!" he yelled. "Run! I'll catch up!"

With a crash of splintering wood, a reptilian snout burst into the row ahead, snapping at the empty space between Jason and Blakely. It hissed and wrenched its neck in the direction of Blakely's penlight; with massive shoulders, it tried to push itself farther through the wall of boxes. Blakely scrambled for his shotgun, but it had skittered beyond his fingertips. As the creature lunged at him, he twisted to the side as far as his pinned legs would allow. Luckily, it was enough.

The snout brushed his shoulder, missing him. The head collided into the crate atop his legs, bouncing it off of him. Not waiting, he rolled away. His instinct was to cram himself between the boxes, but they refused to budge. Trapped, he prepared to make a desperate run after the others.

The beast snarled and hissed, drawing back for a second attack. As the beast's neck tightened to strike, Jason bounced in front of it, twirling his gym bag in circles.

Startled, the beast froze.

The boy used his entire upper body to slam the bag forward, cracking the creature solidly on the nose. Its head flew back from the force of the impact.

Blakely didn't wait. "Run!" Adrenaline ignited his heart, fueling a hot panic. He bolted forward, grabbing his shotgun in one hand. He pounded down the aisle. Jason, agile as a monkey, raced ahead. The creature thrashed behind him as it tried to extricate itself from the piled boxes. He kept running, oblivious to the strain. His sight fixed ahead.

Bright light exploded in front of him.

Roland had reached the other exit. He stood silhouetted against the glare, waving them on. "Hurry!" Roland yelled. "It's coming!"

Blakely tried to increase his speed, but his legs began to buckle. He stumbled to his knees. The sound of crashing boxes got closer. Blakely heaved to his feet, lightheaded and wobbly. Then a sharp pain, burning like bile, blossomed in his chest and shot down his left arm. His heart.

The room tilted . . . blackness tried to swallow him up . . .

Suddenly Roland was there, supporting him. He allowed himself to be dragged, knowing he should protest, insist that they leave him. But he was too weak to utter a sound. They tumbled as a group through the exit.

Jason kicked the door shut behind them.

As they limped away, a bellow of rage erupted from within the Quonset hut. Claws gouged metal as it tried to rip after them.

Blakely, his hand tremoring, pointed forward. "The noise'll attract more of them."

They hurried back toward the center of camp, abandoning any hope of reaching the elevator. Gunfire burst sporadically around them. Clouds of smoke billowed in the cavern breeze. Near the north end of the camp a fire burned, flames flickering halfway to the ceiling. They stumbled across the camp, hiding from every sound.

Resting in a sheltered doorway, Roland was the first to speak since the ordeal. "Where do we go? They're attacking from all directions."

"No," Blakely whispered hoarsely. "They're only attacking from land." Wheezing, he pointed toward the lake.

His aide nodded. "It could be safer there. If we could get a boat, get on the water . . ."

Jason spoke up. "What if they can swim?"

Blakely tried to joke. "Then we better get a speedboat. Let's go." He pushed off the stairs. The slow pace across the base had allowed him to recuperate enough to proceed on his own. With Roland leading, he and the boy followed. With a little luck . . .

Then, from around a corner, one of the reptiles, a smaller one, muscled and scarred like a street bully, burst into their path—only six feet away. It crouched and hissed at them, bristled hackles raised.

Blakely raised his shotgun and blasted wildly. The creature howled and took a step backward, a bloody gouge torn from its right flank. Roland fired, shredding its upper arm, spinning it away.

"Move!" Roland screamed, grabbing Blakely's shoulder and Jason's arm. He shoved them toward a narrow alley between the mess hall and a wooden dormitory. "Run!"

Scrambling away, Blakely heard the rapid explosions of Roland's pistol fire and a loud crash, wood splintering. Then silence.

In a heartbeat, Roland was beside him again, hooking an arm around Blakely so they could travel faster. "I knocked it down, but it's getting back up—

A trumpeting of red anger buffeted them from behind.

"In here," Blakely said between gasps for air, indicating the dormitory.

"It could break in. We'd be trapped again."

"No, follow me." Blakely led the way into the dormitory, empty and silent except for a radio rasping an old show tune. "This way." Limping across the recreation room, he waved them to follow.

A pool table with torn green felt sat empty, a cue leaning against it as if the player had stepped out for a smoke. A pinball machine pinged and blinked in a corner.

"Where are we going?" Roland asked.

"Motor pool . . . get transportation." He nodded toward the hall that exited the room.

His assistant nodded. "C'mon."

A window exploded behind them, shards of glass spraying everywhere. The pursuing beast, bleeding from several wounds, landed with a thud. The worn pool table blocked its path, diverting its attention, buying them the seconds needed to escape into the hall. The creature attacked the table like wounded prey, stripping it apart with tooth and claw.

"Through here," Blakely whispered, pushing open a side door. The garage reeked of burned oil and spilled gasoline. His tiny light scanned nothing but open space. Then he spied a single Ford Bronco in the last stall. One of the few regular trucks still remaining since the arrival of the electric Mules. Thank god. They might still have a chance.

Roland hustled him forward through the darkness.

Looking down, Blakely felt a stab of fear. No tire! The front left wheel rim was empty. No wonder it was still here. He tried to protest to Roland, but his assistant nearly threw him into the vehicle. Resigned, he leaned back into the seat as Jason flew into the backseat. The keys, thankfully, were still in the ignition.

"It's going to be a bumpy ride," Roland said as he tapped the remote opener. "Buckle in." The metal-paneled garage door rattled upward—much too slowly. They all held their breaths as the door trundled higher, revealing the outer lamps. The way forward appeared clear.

"The engine noise," Roland said as he revved the motor, "is gonna attract them like cats after a mouse." Slipping into first gear, he slammed the accelerator, sending the Bronco careening forward. The empty wheel rim spat blue sparks as metal chewed stone.

Just as they cleared the dormitory, the beast crashed through a door, and with a keening cry, it leaped toward the truck. Even injured, it flew at them.

Jason leaned away from his window as jagged teeth snapped at him. Claws scraped paint from the door. "Move!" the boy screamed.

Roland popped the car into second gear and ground his heel on the accelerator. The Bronco seemed to pause mid-shift, allowing the creature to strike the window, creating a spiderweb of thin fractures. As if spurred by the damage, the truck leaped forward and away.

A howl of rage could be heard above the engine noise but soon faded behind them.

The Bronco bounced between buildings, tents, and huts. Here and there, from a distance, an ashen face would pop into view, some panicked straggler peeking from a hiding place.

Roland fiddled with the radio, trying to raise someone, but only static answered. Just as they trundled across the bridge to the north side, a barrage of grenades exploded farther in front of them, near the base periphery.

"Sounds like the troops have regrouped," Roland said, a hopeful edge to his voice. "Making a concerted effort now. Perhaps they can win back the base."

"Maybe," Blakely said, his chest aching. "But we can't risk it. Water's still our safest bet."

Roland pointed ahead. "We're gonna pass damned close to that fighting. Maybe we should lay low in the truck. It'll offer some secur—"

The Bronco rumbled around a corner, almost side-swiping a vehicle that lay on its side in the road. The doors had been torn off, the roof ripped open in curled strips. A severed arm lay on the ground next to the vehicle, a pistol still in its grip.

"Never mind," said Roland.

Blakely clenched his jaw as they slowly edged around the wreckage. As if it were some gory traffic accident, he couldn't take his eyes from it. Through the shredded metal, the interior was spattered with splashes of tissue. He twisted his head forward, away from carnage, his teeth aching.

As he focused on the headlight beams, a beast pounced directly in front of them, cutting off their way forward. Huge, the size of a bull elephant, this one was twice as big as any of the others seen so far, legs like tree trunks, ending in sicklelike claws, jaws that could swallow a calf in one bite.

Roland's neck wrenched around, checking behind them as he searched for reverse with the stick shift.

Jason sat in the backseat, eyes fixed forward. "Go, go, go, . . ." he mumbled.

With a bone-jangling grind, the Bronco popped into reverse, but another monstrous creature stepped behind them, pinning them where they were. Both creatures lowered their snouts and bellowed at the Bronco, tails thrashing, readying to attack.

"Goddamn it!" Roland swore as he slammed the vehicle back into first gear. Each creature looked like it could pick up the truck and juggle it like a Tonka toy. Roland pounded a fist into the steering wheel.

Blakely's panicked breathing tore at his chest.

Suddenly the Bronco jerked forward. It looked like Roland was trying to slip past the beast ahead, but Blakely knew it wouldn't work. The damn things were too fast and too big.

Jason let out a squeal as Roland aimed for the monster. But just before impact, he jerked the wheel to the right, grinding the empty wheel rim across the beast's toes, crushing the tissue between sharp metal and coarse stone.

The creature jerked upward, its neck stretched as taut as a bowstring, howling at the roof. It ripped its damaged claw from under the truck, almost flipping the Bronco. The truck teetered on two wheels for a second, then slammed to the ground.

Roland didn't wait; he edged past the injured beast. The pain of its crushed toes had inflamed the beast's rage. It charged the truck, ramming the Bronco a solid blow, jarring it two feet to the right, almost shoving them into a Quonset hut.

Roland wrestled with the wheel, trying to keep them moving forward. After a moment's struggle, the Bronco cleared the irate monster. The beast bellowed its protest, but its injury kept it from pursuing. Soon its pained roar faded behind them.

As they approached the lake, close to the fighting, Roland was forced to slow. The smoke was so thick from the fires and explosions that even the Bronco's lights could cut only a couple yards into the darkness.

"Are we heading in the right direction?" Roland asked.

"I think so." Blakely leaned forward, his nose almost touching the windshield. Between his blurred vision and the smoke, it was difficult to tell. "If we keep the big inferno to the left of us, we should head straight to the lake."

Blakely glanced in the rearview mirror. Jason still sat frozen in his seat belt. "How're you holding up, Jason?"

The boy remained quiet; only his eyes moved, making contact with Blakely's in the mirror. "This summer sucks," he said, shifting the gym bag in his lap.

That it does, Blakely thought. He nodded to the boy and again concentrated on the road ahead.

A sudden gust of cavern air cleared a narrow tunnel in the smoke. Blakely sat straighter. Just before the tunnel collapsed under the weight of the smoke again, he spotted it.

Lapping water. The lake! They had made it.

Roland had seen it too. A large bump tossed them all a few inches off their seats.

"I hope you can steer a boat better than this Bronco," Blakely said weakly.

The Bronco suddenly crashed to the left. The wheel spun under Roland's hands.

"Hang on!" Roland managed to yell just before the truck careened into the side of a building, knocking over a lamp pole.

Blakely's seat belt cut into his shoulder as the momentum slammed him to the side. Hitting the door, he groaned as he touched the welt on his head.

Roland unhitched his seat belt and reached for him. "Are you okay?"

"What did you run over?" Blakely asked.

Jason screamed behind them, "Watch out!" He already had his seat belt undone and was clambering over the front seat to join them.

The rear window of the Bronco shattered inward as a crocodilian head rammed through. The safety-glass coating kept the pane together, draping over the snout of the beast. The creature struggled to shake it loose.

"Out!" Roland commanded. "Run for the water."

Roland pulled Jason after him. Blakely clambered over to the driver's seat and dropped out of the Bronco.

Smoke enveloped them as they struck for the water. Blakely desperately hoped he was right and the dock was nearby. Glancing back, Blakely glimpsed the beast struggling to free its head of the Bronco, screeching its frustration. Once free, it would be upon them in seconds.

He stopped.

Roland turned to him. "What are you doing?"

"Keep going. Take the boy. I'll delay it."

"Are you insane? You're not in any shape." Roland shoved the boy toward him. "Take Jason. I can catch up. Leave me your shotgun."

Blakely hesitated. He could order him.

Roland snatched the shotgun from his grasp and pointed it at Blakely. "Move it!"

Blakely knew he wouldn't shoot, but they were losing time arguing. The timbre of the beast's bellow had changed. It was free. "We'll get the engine running."

Blakely ran stumbling after Jason. A shotgun blast tore the air behind him. He prayed for his friend.

Jason ran a few steps ahead. "I see it!"

The lights of the dock bloomed through the smoky air. Thank god. Within moments they were pounding across the wooden planks of the pier.

Shots rang out in the distance.

To the left, a green Zodiac pontoon boat was moored with two ropes.

"Hop in," he wheezed, but the boy was already in. "I'm going to start the engine. I want you near the rope. When I say pull, you yank the end of the rope to free us."

"I know," Jason said, staring back down the dock.

Blakely turned to the ignition cord and pulled it. The engine sputtered but didn't catch. He yanked it again. The same. Shit.

"Here comes Roland!"

Blakely looked up. His aide sprinted toward them, barely visible through the smoke. He yanked on the cord again. It almost caught this time, sputtering longer before dying. Blakely prayed as he watched Roland scramble toward the dock.

From out of the smoky blanket, a reptilian head shot forward, grabbing Roland by the shoulder. His body was flipped into the air, his momentum carrying him down the length of the dock. He landed beside the boat, the cracking of bones audible as he crashed to the planks. In thick pulses, blood flowed freely from his torn shoulder.

Blakely strained toward him, meaning to pull him into the boat.

The creature had stopped at the dock's edge, suspicious of the water.

Blood seeping from his lips, Roland struggled to rise but toppled over. He turned to Blakely and shook his head. With his good arm, he pulled the last mooring free. The boat drifted from the dock's edge.

"Go," he sputtered. He struggled to remove a ring from his left hand. He tossed it toward the boat.

Blakely caught it, recognizing the ring from Roland's partner in Seattle.

"Tell Eric . . . I love him." Roland pulled his pistol from his belt as the creature placed a tentative claw on the dock.

Blakely yanked the cord, and the engine caught with a clanking whine. With a twist of the gasoline feed, the prow of the boat tilted up as the craft accelerated from the dock. He watched as the monster crept down the dock, hissing toward his friend.

Roland tried to steady his pistol, but he was rapidly weakening. His first shot went wild. The creature was on top of him now. Roland raised the pistol to his forehead.

Blakely looked away.

A shot rang out, echoing over the water.

When Blakely turned back, the smoke had drawn a curtain between him and the dock. Just a dull glow marked its location through the grime.

A sudden bellow of frustration trumpeted across the water. It had been denied its kill.

SEVENTEEN

"What do you mean, Linda's gone?" Ashley said, raising her nose from the radio. She wasn't able to reach anyone either. "Why can't people stay put? I told everyone to stay inside the tunnel."

Michaelson packed away the radio and pointed behind him. "Sorry. I turned my back on them for a second, and she and Khalid were gone. The tunnel exits another hundred yards ahead."

Ben spoke behind her. "It's the claustrophobia. It's too tight in here."

"Well, it's a damned sight tighter in the belly of one of those predators."

"Khalid already reconnoitered the next chamber," Michaelson said. "I haven't seen it, but he told me it's safe: Only a second wormhole enters the chamber. Too small for one of those creatures."

"Yeah," Ashley said, "but what about other predators? Things that *can* travel through these wormholes."

Michaelson shrugged.

"Fine. Let's head on. I want the team to stick together." She helped Michaelson with the sleeping Villanueva; he moaned as he was moved. She checked his forehead. Damp, but not feverish. He needed help soon too. Damn this shitty radio.

Michaelson backed down the tunnel, pulling the SEAL along. Ashley pushed from behind, her knees raw by the time the glow of the exit appeared. Ben brought up the rear, lugging the packs. With a final heave, the SEAL was extracted from the tunnel. Ashley tumbled after him—into a natural wonderland.

"Holy shit!" Ben said as he crawled from the tunnel. "I've died and gone to heaven."

Ashley stood stunned. Before her opened a chamber the size of a small ballroom. Almost cozy. Iridescent crystals, some as small as thumbnails, others the size of ripe watermelons, encrusted the walls and floor, casting back the lamplight in scintillating sparks. Rainbows reflected everywhere. Stepping gingerly across the uneven floor, Ashley crossed to the center of the chamber, her mouth hanging open.

"Do you know what this is?" Ben asked, slipping his hand in hers.

She just shook her head. Linda and Khalid crouched a few yards away, noses together, examining one of the larger crystals.

"We're in a gigantic geode," Ben said.

"What's that?" she asked, only half interested, unable to turn away from the natural splendor.

"You've seen them. Those hollow stones sold in naturalist shops that are cracked open and lined by clear quartz or purple amethyst crystals. They form predominantly in volcanoes and are usually spurted out during an eruption."

"Yeah, I've seen those, but they're seldom bigger than beachballs."

"I know." He waved a hand to encompass the room. "Nothing like this has ever been discovered. But hell, we're miles under an active volcano."

She looked at his face, ruddy in the reflected light, strong chin raised as he stared at the ceiling. His excitement was contagious. She squeezed his arm.

Michaelson intruded, stepping up to them. "If this is quartz, maybe the sheer load is somehow affecting the radio. But I doubt it."

She hadn't thought of that. Hope flooded her. Perhaps . . .

Khalid called to them. "It's not quartz."

"What?" she asked, surprised to hear him join the conversation. He was usually so tight-lipped. "Then what is it?"

"It's diamond."

Ben laughed. "Sure it is."

"Who's the geologist here? Look at the angle of crystal fracturing. It's diamond."

Thunderstruck, everyone looked again at the pure mass of stone around them. Khalid smirked at their surprise.

Linda held up a chunk of diamond the size of a softball. "My god!"

Ashley thought of the diamond statue. How many other, similar chambers were down here? This much wealth . . .

The sharp edge of her excitement dulled with concern. She shook her head and released Ben's hand. "Before everyone starts counting their pennies, we still need to get out of here. Michaelson, try the radio one more time. Everyone else, set up camp for the night."

As she made her announcement, her exhaustion finally hit her. Every muscle burned. Every square inch of skin felt bruised. It seemed like they had been running for days. She glanced at her watch. After midnight.

"Still no response," Michaelson said, turning off the radio.

Ben spoke from where he had set up an air mattress. He had his geopositional compass open. "This isn't working either. Maybe Michaelson's right about some sort of interference. My compass uses a radio beacon at the base as a stationary reference point to home in on." He snapped the compass closed. "This bloody thing keeps searching, but it's not picking up the beacon."

She nodded, too exhausted to think clearly and too worried about Jason. "Perhaps it's some power outage at the base. We'll try again in the morning," she said, rubbing at her eyes. Her mind kept pushing Jason's face before her. If she thought about him too much, she'd begin to cry. What could they do anyway? Tomorrow would have to be soon enough.

Ben stepped up to her; he had finished inflating her air mattress. "Your bed awaits." He made a sweeping bow.

She took the mattress with a weary smile. "Thanks, Ben."

"I found a relatively flat area over there. Just enough room for two people." A grin played about the corner of his lips, the invitation clear.

In answer, she crossed to the spot and placed her mattress down. His smile had widened with each step she took. "Who's going to take first watch?" she asked.

"Watch?" Ben said.

She nodded. "We're in uncharted worlds down here. Carnivorous snails, whale-sized sharks, and now marsupial predators. We don't know what else might be lurking out there. Just in case, someone needs to stand guard. . . . We'll rotate shifts."

Michaelson spoke up. "I'll take the first shift, but with two entrances to the cavern, I recommend two people per shift."

"Good idea. Any volunteers to join Michaelson on first watch?" She stared directly into Ben's eyes.

He resisted for a few heartbeats, then sighed and raised his hand. "Gosh, I feel a second wind coming on."

With the schedule established, those not on watch retired to their respective beds. Ashley sank into her mattress as if in a lover's embrace. Soon all but a single handlight clicked off. Expecting to be swallowed by darkness, her lids drooped downward. What the . . . ? She sat back up. The chamber had not darkened; it continued to glow.

Ben stood up. "Bloody hell, this'll save on batteries."

Linda sat up. "It's coming from the walls," the biologist said, glancing around. "Reflecting off the diamonds." She crawled up and crossed to a wall where a section of diamond had fallen away. Scraping with the edge of a blade, she studied the rock, then turned to them with the blade upheld. It glowed a soft yellow. "It's fungus."

Great, Ashley thought. With our luck, it's probably emitting some toxic radiation.

"What a find!" Linda settled onto her mattress and wiped the blade off in a specimen bag. She wore a huge grin, talking rapidly as she worked. "This makes the fifth phosphorescent species I've found down here so far. Even the fish back at Alpha Base glowed due to the buildup of a type of fungus on their scales. But this . . ." She waved her arm. "This is almost worth, being chased by monsters."

Michaelson sat back down and rested his rifle across his knees. "Is it worth someone dying for?"

Linda's smile deflated, and she sealed the bag.

The major's words sobered the team, and exhaustion overcame wonder. Everyone settled back to bed.

Ashley stretched and curled her wool blanket around her bare feet, retreating into a cocoon. She peeked at Ben's empty mattress. She could hear the two men mumbling quietly together as they stood watch. She closed her eyes, touching the tip of her tongue to her bruised lower lip, remembering his kiss, and fell into a dreamless sleep.

A hand on Ashley's shoulder woke her too soon. She rolled away from the lantern light.

"Wake up, Sleeping Beauty. It's your shift." Ben's lips brushed her ear. "I even made some coffee."

She moaned and pushed herself upright, rubbing at her gritty eyes. Her muscles felt like stone weights. "Thanks, Ben . . . coffee sounds wonderful."

He helped her stand. "It tastes like mud, but it'll crank those pretty eyelids up."

She offered him a weak grin. She noticed Michaelson was already bundling up in his blanket. "You'd better get what sleep you can. It's only a few hours until morning."

He nodded, sliding out of his boots as he sat on his mattress. "I'll be out as soon as my noggin hits the pillow."

She envied him. Her rumpled blanket never looked so inviting. Yawning, she crossed to the makeshift guard station by the camp stove. She was surprised to see Linda sitting next to Khalid. "What are you doing up?" she asked as she approached. "This is supposed to be Khalid's and my shift."

"I know," Linda said, sliding over to make room on the boulder. "But I couldn't sleep. Too excited.

I wanted to run a few tests. Besides, I took a little nap and that's all I usually need."

Ashley noticed the biologist's test kit spread out on a relatively smooth table of rock. Linda raised a small vial in front of the lantern light and shook it. The phosphorescent glow in the vial increased. "Amazing," she said, then jotted a note in her logbook.

Ashley glanced at Khalid. Holding a pistol in his left hand, he cautiously lifted the hot coffeepot from the camp stove. He sloshed some of the syrupy drink into a tin cup.

Absently, Linda held up her cup for a refill, not even glancing in his direction. Almost like an old married couple at breakfast.

Once her cup was filled, Linda took a sip from her cup and grimaced. "This is awful." But she took another sip, then sighed. She sat back and glanced at Ashley. "You know, since I'm up anyway, why don't you go back to bed?"

This option hadn't occurred to her, but it made sense and was damned attractive. "I suppose if you really think that you—"

Linda nodded. "You need the sleep. You should see your eyes. They're blood-red."

And they felt like it too. Ashley glanced over to where Ben was snoring. Linda didn't have to offer twice. "I'll see you in the morning."

"Before you go, though," Linda said from behind her, "there's a question that's been naggin' me."

Ashley turned back reluctantly, the pull of her mattress strong. "What's that?"

"Those marsupial creatures. They're obviously predatory. How does something like that get enough food to eat?"

She shrugged. "I don't know."

"I mean, they have to be at the top of the food chain. But who's below them? Look at the lions in Africa. To support even a small pride of lions, it takes a huge reservoir of herbivores—antelopes, water buffalo, zebras. From a biological standpoint, these beasts would need a huge supply of prey."

Ashley rubbed her sore eyes. "Yeah, I guess so."

"So, where are they?" Linda took another sip of coffee. "Where is their food supply?"

Khalid snorted. "Hell, all I know is that I don't want it to be us."

Ashley nodded. The question was intriguing. What did they hunt? From their demonstrated teamwork in the other chamber, they had a rudimentary intelligence. Almost cunning. "I'm not sure. It's a mystery that'll have to be answered by a future team."

Linda nodded. She held up a second vial of yellow phosphorescence. "So many mysteries down here . . ." She checked a note in her book and pursed her lips.

Ashley said her good nights and retired to her mattress. She snuggled into her blankets, still warm from her recent slumber. Sighing, she closed her eyes, but the biologist's questions nagged at her. What *did* they eat?

Ben struggled in his sleep, knowing he was dreaming but unable to stop it. He was in that damned cavern once again. He walked among the fruit-laden trees, red pulpy gourds drooping obscenely.

"Hello," he hollered into the grove of trees.

No answer.

He had seen an image of his grandfather the last time he was down here. In a cave. Now, just where was that? He headed in a direction that seemed familiar. He brushed past a low mass of foliage with petite blue flowers. Didn't he pass a similar bush before? It was like returning to your hometown after being gone for decades. His feet seemed to remember their previous steps.

As he approached the far wall, he knew he was going the right way. He could even see the black hole in the glowing wall. Glowing? It was the same fungus growing in the geode room. Strange.

He continued toward the wall, expecting the trees to block his way forward, like his previous visit. But this time no trees stopped him. Taking a handful of steps, he found himself standing before the wall, a soft muskiness enveloping him. The fungus was sporing little pods the size of pinheads. He brushed a hand against the wall. With the sweep of his hand, the odor became overpowering. His mind reeled. Explosions of colors flashed before his eyes. He swooned to his knees, fighting to stay conscious, but his vision swirled in fantastic eddies of colors and textures. He slipped to the floor, the back of his head exploding as it hit the ground.

A voice arose from beside him. "Benny-boy, enough of that bloody crap."

He knew that voice from childhood. It was his grandfather.

"Jesus, snap out of it, mate."

His vision cleared as his grandfather waved a twisted leaf under his nose. It smelled of mint with a hint of cherry. With each wave, the swirls of colors were wiped away, as if erased by the passing of the leaf. "There you go, Benny-boy. 'Bout time you got your bloody arse down here."

Of course, he was dreaming—but it seemed so real. He could see the spiderweb of broken blood vessels at the tip of his grandfather's nose. The tufts of white hair at the edges of his ears. The ever-present laughter in his eyes. "Granddad?"

"Who'd ya think?"

"Well, considering you're buried six feet under Aussie soil, I didn't much expect to run into you anytime soon." He pushed himself upward, the musky odor still strong, threatening to overwhelm him again. "Why are you here?"

"I've been sent to warn you."

"We know about those black beasties. You're a little late."

"Those wankers? Don't let them pests get to ya."

"Pests? Those 'pests' just about consumed our entire crew."

His grandfather sat down beside him, crossing his legs. "Benny-boy, you have to continue down. Don't go up."

"But—"

"Down, Bennie-boy. Down."

The muskiness intruded again, smearing the image of his grandfather with wide swatches of purple and orange. "I don't understand . . ." He felt himself falling away again.

Only his granddad's words followed him as he faded away: ". . . down . . . down . . ."

"**Wake** up, Ben." Ashley patted his shoulder, surprised at how deeply he slept. The others were already up and about. He was the last still in his bedroll. Even Villanueva was sitting up, doing much better, his arm in a crude sling.

She shook Ben's shoulder. "C'mon, breakfast is about ready." She glanced over to where Michaelson was bent over the campstove. How he managed to turn dehydrated eggs into a damned close approximation of a Denver omelet was a mystery that would baffle Betty Crocker. Her stomach rumbled in response to the tantalizing scent of grilled onions and tinned ham.

Ben groaned, rolling onto his back, eyes cracked open a slit. "Bloody hell, what is that stench?"

"It's breakfast, and if you don't hurry, you'll be eating cold cereal."

He propped himself up on his elbows, his hair sticking out in all directions. He scratched at himself under the blanket. "Blimey, my head's aching like she's about to blow. It's not fair that I get a hangover without a fine evening at the pub."

Concerned, Ashley placed her hand on his forehead. Thankfully, Ben had no fever. "It's just a headache. I'll get you a couple aspirin."

"How about a fistful?" he said with a tired grin.

She crossed over to the bag that held the first-aid kit, shaking out three aspirin from a small plastic bottle.

Villanueva sat next to the kit. "He doesn't look too well."

Ashley couldn't help but smile at his observation. This from a man whose shirt was still soaked in his own dried blood and whose arm had just about been torn off. "I'm sure Ben will be fine. You, on the other hand, need to rest. You shouldn't even be sitting up."

He looked at her stonily, as if she were speaking a foreign language.

Michaelson stepped up behind her and handed the SEAL a steaming bowl. "Chicken broth," he said when Villanueva raised his eyebrows. "You lost a lot of blood. You need plenty of replacement fluid. Drink up."

Ashley crossed over to Ben, a slight smile on her face. Major Michaelson was turning into a regular Florence Nightingale.

"Thanks," Ben said, when she offered him the aspirin, "but I'm already feeling better. Once I'm up and moving, I'll be more chipper than a 'roo with a full pouch."

"Take the aspirin anyway." She pushed the tablets into his hand and passed him a cup of water. "We've still got a big day ahead of us."

He pouted but took the pills. "Now, weren't you saying something about breakfast earlier? I always wanted to be served breakfast in bed."

"If you're feeling hungry, then you're fit enough to get your own meal. Besides, we need everyone together at breakfast to discuss our options, and I want your input."

"Oh, all right. But that's a good way to give everyone a bad case of indigestion."

She helped him stand. "Quit griping."

With a mock scowl, he accompanied her to the camp stove, where Michaelson was already scooping out platefuls of omelet and fried potatoes.

"Quite a spread of tucker, mate," Ben acknowledged, hefting a tin plate from the major's hand.

"Since we haven't had hot food since breakfast yesterday, I thought everyone could use a big meal." Michaelson filled Ben's plate with a tap of his ladle.

Ashley took a smaller helping and sat down on a flat boulder. Khalid and Linda were already seated around the camp stove, forkfuls eagerly being consumed. Villanueva sipped at his chicken broth, lustfully eyeing their greasy meal.

Once Michaelson was settled in with them, Ashley spoke up. "We need to decide a course of action from here. We have only supplies for another eight days."

Nods and chewing were her only answer; the others waited for her to elaborate.

"Our options are to go back and try to make it through monster alley back there; stay here and hope that after a period of time the lack of radio contact may generate a search party; or push forward and try to find an alternate route up, knowing that there may be other nasties awaiting us."

Linda put down her fork. "I think we should stay here. Eventually someone will come looking for us."

"Perhaps," said Michaelson, "but consider the previous team. We were sent three months after the first. It could be a long wait."

"That's true," said Ben, "and those beasts will be waiting for them too. It's not fair to ask someone to walk into the same lion's den without warning. And going back through there ourselves is not an option. I say we push on."

Ashley nodded. She felt the same way, but there were other concerns to take into account. She pointed to Villanueva. "We have an injured teammate here, and additional traveling will risk further injury."

Villanueva lowered the bowl from his lips. "I'll manage just fine. I know how far I can push myself."

Ashley looked over at him. "I'm sure you do. But what if we run into more trouble? Your injuries are a serious hardship on the mobility of the team."

"If that happens, then leave me behind. Don't risk the team for my sake."

"Noble words, but it's us abandoning you. I, for one, won't do that."

"Me either, bloke. If we get in a scrape, we all go or no one goes."

Villanueva shook his head and raised the broth to his lips. "Civilians . . ." he mumbled across the steaming bowl.

Khalid spoke up. "So then, what do we do? Push forward or not? It sounds like we're damned if we do and damned if we don't."

"I have a suggestion," Ashley said. "We split up. Linda and Khalid stay here with Villanueva where it's safe. The rest of us will head out. We'll try to find a way back up and come down with a rescue team."

Everyone was quiet as they pondered her plan, then Michaelson nodded. "It's a sound plan. An efficient team has a good chance of making it back up. But, Ashley, there's no reason for you to come along. Ben and I—"

Ben interrupted. "The major's right. Two could move faster than three."

"Bullshit. I can move as fast as you, and I'm a sharper shot. Besides, the more eyes watching the trail, the better. I'm going."

Both men tried to beat her down with stubborn stares, but she didn't budge. Finally, Ben turned to

Michaelson. "It's a lost cause, mate. We got us some female company. Have to watch our language and be careful where we spit."

"Fine," Michaelson said. "Then let's divvy up the supplies and get going. We're gonna have to travel light. Just the necessities: guns, radio, canteens, ropes."

Ashley picked up her holstered pistol. "And lots of ammunition."

Khalid stood off to the side as the others readied themselves for the journey. From under heavy brows, he eyed Ben and Michaelson packing supplies. Villanueva struggled to be of use, disassembling the radio and wrapping key components in waterproof seals. Khalid studied the SEAL, weighing the strength left in Villanueva.

Linda stepped beside him. "Look at this!"

He turned to her.

"There's actually a phosphorescent species of mold growing *within* this diamond." She cupped the glassy chunk in her hands and leaned close to him, blocking out the surrounding light, her hair brushing his cheek. "See!"

The golf-ball-sized crystal glowed a soft yellow between her palms. "Why don't you add it to your specimens?"

Specimens? It took him a heartbeat to understand her. Then he realized she meant the collection of fist-sized diamonds he had stored in his pack. He'd told her they were geologic samples, scientific research.

"I will," he said, accepting her gift. He fumbled his bag open and snuggled the diamond carefully among the others. He ran a finger across the other diamonds. Twelve of them.

Regardless of his employer's desire, he wasn't leaving this cavern empty-handed.

Linda watched with mixed feelings as the others exited through the wormhole. She waffled between trepidation that the team was splitting up and relief that she was safely ensconced in a cavern secure from the predators.

She noted Khalid had already returned to studying the diamonds; he seemed fixated on the wealth around them, constantly drawn back to collecting stray fragments. Villanueva dozed nearby on his mattress.

Only she stared as Ben's light faded around a curve in the wormhole. She wondered what new discoveries they would encounter, what marvels she would miss by staying behind. A small spark of envy tried to blossom into a flame, but the horrors that could also lay ahead lessened her regret.

Glancing around the small cavern, iridescent in the lamplight, she smiled at the thought that she, Linda Furstenburg, claustrophobic extraordinaire, was happy to be trapped in a confining chamber miles below the earth's surface. Let the others discover new wonders. At least here she wouldn't be something's dinner.

She crossed to the miniature laboratory she had set up. Besides, there was plenty to research right here. She sat down and checked her figures twice, then monitored the new hyphae growth under a microscope. She pulled out a slide of the older fungus and studied it too. "My god, if that isn't a chloroplast," she muttered.

Villanueva, who had been dozing nearby, opened an eye. "Are you talking to me?"

Linda blushed. "No, sorry. It's just this mold is fascinating."

Villanueva pushed into a seated position, obviously still groggy, but bored too. "What did you find?"

"I thought at first it was a dimorphic species, two forms of the same fungus. But now I don't think so. I think they are two unique species surviving symbiotically. Each sustaining the other."

"You lost me, Doc."

"One type of mold—the one with glowing hyphae— gets its energy from hydrogen sulfide in the trace volcanic gases, but its rate of growth is too fast to attribute to the amount of gas present. Plus it wastes a lot of energy to produce the glow."

"So how come it does that?"

"That's just it! There's a second species of fungus interwoven with it. This second fungus is full of a type of chloroplast!" She pointed at the microscope slide as proof.

The SEAL shrugged. "So?"

"So the second fungus uses the glowed energy from the first, like a plant uses sunlight. It feeds on this energy and in turn not only thrives, but also produces hydrogen sulfide gas to feed its glowing counterpart."

"So each mold feeds the other."

"Exactly! But obviously there must be more to it. More energy is needed to sustain this relationship. Whether from thermal heat, or from something in the rocks here, or from decomposition, or something else. I don't know. There's so much to learn. I could spend years studying just this relationship."

Villanueva seemed to be losing interest in her revelation. "Uh-huh. I'd still rather just get out of here."

"Me too, but the fungus explains a lot."

"Like what?" Villanueva yawned.

"Like why the predators down here still have eyes. Why they camouflage so well with the rock. It was strange why creatures isolated for millennia in perpetual darkness should still have eyes and need to blend into the background. Most isolated cavern species are blind and albino due to the darkness."

"Hmmm. So what you're saying is that these creatures have been mostly hanging out in lighted areas."

"Or at least at their fringes."

"That's good to know. So anywhere there's fungus, there might be predators around."

"Exactly!"

Ashley noted two things as soon as she exited the newest wormhole. It was getting damned hotter, and the fungus grew thicker and brighter the farther they descended.

They had been traveling for half a day now, stopping only to check the radio periodically. No one ever answered their call.

"We'd better conserve our batteries while we can," Ben said. "The glow here is sufficient to see by."

He was right. When all the lights were turned off, she could see just fine. She wiped her brow. The cavern ahead was spotted with bubbling pools of steaming water, the room as hot as a sauna. It reeked of rotten eggs.

Ben offered her a sip from his canteen. "We must be approaching a hot vent of the volcano."

She nodded. "We need a way *up*. Soon!"

Michaelson called from yards away, "Your wish has been granted, Ashley. There's a crack over here. It's scalable and seems to climb at least a hundred yards up. This may be the break we were searching for."

Ashley hurried over to him. She would climb a sheer cliff if she could get away from this sulfurous heat. She clicked her flashlight back on and probed the way up. The fissure was craggy, with many handholds and footholds. The top extended beyond her light. Excellent.

Ben approached her side. "There's another wormhole on the south wall. It heads down again."

"Who cares? We're going this way."

Ben peered up. "I don't know," he mumbled.

"What do you mean?" She gave him a perturbed look. "This is perfect."

"We can't tell where it ends. Who says it ends in a chamber? It may just peter out."

"Ben, feel the breeze. It practically sucks you up this crack. Didn't you say that meant there were continued passages?"

"I guess so." His voice was a whisper.

She glanced at him, wondering what he balked at. Surely not the climb. It looked like a piece of cake to her. "Ben?"

He shook his head as if clearing cobwebs. "Of course, you're right. Everyone hook on your quick draws and belaying harnesses. We're going up."

Ashley stared at the Aussie. She had only known him a short time but already knew his moods. Something was bothering him. "Ben, you're the expert here. . . ."

He fastened his rope in place and approached the rock face. "I'm fine with this. Just had this urge to . . ." He shook his head again. "Hell, never mind. Let's go."

She watched his left hand jitter as he gripped his first handhold.

Linda woke with a snap, her head pounding. Khalid lay on a mattress nearby, snoring loudly. It was one of his rasping snorts that had startled her. She glanced at her watch. Four hours had passed since the two had retired for a nap after lunch. She glanced at Villanueva. He too was sound asleep.

Odd. She was never one to take naps, let alone allow hours to slip by like that. She sat up and stretched. Of course, the present circumstances were unusual. After running all day yesterday from monsters, her body deserved a rest.

She stood up, and the room spun; pinpoints of light exploded across her retinas. She almost stumbled to her knees, close to blacking out. After a few wobbly seconds, the spinning stabilized. Must have stood too fast, she thought, shaking her head. Her heart pounded loudly in her ears, each beat throbbing at her temples. She reached for her canteen and took a deep swallow.

Breathing heavily, she saw something that almost made her drop her canteen. The walls! The smooth-surfaced fungus was now festooned with protruding balls of growth. As she watched, several hundred pods burst, releasing a small puff of smoky dust. Spores! In the lamplight, billowing clouds of spore dust wafted through the chamber. She watched as Khalid inhaled a stream of the smoky air.

This couldn't be healthy. She knelt by Khalid and shook his shoulder. He didn't awaken. She shook him harder. Nothing. She raised his eyelids; his pupils were dilated in the bright light, nonresponsive. Damn, the spores were acting like a drug. Anesthetizing them! She realized that if they kept inhaling the drug, an overdose pended.

The fungus was trying to kill them!

Agitated, her breathing grew ragged. Blossoms of color flared across her sight. The spores! Must remain calm. Must breathe slower. Take in less of the drug. She held her breath. Still the room began to spin again. Think, damn it!

An idea occurred to her. She grabbed a handkerchief and splashed water over it, soaking it. She wrapped the dripping fabric over her mouth and nose. The moistened fabric should filter the spores. At least she hoped it would.

Hurrying, she applied a similar wrap to Khalid's face, trying to prevent him from taking in any more spore dust. Don't you die on me, she thought.

She scooted to Villanueva. For a moment she thought he had stopped breathing. But on closer inspection, she could see his chest rise and fall. Still, his complexion had a blue tinge. Cyanotic. She prepared a third handkerchief and wrapped it around the SEAL's face.

Clenching her fists, she studied him. The SEAL's breathing was ragged and shallow. In his debilitated state from yesterday's attack, he was more susceptible to the drug.

She glanced around. The glowing fungus had dimmed slightly while sporulating, probably to conserve energy for the production of the spore dust. But what had set it off? Their body heat? A change in the level of carbon dioxide from their breathing?

She did not have time to seek answers. Right now she had to get them out of here. But where? There was no telling if the monsters still lurked in the other chamber. And who knew what awaited them if they followed in the other team's footsteps?

Only one thing was certain. If they stayed here, they would die.

She crossed to the wormhole that Ashley and the others had gone down several hours ago. A slight breeze blew up from below, wafting a few blond strands of her hair.

The air was fresher, free of spores.

She made a decision. She would have to drag the two men through this wormhole. If anything threatened beyond, they could at least stay in the passageway. But more importantly, the direction of the breeze should keep blowing the spores clear of the wormhole.

At the thought of hiding for days in the narrow tunnel, a twinge of anxiety threatened, but she squelched it. She turned to the men. It would be difficult hauling them over the rough terrain of the floor. The jumble of diamond made the sleds useless, but once at the wormhole, she could use the sleds to easily maneuver them from there.

She crossed to the two sedated forms. Grabbing the SEAL's legs, she hauled him toward the wormhole, grunting with the effort. After fifteen hard minutes, she had both men in the wormhole, sprawled across their sleds. Her head pounded and sweat stung her eyes. By now she weaved drunkenly as she stood, unsure if from the strain or from the drugged spores.

She splashed her face with more water, readying herself. Holding her breath, she dove into the wormhole, trying to ignore the walls pressing around her, concentrating on maneuvering the men ahead of her. She shoved Khalid's limp form forward, bumping his shoulder into Villanueva's sled, causing the SEAL to roll several yards ahead before settling to a stop.

Bumping her way forward, it was slow progress. But the farther away from the cavern they progressed, the clearer her head became. She stopped for a moment and rested, leaning a cheek on her arm. She had done it! The air was clear here.

A groan arose from Khalid. He was waking. She allowed herself a weary smile. Only a vague sense of unease because of the closely surrounding rock intruded on her satisfaction. But it was only that of a buzzing gnat, not the usual panicked roar. No, the enclosing grip of the tunnel had lost its hold. She had saved them.

Ashley followed Ben's lead, placing her hands and feet where he placed his. Her fingers stung and her thighs screamed. The fungus growing on the walls made the grip slippery, but at least the farther they climbed, the less prevalent the fungus was. As they progressed, they eventually had to turn on their helmet lamps. With the disappearance of the mold, the perpetual darkness had crept back to smother them.

Michaelson followed, pushing her over some of the rougher spots.

She watched Ben jam a quick-draw bolt in a crack above and secure a loop of rope. He was humming roughly under his breath as he worked. After two hours of climbing, she was sick of that tune.

"Ben," Michaelson called from below. "How much farther?"

"'Bout another hour."

Ashley groaned, leaning her face into the rock.

Ben continued, "But there appears to be a wide ledge about ten yards up. We should be able to take a lunch break before we challenge the last leg of the climb."

Grasping that small hope, Ashley thanked the gods of climbing. "Then let's get up there, Ben. I'm tired of hanging around here."

She watched Ben reach for a handhold and pull himself upward. "You wanted to come this way," he said in good cheer. "I was the one who wanted to go the easy way, so quit your bellyaching."

At least his initial trepidation had seemed to fade as the strain of the climb progressed. The first hour of the climb had been easy, but it was only a warm-up for the nearly vertical climb they had been struggling with for the last hour.

Ashley stretched up to secure her hand on Ben's previous foothold. She couldn't quite reach. She searched for an alternate hold on the sheer face. Only a blank wall faced her. Damn. "Ben, I can't get past this point," she called, trying to hide her increasing panic.

Ben glanced down at her. "No problem, Ash. Just let go. I'll haul you with the rope to the level of the next quick draw. Then you can reestablish your holds. I've got good leverage here."

She swallowed hard. Common sense kept her clutched to the wall.

He winked down at her, seemingly reading her mind. "I won't drop you."

Embarrassed by her doubts, she willed her hands to let go. The carabiner brakes held her in place as she hung from the rope, swinging away from the wall and out over the hundred-yard drop. Suddenly she jerked upward as Ben's arms pulleyed rope through the quick draw.

In two pulls, she was hauled next to him, still swinging a couple feet from the wall. He held his hand out to her. She reached for him. His fingers slid across her palm before gripping her hand. His eyes never left hers as he pulled her toward him. He held her waist steady, his palm hot through her damp T-shirt, as she planted her feet and gripped the wall.

"Thanks, Ben."

"Anytime, love," he whispered in her ear, then brushed her cheek with his lips.

She blushed and glanced away. "We'd . . . uh . . . better get going. Michaelson's waiting."

He turned back to the wall and continued. She watched him climb with the ease of a mountain goat, his legs spread wide. She had to force her eyes away before she could continue, her cheeks still flushed.

Within ten minutes, all three were sitting on the ledge, sipping warm water and chewing on jerky and dry cheese.

Ben sat close to Ashley's side, his leg brushing hers. They ate in silence, all of them exhausted. Michaelson seemed lost in his own thoughts.

Finally, Ashley dusted crumbs off her lap and pushed to her feet, her leg muscles wobbling. Planting her fists on her hips, she glanced up the pocked slope. Thankfully, it was a short, easy grade. If she had to climb another vertical wall, she'd need at least a day's rest.

Ben stood up beside her. "Ready?"

She nodded.

"Okay," Ben said, "then let's cinch up and head on out." He grabbed the bundle of climbing rope and hooked her to him. He stood close as he knotted her up, then leaned toward her. "Sometime we're going to have to try this when we're not rock climbing," he said with a jaunty grin.

Rolling her eyes, she shook her head. "Let's get going."

Whistling that damned tune again, Ben tackled the slope. Ashley followed. For a good part of the ascent, she found she could simply walk, only needing to crawl over short sections of the climb. Near the very top, though, the climbing became tricky again. Footholds and handholds had to be searched for carefully, each yard gained only with planning and muscle.

Sighing, Ashley glanced up, wondering if they would ever escape this damn crack. She watched Ben suddenly heave himself up and roll out of sight. He had reached the lip of the cliff! With renewed energy, she followed, scrambling from handhold to handhold.

Suddenly Ben's face popped over the lip, only feet from her. He wore a huge smile. "C'mon. What's keeping you?"

"Just get out of my way," she said with a matching smile.

He reached down and hooked a hand into her harness.

"I can manage on my own. Just—"

He yanked her up to him, kissing her squarely on the lips, then rolled backward, hauling her over the edge and on top of him.

She laughed convulsively as she lay sprawled across his chest. Relief at finally surmounting the cliff washed over her. Ben's nose was only inches from hers. But he wasn't laughing—only staring into her eyes. His seriousness sobered her.

There was a hunger in his stare, a desire she had never seen so openly offered. And in his eyes, a question. As she stared, her laughter died in her throat. Restraining for only a heartbeat, she answered his question, leaning down and returning his kiss, at first gently, then with a passion that had been too long suppressed.

In response, he wrapped his arms around her, swallowing her up, enveloping her deeper to him, bodies crushing together as fervently as their lips.

Words intruded: "If you lovebirds are done, I could use a hand."

Blushing furiously, Ashley rolled off Ben and sat up.

Michaelson, with the biggest backpack, struggled to pull himself up over the edge. Ben scooted over and by pulling on his pack was able to wrestle the major up.

Michaelson shoved to his feet. "Well, we're up here now. But where the hell is *here*?"

Clearing her throat, Ashley shot Ben a guilty glance. They should have been checking out the site. She unclasped her hand lantern and clicked it on. The men followed her example. "Let's find out," she said.

Ben freed the geopositional compass from his pack and fiddled with it. "Still not working." He snapped it closed and rummaged through his pack. "Forget all that newfangled computer crap. Sometimes you have to resort to old-fashioned methods." He pulled out a scratched silver box the size of his palm and kissed it. "Ah! Here's my darling. Simple magnetic compass with built-in barometer for measuring pressure. Great for approximating depth." He studied the tiny tool's measurements. "I'd estimate we've just climbed two hundred meters. Bringing us just that much closer to home." He pointed the compass forward. "We should head this way."

Ashley took the lead, Michaelson limping behind her.

Ahead of them, the surrounding rock opened into a spacious cavern, a short rise blocking the view into the main chamber. Leading, Ashley reached the crest first.

She froze as she waved her light across the cavern floor ahead.

Ben tromped up beside her. "Shit!" he said as he looked down.

"Goddamn," Michaelson whispered.

Ashley widened her lantern beam. Before them, strewn across the cavern floor, lay thousands of white eggs the size of ripe watermelons. Most were clustered into distinct groups. Nests. Several patches of cracked empty shells dotted the field. Halfway across the cavern, three immature marsupial creatures, about the size of small ponies, huddled together, necks entwining. As Ashley's beam settled upon them, they began a strident mewling.

Linda was right, Ashley thought. Egg-laying, like the platypus. "This is not good," Ashley said. "Not good at all."

Only one other passage exited the chamber. A tunnel large enough for a train to pass through. The babies' cries continued, grating like a fingernail scraped across a blackboard. The trio quieted, cowering in their nest, when a bellow erupted from the tunnel ahead.

Something large and angry barreled this way.

EIGHTEEN

Leaning over the green pontoon, Jason watched the triangular wake his fingers made in the water. He wished his mother were here. Not that he was scared. Actually, the initial terror of their escape yesterday had dulled to a mere worry. He just missed her.

Behind him, Blakely snored, slumped in his seat. For nearly a day they had anchored here, a hundred yards offshore. Nothing to do, nothing to see. A smoky pall obscured the shoreline. Yesterday, brief explosions of fire had brightened the water's edge. Today, though, nothing but oily smoke and darkness. It was hard to tell in which direction the base even lay. Just walls of emptiness, like they were adrift in space.

Jason rolled onto his back. A buckle on his orange life jacket gouged his side. He squiggled into a more comfortable position, studying the world above him. The single lantern cast a splash of illumination toward the ceiling. Poking through the black mist, stalactites pointed down to the boat. Like they were pointing at him. Even as the boat drifted, the rocky spears seemed to bend and continue to accuse him, before finally disappearing into the smoke.

Jason sat up suddenly, rocking the boat. Wait a minute. They were anchored. The boat shouldn't be gliding past stalactites. They were moving! Drifting!

"Dr. Blakely!" Jason crawled across the bouncy floor to the doctor. "Something's wrong."

Blakely groaned and pushed back into his seat. "Now what, Jason? Did you see another fish?" He straightened his glasses, one lens of which had been knocked out sometime yesterday. He kept squinting the unprotected eye, almost like he was winking.

"Look up, Dr. Blakely! We're moving."

Sighing, Blakely craned his neck back, his lip cemented in a disapproving line. Then his expression jumped to a startled look, both eyes wide. "Damn, we *are* moving."

Blakely reached over the side and began hauling the anchor's line, tossing dripping loops of rope onto Jason's toes.

Jason nudged the slimy, smelly loops away with a scowl.

"Damn!" Blakely held up the frayed end of the rope. No anchor. "Looks like something chewed through it." He dropped the end of the rope and sat down by the rudder. "The current's strong here. We're moving at a fair clip."

"What are we going to do?"

Blakely crossed to the motor. "First, we need to find out where we're heading. Jason, go to the front and turn on the searchlamp."

Jason scooted to the prow of the boat, grabbed the handle of the lamp, thumbed the switch, and swung the beam forward. A thick blade of light shredded the darkness ahead. But the smoke fought it to a standstill. An endless shroud of oily mist blocked the light only yards from the prow.

"Jason, why don't you free those oars? We may need to paddle."

"Why? We could just use the motor."

Blakely shook his head. "There's not much gas in the engine. And with the smoke this thick, it would be suicide to go too fast. We could barrel right into something or into shore. And besides, if we're close to shore—and who the hell could tell in this pea soup?—I don't want to draw attention. So let's paddle."

Nodding, Jason locked the light in position and slipped to where the two plastic paddles were housed.

As he was lifting one free of its berth, Blakely suddenly swore. Jason glanced up.

A wall of jagged rock raced toward them, stretching wide ahead of them. Black daggers jutted from the walls and water. The current was aiming their boat right for the thickest cluster of sharpened stone. Suddenly floating on big rubber balloons seemed a stupid way to travel.

Blakely yelled while he leaned his full weight on the rudder. "Boy, get on the right side and paddle like mad!"

Jason understood the danger and flew to the right side, lunging over the pontoon to plant his paddle. He pulled as his mother had once showed him while canoeing down the Colorado River. He dug deep with the blade of the paddle, making his strokes long and fast.

"We're not going to make it," Blakely yelled, each word louder than the last.

The note of panic in his voice was contagious. Jason's studied paddling grew frantic. He concentrated on the water he was churning. Still he kept listening, blood pounding in his ears, expecting to hear at any moment the rip of shredded pontoon.

His shoulders burned with the strain, but he kept digging with his paddle.

"We're turning!" Blakely's voice had an edge of hope.

Jason glanced over his shoulder. The boat was now running at an angle toward the wall, rather than straight. He continued pulling with his paddle. "Get the motor started!" he yelled.

"Not enough time. I don't dare let go of the rudder."

Jason had been on enough canoe trips to know that they weren't going to make it. Still he wrestled with his paddle. Then, through the smoke ahead, an opening appeared in the wall as their boat angled to the side. A wide black mouth. If they could aim for that, maybe they could miss the jagged wall.

Blakely saw it too. "It's our only chance."

Jason dug savagely. Luckily, the current aimed for the hole too. As he worked the paddle, the prow of the boat crept deeper into the current.

"Watch your head!" Blakely called out.

Jason ducked as a shelf of rocky overhang passed over the boat. They were about to hit the wall! He crouched low in the boat, anticipating the collision. But the strength of the flow suddenly grabbed the boat and pulled the prow around the bend and into the black tunnel.

"We did it," Jason said.

They glided smoothly into the tunnel. Jason crawled forward to the light at the prow. He swiveled it about, examining the walls. No rocky spars awaited to jab them. Instead the walls were glassy smooth.

"It looks safe," Blakely said. "This is the river that drains the lake. Luckily for us, the years of running water have polished these walls." His words echoed, giving them a hollow feeling.

The river carried the boat deeper into the tunnel. The light pierced the tunnel to a bend ahead. "Where does it go?" Jason asked.

"I don't know, and I don't think this is a good time to explore. Let's see if we can swing the boat around, and I'll get the motor running."

Jason passed Blakely a paddle and each took a side. Jason paddled forward while the doctor backpaddled. The boat began to turn on its axis just as the current passed around a bend in the tunnel. The river beyond the curve suddenly dropped at a steep slope. The increased speed of the flow ripped the prow of the boat forward again.

"Hang on, Jason!" Blakely said, as the boat was dragged toward the racing waters.

Jason swallowed hard, winding one hand into a rope handle. The boat plunged into the trough, accelerating rapidly. The prow's light bobbed across the churning waters. The sight ahead caused Jason to wrap a second hand into the rope.

The tunnel curved around a tight bend. The river swung in an arc up the side of the wall as it coursed around the turn, tilted at an impossible angle.

"Shit!" Blakely blurted, quickly wiping spray off of his glasses with the cuff of his shirt, then frantically grabbing his handle.

The boat shot into the curve, climbing high on the wall as they made the turn. Like riding some water slide down a sewer drain, Jason thought. He watched as Blakely's side of the boat tilted up over his head. The doctor struggled to maintain his seat, legs scrambling on the slick rubber floor. Jason cringed, praying the boat wouldn't flip.

Then the boat slammed back down as the corner straightened out, throwing Jason to the floor.

"Another turn!" Blakely yelled.

Jason braced for it. This time his side of the boat was thrown high. He saw the bald spot that crowned the doctor's head. Then the boat leveled again. "How do we stop?"

Blakely squinted at the tunnel ahead as the boat raced past the walls. "I don't know. Just hope that eventually it levels out so we can slow down . . . Hang on! Here comes another turn!"

After five more turns, Jason's stomach began to get queasy. The dry rations he had eaten for breakfast felt like a gnarled lump in his stomach. "I'm going to be sick," he mumbled.

"Shhh!" Blakely said. "Listen." The boat had slowed somewhat, the river leveling out, but the current was still strong.

Restraining a groan, he cocked an ear. Now what? Then he heard it too. It sounded like someone gargling. It swelled louder and louder until it was thunderous.

Blakely said the next word as if it hurt his mouth. "Waterfall." He grabbed the rudder. "We've got to turn around and get the motor going!"

Jason looked at the rocky tube tight around them. No room to turn, even ignoring the torrent of water. Then he remembered something his mother had taught him. "Spin in the next curve!" he yelled above the thunder.

"What?" Blakely looked at him as if he might be insane.

"As we turn, the force of the water can help spin us."

"That's too dangerous."

Jason pointed ahead. "Yeah, but what about that?"

"Good point. How do we spin?"

Jason pantomimed frantically while trying to explain, "Lean the rudder in the opposite direction of the next turn. Force the prow up the wall. The current will whip the stern around. Spinning us backward. My mom and I tried it once."

"Did it work?"

"Well, no. We flipped the boat."

"Great."

"It's supposed to work. We just did it wrong."

"Well, we have only one chance to do this right. There's the next corner!" Blakely had to holler to be heard above the roar.

Jason scooted back beside Blakely, ready to add his weight to the rudder. "Push when I say!" he shouted.

The doctor nodded.

Jason waited until the tip of the boat entered the curve. "Now!"

Blakely shoved the rudder, leaning hard on it. Jason pushed too. The prow shot up the wall, tilting the boat vertical.

"Don't let up!" Jason yelled, sensing that the doctor was beginning to ease up on the rudder. "Not till we're around!"

The boat shuddered for a heartbeat, then the stern of the boat flipped around, the light pointing back the way they had come.

"My god!" Blakely said, wide-eyed. "We did it."

Jason swung around to check where the current was still dragging them. A hundred yards farther, the river emptied into a large cavern. He squinted his eyes at the approaching hole. That's weird, he thought. He rubbed his eyes, glancing at the tunnel walls around him. It didn't go away. "Look, there's some sort of light coming from the walls here."

Blakely craned his neck to see. "Some sort of glowing mold." He pulled on the motor's starter cord. The engine click-clacked but died.

"Uh-oh!" Jason said. "Look!"

Blakely had already seen it and yanked frantically on the cord.

Downcurrent, the glow revealed a whitewater turmoil. The roar now pressed on the eardrums, rattling inside his skull. The river disappeared beyond the churning water. Over a cliff!

Jason turned to the doctor as the boat raced toward the plummet. "Hurry!"

With a fierce pull, the engine sputtered—then caught! Blakely twisted the throttle wide open. The motor fought the current. At first, there was no effect. The current still pushed the boat toward the waterfall. But finally, only yards from the whitewater, the engine started winning. The boat now sat still in the river, engine struggling with the current.

"C'mon, c'mon, c'mon . . ." Jason willed the boat forward.

As if the boat heard him, it inched forward, at first slowly, then faster and faster.

Jason whooped. Blakely wore a fierce smile.

Until the engine died.

NINETEEN

Another piercing scream. It had almost reached the cavern.

Ashley searched for any other exit from the nesting area. Even a small crevice in which to hide would do. A hurried scan with her hand lantern revealed only rock.

"Back down!" Ben said, pointing his lantern back to the cliff.

Michaelson already had his sawed-off shotgun in his hand. "No, we stay and kill it."

Ashley shook her head. "Might be others. Gunfire could draw a whole flock of those damned creatures. We only shoot if cornered."

Ben glanced back at the cliff. "I'd say we're cornered."

"We just need somewhere to hide," she said. "If Big Mama finds the cavern empty, hopefully she'll lose interest and go away again."

"But where could we hide?" Michaelson asked. He checked his rifle to make sure the clip was secure.

Ben tugged on the coil of rope over his shoulder. "We could hang over the cliff edge. Wait for it to leave. If it finds us, we can rappel farther down the cliff face."

Ashley's arms still felt like limp noodles, but what choice did they have? "Good idea. Let's go."

Ashley slid down the ridge, following Ben to the cliff's edge. From the ridge, Michaelson guarded their backs, watching the tunnel for Mama's appearance.

"Loop your rope over that stalagmite," Ben instructed. "Like this."

She followed his example, pulling on her knot even more strongly than him. She gave it a third yank.

"That's plenty tight, Ash."

"Just making sure." She watched Ben set up the major's rope on a third outcropping. He threw the coiled rope over the edge, letting it drape down the cliff face.

A bellow of anger thundered through the chamber. She glanced toward the nest.

Michaelson scrambled down the slope toward Ashley, clutching his shotgun in one hand. "Here she comes!"

"Ash! Get going. I'll make sure Michaelson gets hooked up."

She nodded, clipping the rope through the carabiner. "Don't take any chances."

"Who, me?" He winked at her, herding her toward the edge. Another bellow erupted. "Hurry!"

Grasping the rope, she leaned over the edge and hopped down a few yards, then braked to a stop. The cliff's edge blocked her view of Ben as she descended. Damn, she couldn't see what was happening up top, but she could hear.

"Don't wait, Ben! Get your ass over the edge!" Michaelson's voice was near-hysterical. "She's right behind me!"

"Just get your butt over here, mate."

A scattering of loose shale rained over the edge as the major skidded to a halt. "She sees us! Here she comes!"

The sound of claws ripping at rock sent a cataract of tremors up Ashley's back. A deafening scream blasted from above, sounding as if it were coming right from the cliff's edge.

Michaelson suddenly leaped over the precipice, rope zinging through his carabiner. His boots hit the rock yards to her left. His face was beet-red in the glow of her helmet lamp.

"Ben?" she asked, searching the cliff's edge.

Between gasps for air, Michaelson shook his head. "He . . . he . . . had turned off his lamp . . . then bolted behind a boulder fall. I don't think it saw him. Instead it fixed on my light."

She prayed he was safe, eyeing the empty dangling rope to her left. She could hear something snorting just overhead. More shale tumbled down, pelting Michaelson.

A reptilian head shot over the edge of the cliff, searching with one black eye, then the other. It was right above the major. Its scanning halted, one eye pointing toward Michaelson. Opening its jaws, it screamed at him.

Michaelson leaped another yard down, now well beyond the reach of even its long crested neck. The predator hissed at its escaping prey, then cocked its head a final time before snaking back over the edge. Ashley blew suppressed air from her chest as Michaelson gave her a thumbs-up. They were safe. But what about Ben? She searched again. A gasp from the right drew her attention back to Michaelson. He had lost his footing, slamming into the wall as his rope was yanked upward. She watched wide-eyed as his flailing figure was dragged another several feet up. He hit the wall hard with his shoulder.

"Jesus Christ! It's got my rope!" He was hauled farther up, now only two feet from the top.

Again the beast peeked over the edge, eye cocked toward Michaelson, the rope clamped in its jaws. It reared up, dragging Michaelson straight up into the air to dangle from the jaws of the creature.

Ashley tried to loosen her pistol with one hand while gripping the rope with the other. Her fingers struggled with the clasp over the gun. Damn it! She fought the holster, then froze when she heard Ben.

"Hey, there, Big Mama. Is that any way to treat a guest?" He followed his words with a loud whistle.

Ashley watched as the beast twitched in the direction of his voice, swinging Michaelson wildly. The creature opened its mouth to hiss at the new intruder, dropping the rope.

Michaelson plummeted past her, his arms and legs wheeling. The slack in his rope snapped taut. He crashed into the wall. The sound of snapping bone accompanied the collision.

She stared down at him. He groaned, eyes narrowed with pain, as he struggled into a rappelling position, using only one leg. Satisfied that the major had survived the fall, she turned back to the cliff's edge.

The monster had disappeared beyond the horizon of her view. She could hear it snorting and sniffing up there, claws tentatively scratching at rock, searching.

C'mon, Ben, get down here. She listened for any further sign of what was going on up there. Silence. She glanced to her left. Ben's rope was gone! When had that disappeared?

A loud snort of glee drew her attention. The hunter had found its prey. A frantic scraping and scrambling erupted.

"Look, Ma!" Ben's voice was savage. "I knitted you a new scarf."

A bellow of rage.

Suddenly Ben leaped over the edge, shooting over empty space, rope trailing. As he reached the end of the slack, he twisted in midair to face the cliff and plunged toward the wall. Using his legs, he absorbed the brunt of the impact. Only an explosive "Oof" indicated that the collision had any effect on him.

"Ben . . . ?" she said, relieved and confused. "What about the—"

Ben pointed up.

She turned her eyes back to the cliff's edge. The marsupial's head dangled over the cliff, its blubbery tongue hanging from its slack jaw. Ben's rope was looped around its neck, digging a trench in its flesh.

Ben pushed a pouted lip at the beast. "Now, how's that for gratitude? I don't think she likes my present."

As the SEAL groaned and opened his eyes, Linda checked his pulse. "He's coming out of it," she said. She had been worried that in his weakened state the fungal spores may have been too strong for him.

"That's good," Khalid said. From his queasy expression, he was still suffering from the aftereffects himself. He closed his eyes and pressed fingers to his temples.

"Here. Try this." She passed him a damp towel. "Lay back and place this over your eyes."

He smiled wanly at her but accepted her offering.

As he lay back, Linda turned to Villanueva. She wiped the SEAL's forehead. With Khalid's help, she had been able to transport him to a relatively fungal-free chamber. A stream of cool water coursed through the cave, slightly tangy with dissolved minerals. The only entrance to this room was a narrow hole, too small for any large predators. Still she kept a pistol resting on a rock within arm's reach.

Villanueva struggled to speak between sticky lips. "W-w-water . . ."

She helped him sit up and raised a cup to his lips. With shaky hands, he collected the cup and managed himself.

"What happened?" he asked, glancing at Khalid, who now snored quietly from under the wet cloth.

She explained the story of the poisonous fungal spores while he finished his water.

He handed her the cup. "Is there anything down here that doesn't want to eat us?"

She grinned at him. "This is a hostile environment. I think for anything to survive it must learn to utilize the scarce resources to the fullest. That means intense competition and varied modes of attack."

"Great. What's next? Carnivorous butterflies?"

She shrugged.

He shook his head. "Damn, I could use a smoke."

"I don't think that would be good for you."

He raised his eyebrows. "I've just about had my arm yanked off, I've been a chew toy for a monster, and now some freakin' mold tried to poison me. I think I can survive one cigarette."

She nodded. "I could check in Khalid's stuff. He has a few extra packs. I'm sure he wouldn't mind sharing one." She tugged his pack over to her, surprised at how heavy it was, then fumbled the flaps open. She rummaged through the extra clothes and climbing gear. "It's got to be in here somewhere."

"That's all right. I could—"

"Here, I think I found one. Still in its cellophane." With her arm buried to the elbow, she felt the plastic crinkling with her fingertips. "Got it!" She pulled her arm free, clutching her find. Embarrassed, she realized it wasn't a pack of cigarettes. Curious, she held it up to the light to see the object better.

Villanueva's eyes sprang wide when he saw what she held in her palm. "Careful with that."

"What is it?"

"Plastic explosive. Let me see it."

"Explosive?" She handed him the cellophane-wrapped block of clay.

He flipped the package around. "This insignia stamped into it . . . it's German manufacture."

"Why would . . . ?" She glanced at the sleeping man. "As a geologist, maybe he thought he might need to explode some sections to get to samples."

The SEAL shook his head. "I was briefed. I would have been told if someone had plastique. This is obviously contraband. Pass me his pack."

She held her breath, and a thousand thoughts bounced around her head as she passed him Khalid's pack. She now recalled how guarded he was at times when anyone handled his pack. How odd some of his expressions were when anyone asked about his past. But she also remembered his strong hand pulling her up steep slopes and his kind words of encouragement.

Villanueva closed the pack. "There's twelve packages in here. Enough to bring the entire volcano crashing down on us." He reached for her pistol, but his injuries prevented him. "Give me your gun."

Instinctively, she started to obey, but with her hand on the pistol grip, she froze, suddenly unsure what to do.

With a rattling snort, Khalid coughed himself awake. He pushed the cloth off his face and sat up. "What are you . . . ?" His eyes shifted from Villanueva with the pack to Linda with the gun. His brows drew together, lowering over his eyes. His accent became thicker. "What the hell are you doing with my pack?"

His words were directed at the SEAL, but the heat of his anger scorched her too. Embarrassed, words flowed from her. "We were just looking for a cigarette and—"

Villanueva cut her off. "What is your game here, Khalid? Who sent you?"

"I don't know what you're talking about. Give me back my pack."

The SEAL shook his head. "Go to hell."

Linda backed a step away from the combatants. Her gun hung limply in her fingers. She kept staring at Khalid. He was the same man who had shared his canteen with her. The same man who had pulled her free when she was trapped in the narrow crack.

Her motion attracted Khalid's eye. He spoke to her, pointing a thumb toward Villanueva. "Is he feverish? Is it the fungal poison? Why is he acting like that?" He waved her away from the SEAL. "Be careful. He may be dangerous."

Numbly, she watched as her feet started stepping toward Khalid. "He's fine. It's just that he doesn't understand why you have explosives."

"Get away from him!" Villanueva struggled to stand but was too weak and unstable. He toppled back down. "Don't trust him. Give me the gun."

Khalid turned to her. "Don't. He'll kill me."

She glanced toward the SEAL.

Villanueva's lips were a cruel line. "And what did you have planned for us with all these explosives?"

Khalid lowered his head. "Linda, let me explain. He's twisting it all around. I'm not some Arab terrorist. He's letting his prejudice delude him."

"Khalid . . . ?" She took a single step toward him, now only a few feet between them.

"Watch out!"

Villanueva's words were too slow. Much slower than the sudden speed of Khalid's leap. He was upon her before she could gasp. He held her in a tight hug. One hand reached down and freed the gun from her trapped hand.

"I'm sorry," he whispered in her ear. "It wasn't supposed to be like this." With the gun in his hand, he released her.

She stumbled a few steps away, tears pooling in her eyes.

He pointed the gun at Villanueva.

"So now what, Khalid?" he said with a sneer. "How do you think you're gonna get out of here?"

"By lightening the load." He pulled the trigger twice. Villanueva's head bounced back, two small holes appearing in his forehead. His body slumped to the floor.

Linda screamed. Covering her face, she dropped to her knees, sobbing, expecting at any moment to feel bullets ripping into her too.

A hand touched her shoulder. No words.

She cringed from his touch and continued crying. The hand did not try to touch her again. Eventually her wracking cries dissolved to a simple flow of tears. She glanced up.

Khalid sat on his haunches, hanging his head. The gun still rested in his hand, as comfortable and easy as a pen. He must have noticed her look.

She sniffed. "Why?"

His words were dry, unemotional. "I was assigned this mission." Khalid shifted to face her. "Blakely was naive. News of his discovery of a huge diamond statue reached many ears. A South African diamond cartel approached my employer. If the source of such huge diamonds were ever discovered, it would destroy the diamond market. Current prices would plummet. I was assigned to find the source of the diamonds, then sabotage the site. Explode the entire system."

She lowered her head. "All those deaths just for money."

He reached over and tipped her face toward him, his fingertips warm from the hot gun. "No," he said. "I accepted this assignment from the South Africans for another reason too. One closer to my heart. Like the diamond market, if this continent should open up as a major oil competitor, it could devastate the Middle East economy. Oil is my country's lifeblood. Before oil, my country was poor. No education, no health care, no way out of the sand. I will not see that happen again. Not after so much progress." A flash of pain in his eyes. "I care for my country as much as you do yours. Would you kill to save your country?"

Unsure herself, she did not answer, only turned her face away.

Releasing his grip on her chin, he stood up. "I need to head back up. Complete my mission." He walked to Villanueva's body. "He had to be killed. His knowledge was a threat to my mission. But . . . you . . . I need. Another pair of eyes, another pair of hands. It's a long journey back up."

She allowed herself a moment of hope.

"I have my mission and won't fail," he said. "You could stay here . . . or you can come with me. But you must understand. If you come along and betray my secret, then I will be forced to kill again." He held a hand out to her. "Can I trust you?"

Linda stared at his calloused palm. To go with him, he might turn on her as swiftly as he had turned on Villanueva. But to stay alone down here, unarmed, meant certain death.

Wrapping her arms around her body, Linda ignored his hand and made a decision. "I'll go with you."

Thank God, Michaelson thought, as Ben stopped in front of him. He steadied himself with a hand on the Aussie's shoulder, the crude splint on his ankle biting into his calf. The half-assed contraption had been hurriedly slapped on his leg after climbing back to the nest area. Walking was possible, but slow and wobbly. Michaelson winced when he saw how far they still had to go to reach the nursery's exit.

"Did you hear something?" Ben asked, his head cocked to the side.

Ashley shook her head. Michaelson listened.

From several yards behind, the infant marsupial predators hissed at the group, tiny crests twitching up and down. Their protests had become less strident as they became aware that the group was leaving the nest. Still the tunnel was some distance away, a black slash in the wall.

"No," Michaelson said. "Nothing. Sounds clear."

Ben nodded, using a finger to clear an ear. "I could have sworn . . ." He proceeded forward.

Michaelson followed, his steps clumsy on his bad ankle.

Ashley stepped up beside him. "How are you holding up?"

"Fine, but I still think you should proceed without me. I'm holding you up."

She frowned. "It's best if we go slowly anyway. No telling what lies ahead."

Resigned, he tromped after Ben, keeping an eye on the tunnel entrance. A goal. He began counting his steps, each odd numeral painful as he hopped his weight on his splinted ankle.

On his thirty-third step, he finally reached the opening. He leaned on the wall of the tunnel, perspiration soaking his forehead. A stitch of pain had started throbbing on his right side. Damn it, must have cracked a rib too, he thought, rubbing a hand over his side.

Ben stepped up to him. He had reconnoitered the passage ahead while waiting for Michaelson to hobble up. He glanced at where Michaelson rubbed and raised an eyebrow, but thankfully didn't ask any questions. It was already embarrassing enough to have the Aussie pull his butt out of the fire when that enraged creature had caught him up. If it wasn't for Ben's foolish stunt, he would have been dead by now.

He dropped his hand from his side. "What did you find?"

"It's a bloody maze down there. Passages crisscrossing every which way. Some lighted by fungus, some clear. We need to be careful."

"At least we have plenty of escape routes."

"Yeah, but which passage gets us out of here?"

"There's only one way to find out." Suppressing a wince, he pointed down the tunnel. "After you."

Ben flashed his light forward and entered the tunnel. After several yards of careful progress, Michaelson realized Ben's description of the passages ahead was an understatement. The first intersection had five rocky passages sprouting in all directions.

"Now which way?" Ben asked, his question directed at Ashley.

Michaelson hopped forward, irritated that Ben should exclude him from the decision-making process. Even if he was an invalid, he was still the senior military presence here. Their safety was still his primary responsibility.

Ashley pointed to each of the tunnels with a beam of light. She settled her light on one of the passages. "This passage seems to be heading up. And it has some of that glowing mold on the wall."

Michaelson peered down the tunnel selected. He made a noncommittal grunt.

Ashley looked at him. "The mold will allow us to conserve batteries. We still don't know how far we have to travel before we find our way out of this hellhole, so we better think conservation. Try to stick to lighted passageways as much as possible. Besides, the more light around us, the safer I feel."

Michaelson nodded. As much as it grated on him, her assessment of the situation was sound. He couldn't have planned any better. "Let's go, then," he said.

Ben took the point again. He turned his light to a weak diffuse setting, just enough to highlight some of the blacker nooks and crannies. Otherwise, the thickening mold added sufficient glow to see by. Ben waved them to turn off their lights, including their helmet lamps.

Michaelson followed Ben. Ashley covered their rear, pistol in hand. Michaelson ground his molars, both from the pain and his frustration with his physical shape. He should be guarding their retreat or sweeping ahead for dangers. Not sandwiched in the middle like some sheltered mama's boy.

Still, he couldn't argue with the order of their procession. Ben had already skipped several yards ahead while Michaelson hobbled to keep up. Glancing behind him, balanced on his good foot, he watched Ashley check the passage behind her. She swung forward and caught him staring at her. She smiled weakly at him, almost like she was trying to reassure him.

Pinching his brows together angrily, he increased the pace of his hopping. Side passages and crossways flew past. He didn't try to memorize his route, only kept his eyes fixed on Ben's back, struggling to match his pace. As much as his hot blood drove him forward, past the pain, past his incapacitation, eventually his feverish pace dwindled back again to a pathetic crawl. Ben disappeared around a bend in the corridor. Panting now, sparks of lights danced across Michaelson's vision; pain shot in electric bolts from his ankle.

He stopped, leaning on the wall, his side now burning with a hot flame.

Ashley stepped to his shoulder, her voice a mixture of concern and anger. "Quit pushing yourself. We're not in a race. Careful progress is what will get us out of here."

"I'm slowing you up," he said between pain-clenched teeth.

Ben's face suddenly appeared in front of him. Damn, that Aussie moved silently when he wanted to. Ben wore a concerned expression.

Michaelson glared at Ben. "I'm fine." He dared him to argue.

"That's good," said Ben, his voice an urgent whisper, "because I think we're being stalked."

Ashley crossed next to Ben. "What do you mean?"

"I keep hearing something scraping and shuffling in neighboring passages. Keeping pace with us."

"Maybe they're just echoes of our own progress," Ashley said, but her eyes darted behind her. "I haven't heard anything." She glanced at Michaelson. "Have you?"

He shook his head, but he was no judge. All he could hear when he moved was his own wheezing pants and his heart pounding in his ears. Hell, he hadn't even heard Ben approach until he was on top of him.

Ben hissed his words. "You've got to know what to listen for. I know noises that are natural for a cave. And these aren't normal."

"So what do we do?" Ashley asked.

"We need to shake this tail, but it knows these passages better than we do. Our only hope is speed. Outrun it."

Michaelson was very conscious that Ben didn't glance his way. Ashley didn't either, but an uncomfortable silence descended like a weight upon them. He knew what they were thinking. They needed to move quickly but wouldn't leave him behind.

Rolling his eyes, he started to speak when he heard it too. They all did. Six eyes turned in unison to their back trail. Something scraped rock behind them, out of sight, followed by the sound of a single pebble displaced and bouncing. Something was back there.

"Leave me," he said. He pulled his pistol and pointed it. Not down the trail but at Ashley and Ben. "Now."

"Quit that shit," Ben said. "We're not in some damned Rambo movie. We know you're not gonna shoot us."

"I won't allow my injuries to get us all killed." He raised the barrel to his own temple, pressing the cold muzzle to his heated skin. "Go or I'll shoot."

"Michaelson . . ." Ashley's voice was tight with fear. "We're a team."

"Go. I'll cover the back trail for as long as possible."

"No!" Ashley said. "You're coming with us."

"Go." He cocked the pistol with his thumb. "Now. Or in three seconds you'll have no one to cover your escape."

He watched Ashley swallow hard and glance at Ben for help. If either rushed him, he would pull the trigger.

He knew he needed to force them to leave him behind. A second pebble tripped somewhere behind them.

Ben turned to Ashley, the stubborn set of his shoulders slumped. "He's right. We've got to think of the others. If we don't reach help, they'll all die too."

Ashley's fists clenched, her knuckles white. "I hate this."

Ben rested a hand on her shoulder. He turned his eyes to Michaelson. "I know you're keen on this suicide mission. Kamikaze and all that. But up five yards ahead is a small alcove with a tiny pool of water. It's large enough to hide three Marines in there. I suggest you hole up. It'll be a secure spot to keep out of sight and offers good coverage if you need to shoot."

Michaelson nodded, suspicious. "Go. I'll check it later."

Ben pulled Ashley away. "C'mon. Maybe we can lead the pursuers away from him."

She allowed herself to be shifted away, but not before her eyes locked on the major's one final time, tears at the corners of her lids. "Dennis, be careful. Don't do anything stupid."

He waved her away with the muzzle of the gun. He watched her twist around and leave with Ben's arm around her. They disappeared around the bend without a glance behind. He listened as their footfalls faded down the tunnel until there was only silence. He listened carefully, ears straining, making sure they had definitely left, as well as trying to hear any telltale sound of the stalkers.

He heard nothing other than his own pulse throbbing at his temples. He continued to wait. Still after nearly an hour, nothing appeared or was even heard. Maybe Ben had been panicked over nothing, but he couldn't convince himself. Ben was too wise in cave lore to be fooled by an echo or natural noises.

He licked his dry lips, caked with dust and dried sweat. He swirled the canteen at his belt. Almost empty. He'd better take Ben's advice and check that alcove. Fill his canteen and hole up there.

Wincing, he stumbled as quietly as possible down the tunnel, searching for the side cave. The scrape of his boot on the rocky floor sounded explosively loud in the empty tunnel. Luckily, only steps past the turn in the passage, a small black aperture appeared in the right wall of the tunnel. He clicked on his lantern and flashed the opening with his light. It was dark in there, no glowing fungus, just emptiness. The roof was low. Too low to stand up in, but by crouching he could enter and move around. In the corner, a small trickle of water ran down the rear wall and accumulated in a puddle.

He tested it with a finger. A strong mineral tang but should be okay to drink. After finishing the dregs of his canteen, he positioned his canteen under the trickle to collect the fresh water.

Satisfied, he settled by the opening, hidden in shadow; the glow of the mold-encrusted passage allowed him to view both directions in secret. It was a secure post. He waited, his gun pointing forward.

Cowards, she thought, that's all we are—cowards. No matter how logical their decision to abandon Michaelson was, Ashley still felt like a dog running with its tail between its legs.

She followed Ben's back through the twisting maze. Almost five hours had elapsed, and during brief rest breaks to sip warm water from her canteen, she still heard the noises trailing them, sometimes from a long distance away, sometimes from just around a blind bend.

Ben stopped ahead of her, his brow drenched in sweat, and unscrewed the lid of his canteen. He raised it to his lips and took a short swig. Wiping the cuff of his sleeve across his mouth, he said, "It doesn't make bloody sense." He shook the canteen and frowned at it.

Hers was almost empty too. "What do you mean?"

"By now we should have either lost this tail or been caught. This stalemate is bloody odd."

"Maybe we've just been lucky."

A tumble of loose rock down a tunnel to their right caused them both to jump.

Ben scrunched up his nose as if he smelled something foul. "I don't trust luck any more than these caves."

She capped her own canteen after sipping just enough to flush the rock dust from her mouth. "Let's go."

Ben set a faster pace, his shoulder muscles knotted with tension, his gun tight in his hand.

This constant waiting was getting to her also. What the hell was stalking them? And why wasn't it attacking? Her stomach churned with hot acid. She almost wished their pursuers would pounce. At least then she could fight . . . do something instead of running in fear.

For the next hour, they traversed numerous tunnels, some heading up, some heading down, some with smooth floors, some tumbled with boulders, some illuminated with fungus, some black as pitch.

Ben held his silver compass in his free hand. "We're heading in the wrong direction. Away from the base."

"What choice do we have?" Hunger and the twisting passages were making Ashley dizzy. She had been nibbling dry rations as they moved, but she needed a meal. She found herself dreaming of a cheeseburger with an extra-large order of fries. And, of course, a Coca-Cola. This warmed spit in her canteen failed to even moisten her mouth.

She tripped over a rock, dulled reflexes causing her to stumble to her knees. She tried to push herself up, but then her legs protested, muscles tired and strained. She collapsed back down with a sigh.

Ben returned to her and crouched down. "We can't stop now."

"I know," she said heavily. "Just need a minute, that's all."

He sat next to her, resting a hand on her knee, squeezing her thigh reassuringly. "We'll get out of here."

"Will we?" she whispered. What if they didn't make it out of here? She thought of her son, ensconced in the security of Alpha Base, and hung her head. At least Jason was safe. If something happened to her . . .

She gritted her teeth. To hell with that type of thinking! She *would* see her son again. She pictured his silly grin when something surprised him, the way his hair had a stubborn cowlick, causing it to stick out behind one ear. She pushed Ben's hand off her knee and stood up. Even if it meant wrestling every damned predator in this hellhole, she would see her son again. "C'mon," she said, offering her hand to help Ben stand. "We've got to find a way home."

"Sounds bloody fine to me." Ben grinned one of his wide smiles, every tooth showing, then set off down the passage.

She tramped after him, determined now, ready to run miles if necessary. But after only a hundred yards, Ben stopped. He held a hand up in the air, his ear cocked.

She remained silent, straining to hear. But she heard nothing unusual. "Ben . . . ? What is it?"

"A breeze." He pointed to a side tunnel.

She stepped next to him. Now that he mentioned it, she could feel a slight wafting from the passageway, raising a few stray strands of her black hair. "What does it mean?"

"I think . . . it's the end of this maze."

"Then let's go." She headed out, taking the lead this time.

As they progressed, the passage narrowed with sudden knife-sharp turns, the breeze becoming stronger and stronger. The fungus on the walls had thinned as they followed the turns; eventually they were forced to click on their hand lanterns and helmet lamps.

After almost a mile of trekking, Ben spat, "Bloody hell."

"What?"

"We've yet to cross a single side passage in this chute. It would be easy to get pinned down in here. No escape routes."

She frowned and continued. Great. One more thing to worry about. But they were committed, with only one way to go: straight ahead.

As she worked around the next tight bend in the corridor, the roof lowered. Crouching, she continued. The breeze had become a wind, blowing hair about her face, whipping it behind her as if pointing for them to turn back. The rushing air whistled in her ears.

Ben poked her from behind. "Did you hear that?"

She twisted around. "What?"

"They're behind us now—and they're coming fast."

She turned around, her lips drawn into tight lines. She increased the pace, crouching and running into the wind. She turned the next corner, and the passageway ended just yards ahead. Wind blew from a wormhole opening at the end of the tunnel. The first they had seen since entering the maze.

She ran forward, praying that this tunnel would lead up, toward home. She knelt beside the opening and pointed her lantern. The sight forced a groan from between her lips. It not only led downward, but at a frighteningly steep slope, deeper into the heart of the continent.

Ben leaned beside her. He already had his sled out and was releasing the catch to expand it. "Better hurry, Ash. They're about a hundred yards behind us."

She pointed at the wormhole sullenly. "It heads down. Pretty far too, I'd say."

"We can't go back." He helped her unstrap her sled. "I have the sneaking suspicion that we've been herded to this place."

"What?" She unhooked the catch to expand her sled.

A scrabble of rock echoed from behind them.

"No time," Ben said. He waved to the hole. "Ladies first." He pointed his gun to their back trail.

Ashley glanced at the black tunnel behind them, then at Ben. She took a deep breath and shoved into the wormhole on her sled. The steepness of the slope quickly accelerated her plummet. She braked with the heels of her gloved hands and toes of her boots, but succeeded only in slowing her pace slightly.

She heard Ben enter the wormhole behind her, his wheels whisking toward her.

"Hell!" he called to her. "It's like a slide. Let's see those bastards catch us now!"

By now, her rate of descent was such that it burned her hands to brake, even through her climbing gloves. And as they flew farther down the tube, the fungus began appearing in patches on the walls.

"We're in a big corkscrew!" yelled Ben. "Can you feel the centrifugal force?"

She did. Her board kept climbing higher on the walls as their speed increased and the tunnel's curves tightened. To try to brake now was impossible. During their flying descent, the fungus had grown thicker and thicker, its glow almost blinding now. The mold also made the walls slick so even the tips of her boots dragging across the floor failed to offer any significant braking.

She hoped the tunnel would level out before ending. Give them a chance to slow down. At this speed, she'd hate to be spewed out of the tunnel right into a slumbering stalagmite. She watched the tunnel ahead, praying for an easing of the slope.

No such luck. The tunnel exit appeared around the next bend. No time to brake. No time to slow down. Only time to cover her head with her arms and cringe.

She shot out of the tunnel, blasting into the next cavern. Blinded for a moment by the bright light, she jolted and bounced across the slightly rugged floor. When her eyes adjusted, she saw herself barreling toward a solid wall of yellow vegetation. Closing her eyes, she slammed into the thick stalks of growth. Her collision tumbled her from her board, but the field cushioned her fall as she rolled for several yards.

Once stopped, she pushed to her knees. She was almost up when Ben tumbled into her with a wild yell. She fell in a tangle of arms and legs.

"Well, that was different," Ben said, speaking to her left knee.

She untangled herself and stood up with a groan. Bruised everywhere, she glanced around as Ben stood up. The field of yellow vegetation, like wheat, stood chest-high and spread for miles across the rolling cavern floor. Miles! She craned her neck around. The cavern was monstrous, dwarfing even Alpha Cavern. Almost like the Grand Canyon—but with a lid. The walls stretched hundreds of stories high. The roof, far overhead, glowed with thick fungus, some patches glowing as bright as sunlight. She glanced across the smooth yellow fields that undulated across the wide plain, broken only by tiny groves of spindly trees, like islands in a sea.

"I don't think we're in Kansas anymore," Ashley said, with her mouth hanging open.

A rustle of vegetation drew her attention from the panorama around them. From several yards away, something was working through the field toward them, maneuvering around clusters of trees. Too low to be seen except for the wake of bending stalks, like a shark through water.

She glanced at Ben as she backed away. He pointed off to the left. Two more wakes arrowed toward them. She studied the field more closely, now noticing three other trails moving in their direction. Six in all.

She backed away, pulling Ben's sleeve. He didn't resist.

Almost tripping, she stepped from the field onto bare rock and stumbled back until she stood by the wormhole opening. Their sleds were lost somewhere in the field. Reaching for her pistol, her hand touched the empty holster. Damn, the gun must have been knocked away by her fall.

She turned to Ben. Thankfully, he had his pistol already gripped in his right hand.

"I lost mine," she said between tight lips.

"That's all right. I lost my extra clips. And I've got only three shots left on this clip."

She stared at the six trails inching slowly toward them. Not good. The nearest one was only ten yards away now. It had stopped and held its position. Waiting. Soon the others had drawn even with it.

"The wormhole?" she asked.

"Sounds good to me. Go on in."

Their words seemed to jar the stalkers in the field. They rushed with lightning speed. With their sudden movement, Ashley froze crouched by the wormhole, like a deer in headlights. The six creatures burst through the wall of vegetation, then stopped in unison, hunkering on all fours, haunches raised, ready to spring, tails slashing.

They looked like a cross between a wolf and a lion. Amber-furred, a cowl of thick mane around their necks, huge eyes, slitted pupils, long jaws bristling with fierce teeth. A steady growl arose from the pack.

"Freeze," Ben whispered. "No sudden moves."

She wasn't about to move, still frozen in her crouch, her eyes glued to the six sets of unblinking eyes that stared at her. And she was willing to stay that way for as long as it took, until something shot from the worm-hole and grabbed her ankle. A high-pitched scream burst from her throat.

TWENTY

"Try the paddles!" Blakely called above the roar of the approaching falls. He gave one final pull on the engine's starter cord. It sputtered and died. He watched as the current dragged the boat toward the precipice. It was impossible to determine from here how high the waterfall dropped. But the noise! The crescendo of rumbling water and rock suggested a deadly fall. He grabbed his paddle and scrambled to the side of the boat. He noticed Jason digging with his paddle on the other side.

"Harder, Jason, harder!" he called to the boy as he added his strength to fight the current, his shoulders burning with exertion.

"I'm trying! It's not working! We're not slowing down!"

Blakely darted a look behind them. The stern of the boat was at the edge of the falls. He watched as the current pushed the boat over the edge. "Grab on! Tight!" he hollered, and grabbed the strap handles on the pontoons while Jason did the same.

The boat seemed to hover at the edge of the waterfall, teetering. Blakely held his breath as the boat flipped over the edge. For a moment, walls of water encircled the boat as it plummeted. He watched the boat try to tumble on top of him. He opened his mouth to yell when the boat slammed into the bottom of the waterfall, both of them pressed to the floor of the boat, sprays of water flaring in jets around them. Luckily, they hadn't flipped.

Blakely raised his head. The waterfall was only about fifteen feet high. "I can't believe it. We—"

The boat tipped over a second waterfall. Blakely almost lost his grip in his surprise as the boat slipped over the edge, crashing downward. Even above the noise of the thundering water, the sound of a ripping pontoon was terrifyingly clear. Damn it! The boat smacked into the bottom of the falls and rapidly filled with water, the remaining trapped air in the damaged float barely keeping it above water.

He pulled Jason away from the sinking side so the boy could grip the intact pontoon's straps.

Jason stared back behind his shoulder. "Here comes another one!"

Before he could even glance behind to confirm the boy's panicked statement, the boat twisted over the edge of another fall. The sinking pontoon, acting like a drag, spun the boat. The uneven motion tumbled the boat over the falls, capsizing it into the surging water.

Just before Blakely plunged beneath the water, he saw Jason fly from the boat, his hands still reaching to regain his hold as he was launched from his seat. Then salty water surged around Blakely, swirling up his nose, triggering a fit of coughing, which only emptied his lungs of life-giving air. He clamped his mouth closed, his chest screaming in protest. He fought the current to free himself of the foundering boat. With a final push off the intact pontoon, he shoved himself away and into clear water. With the aid of his life jacket, he popped to the surface of the roiling waves.

Gasping air, he searched the waters. Before him crashed the series of three cataracts down which they had fallen. He twisted to see if any new falls threatened as the current pulled him away from the others. Luckily, that was the last of them. They had reached the bottom of the deep cavern. The current pushed him into a pond-sized eddy, where the waters swirled torpidly.

Treading water, he searched around him. The cavern glowed with wide patches of phosphorescent fungi. In the faint light, he spotted an orange object bobbing near the far shore. Jason. Blakely kicked vigorously, his boots heavy with water. Jason did not seem to be moving, just drifting in the eddy. The current threatened to pull the boy from the shoreline and back into the main flow.

It was taking too long to reach Jason. As he swam closer, he could see blood trailing from a gash in the boy's scalp, but at least the jacket had kept his head above water.

"Hang in there, son!" He increased his effort and within a minute had the edge of the boy's jacket in his grip. He allowed himself a moment of relief when he heard Jason's breath, raspy but strong. He kicked for shore, hauling Jason behind him, careful to keep the boy's nose and lips above water.

His shoulder bumped into rock. He had reached land. Letting go of Jason for a moment, he clambered onto the slippery shore. Once up, he lay on his belly and reached out to Jason where he listed by the shoreline. Catching the jacket with the tips of his finger, he pulled the boy close enough to grip handfuls of jacket.

Just as he started to yank him up, Jason's lids fluttered open. Confused and dazed, the boy panicked, thrashing his arms wildly, garbled protests burbling from his lips.

A wild hand struck Blakely in the temple, and he almost lost his grip on the boy. He raised his voice, trying to be stern and comforting at the same time. "Jason, calm down! It's me. You're safe."

His words seemed to penetrate the boy's haze. Jason's thrashing quieted to a dull squirm. "That's it," Blakely said soothingly as he hauled him up onto shore. He dragged him back from the edge, then collapsed beside him. Jason struggled to sit up, but Blakely, his breathing ragged, held him down. "Don't move. Rest," he gasped.

Blakely's adrenaline rush from the falls seeped away into the slick rock, his limbs suddenly waterlogged and heavy. He hung his head a moment, taking deep breaths. What were they going to do now?

Jason coughed moistly beside him, drawing Blakely's attention once more. He reached over and unbuckled the boy's life jacket, then checked for any additional injuries. No broken bones. No other lacerations. He gently palpated the wound on the boy's scalp, where he must have hit his head on a rock. Grimacing, he decided that it looked worse than it was, but nevertheless he needed the first-aid kit from the boat for antibiotics and a dry dressing.

He glanced to where the damaged boat had eddied out a few yards from shore. Before the boat drifted back out, he decided he'd better salvage what he could—rations, flashlights, first-aid kit. No telling how long they would be down here.

He glanced at Jason. The boy was now staring back at him. A clear lucidity had returned to his gaze. Jason licked his lips. "My head hurts," he said, his voice a throaty whisper.

"I know, my boy. You got conked pretty hard."

Jason reached up and touched his head. He then stared at his bloody fingertips, his eyes wide.

Blakely patted his shoulder. "You're gonna be fine. It's only a small cut. I'm gonna swim out to the boat and get a bandage for it."

"But—"

"Don't worry, I'll be right back." Blakely pushed himself up with a groan, his chest sending flares of warning pains. He did not want to enter the water again but had no other choice.

Jason raised himself up on an elbow, watching silently.

Slipping into the water, Blakely struck out for the boat. Thankfully, it had drifted even closer to shore while he had consoled Jason. Only a few kicks and strokes and he was at the half-submerged boat. Though everything had been secured with ties and straps, some things had knocked loose. At least the rations and first-aid kit were still there.

He searched the remainder of the boat. Damn it, the plastic carton that housed the spare flashlights and batteries had been knocked free. Leaning on the remaining pontoon, he rested for a moment. In this cavern, it was no problem—the fungus gave off sufficient illumination. But if they should need to leave . . . ?

Shaking his head, he explored the remainder of the boat. He found Jason's gym bag tied to a strap. He fingered the bag. Hmmm, made of waterproof material. This discovery should offer some consolation to the boy. He picked loose the swollen knot and added the bag to his armload of supplies. With a final cursory exam, he kicked away from the boat and headed to shore. Luckily, the rocky coast was near; still, by the time he reached shore, his lungs burned and a pain had developed in his left arm.

He threw his collected items up on the edge of the bank, then followed them, slipping a few times in his attempt to get up. Finally, after severely scraping a knee, he managed to clamber up onshore and stand.

He froze, staring at the empty life jacket. "Jason?"

The boy was gone.

Linda reached up and grabbed Khalid's offered hand, fighting back a wave of revulsion. At his touch, she almost pulled back, but his grip, dry and warm in her palm, held her tight. Reluctantly, she allowed herself to be hauled up the last yard of the rockfall. She risked a glance back down the cascade of boulders they had just climbed. Lit by the ubiquitous fungus, the cavern floor was hundreds of yards below them.

"I was right," Khalid said, pointing to the crack in the wall at the top of the rockfall. "Look. It is a fault-line crack. And it goes up." He turned to her with a huge grin. "Do you feel it? The wind?"

She felt a soft brushing of air across her cheek as the crack drew a breeze down its dark throat, almost like it was trying to suck them in, the draw of air whistling down the passage away from them. "It seems promising." She forced the corners of her lips up.

In answer, his grin became even wider. She stared up into his eyes, two black holes in this light. As he turned, she was tempted to twist free and rush down the rock face. But her feet followed Khalid into the V-shaped crack in the rock.

After a few yards, Khalid clicked on his helmet lamp. No fungus grew on these slanted walls. His beam of light thrust forward, ripping into the virgin darkness. She unharnessed her own hand lantern, twisting it to a diffuse setting to wash broadly across the rock.

Walls spread to either side like wings of stone. The roof far above their heads looked like a single slab of rock tilted and resting precariously in place. So fragile, it seemed even a loud noise might shake it loose, crushing them under miles of rock.

"I think this is a relatively new formation," Khalid said. "From a geologic standpoint, that is. Maybe only a thousand years or so. The rock"—he patted the wall on his right—"is not as water-worn as the rock in the previous cavern. Notice how sharp the rock is, like it was sliced with a knife. A recent seismic event must have created this crack."

"There's no fungus either," she mumbled.

"What?"

She waved her light on the walls. "No fungus here. I think if it was a million-year-old crack the fungus would have invaded here too."

He nodded. "True."

"We need to be sure that wherever we make camp tonight there's no fungus nearby. Or if there is, that I check it first," she said. She found talking seemed to push back the clinging terror around her heart. "During the rest breaks, I've analyzed several samples of the fungus. They're not all the same. I'm pretty sure that most of this glowing fungus is safe. The predatory species, though, has a distinct hyphae structure. So we need to watch out for it."

"Of course. We must be more wary." He turned forward.

She wanted to continue talking, to keep herself distracted from the thought that she was following a cold-blooded killer. "How did you get picked for this mission? Was it because of your geology background, or were you always a . . ." She almost said "terrorist," but she allowed the word to die in her throat.

"I'm not a geologist," he said. "I was assigned this mission two years ago and was taught as much geology as I could learn in that time. Not only to impersonate Khalid, but also to better understand what I might discover down here. I had plenty of time to study as I recuperated from my plastic surgery."

Her mind spun with his revelation. "You're not the real Khalid Najmon?"

He helped her over a blockage of tumbled stone. "I already looked much like the original Khalid. That's why I was chosen. But my superiors are thorough. They wanted a more exact match."

She watched his back as he climbed ahead of her, beginning to understand the depth of his drive, his fanaticism. "What happened to the real Khalid?"

He turned his dark eyes toward her, his gaze disapproving, as if her question were foolish.

"What is your real name?"

He ignored her question and turned away. "There's light up ahead."

She sidled next to him to look ahead, suddenly hopeful. Maybe a way out? The tunnel here widened to the size of a small cavern. A glow emanated around a turn in the tunnel. The characteristic green light left no doubt what lay ahead. "Fungus," she said tiredly.

He nodded. "But listen."

Now that he mentioned it, she could hear it too. A low roaring. She recognized the sound from her grandfather's home outside of Quebec City. "Sounds like a waterfall."

"Yes, I think so. But it's getting late. And with fungus ahead, we should make camp here. We can strike out in the morning for the falls."

She nodded. She too had no desire to battle another attack by the predatory mold, but she had been dreading this moment as well. Camping. Spending the first night with the man she now knew as a murderer.

Suddenly a yell echoed from the tunnel ahead. Startled, Linda involuntarily stepped closer to Khalid.

Someone calling. It was from far away, but it was human!

"Jason! Where the hell are you?"

Gosh, Jason thought, can't a guy get a little privacy? Zippering his pants, he stepped back around the stalagmite into view. "I just needed to take a leak," he called to Dr. Blakely. "I've been holding it all day."

The doctor hurried over to him, still dripping from his swim, his eyebrows knit with anger. "Don't ever do that again!"

"What?"

"Run off like that."

"I was only over there." Jason pointed at his rest station.

"I don't care. There are all sorts of hazards around here." Blakely's face relaxed, but his breathing was still raspy. "Listen, Jason, we need to be careful. Stick together."

"All right. I didn't mean to . . ."

"It's fine. Now let's see about that bump on your noggin."

Dragging his feet, Jason crossed to the small boulder and sat. With a grimace, he let Blakely clean his wound. It wasn't too bad when he flushed the wound.

Heck, it almost felt good. He relaxed, closing his eyes. Suddenly his forehead stung as if it were on fire. "Owww!"

"Oh, quit fidgeting. It's only a little iodine."

"It burns."

"That's good. That means it's working." Blakely strapped a sticky bandage over the cut. Then he sat back, seeming to admire his handiwork. "We'll need to change this twice a day."

Jason rolled his eyes. Great.

Blakely crossed to fish through the collected salvage from the boat. "Are you hungry?"

"No. I'm fine. Unless you have one of those chocolate bars."

Blakely hauled out the box that held the food and cracked it open. He reached in and pulled out a foil-wrapped bar.

Jason's eyes widened. He held out a hand.

The doctor split the bar into quarters, then passed him a single section. "We're going to have to strictly ration our supplies."

He accepted his share with a frown. Man, this sucked. "So how do we get back up?"

"We don't. We have no flashlights."

"So what do we do?"

"We wait. A day or so. Someone will find us."

Jason knew a lie when he heard one, but he kept his mouth closed. The doctor had enough on his mind, and Jason didn't want to be a bother.

Slumping on the rock, he noticed a familiar red bag. "Hey, my gym bag! You saved it. Thanks!" Scooting over to his bag, he opened it up and pawed through it. Still here!

He pulled out his Nintendo game and sat back on his heels with a sigh. He thumbed on the power button, and in a few seconds, a familiar theme song jingled from the game. "Cool!"

Jason leaned back against a stalagmite and attended to his game. At least he would have something to do while they waited. Immersed in the world of Nintendo, it was almost like he was back home. By now his mother was usually complaining about the noise from his Game Boy. Sighing, he plunged his character into level twelve.

"Jason, could you turn that off," Blakely said, standing up. "The noise."

Jason grinned. Just like his mother. What was it with grown-ups anyway?

"Please, Jason, hurry." There was a note of urgency in his voice.

He clicked off the game and stood up, crossing closer to Blakely. "What—"

"Shhh! I thought I heard something."

Jason held his breath, picturing another of those creatures sneaking up on them. He shifted farther behind the doctor. They waited for several tense heartbeats. It was difficult to hear with the waterfall crashing so close. Straining with so much churning water nearby was beginning to make his ears ring. He swallowed hard, his mouth dry. Maybe the doctor had just thought he heard something. Like one of those desert mirages, but with sound. He sure as heck hoped so.

Blakely shook his head. "I don't know—"

"*Hellooo!*" The call echoed through the cavern, causing both of them to jump.

Blakely looked at Jason. "Someone's out there! I can't believe it!"

Jason watched as Blakely climbed on top of a boulder. It took the old man a few tries to boost up on top. Jason clambered deftly up next to him. "Who do you think it is?"

"I don't know, but let's find out." Blakely cupped his hands over his mouth and yelled, "*We're over here! By the foot of the waterfall!*"

Jason listened for a reply. Nothing for several heartbeats, then an answer: "*We're coming! Stay put!*"

"I told you someone would find us. I told you." Blakely suddenly sounded exhausted and wheezy as he scooted from the boulder.

Jason watched the doctor slump to his knees beside the rock. Something was wrong.

Jason hopped down and crossed to the doctor. Blakely coughed raggedly, then slipped to his side and collapsed.

"Dr. Blakely!" Jason tugged on his arm. He didn't respond.

Jason's heart seized in his throat. He searched around him, desperate, his hands shaking. Jason darted to the boulder top and screamed at the shadows, "*Help!*"

Linda hurried to catch up with Khalid, her pack dangling from one shoulder. She stared across the cavern. "That sounded like Ashley's son."

Khalid grunted and continued deeper into the cavern, aiming for the foot of the falls. He held a pistol in his left hand. "If it is Jason," he finally said, "then we must be near the base. Blakely would not let the boy travel far from the security of the camp."

She eyed the gun. "What're you going to do?"

"Complete my mission."

"What do you mean?"

"That depends on you."

Linda swallowed hard. "Listen, Khalid, I don't want *anyone* else killed."

His eyes became shadowed under heavy brows. "Then keep your mouth shut. As long as they stay blind to my mission, I'll spare them."

She remembered Villanueva murdered so suddenly and needlessly. "I won't say a word."

Khalid nodded and set up a quicker pace again. Within a few yards, he pointed forward. "Over there. On top of that rock. I can see him. It's the boy."

She squinted. There were boulders everywhere. Then she saw the tiny figure waving his arms. She called to him, *"Hang on, Jason! We're coming!"*

Jason saw them. Two people wearing helmets; their lamp lights sparked across the fungus-lit cavern. They had seen him. Someone called to him, but the falls drowned out the words. Still, it didn't matter. The important thing was they were coming.

He clambered off the rock to check on Blakely. The doctor's color had blanched, his lips purplish. He still breathed, but each inhalation rattled, as if pebbles filled his chest.

Jason hugged himself, shifting from foot to foot. "C'mon, Doc, don't die. Help is coming." He turned in the direction of the rescuers. Hurry, he prayed.

He sat down next to Blakely, picking up one of his hands. So cold, he thought. He rubbed the hand, like

Aladdin with a lamp, wishing for the doctor to get better. As if in answer to his wish, a groan escaped the old man's lips. Jason rubbed harder, then darted to the other side and rubbed his left wrist and hand. "C'mon, Doc, c'mon."

The doctor's eyelids fluttered apart, pupils crossing, then his eyes snapped back into focus. He let out another loud groan, then just breathed thickly. Finally, he spoke: "J-Jason?"

"Are you okay?"

The doctor's lips were taut with pain as he whispered, "M-my m-medicine. Nitro . . . nitroglycerine."

Jason looked around him. "Where?"

The doctor lifted his hand, but it dropped limply. "M-my pocket. Inside . . . my jacket."

Jason patted the doctor's clothes and discovered a telltale bulge in the inner breast pocket. He fished out a red plastic bottle. "Is this it?"

"Y-yes."

"What do I do?"

"One . . . no, two pills."

It took Jason a minute to get the childproof cap off the bottle. He tapped two pills into his palm.

The doctor's eyes opened again. "Good boy." His voice sounded ghostly. Almost like he was some ventriloquist doll and the speaker was miles away. "U-under my t-tongue."

Jason reached across and dropped the two pills inside the doctor's mouth. He watched as Blakely worked the tablets around. Then the doctor closed his eyes and took several deep breaths.

Letting his head hang in relief, Jason thanked whoever was watching over them.

Just then a voice spoke directly behind him, causing him to jump in fright. "Jason? My god, what happened?"

He whirled around and stared into a familiar face. Her hair was stringy with mud, and dark shadows circled her eyes, but she was still a wonderful sight. "Linda!" He jumped up and ran into her arms.

She hugged him tight, and tears burst forth from his eyes. He cried into her shirt, all the pain and terror of two days releasing in a single torrent.

"Oh, Jason." She rocked him in her arms. "You're okay."

He continued to cry, knowing he should stop, but he found he couldn't. He let himself be held and rocked, his body wracked with sobs. He didn't ever want to leave her arms.

An accented voice intruded.

Jason peeked a moist eye open and saw the blue-steel pistol in the Egyptian's hand. He stiffened in Linda's arms.

"So what the hell happened here?" Khalid asked.

BOOK FOUR

Drums and Death

TWENTY-ONE

With Ashley's panicked scream, the furry grip tightened on her ankle, like a closing vise. What the hell? She sprang to the side, yanking her leg and breaking the hold of the attacker. She collided with Ben, accidentally knocking his gun aside. A shot rang out as his pistol fired, shooting toward the distant roof, the waste of a precious round.

"Christ, woman!" Ben blurted, shoving her behind him, his eyes still glued to the pack of slathering wolfish creatures pawing the ground.

"Something's in the wormhole. It g-grabbed me."

He darted a look toward the hole. Nothing was there. "I don't see any—Bloody hell!" It was Ben's turn to hop away from the wormhole as something crawled from the passage. "Shit!"

Ashley thought at first it was a small dirty child, naked and covered in filth. But when it straightened and turned to her, she knew she was vastly mistaken. She took another step back.

It stood four feet high, squat and unclothed, and from the exposed genitalia, it was obviously male. His muddy black hair was tied back from his face with a leather ribbon, and his chest and legs were covered in coarse matted hair.

Ashley's first thought was that she faced a hominid or protohuman. Maybe some type of dwarf Neanderthal. Several of the features supported her supposition: the thick bony brow bulging above huge eyes, the wide blunt nose that sniffed in her direction, the protruding jaw and maxillary bones that created a muzzlelike countenance.

Ashley, though, had studied the fossil record of all the hominid and protohuman species. And this breathing (and stinking) specimen conformed to none of them. The closest might be the Australopithecine species, but this creature was vastly different. The body, though thick with muscle, was not as bulky as the early hominids, and the neck was too long and slender. His ears too were striking: slightly tufted and pointed, they actually swiveled back and forth, wary. None of these features matched the fossil record of any ancient protohumans!

Suddenly the creature stepped toward them.

Ben raised his gun.

Eyeing the pistol, the creature opened his mouth, baring short fangs, then turned away and waved a muscled arm toward the pack of beasts and grunted toward them—"*Unkh! Unkh!*" Like a precision drill team, they all turned and vanished back into the field. He turned back to Ben, crossing his arms.

Ben lowered his gun. He spoke out of the side of his mouth. "What do you make of this, Ash?"

"I'm not sure," she said with wonder in her voice. "But I think we've just met one of our cave dwellers."

One of the creature's ears swiveled away from them. He seemed to be listening, his eyelids drifting closed. After several heartbeats, his lids snapped back open. He swung around and began walking away with a rolling sort of gait.

Ashley watched him, dying to run a hand over his pelvic structure. It didn't appear right either, matching none of the hominid species. Who was this? What was this?

The creature walked several yards, then stopped and turned back to them. His arms crossed again. Waiting.

"I think he wants us to follow," she said, stepping forward.

Ben touched her elbow, stopping her. "We don't know where in bloody hell it's taking us," he whispered. "For all we know, we may be on tonight's dinner menu." Ben raised his voice, calling to the waiting figure. "Hold it right there, my hairy buddy. Where are we going?"

The creature glanced toward Ben, then turned and walked away.

Ashley stared at the retreating figure. She had to find out more about these creatures. Deciding she had nothing to lose, she started to follow, calling over her shoulder, "I think it's safe, Ben. He could've let those wolf things attack if he meant us harm."

Ben shook his head, but he followed cautiously.

Trailing several yards behind their guide, they were led to a thin path in the field of yellow vegetation. Before the creature started down the track, he took a long dagger from a belt, which was his only piece of clothing. The blade was a long crystal shard. It was diamond!

Ben held a restraining arm across Ashley's chest, obviously worried that their guide was about to attack.

"*Dogaomarubi*," their guide said, as if explaining, hefting up the knife.

Ben nodded. "Uh-huh. Whatever, little fella. Just keep that little poker in your pants."

"My god," Ashley said, "he's trying to speak to us. Verbal communication! It's incredible."

The creature swung away and led them into the yellow fields. The grainlike seeds at the tip of the stalky vegetation waved above the head of their guide, while reaching only chest-high on Ashley. She had to push down the narrow path, shoving her shoulders through the barrier of vegetation on either side, while their guide seemed to glide down the path without disturbing a single stalk. Ashley felt like some lumbering elephant. After an hour, she stumbled more than pushed through the growth.

Ben followed, grunting with effort to haul through the dense growth. "I'd love a machete," he said, huffing.

"Or a four-wheeler," she added. "I need a rest."

As if in answer, they entered a clearing in the field. A small creek crossed the path, forded by a stone bridge. Their guide waited at the foot of the bridge, sitting on a stone seat, the dagger in his hand. "*Dogaomarubi*," he repeated. He pointed to two smooth rocks.

Ashley looked at Ben, mystified. Ben looked at their guide.

She watched as their guide pantomimed sitting down. "*Dogaomarubi*," he said more forcibly.

"He wants us to sit," she said, crossing to a stone, taking off her pack. "*Dogaomarubi* must mean 'rest break.'"

Ben sat on a neighboring rock, dropping his pack with a sigh. " 'Bout time."

The creature crossed to Ben and offered him his dagger.

Ben accepted the dagger. "Thanks . . . I guess." He turned to Ashley. "So is this a gift? Do I give him something in return?"

"I don't know. Cultures vary. Sometimes it's an insult to give a gift in exchange for another."

"Then what do I do? Does he want me to do something with this? Cut my palm? Become blood brothers?"

She shrugged.

Their guide stared at them during their conversation. Ears swiveling back and forth as they spoke. Finally, he grunted loudly and stepped forward, snatching the knife from Ben. He knelt by Ben and yanked his pants leg up.

Ben began to snatch his leg away—then froze.

Ashley saw it too and gasped. "What is that?" She crossed to examine it closer, bending down beside Ben. A palm-sized black slug was attached to his shin. As she watched, its body quivered in a wave of undulating tissue; it grew a few millimeters larger.

Their guide reached forward with his blade and deftly scooped the creature off Ben's leg. Its suckers caught stubbornly on his flesh, then popped free. Two small pink circles with pinpoint holes in the center marked Ben's leg where the creature had attached. A couple drops of blood oozed out.

"Fucking leeches!" Ben exclaimed, a shiver passing through him. He stood up and stripped off his pants, his face frozen in a look of disgust. Five more leechlike parasites were attached.

Grimacing, Ashley noticed one had climbed as high as his right buttock. She glanced down at her own pants. Suddenly it felt like thousands of scabrous creatures were crawling up her legs. Knowing it was only her imagination, she still quickly unbuckled her belt and climbed out of her pants.

Holding her breath, she looked down. Two black patches covered her left thigh and there was one on her right. Shit! There was no telling what sort of diseases these slugs might be carrying.

Ben, standing naked from the waist down, looked green as his last parasite was extracted. Once finished, the guide came toward her with the knife.

"I can do this myself," she said, holding out her hand for the knife.

Their guide glanced at her hand, then up to her face. She pushed her hand out further, insistent. He paused and seemed to understand . . . even nodded! He placed the hilt of the knife in her hand.

Goddamn leeches! She used the tip of the knife to pry the posterior sucker loose, then lifted the parasite's trunk with the blade until the anterior sucker was reached. It took a bit of tugging to dislodge this last sucker. Carrying the leech on the diamond blade, she tossed it in the creek like their guide had. She then went to work on the other two.

Once the last one was scraped off, its black body still balanced on the blade, their guide carefully picked up the leech. He pointed at it. "*Dogaomarubi!*" he said, then threw the parasite into the creek.

Ben buckled his pants. "I *don't* think *dogaomarubi* means 'rest break.' I think it means 'goddamn fucking land leech.'"

Hooking the pack over her shoulders, she nodded. "Notice how he didn't destroy the parasites. He was careful cutting them free. I watched one of the leeches in the water. It swelled with water, then crawled back into the fields."

"Yeah, so?"

"I think they're used in maintaining the fields. Like a farmer uses bees. They use the leeches as some form of irrigation. A biological tool."

Ben quivered. "Yeah, but bees don't suck your blood," he mumbled.

Ashley rolled her eyes and followed their guide over the bridge and into the fields again. After an hour, a herd of lumbering creatures could be seen in the distance, apparently grazing. They raised blocky heads on short necks to stare at them as they passed.

"Sorta look like wallabies on steroids," Ben said.

"*Turituri*," their guide said, pointing at them.

Ashley nodded, amazed at the ecosystem evolved here. Phytoplankton and volcanic gases as a base energy source, initiating a food chain based on fungi and microorganisms. The system must be incredibly fragile, requiring constant manipulation to maintain. Like the leeches, each organism played a key role in fortifying and protecting the environment.

She eyed their guide's back. What level of intelligence did this ecosystem require to maintain itself? Mere chance would not allow such a rich and varied environment to flourish.

As she continued, a flock of birds exploded nearby. Quick as lightning, their guide whipped out a sling and chucked a stone at the birds, knocking one from the sky. He bolted into the field to retrieve his kill, returning shortly with the bird tied to his belt. Ashley stared at his catch. No feathers. What she had thought was a bird was a winged lizard.

Ben had been eyeing the "bird" too. "I hope that's not our dinner."

"Probably tastes like chicken," she said, tugging him along.

Their guide stopped several feet ahead and squatted down. Ashley followed his example and slunk lower, fearing a predator might be approaching. She cautiously surveyed the savanna.

"What is it?" Ben asked, slipping behind her, crouching too.

Ashley glanced ahead toward their guide. He squatted a few feet away, defecating beside the trail. Ashley was speechless.

Ben wasn't. "Not exactly a private sort of folk, are they?"

Their guide finished and cleaned himself with a frond from the field. He then turned around and used the same frond to pick up his stool and store it in a small pouch on his belt.

"Tidy too," said Ben.

Ashley shook her head. "Conservation."

"What?"

"This ecosystem's energy is limited. Everything must be put to use. For this fragile system to survive, nothing can be wasted."

"Still . . . remind me not to shake this fella's hand."

Their guide continued forward with hardly a glance back. Ashley followed.

After two more hours of travel and two more stops to remove leeches, Ashley dragged at a snail's pace, drenched in sweat, every part of her anatomy scratched and poked.

Their guide turned to her. "*Daga mond carofi*," he said, his slit-pupiled eyes narrowed with concern.

She shook her head, not understanding. She uncapped her canteen and drank.

He pointed toward the distant wall; the path now turned in that direction. "*Carofi!*"

She wiped her forehead and squinted where he pointed. Just barely distinguishable from the shadows on the far wall was a pattern of black dots, arranged in rows and levels. She recognized the pattern, similar to the grouping of dwellings in Alpha Cavern. Even from this far away, she could see plenty of motion. Little figures clambering among the dwellings.

"My god, Ben. Look! A village!" she said, turning to him.

Pulling on his right ear, he wore an odd expression, a mixture of surprise and fear. "Do you hear . . . ? A buzzing . . . ?" His eyes rolled back, the whites of his eyes showing.

"Ben?"

He began to sway a bit, teetering, then collapsed into the field.

Ben struggled against the darkness. He could hear Ashley call to him, but it sounded like she was down a deep well, so far away, fading. The blackness swallowed him further.

He felt a tugging on his shoulder, at first tenderly, then more urgently. Ben's eyes fluttered open. His grandfather shook him again. "Benny boy, no time to take a nap. We need you up and about."

Not again, he thought, as he looked around at the familiar cavern. Trunks of rock, bearing red bulbous fruit, surrounded him. He was dreaming. But how could that be? His grandfather was naked except for a loincloth, his chest painted in primary colors.

"What do you want?" he asked.

"Come. Follow." His grandfather stood up and pointed to a cavern opening with a star scrawled above the doorway. "This way." His dead grandfather crossed to the opening and climbed inside.

Ben tried to follow but found he couldn't sit up. He was paralyzed. "I can't move!" he called.

Only a voice from the cavern answered. "Come when you can. You are one with us!"

Blackness swallowed him up once again. He tried to push it back, succeeding this time. Light burst around him, and he found himself staring into Ashley's worried face.

"Ben?" she asked. "What happened?"

"I don't know." He sat up. "I don't know."

· · ·

As they approached the encampment, Ashley stared up, her mouth hanging open. She tried counting the number of dwellings carved into the wall but lost her concentration after a hundred. The grouping of homes was crowded in a scalloped declivity about a mile wide, forming a natural amphitheater. The level of homes climbed some twenty tiers up, carved stairways joining landing to landing, thick ropes and crude pulleys draped down the face of the cliff in several locations.

These cave dwellings, though similar to the ones found in Alpha Cavern, were not the stark spartan dwellings found there. Rather, they had been transformed into comfortable-looking homes. The walls were festooned with multicolored weavings; entryways were draped with blankets in intricate designs; woven banners hung from various levels depicting strange animals and complicated hunts. Stone pottery painted in yellows, reds, and blues dotted many landings.

Ben reached across and took her hand as they left the yellow fields and entered the curve of homes. Squeezing his hand, she noticed the rock floor had been polished to an almost smooth surface—whether from years of arduous labor or simply from centuries of ordinary foot traffic, she wasn't sure.

She followed the guide through an increasing throng of spectators. Some hung back with wide-eyed awe, some crept up to gently touch her arm or pluck at her clothes, and some hid behind others, peeking around a shoulder. She stared up at the cliffs surrounding them. Small hands held blankets aside to stare at them. The carved stairs between levels were crowded with thousands of sharp faces peering from above. A scattering of toddlers ran between the legs of their parents.

All were naked, like their guide. A few, however, were adorned with various crude necklaces, and some wore caps of woven reed. One group of males, all charcoal-haired, had some type of sharpened bone piercing their noses.

Their guide stopped and knelt on a stone, head bowed, waiting.

Ashley and Ben stood behind him. Looking over their guide's shoulder, Ashley caught sight of one adult female who drew her attention. While only slightly less furred than their guide, her pendulous breasts were bare, with wide tan nipples drooping down to her bulging belly. She exhibited all the signs of pregnancy. Ashley was about to turn away when a sudden motion caught her eye. A tiny hand popped out of the bulge in the female's belly; it reached up and grabbed a handful of fur beneath a breast. Using this handhold, a mewling infant, pink and hairless, pulled itself from her belly and began suckling. The mother seemed unaware and just continued to stare at Ashley. Ashley squinted, fascinated. The infant, made nervous by the commotion around it, lowered itself back down into its hiding place. Into a pouch!

"Look, Ben!" Ashley said, her words causing the spectators to back a step away. "That mother over there. She's carrying a child in a pouch."

"Yeah, so what? Did you see those guards at the entryway with the spears and leashed wolf creatures? If we want out of here, it ain't gonna be easy."

"I don't care. I'm not leaving here until they push me out kicking and screaming. There's too much to study. Do you realize what this means?" she said, nodding toward the female.

"What?"

"Only marsupials carry their young in pouches. These creatures must be evolved from marsupial origins!"

"Great, we've been captured by a bunch of kangaroos."

She ignored his remark, still thinking out loud. "The huge predators that attacked us were also a type of early marsupial. It's like this whole ecosystem's environmental niches have been filled with various marsupial species. But how? How did they get here? How did they survive?"

Ben shrugged.

"I mean, think about it, Ben. A whole marsupial ecosystem, separate from mammalian competition and intrusion, has evolved here. In these caverns, evolution has taken an entirely different branch to sentience."

Just then a hush descended on the whispering crowd. Total silence. Ben nudged her and nodded forward.

A towering creature strode out of the entrance to the largest dwelling. He was black-haired, but a spattering of gray dotted his beard, his eyes so richly yellow they almost glowed. The creature stood a head taller than their guide, shoulders wide and muscular. He carried a walking stick taller than himself in his right hand, topped by a ruby the size of a grapefruit.

Their guide raised his head for the first time and began speaking rapidly. The other, clearly the leader of the community, blurted a word here and there. Ashley watched the exchange, curious what was being said. Their guide spurted out a last growl and lowered his forehead to the stone before him.

The leader finally turned to them, eyeing Ashley first, then Ben. He seemed to be studying them, absently scratching at his belly. He barked something at them. Though unintelligible to Ashley, his words caused the crowd to gasp and step away from them. Some even darted away, scurrying behind drapes.

Ashley turned to Ben.

He shrugged, then whispered, "I don't think this is good."

The leader stamped his stick on the stone and turned away.

Just then a tottering figure with coarse silver hair emerged from a neighboring cave. He moved so slowly and carefully that Ashley was sure she could hear his bones creak. Like the leader, he carried a walking stick, but unlike the leader, he needed it, leaning heavily on the staff with each step. Also, rather than a ruby, his stick was topped by a pear-shaped diamond.

Ashley noticed as he approached that painted on his chest was a design in reds and yellows.

Ben started fidgeting beside her. "I gotta be going crazy."

"Shhh!" she said. "I don't think it's polite to talk."

The ancient one looked toward her. Though his body was obviously old and decrepit, there was a sharp intelligence in his eyes, revealing an agile mind. He turned to Ben and nodded toward him, then began talking to the leader.

Ben shifted back a step. "Ash, I've seen that design before. That painting on the ol' bloke's chest."

"What? Where?" she whispered.

He swallowed hard. A trace of fear frosted his voice. "In . . . a dream. Painted on . . . my dead grand-father."

She took his hand. "Listen, we'll figure that out later. Right now we need to find out what they intend to do with us."

While they had been whispering, the discussion between the old man and the leader had become heated. Voices were now raised, punctuated by the stamping of walking sticks. Finally, the leader bared his teeth and cracked his walking stick across his knee, snapping it in half, and stormed away.

"Now what?" Ben asked.

The ancient one turned to face them and pointed his stick in their direction. He uttered one word: "Death."

TWENTY-TWO

Exhaustion lulled Michaelson from his surveillance of the tunnel outside his tiny refuge. It had been hours since Ashley and Ben had disappeared, leaving him alone. He strained to listen for any sign of the stalkers. Nothing. Silence pressed like a physical weight against his eardrums.

He sighed. At least his ankle's throbbing had dulled to a mild protest. Eventually he'd have to adjust the ankle splint, but he was too tired for that now. He closed his eyes so he could concentrate with less distraction. Still, there was only silence and more silence.

A yawn escaped him, and his head sagged to his chest. He shook his head, knowing he must stay alert.

He checked the corridor. Still clear. After several minutes, like sinking suns, his eyelids began to droop downward again. His breathing deepened. He hung suspended in that fuzzy haze between dream and reality.

It was then something brushed across his hand.

His eyelids snapped open, and he threw his head back, almost cracking the back of his skull on the wall. He fumbled with his gun and pointed it at a man dressed in a ragged Marine uniform, the sleeves torn off at the shoulders. It was impossible. He blinked a few times. Must be dreaming, he thought. But the figure persisted, smiling down at him.

Michaelson stared up into the eyes of his long-lost brother. "Harry? My god! You're alive!"

His brother pushed the muzzle of Michaelson's gun away with a fingertip. "Not if you pull that trigger," Harry said, a tired grin on his face.

Michaelson threw his gun to the side and, ignoring the protest from his ankle, jumped and grabbed his brother in a bear hug. He squeezed back tears, praying he wasn't hallucinating, but his brother's amused chuckles were not those of his imagination. He was real. "Thank god thank god thank god," Michaelson chanted into Harry's shoulder.

"Brother, you gave us quite a chase," Harry said, breaking their hug and swiping a hand through his black hair, a familiar mannerism.

Smiling, Michaelson realized he hadn't seen that gesture in ages. It had been decades since Harry's hair had been any longer than a tight military crewcut, but after the months down here, the gesture, like an old friend, had returned.

Michaelson's voice caught in his throat. He almost took his brother again in his arms, but then noticed the scar that ran the entire length of Harry's right arm. It was still pink and raised, something recent. He reached out and touched it. "What happened?"

Harry's expression sobered. Michaelson studied his brother's face closely and noticed the circles under his brother's blue eyes. A haunted look. Harry had lost weight; the remains of his uniform hung on his frame. "It's a long story," Harry said.

"Well, I think we have the time."

"No, not really. We need to hurry. The crak'an are close."

"The who?"

"Those monsters." Harry waved him to follow. "Gather your gear, soldier, we're bugging out."

Michaelson tossed him his gun and climbed into the alcove to collect his pack and canteen. As he crawled back out, he noticed his brother checking his gun with an appreciative smile.

Harry handed back the gun reluctantly. "Nice tool. I could have used that firepower when I was escorting those scientists. Maybe then . . ." He stopped talking, a fierce set to his lips.

Michaelson approached his brother's back, laying a hand on his shoulder, still half expecting him to vanish in a puff of smoke, like some trickster spirit, teasing him with his brother's image. He noticed his brother's hands were empty. How had he survived running around here without a weapon? "I've got another gun in my pack—" he started to say.

"No need. I've got friends."

Friends? Michaelson searched the empty passageway, shifting his pack to his shoulder. Who was Harry talking about?

His brother then growled something that sent a chill up his back, half howl, half moan, inhuman. Low but penetrating.

Michaelson stared at his brother's back as he howled. Had his brother gone mad during his isolation?

Harry turned to him, dead serious. "Don't shoot at them."

"Who the hell are you talking—" There was movement along the walls farther down the passage. Small figures, camouflaged against the rock, stepped into the passage, knives and spears glistening in the greenish mold light.

Michaelson heard a pebble shift behind him. Glancing around, he saw more were approaching from the rear. "Harry?"

"They're friends. Saved my life."

One of the creatures separated from the others and approached. His eyes fixed on Michaelson as he edged toward Harry. Michaelson held his gun tightly. The creature, naked, stood only four feet high but was wiry with well-defined muscle. Its shaggy, sandy-colored hair was secured with a blood-red headband. Large eyes searched Michaelson from toe to head, while its prominent ears swiveled in all directions like radar dishes.

As the small figure approached, Michaelson judged the weaponry he carried. A long knife with a crude crystalline blade was belted around his bare waist, and in his four-fingered hand, he clutched a long spear.

As Michaelson watched, the creature crossed to Harry and handed him the spear. Then it backed away.

"Who are . . . No, *what* are they?"

"They call themselves *mimi'swee*."

One of them darted from behind, startling Michaelson, and slid past him to approach Harry. He pointed behind them. "*Doda fer'ago*," he said. "*Doda crak'an!*"

Harry glanced over to Michaelson. "He says we've got company. They've caught our scent and are closing in on us. Time to hightail it."

As if on cue, a roar erupted from behind them. A second and third answered it, coming from all around them. They were being boxed in.

Michaelson thought of Ashley and Ben, lost out in the maze of tunnels. He stepped next to Harry. "Listen, I've got friends, and—"

"I know. A small team of my buddies were dispatched after them." He pointed a thumb forward. "Your friends have been herded to safety."

"Where?"

A second volley of roars echoed through the tunnels. "I'll show you. C'mon, before we're someone's dinner."

Michaelson stuck close to his brother. The tiny figures scurried around him, some passing him and running forward, others hurrying behind him to check their trail. He struggled to keep up, biting his lower lip, but his bum ankle soon began throbbing in protest again. A gap started forming between himself and his brother.

Harry slowed down, grabbed Michaelson's arm, and hooked it over his own shoulder, supporting his injured side. By now, only two or three of the little hunters still jogged behind them, guarding the rear. "I'm not leaving you behind, Dennis."

"I'm slowing you down. I didn't come down here to get you killed."

"Shut up, brother. No one is going to get killed today." He squeezed Michaelson's shoulder. "Besides, hooked together like this, it's just like the three-legged race in Kearney when we won the blue ribbon at the fair."

Grimacing with pain, Michaelson spat out, "It's because you cheated!"

"I didn't see you giving back your ribbon."

There was a sudden eruption of commotion from behind them. One of the hunters scurried toward them and growled something to Harry. Harry's expression sobered. He answered something unintelligible. The figure nodded its chin and scrambled forward. Only one tiny figure remained behind them now.

"What did he say?"

"One of the *crak'an* is closing the gap. We won't make safety."

Michaelson ground his molars. Now he had put his brother in new danger. "I told you—"

"Yeah, yeah, you're always right." His brother stopped their shuffling gait. The remaining hunter, black-furred with a scar down the right side of his face, halted beside Harry. "Dennis, go on ahead, try to keep up as best as you can. Nob'cobi and I'll try to slow it down. Buy some time for the others."

"To hell with that! I've got the gun."

"Yeah, and I've got the experience. Now move it!"

He recognized the stubborn set to his brother's eyes. There would be no arguing. "Well, at least take my gun, then."

Harry shook his head. "You may need it." His brother then hefted the long spear still held in his right hand. "Besides, using nontraditional weapons lessens our chance to gain *il'jann* from the kill."

"What?"

Harry waved him on. "It's sort of like counting coup. A measure of honor." A scrabbling of claw on rock could now be heard coming from down the tunnel. "Now get going!"

Michaelson nodded and started down the tunnel. No way was he going to leave his brother to fight with only a spear. As soon as he reached a side tunnel, he ducked in and checked behind him. His brother and the other hunter had their heads together. The little figure was gesturing with his hands and nodding.

Dropping his pack, he unhooked his gun and lay flat in the tunnel, sighting back down the passageway. He waited, listening to the increasing noise of the approaching predator.

Suddenly his brother tensed and swung his spear forward, apparently seeing something still out of sight from Michaelson's position. The tiny hunter pressed himself flat against the passage wall. Harry planted the haft of his spear in a divot on the floor and held it in place with his foot, leaning the length of the shaft forward, blade pointing down the tunnel. He crouched, holding the spear steady.

A roar of rage echoed down the tunnel; then the monster stalked into view, filling the entire tunnel, massive, larger than any Michaelson had seen before. Black as if soaked in pitch, it twisted its head back and forth, snorting explosively. When it spotted Harry, it froze, tensing on its two thickly muscled hind legs. It backed a step, stretching its neck forward, then opened its mouth and screamed.

Harry held his position, but answered the monster with his own yell: "Fuck you!"

Michaelson let a small smile come to his lips. Nothing intimidated the foolish bastard. Lying on his belly, Michaelson narrowed his eyes, raising the rifle's butt to his shoulder, eyeing through the sights. His shot was blocked by his brother. Shit.

With a howl of fury, the beast burst toward his brother, barreling across the gap between them. Everything happened too fast for Michaelson to react. Harry ducked down as the head lunged at him, then braced himself as the beast rammed into his planted spear, impaling itself through the chest. The shaft snapped in half as Harry rolled away.

Just then the tiny hunter leaped from the side wall and landed straddled on the neck of the monster, a long knife clutched in his fist. He drove the blade at the eyes of the beast, gouging viciously.

The beast reared with an agonized roar, throwing its head back, dislodging the hunter. The long knife, though, protruded from the monster's left eye.

The tiny hunter landed hard where he was flung, but he quickly scrambled away from the thrashing beast and crawled toward Harry.

The predator spotted the hunter with his one good eye, and snapped at him. Harry tried to reach his fellow hunter first and yank him out of reach of the beast, but his hand fell just inches too short. The little man was snatched up in the jaws of the monster. Still Harry scrambled forward with the snapped half of his spear, apparently intending to use the sharpened remains as a weapon to free his friend.

Michaelson gritted his teeth. His brother still partially blocked his shot but obviously wasn't going to leave the tiny hunter to the jaws of the beast. Damn him! Holding his breath, Michaelson squinted and pulled the trigger, the explosion from the rifle deafening in the narrow space.

The sudden noise froze everyone. Harry stopped his approach to strike the creature, the stump of his spear still gripped in his hand. The beast paused in midstride.

"Harry!" Michaelson called. His voice shattered the tableau. The beast collapsed to the floor, dead, a bullet through its brain. As it fell, it released its prey, the hunter tumbling from its jaws. Harry ran forward to his friend.

Michaelson crawled from his hiding place and approached his brother, eyeing the bulk of the beast that blocked the passage. "How is he?"

Harry helped the tiny hunter stand. "He'll live. They're a tough-skinned lot. A few punctures in his shoulder. Nothing seriously damaged, though."

"Good." Michaelson knelt beside the *mimi'swee* hunter and lay a hand on his good shoulder.

Harry sat back on his haunches. "Dennis, I thought I told you to get out of here."

Michaelson frowned. "Besides being your older brother, I also outrank you."

"Suddenly I'm glad you rose through the ranks faster than me. Otherwise you might've actually listened to me." Harry then turned to him, his eyes serious. "Thanks, Dennis."

The tiny hunter started spouting gibberish, a pained expression in his eyes. Harry nodded soberly. The tiny figure reached to his injured shoulder and dabbed a finger in the seeping blood, then turned to Michaelson.

"Nob'cobi wants to share his *il'jann* with you," Harry explained. "It's a distinct honor among his people. Equivalent of blood brothers."

The furry hunter reached forward and placed a bloody finger to Michaelson's forehead. "Br . . . brother," he said in a half growl.

TWENTY-THREE

Khalid watched as Linda embraced the frightened boy, her cheek resting atop Jason's head. She whispered consolations in the boy's ear. Khalid crossed to Blakely's form sprawled on the rock. The doctor's eyes were open and staring at him, his breathing still ragged and hissing. The doctor had information he needed, data necessary to complete his mission. He knelt beside Blakely and offered his canteen, pouring a small stream of water into the doctor's mouth.

Blakely closed his eyes and swallowed greedily, then pushed the canteen away, sloshing water across his chest. "Thanks," he muttered.

"What happened?" Khalid asked. "How did you end up here?"

Blakely spoke with his eyes closed, as if remembering. "The camp . . . it was attacked . . . destroyed." He breathed thickly, catching his breath.

Khalid's first thought was that someone had outmaneuvered him. A second agent? But the doctor's next words dismissed this idea.

"Huge creatures . . . hundreds of them . . . overwhelmed the camp. We escaped in the raft. Ended up stranded here."

Khalid frowned at the bad news. Damn, so there were more of them. He had hoped the few they had run into were the only ones. He looked up at the series of waterfalls. If they should eventually find their way back up, awaiting them lurked a herd of those predators. He sat back on his haunches and holstered his pistol.

"What now?" he mumbled to himself.

The doctor heard him and answered, his voice still hoarse but steadier. "We wait. Leave it to the military. Once they realize what happened, they'll be swarming through here. Let them find us."

Khalid rubbed the thick stubble on his cheek. The doctor was right. The military *would* be mobilizing shortly, reestablishing the security of the base. And with the entire U.S. Navy down here, combing the place, his mission would be that much more difficult, if not impossible.

He rubbed at his tired red eyes, sandy grit ground under his lids. He would have to reach Alpha Base somehow before military reinforcements did. And with enough spare time to finish setting his charges and get the hell out of the place. A tall order, even for himself.

Perhaps this was a test from Allah. The forces of nature pitted against him, testing him. How else could one explain the vile monsters that blocked them, the innumerable obstacles, the new horrors at every turn? It had to be a test from the Almighty.

He closed his eyes, placed his palms across his face, and prayed for the strength to succeed and for a sign that he was honorable in his mission. He prayed for five minutes, his heart beating in his ears. But still no sign appeared. Finally, he sat back with a sigh, placing his hands on his knees. Nothing.

Then, when he raised his eyes, he saw it. A plume of oily smoke curling out from an opening halfway up the wall of the cave. Khalid sat up straighter. "Doctor, was the camp burning? Was there lots of smoke?"

The doctor cleared his dry throat. "Yes, thick with smoke. Why?"

Khalid pointed to the far wall, a smile of delight on his features. "Look, over there! The smoke! It must be the way back up!" He continued to stare at the billowing smoke, like some cloudy finger of god.

. . .

Still holding Jason under one arm, Linda stared at the smoky tunnel opening. Emotions warred within her: relief at finding a way back up and dread for the events that might transpire. What would Khalid do? He couldn't let Blakely and Jason know his plans without killing them.

She turned to stare at Khalid. His expression as he stared up the cliff face was one of strange exaltation, his eyes wide, glassy. A shiver passed through her when those eyes met hers. He smiled at her. "It's almost finished," he said.

She nodded. It had all happened too fast. She had expected days of searching before the way home was discovered, giving her plenty of time to formulate a plan, extra hours to decide if she should try to stop him or just save her skin and let him do what he wanted.

A tugging on her arm distracted her. She looked down at Jason. "Linda, what about my mom? Do you think she's okay?"

She squeezed the boy's shoulder as he stared up at her. She should lie, tell him everything would be just fine, but Jason was an astute kid. His eyes as he looked at her were dry and serious. He wanted an honest answer. "Jason, I truly don't know. But Ben and Major Michaelson are with her. She's in good hands."

Jason nodded.

Khalid touched her shoulder, startling her. He gestured for her to follow him a few steps away, to talk in private. Her heart pounded in her throat as she followed.

He checked over his shoulder to make sure they were alone. "Listen, I want us to head out tonight."

Her mouth dried. This was happening too fast, like a freight train racing toward a demolished trestle. "But Blakely shouldn't be moved so soon."

Khalid didn't blink. "I wasn't planning on taking him. Or the boy."

Her words were a whisper. "You promised me that you wouldn't kill anyone else if I stayed silent."

"I'm not going to kill them. Just leave them."

"Is that any different?"

He shrugged. "As I told you, if they find out about my plan, I would be forced to kill them. At least by leaving them, they have a chance to fend for themselves."

Staring at Khalid, she pictured Jason starving to death and Blakely being devoured by a beast. How easily he condemned Blakely and Jason to a lingering death. Where was the heart in this monster? She swallowed. "I hate this."

"We'll leave after the other two fall asleep," Khalid whispered in her ear, like a lover passing secrets. "You won't have to face them."

His words threatened to destroy her sanity. How could he so casually plan their deaths? Just stroll away from them in the night? How could . . . ?

Then an idea formed in her mind.

She chewed on the idea, but there wasn't much time, and the risk was great. She bit her lower lip, unsure. She watched Jason grin at something Blakely said. She saw his eyes shine brightly in the fungal glow. Shining with young life, with so much of life yet to explore.

She closed her eyes, firming up her plans. She could do this. No, she *would* do this. "Okay, we'll leave tonight," she said with resolve.

While Linda feigned sleep, Blakely and Jason slept, wrapped in spare blankets. Blakely snored, a whistling gurgle heard over even the rushing falls. But Linda's slitted eyes stayed focused on Khalid's profile, where he sat, half in his sleeping bag, leaning on a boulder. She waited. She watched his head slip down, then bob back up as sleep almost overtook him. Almost.

Linda had talked Khalid into resting a bit, pleading exhaustion herself. Just a nap of two hours, she had begged, enough to charge her batteries for the next leg of their journey. He agreed. She then secretly dissolved several of her prescription anti-anxiety tablets in Khalid's water and made sure he drank his fill. The strong mineral tang of the local water disguised the taste of the tablets. The pills wouldn't knock him out—they only had a mild sedative effect—but in these numbers, the medication should make him so drowsy he might accidentally fall asleep while standing guard. It was all she needed.

She saw his chin hit his chest again. This time his head stayed down.

With her heart pounding in her ears, she listened, tense in her sleeping bag, close enough to Khalid to recognize when his breathing deepened into a regular rhythm. She knew she did not have much time.

With agonizing slowness, she inched from her sleeping bag. Thankfully, the roar of the neighboring falls muffled her movements.

She slipped next to him and collected his lantern and helmet from a nearby rock. She had originally planned to snatch Khalid's pistol, but he had fallen asleep with it tucked in his sleeping bag. To try to get to it now was too risky.

So she resorted to a backup plan. She removed the batteries to his lantern and helmet. He may still have the gun, she thought, but let's see if he can travel blind.

Once finished, she turned her attention to the dozing doctor. Linda placed her hand over the doctor's lips, pressing hard when he jerked awake. She leaned over him and pressed a finger to her lips, indicating silence. Once he settled from his shock, she removed her hand and waved for him to follow . . . quietly. She led him off several yards.

Once far enough away, she pressed her lips to his ear, hoping the roar of the falls kept her words from reaching the sleeping figures. "We need to sneak away. Now. Can you travel?"

He squinted at her. "Yes, but why? What's going on?"

She gave him an abbreviated version of the events that led her to him. By the time she had finished, her voice was trembling.

Blakely's eyebrows had risen higher and higher as she told her story. "The asshole! I didn't think . . . Hell, it's my fault. I should have checked more thoroughly. Too damn naive. About everything!"

The doctor looked decades older than just a week ago. Sunken eyes, slumped shoulders, even his hair looked grayer. She placed a hand on his arm. "We need to get Jason and steal away now."

He shook his head. "Why don't we just jump on him and wrestle the gun away? Or grab a big rock and clobber him."

"He's a trained killer. A machine." She could not keep the fear out of her voice. "We're no match for him. If he's attacked and only injured, then we're dead. It's safest if we just run. Try to get into the darkened tunnels, where without light, he can't follow."

"What about the other hazards out there?" He pointed toward the far wall. "We won't survive long without a weapon."

She hugged her arms around her body. "I know. But I'd rather take my chances on the unknown than with him."

"Okay. But we travel light. Only canteens and rations."

She nodded. "Let's get Jason."

Jason panicked when he was shaken awake. He couldn't breathe! He struggled violently for several heartbeats until he realized his respiratory distress was due to Linda's hand clamped over his mouth.

She hushed him, her lips at his ear. "Quiet, Jason."

He stopped struggling, but his heart still pounded, his head ached. What now? More monsters? He scooted up into a seated position and saw Blakely collecting the boxes of dry rations, creeping like a thief in the night, careful where he placed his feet.

Khalid slumped in his sleeping bag. Both Blakely and Linda kept glancing toward the snoring man. Jason turned to Linda with a question on his lips. She held a finger across her own. He didn't know why he had to be so darned quiet. The crashing waters were noisy enough. Still, he did as he was told and sat silently.

Within less than a minute, Linda and Blakely had piled three canteens, flashlights, and a bag of rations near him. Blakely showed Linda a wide-muzzled pistol he had found in the supplies from the boat. A flare gun, Jason noted.

Blakely crouched by him and whispered, "Listen, boy, we need to sneak away. Leave Khalid behind. We have to move fast. Do you think you can do that?"

He nodded, confused, but from Linda's pale face and nervous eyes, there was something to fear here. He eyed Khalid, hunched like an ogre.

Linda and Blakely quickly split up the small pile of supplies and waved him to follow. He stood and picked up his gym bag. Blakely eyed the bag and shook his head. "Leave it," he mouthed to him.

No way! He could carry it. He wasn't a baby. He shook his head and clutched his bag tighter.

The doctor opened his mouth, but Linda touched Blakely's arm and silenced him. She waved for the two of them to follow her. Jason marched behind her, and Blakely followed.

No one spoke as they traveled, even when their abandoned camp was hidden by stalagmites and boulders. The silence pressed around Jason, more frightening than screaming monsters and firing guns. Every odd noise made him jump, every crunch of their steps seemed to holler across the cavern. Thankfully, a half hour later, when they finally reached the tumble of rocks and boulders that led up to the smoking tunnel, Linda spoke. "Look." She pointed to the opening far above. "The smoke has thinned already. That'll make it easier for us to breathe."

"Yes," Blakely said, "but it may make it harder for us to trace the way back up." His expression was grim as he eyed the climb.

"Can you manage?" Linda asked.

"Do I have a choice?"

Linda squeezed the doctor's shoulder, then turned to him. "Jason, what about you? Can you climb up these boulders?"

"Piece of cake," he said with a squeak.

"Then we'd better hurry. I don't know how long the drugs will keep Khalid sleeping."

Khalid dreamed he gripped his mother's robe as the black storm descended on her camp in the desert. He tried to warn her that the gale was coming, but she just continued to talk to the other robed figures, oblivious to the roaring of the approaching sand and winds. He tugged on her robe, trying to get her attention, but she shoved him aside with her hip. He raced to the tent's flap, peeking out at the seething maelstrom as it wiped away the horizon. He turned to the group of robed figures, his mother among them. He screamed at them, his voice a reed before the wind. This time they heard him and turned. He opened his mouth to repeat his warning when he saw the faces peering over the veils. Not faces! Skulls. Yellow, sand-scrubbed bone peering over black veils. Skeletal hands reached for him from folds in the robes. He backed away into the roaring storm, a scream clutched in his throat.

Facing the storm's attack, Khalid jerked awake, confused as the roar followed him from his dream. He cringed against the roar until he realized it was just the waterfall crashing nearby. Swallowing hard, almost imagining his throat was caked with sand, he pushed out of his sleeping bag. He reached for his canteen. It was gone. He bolted up.

In one scan of the empty sleeping bags, like so many discarded snakeskins, he realized he had been duped. Damn her. He raised the pistol as if expecting an attack. He peered around. No sign. He glanced toward the distant smoking tunnel, where only a whispery black trace still seeped from the opening. At least he knew where she had gone.

He kicked through the scattered debris, inventorying the remains. All the lanterns were gone. Batteries too. No light source.

He reached into his pocket and pulled out his cigarette lighter. He flicked it open. A flame burst upward. It would be a fire to light his path.

A smile of determination pressed his lips flat. He would teach her. Soon she'd know his wrath and beg his forgiveness.

He would be like the black storm of his dream. Merciless and unstoppable.

TWENTY-FOUR

Ashley took a step back, wondering if her ears were playing tricks. How could this creature speak English? It had to be a coincidence, a common series of sounds that just happened to match an English word.

"*Death*," the old silver-haired creature repeated, pointing his stick and shaking it at her as if trying to get her to understand. He then planted his staff and leaned heavily on it, a saddened set to his shoulders. "*Dobori dobi!*" he finally said in a tired voice.

At his words, a gasp arose from around her, igniting a scurry of commotion. The few curious onlookers who still thronged around her scrambled away, disappearing into cave openings, cloth flaps quickly drawn across entryways. Not a single face peeked around a corner.

Only a scattering of the small creatures remained—those armed with diamond spears. And even these warriors shifted their feet nervously.

Ben spoke up beside her. "Ash, we've got trouble."

She glanced at him; his eyes were huge. "Ben?" she whispered, feeling exposed under the eyes of the creatures. "What do we do?"

"Hell if I know. You're the anthropologist."

"Maybe we should—" Ashley was interrupted by a firm stamp of the old creature's staff on the rock, demanding their attention.

"*Dobori dobi!*" The creature boomed, pointing at Ben with a long crooked finger. Then he turned and hobbled away.

"Wait!" Ben called.

The creature turned to face him, but it took much effort. He was obviously exhausted, coughing raggedly and leaning heavily on his staff.

With large, moist eyes, he stared back at Ben. He lifted a finger and placed it at the tip of his ear, then lowered his finger to the center of the design painted on his chest, just above his heart. He turned away and thumped across the empty rock to vanish into a cave opening.

"Ash, what do you make of that?"

"I'm not sure. He was trying to tell us something. But who knows what?" She swallowed hard, trying to dislodge a solid lump that had stuck in her throat. She swiveled around to check behind her. Nothing. She and Ben stood alone at the edge of the yellow fields. The cliff walls that contained the village cupped around them.

Swinging back around, she counted ten guards who remained out in the open, stationed at the ramps that led up to the second level of dwellings. No guards blocked them from just heading out into the fields.

As she was about to suggest that maybe they should just leave, try to find their own way back across the fields, a deep booming erupted from the cliff face, rhythmic and slow. The low resonant throb cut to her diaphragm, vibrating through her as if she were a plucked, bowstring. She knew even if she crammed her fingers in her ears she would still feel the sonorous beat.

"Drums," Ben needlessly explained.

She nodded. "Cultures use drums to mark ceremonial rituals." She turned to stare again across the yellow fields. Especially rituals of death, but she left that unsaid.

Ben, though, knew what the drums meant. Hell, he had watched enough Tarzan movies to know the natives were restless. Still, a strange calm enveloped him. He knew his heart should be racing, and his palms should be clammy with fear. But no, instead he felt detached as if viewing events through another's eyes. Ever since the old man had touched his finger to his chest, a sense of peace had descended upon him.

With each new drumbeat, odd thoughts intruded upon him, almost as if the drums spoke to him. *Boom* . . . Death approaches. *Boom* . . . Survive and live. *Boom* . . . One way out. *Boom* . . . Prove your blood.

"Ben?" Ashley's face appeared before him, seeming to appear out of nowhere, her voice tiny when compared to the call of the drums. She waved a hand in front of him. "Are you okay?"

"I'm fine." He shook his head. "Just trying to think."

"You were mumbling something. Something about blood."

"It's nothing."

"Are you sure you're all right?"

"Considering our predicament, I'm peachy keen." He offered her a weak smile, hoping she would swallow his lie, while wondering himself just what the hell was wrong with him. "I'm fine," he repeated.

Still she wore a worried expression on her face. "Any idea what they might be planning?" she asked while searching the cliffs for movement.

He shrugged. There might be any of a number of ways the creatures could murder them: rush at them with spears, drop boulders on them, sic those wolf creatures on them, let those damned leeches suck them dry. Who knew? He rubbed at his temples. Oddly enough, he did know. They would be attacked by air. *Death approaches*. But just how the hell did he know this?

He turned around and searched the skies above the fields, trying to see if anything was visible. Nothing but glowing fungus roofed the world. But he was sure. He even knew from which direction. He squinted his eyes to the left. Then he saw them, black specks against the greenish background glow, approaching swiftly, growing rapidly in size as they closed the distance. He pointed. "Over there, Ash. Do you see them?"

"What? Where?"

He tilted her chin until she was looking in the correct direction. "The drums must be calling them," he said. "My guess is they're acting like a dinner bell."

"What are they?" she asked.

"Something hungry. 'Cause they're coming in bloody fast!"

Ashley pointed to the gun at his waist. "How many bullets did you say you have left?"

"Only two." He scanned the horizon, counting the flying black figures. Larger than specks now, their wide wings could be seen beating the air. "I'd say there's a flock of at least fifteen aiming our way."

"So we can't shoot our way out." Ashley eyed the fields. "Maybe we could run for it. There are no guards out in the fields anymore."

"No, we'd be just sitting ducks out there. We need to find cover." Ben turned to the village. The drums had increased in fury, pounding wildly, making it harder to think clearly. He surveyed the village. All the dwelling openings were now securely covered with thick drapes. Nervous guards stationed at the ramps watched him with narrowed eyes, clutching spears tightly. No guards stood between him and a handful of openings on the ground level. He nudged Ashley and nodded to the six black openings. "How about we take cover in one of those?"

"Will the guards let us? Those spears don't seem too inviting."

"Notice they're only guarding the way up. These dwellings," he said waving an arm to encompass the six black openings, "are uncovered and unguarded."

"We'd better take a chance, then. Look!"

Ben swung around. "What the hell are they?" The flock had approached close enough to make out details.

Leathery wingspans spread several yards wide, armed with hooked black beaks and ebony talons longer than his forearm. And their eyes! Black dull orbs, unblinking, like those of a great white shark.

"Some flying predator! A descendant of the pterodactyl, maybe," Ashley said, tugging on his arm. "Let's go. They're almost on top of us. We need cover."

He tore his eyes from the approaching flock, now only fifty meters away. "Run!" he hollered as he pushed her forward. The guards made no move to stop them.

The drums suddenly stopped, the frantic pounding ceasing in a single beat, leaving only a heavy silence. He hurried his pace, struggling to keep up with Ashley.

Behind him, he heard a loud thud followed by several others, like boulders crashing to earth. The flock had landed, screeches erupting from several throats.

Ahead, Ashley had almost reached the closest opening, the five remaining black holes spread farther along the wall. Suddenly he remembered the message from the drums, almost like the words blazed across his mind's eye: *One way out!* He again studied the six openings. *Six!* And only *one way out!* He noticed a small carving above the entrance Ashley was driving toward: a circle with a triangle within it. Not the correct symbol. Wrong way!

He sped faster and tackled Ashley as she tried to duck into the opening. He rolled across the floor, jamming his shoulder as he cradled her from the fall.

She struggled free. "What're you doing?"

"No time!" He pushed up, yanking her with him. "Follow me."

"Ben! Behind you!"

He swung around, pulling his pistol free as he turned, knowing what he would find. It stood taller than an ostrich, but unlike the thin-necked bird, it was all muscle and beak. It lunged at him, striking low, trying to gut him with its hooked beak.

Bloody hell! He was getting damned tired of things trying to eat him. He fired two shots into its skull, the last at almost point-blank range. "Bugger off!" he screamed, ducking away, pulling Ashley aside.

With Ashley in tow, he sprinted across the cliff's base, searching for the correct symbol. Behind him, the beast's carcass was attacked by the others. Hot blood splashed across the back of his legs as he ran. He prayed the body would buy them the time they needed.

He continued to search. The next opening had a squiggling line with a circle atop, the next a crooked arrow, then a circle within a circle, like a doughnut. Wrong, wrong, wrong! He rushed past these openings.

Then he saw it! Carved above the next tunnel was a crude star. Like an explosion in his brain, he pictured his grandfather in his dream cave, beckoning him inside an opening with an identical star. This was the *one way out!*

He flew into the opening, dragging Ashley with him. As he tumbled into the hole, he almost crashed into a figure standing just six feet from the opening. There was just enough light to make out the design painted on his chest as he leaned on a staff. Teetering, the old man raised a tiny hand and rested it on Ben's shoulder. He growled thickly, but the words were understandable: "You are one of us."

Ashley untangled her hand from Ben's grip. What was going on? She stepped aside as the old one waved his staff to clear room. Using his staff like a crutch, he stomped between them and crossed to the lip of the entrance. He waved them over to peer out.

"Ben?" She gave him a questioning look. He shrugged at her and joined the old man. Frowning, Ashley crossed to join them, having to hunker down to get a better view.

Outside, the flock of predators had finished cannibalizing their dead companion, leaving gore and bones strewn across the rocky floor. A couple of the winged monstrosities were trying to get past the guards and up the ramp to the habitats, but spearing lances kept them at bay.

A whistle sounded from somewhere to the left, and from the other five openings, a small procession of mewling, hoofed creatures burst forth, prodded out by spears held by other tribesmen. The creatures were similar in size to a small calf but more horselike in appearance, except for the sharp curling tusks. They reared and pawed at the rock, eyes rolling white with terror. Once free of the poking spears, they scattered, darting in all directions. Their motion caught the attention of the flock, and the horny-beaked creatures tore into the herd of hoofed animals.

"If we had chosen any other tunnel but this one," Ben muttered to her, "we'd be herded out along with those animals to the slaughter. It was a test."

Ashley started to turn her face from the carnage, but not before she saw one little animal zip away from the rest and freeze, wild-eyed, just outside their cave as it spotted her. She cringed as she saw a predator pounce from behind, its hooked beak swinging forward, intending to impale the tiny creature. The creature mewled plaintively at her, its eyes wide with fear. Without thinking, she darted from the cave, snagging the nape of the terrified animal's neck, and dragged it into the cave. "Then this little one gets sanctuary too," she said, gasping, as she led the small creature deeper into the tunnel.

The old man turned to her, his eyes wide with shock. With his back to the entrance, he failed to see the open beak plunging toward him. The foiled hunter was not going to give up its prey so easily.

Ashley opened her mouth to warn him, raising an arm.

But before she could utter a sound, the old man, without even glancing over his shoulder, swung his staff backward. The crack of staff against beak echoed loudly down the tunnel; there was surprising strength in those old thin arms. Still staring at her, he mumbled to himself and crossed to her, laying a hand on her shoulder. He then nodded to her and continued deeper into the tunnel, pausing only to beckon for them to follow.

A loud clangor erupted from outside, sounding like pots and pans banging together. Ben stepped away from the entrance and crossed to her. "Now that they're fed, the noise is driving those buggers away."

"Like so many trained parakeets," she said. She stood up and followed the old man; the little animal clopped after her, mewling quietly.

Ben eyed the hoofed creature. "You could've been killed."

She said sheepishly, "It was an impulse. I was thinking that if you hadn't chosen correctly, then that could have been us out there crying for help. I couldn't just leave it out there to die." The little animal bumped against her and nuzzled at her boot as she walked.

Ben put his arm around her shoulders and squeezed. "I think you made a friend."

She leaned into Ben's arms. "Jason always wanted a pet."

Together they trudged down the darkened tunnel, lit only by occasional splashes of glowing fungus. After a few minutes, she said, "Now, tell me how you knew which was the right opening."

She felt him tense beside her. "Ash, you're gonna think I'm nuts."

"After this trip, I could believe almost anything." She stared at the back of the old creature, a creature who spoke English and whose tribe predated man by several million years. Yeah, she was feeling pretty open-minded right now.

"Okay." He took a deep breath. "Remember when I told you I had seen that symbol on the old bloke's chest before?"

"Yeah. Something about a dream of your grandfather."

"Right. Well, in that dream, my grandfather led me to a cave opening with the same symbol carved above this opening. He told me it was safe."

She stopped and stared at him. "Are you serious?"

He laughed weakly, pulling her forward. "We're alive, aren't we?"

"Have you had clairvoyant experiences before?"

"Hell, no. If I did, I wouldn't be in this trouble right now. I'd be basking in the Las Vegas sun, waiting for my next performance as Mr. Clairvoyant."

"Then why now?"

He squeaked out a nervous laugh, slipping ahead of her as they followed the old man. "I have an idea. But it's bloody creepy."

"What?"

"These dreams of this place . . . I've been having them a lot since I first got wind of this trip. They've gotten clearer and more frequent since we got down here."

"So you think it has something to do with the cavern."

"No, with him." He pointed at the old man's bare backside. "I think he's been communicating with me. When the drums began beating earlier, strange thoughts and words formed in my mind."

"Telepathy?" she said, pondering the implication. "But why only you?"

He shrugged. "I don't know. My Aboriginal blood, maybe?"

She stared up at his blue eyes and blond hair. "Considering your appearance, that blood is awful thin."

"Well, there must be enough."

"Why do you think it has anything to do with your ancestry?"

"The images in my dreams," he said, counting off his points on his fingers. "First, my grandfather appearing dressed in traditional Aboriginal garb. Then the recent recurrence of my childhood nightmare of the cave. Even the words from the drums—'prove your blood.' It all seems to point to some ability inherent in my ancestral blood."

She took a deep breath. Common sense and logic made her want to scoff at his claim. It had to be pure hogwash. Still, Ben had proven himself by selecting the right cave. She remembered a colleague who researched his doctoral thesis on Aboriginal tribes. "There is a lot of mysticism in Aboriginal lore. Spiritual walkabouts. Elders able to communicate over vast distances using dreaming pools. That sort of thing."

"Right," he said. "I thought it was mumbo jumbo myself. An Aboriginal friend that I used to cave with swore he had seen some pretty weird shit, but I never believed him."

Distracted, Ashley pushed the little hoofed creature aside as it tried to get underfoot. It bleated and took off down a side passage. "What's the connection between a previously undiscovered tribe of evolved marsupials in Antarctica and Aborigines in Australia?"

"Hell if I know. But that drawing you discovered in the cliff dwellings in Alpha Cavern—the oval with the lightning bolt through it—makes me wonder."

"What?"

"Remember when I told you I had seen them before? In Aboriginal cave paintings?"

She nodded. "Some sort of spirit guides of the Aborigines."

"Right, the ones who supposedly taught early Aborigines how to hunt. The Mimis."

The old man glanced backward at them. He mumbled something. "*Gota trif'luca mimi'swee.*"

Both Ben and she looked at each other. "You're the telepathic one," she said. "What did he say?"

Ben shrugged and shook his head.

The old one seemed to sense their confusion and sighed heavily. He pointed at his chest. "*Mimi'swee.*" He waved to encompass the entire warren of village tunnels. "*Mimi'swee.*"

"I still don't get it," Ben said.

Ashley held up a hand. "Mee . . . mee . . . swee," she stammered, concentrating on the correct pronunciation. She pointed a finger at the old man.

His old neck creaked up and down; then he turned away.

Ashley stumbled in shock. This was impossible. "He was telling us the name of his tribe. The *Mimi'swee*," she said. Then, under her breath, she uttered, "Mimis, the Aboriginal rock spirits. They're one and the same."

Ben's eyes widened with sudden understanding. Before he could say anything, the tunnel emptied into a large cavern, lit by fungus on the walls and ceiling. Ashley stared in awe at the columns supporting the distant roof, but it wasn't the rocky colonnades that drew her attention. It was the thick growth that wrapped around the columns, sprouting white limbs laden with a pulpy red fruit, hanging like Japanese lamps.

"Damn," said Ben from behind her. "Not here again."

Ben hesitated before following Ashley and their old guide into the chamber. He studied the room, expecting to hear ghost voices or see his grandfather moving in the shadows. But neither occurred. On closer inspection the fruity growths were the only similarity between this chamber and his dream cavern. The formations were all wrong, and the growths weren't nearly as thick or leafy as in his dream. Taking a deep breath, he followed Ashley's slim back.

Ashley stopped, reaching up to one of the red fruits. "I think they're a type of mushroom," she said, breathless, nodding toward the growth. "Notice the lack of leaf structure. The interconnecting root system. Hyphaelike. Linda would go ape-shit over this stuff."

"Speaking of Linda," Ben said, "this is all very fascinating, but we have friends depending on us."

"I know, Ben. I know. I haven't forgotten. Maybe with the Mimis' rudimentary grasp of our language, they can tell us a way up from here."

"Well, let's ask!"

Ashley shook her head and continued deeper after the old man. "First we need to gain their confidence. Your stunt in escaping those predators helped, but they still seem suspicious of us. Wary. We need to proceed cautiously, or we might still find our heads on the block."

By now they had reached the center of the chamber. Here the floor was clear of the rocky columns and their bulbous growths. A shallow pit was carved into the center of the floor about a hand span deep. Around the declivity, the stone was polished to a glassy sheen and blood-colored drawings encircled the central pit.

The old man leaned on his staff on the far side of the clearing.

"My god! Look at the detail!" Ashley said, leaving Ben's side to study a drawing closer up. She knelt to peer at a depiction of a creature being attacked by a group of tiny warriors. "Look, the red paint is the same color as those weird fruits. The mushrooms are probably some type of home-grown dye."

"Great," he said sarcastically. "Some freakin' artist's den."

"No, I think it's a religious place. Primitive cultures place great stock in graven images. Idols, statues, paintings, that sort of thing. Give me a few minutes to study these. Maybe I can learn something." She slid over to examine the next picture, not even bothering to glance at him.

Ben felt the stare of other eyes, like in his dream, drilling into the back of his skull. He turned around.

The old man stood on the far side, sparing only a quick glance at Ashley before settling those gray eyes back on him. The elder nodded and sat cross-legged down on the floor, his staff balanced across his knees. He motioned for Ben to do the same.

Lowering to the floor, Ben finally noticed how tired his legs were. It had to be evening by now. Late evening. With a rattling sigh, he settled to the hard floor. Stretching a kink out of his back, he allowed his body to slump into a relaxed pose. He dreamed of a tall bottle of warm beer.

Glancing up, he noticed the old man staring at him, not uttering a sound, just peering across at him with those intent gray eyes. He seemed to want something. But what?

Ben smiled across at him one of his patented "charmers" that was known to turn a crocodile into a pussycat. But the elder only frowned back at him, his gaze still expectant. Well, stuff him then, Ben thought, letting his lids drift closed as he relaxed further. He had solved enough mysteries for one day. Now he only wanted to find a soft spot to sleep. His chin slowly sank to his chest. Maybe just a nap.

He drifted into a hazy land, half aware of the tiny noises Ashley made as she scuffled from drawing to drawing. It felt so good to release the pressures of the day, allowing them to seep into the rock. His breathing deepened and a slight snore rattled from his nose. If only he could—

"Ben! Benny boy. Wake it up there, son!"

Ben's eyes snapped open. Who the hell . . . ? He still sat in the same cavern, the ring of columns and pulpy fruit surrounding him. But instead of the old creature, his grandfather sat cross-legged across the pit. He waved a liver-spotted hand in his direction. Ben glanced around. The place was otherwise empty. Not even Ashley was there. He craned his neck, peering. That was odd; he could still hear her, moving off to the left, mumbling something, but she was invisible.

"Benny, whatcha lookin' for?"

"Where am I?"

His grandfather lifted a finger crooked with arthritis and pointed to his skull. "In here, my boy."

Ben took a deep breath, his heart beginning to beat faster. This was insane. His grandfather and the chamber began to fade to blackness.

"Whoa there, boy. Ya need to calm yourself. Can't get all riled up, or this here won't work."

Swallowing hard, Ben began to get an inkling of what was going on. He concentrated on letting his body relax, starting with his toes and working up. The imagery around him intensified with clarity.

"There ya go, Benny. That's better."

He concentrated on breathing evenly and deeply as he spoke. "You're not my grandfather."

"No, I'm not." His grandfather smiled slightly, then his image slowly shrunk and swirled, his brow thickening, his eyes widening; a staff appeared resting across his knees. The swirling settled into the figure of the old crippled creature. "This is, of course, my true image. I am called Mo'amba."

The elder's voice still sounded like his grandfather. It was disconcerting to hear it coming from such an alien face. "How? Why?" Questions tumbled in his mind.

"Benny, neither of us speaks the other's language. So I speak to you with the language of the mind. My thoughts are translated by your mind into images and words you understand."

"So you stole the memory of my grandfather to represent yourself."

"Not me. You did. It was your mind that pulled up your grandfather's image to represent a *heri'huti*."

Ben pictured his grandfather's stern sober face. "And just what the devil is a *heri'huti*?"

"I am. As are you. Someone with the ability to connect on the dream plane. To see farther down the dark paths to the unknown."

"But why me?"

"I can read the history of your blood. A strong *heri'huti* glides in your bloodline from the distant past. Very strong. You are still unlearned, but with time your skill might even surpass mine. A skill that my village needs in order to survive."

"What do you mean, survive?"

"I am the last of my people with this ability," Mo'amba said, his expression suddenly pained. "With the passing of time, I have seen the other *heri'hutis* depart this world until only I was left. Now even I can't lead the hunters to feed our people and protect the boundaries from the *crak'an* anymore. The hunters go out alone. Blind. Without the guidance of a *heri'huti* to see beyond the next bend, it is very dangerous, and we have lost many hunters. Widows wail every night. We cannot survive much longer without a new *heri'huti* to guide our people." He pointed one finger at Ben. "You are the one."

"Me?"

"I have been calling for many years seeking to draw others like me here to our village. But you were the only one to answer."

"Bloody hell, there must be others. Others like . . . well, like you. Maybe another village would share their *heri'huti* with this village."

Mo'amba shook his head. "After the Scattering, the other villages were lost to us. In deep dreams, I sometimes hear inklings of the Lost Ones, but it may just be wishful dreaming rather than true dreaming."

"Still, you can't expect me to—"

Mo'amba's form drifted back into the image of his grandfather, anger lines deep around his eyes. "Blood runs true! You are one of us!"

Ben opened his mouth to protest when Ashley's voice suddenly intruded. "Ben, you must see this!"

With her words, the images around him faded, the face of his grandfather swallowed by blackness. He opened his eyes and shook his head, clearing the clinging cobwebs of his dream.

Ashley stared at him with a crinkled brow. "Jesus, how could you sleep at a time like this?"

"What?" Dazed, he rubbed his temples, a vague throbbing still there.

"Come see this," Ashley said, oblivious to what had just transpired. She crossed a few yards and knelt by a painting, waving him over.

He glanced across the clearing to the old man. He still sat staring.

With a shiver, Ben pushed up to his feet and slid over to Ashley, unsure what to tell her. "What did you find, Ash?"

"Look at this painted petroglyph. It's a triptych."

"A trip . . . what?"

"Three pictures. See the last one." Ashley crouched before three painted red circles and pointed at the third one.

Ben knelt closer, not quite believing what he was seeing. The third circle held a crude map of landmasses of the southern hemisphere. "My god, that's Australia."

"I know. It's crude but fairly accurate. Now look at the other two."

Ben studied the other two circles. The first showed the Australian continent connected to the Antarctic continent by a thick land bridge. The second showed the same huge land mass breaking away. "What about them?"

"It's the connection! It explains how the Mimis of Australia—at least some of them—ended up here."

"I still don't get it."

Ashley sighed as if she had already adequately explained. "Millennia ago, land bridges connected various continents. With the continental plates shifting and ocean levels changing dramatically, land bridges rose and sank frequently, some disappearing in a matter of months. The fossil record also supports the existence of just such a bridge. Many fossilized remains of extinct marsupial species have been found in Antarctica."

He shrugged. "So you think . . . ?"

"Yes! Look at the first map." She pointed to the link between the continents. "That's the land bridge. The second picture shows the breakup of the bridge. The third picture shows how the continents eventually became isolated."

"But how could these people know about this? Map this?"

Ashley sat back on her haunches. "They obviously lived through it. And mapped it, like the American

Indians did their coastlines. And through either an oral or pictorial history, they kept the memory alive." She pointed to both Australia and Antarctica on the third map. "They were once connected. Then something drove these people out of Australia, at least some of them. They were trapped here when the land bridge sank."

Ben studied the images, imagining a people forced to flee to the icy continent across a bridge of rock. He placed a finger on Antarctica. Two tribes separated. "My god . . . the Scattering," he mumbled. "Maybe this was what Mo'amba was talking about."

"Who?" Ashley asked, turning her nose from the middle picture.

"Ash, you better sit down for this one." He watched as she gave him her full attention, her eyebrows knitted tightly together. As he explained what had just occurred between him and the old man, her eyebrows drew apart and climbed high on her forehead.

"You mean he can speak to you!" she exclaimed when he had finished. "They *do* use some rudimentary telepathy." She glanced toward the creature seated cross-legged across from them. "Is he listening to us right now? Reading our minds?"

"I don't think so. We both have to be in a trance-like state. Like the Aborigines do with their dreaming pools when they communicate."

"And he's the last of his people with this ability?"

Ben nodded. "Besides me."

Ashley's expression became thoughtful. "From the standpoint of population genetics, the loss of this trait among the tribe makes sense. This community has been isolated for thousands of generations. The amount of inbreeding in this closed group without the infusion of fresh genetic stock would weaken the complex string of genes that creates this ability, eventually wiping it out." She turned to him, her eyes wide and glassy. "I could spend a lifetime just studying this single trait's effect on a population. It will turn the field of anthropology on its ear. I mean—"

Ben held up a hand. "Ash, that's all just fine and dandy, but we still need to get out of here. Or at least retrieve Michaelson and the others."

Ashley's expression sobered with his words. "You're right," she said, nodding. "There's plenty of time to start investigating after we get back to Alpha Base." She pointed at the sitting figure. "Did you ask Mo'amba how to get out of here?"

"No. And I don't think he'll be too cooperative. He wants me to stay. Take his place in the tribe."

"That could be a problem." Ashley started tapping the tip of her finger on her chin. "Something doesn't make sense. If you're so damned important to the tribe, why did they try to kill you?"

"I don't know."

"Apparently not everybody shares Mo'amba's view. That young buck with the ruby staff, possibly the village leader, sure as hell didn't seem to want us around. Perhaps we could—"

A sudden commotion erupted behind them. Ben turned to see a familiar figure limping toward them from between the shrouded columns. A small group of armed creatures followed, spears knocking the red mushrooms to swinging.

Ashley sprang up. "It's Michaelson!"

Ben's eyes drifted across the legion of spears that followed the major. He studied the score of armed warriors. While most of the warriors held their spears casually across their shoulders, some kept wary hands on scabbarded knives.

Stepping up to Michaelson, Ben clapped him on the shoulder. He noticed the smears of blood on his face. "What happened?" he asked. "It looks like you've been through the bloody wringer."

Ashley joined them, a worried expression frozen on her face as she looked him over for injuries.

Michaelson avoided their eyes, wearing an embarrassed expression. "It's nothin'. Most of it's not even my own blood. Besides, that's not important. Listen, we don't have much time."

The crowd of warriors stirred behind them. Michaelson glanced back. A tall figure wearing torn military fatigues elbowed his way through the crowd of warriors. As he crossed to Michaelson, Ben recognized the family resemblance. Same black hair and blue eyes. Same hooked nose.

"My brother Harry," Michaelson stated.

"You've got to be kidding," Ashley said. "You found him."

"Actually, he found me. He's been living with these . . . these creatures for the last three months."

Ben noticed Harry's eyes wander appreciatively up and down Ashley's physique. "Did you tell them?" Harry asked his brother.

"No. I was just about to."

Nodding, Harry turned to Ben and Ashley. "I'm sorry. I thought you all were refugees."

"What do you mean?" asked Ben.

Harry swallowed hard. "I thought you already knew. Or I would have tried harder to reach you sooner."

"What?" Ashley asked forcefully, trying to get Harry to spit out whatever he was holding back.

Michaelson cleared his throat. "Alpha Base. It's been destroyed. Overrun by those dinosaur things."

Ashley froze, her mouth parted with an unspoken question. Then she turned slowly to Ben, fear bright in her eyes. "It can't be," she whispered. "What about Jason?"

Ben collected her in his arms, holding her tight. "Shhh," he whispered. "I'm sure at the first sign of trouble, Blakely would have whisked him out of harm's way."

His words seemed to calm her, giving her an anchor on which to hook her hopes. Her trembling slowed, then ceased. She wiggled out of his arms, a fierce set to her jaw. "We've got to get up there. I need to know what happened."

Ben could hear the tears just behind the words. "I know. We'll leave immediately."

Harry stepped forward. "Listen, we can't just—" He jumped as a loud crack exploded behind them.

Ben whirled around to see the chief of the village cross toward them. He slammed his new staff again on the floor, the crack deafening in the chamber. "Uh-oh," Ben said under his breath. "Someone's bloody pissed."

Mo'amba struggled to rise at the sudden appearance of the village leader, heaving himself up with his staff. He shuffled across the floor to intervene. Heated words were exchanged back and forth. Finally, in a burst of growls, the chief swiped his staff across the floor, knocking Mo'amba's staff out from under him. Unsupported, the old man toppled to the floor.

A gasp arose from the warriors who circled the group. Several turned their backs. The chief eyed the others warily, his chest heaving up and down. Finally, he seemed to calm a bit and helped Mo'amba up. Quieter words were then exchanged, followed by an awkward moment of silence as they stared each other down. The chief then growled, pounded his staff on the ground as punctuation, and stomped away.

Michaelson turned to Harry. "Did you follow any of that?"

Harry nodded, his face drained of color. "Trouble."

TWENTY-FIVE

Jason knew they were in trouble when the two adults started talking in low tones. Just ahead, the tunnel passage was blocked by an old rockfall. Only a small hole the size of a pumpkin penetrated the tumbled stone. Out of this tiny hole, smoky air buffeted toward them, blowing in their faces. He stared at the two adults crouched by the rockfall.

"We can't go back," Linda said. "He'll be waiting."

"Well, then maybe we can find another way back to Alpha Base. One of the side tunnels," Blakely said, his voice wheezing in the smoky air, his eyes red and watering.

Jason looked back the way they had come. Pinching his nose against the stench, he watched the whorls of black smoke fly away from him, smoke that stank like roasted rubber tires. He could even taste its foulness on the back of his tongue. The dampened cloth wrapped around his face did little to stop the stench.

Still, no one complained, since the smoke was also their guide. For the past day, whenever they had reached a crossroads in the tunnels, pausing to decide which way to go, the smoke wafting through the passageways marked the correct path.

"Turn around? I don't know," Linda said behind him. "None of the other passages had a breeze. The air seemed stagnant."

"What other choice do we have? We can't go forward." The doctor coughed harshly. "And at least we'd get away from this damned smoke."

Jason crossed to Linda's side. "Maybe I can wiggle past the hole."

Linda gave him a weak smile. "No, honey, it's too small."

"Let me see," Jason said, squeezing between Linda and Blakely. He coughed when he got a whiff of the thick smoke coming from the opening.

Blakely put an arm around him. "Hold up, Jason. We don't know how stable that is. Besides, Linda's right. It's much too small."

Jason persisted. "Just let me see!" He shoved past Blakely's hand and crouched down. The column of smoke looked like a solid pillar jetting toward him from the opening. Pushing a fist into it, he was amazed at the pressure of the wind, like sticking his hand out of a speeding car. But his amazement turned quickly to nausea as his probing arm disrupted the flow, diverting a stream directly into his face. Gagging, he pulled his hand back out. Lights twinkled before his eyes as he gasped for clear air.

Blakely placed a hand on his shoulder, a half-amused smile on his lips. "Careful, boy, that's potent enough to kill you."

His face reddening, Jason shrugged off his hand, now even more determined to investigate the hole. Before anyone could stop him, he sucked in a lungful of air and clamped his eyes and lips closed. Then he dove forward into the smoky wind.

He found himself almost instantly buffeted back by the pressure, but he dug his toes in beneath him. Working one arm and shoulder through the hole, he wiggled around, seeking a way to crawl ahead.

If he could just turn his head and twist over this way . . . but rock blocked him at every turn. In a few seconds, he realized it was much too small for him to squeeze through. Disappointed, he pulled back and rolled to the side, letting out his held breath in a long sigh.

He saw Blakely waving his hand before his nose as the disturbed smoke billowed around him. "A lot of good that did you. You almost gassed the two of us with your foolishness."

"But I was just—"

"Enough of this tomfoolery. We just need to accept our predicament and find an alternate route. This tunnel is a dead end for us."

Jason sniffed, trying to save face. "But I did find out that the hole is only about two feet deep. After that it widens again. I think the tunnel is fine beyond this short section. If we can find a way through . . ."

"Well, unless you happen to be hiding a pickax under your shirt, I'm afraid that's not much help."

Jason, finally defeated, hung his head.

Linda laid a consoling hand on his knee. "Hey, at least you tried. And besides, there's no harm done. Heck, if I had been any smarter, I could've stolen a cube of Khalid's plastic explosive. We could have blasted our way out." She lifted his chin with a finger. "I'm very proud of you."

Jason tried to suppress a smile but couldn't stop it. "Thanks."

She tousled his hair, then turned back to Blakely. "I guess we've no choice but to search for an alternate route."

Blakely mumbled something in response, but Jason had stopped listening. Instead, Linda's words repeated in his mind: Cubes? Explosives? He stood up. Could it be?

He crossed to where Linda huddled in conversation with Blakely and tugged on her sleeve. Linda glanced at him, and Blakely frowned down, his eyes narrowed with irritation at his intrusion.

"What is it, Jason?" she said, pushing back a strand of blond hair.

He shifted his feet. "Um, Linda, that explosive you were talking about. I think I may have some of it."

Blakely stepped forward. "What? How?"

Linda placed a restraining hand on Blakely's arm. "Jason, why do you think you have some explosive?"

Scuffing the toe of his sneaker on the rocky floor, not looking anyone in the face, Jason explained about the incident in the bathroom when Khalid's bag spilled into his cubicle. "I have it in my gym bag," he finished, pointing to the red Nike bag at his feet. "I'll show you."

He unzipped the bag and rummaged through it. He should have told someone. Now he was going to get into trouble. He shifted the contents of the pack around. It was difficult to search, full of gym clothes, an orange towel, a pack of playing cards that had fallen loose, and scattered loose change for the video-game machine. Where was it?

After a full minute, Blakely exclaimed in exasperation, "Just dump it on the floor." He tried to take the bag from Jason.

"Wait!" Jason pulled his Nintendo Game Boy from the bag. "It'll break." He shoved the Game Boy in his jacket pocket.

The doctor overturned the bag and shook it. All his stuff tumbled to the floor. The three of them searched through his loot.

Jason carefully tucked his spare pair of underwear out of sight, mortified that Linda might see his boxers. As he was hiding it under his towel, he spotted the familiar gray material.

Picking up the clay, he held it out to Linda. "Here it is."

With a whisper of a smile on her lips, she accepted the sculpted clay, eyeing his handiwork. "Nice airplane."

He shrugged. "I thought it was some sort of hard Play-Doh."

Blakely looked on with disbelief. "Are you sure it's the explosive?"

Linda fished a piece of crinkled cellophane from his belongings. "Yes, this is the same cellophane that wrapped the other cubes."

Blakely took the airplane from her as if handling the most fragile piece of expensive art. "Okay, we've got an explosive, but nothing to detonate it with. We need a blasting cap."

"What's that?" Jason asked.

Blakely just frowned at him, but Linda explained, "They're little explosives that set off the chunk of plastic explosive."

"Like fireworks?"

"That would do the trick," Blakely answered, "but we're not going to find any fireworks stands down here."

Fumbling through the side pouch of his bag, Jason pulled out the little red cherry bomb he'd hidden from prying eyes. "Will this work?"

Linda stared at it. "Do you think . . . ? Will it work?"

Blakely nodded, grinning. "I believe so."

She returned his grin, then turned and hugged Jason. "You're just full of surprises, little man."

Jason blushed purple. "Just don't tell my mom about the cherry bomb. She'd kill me."

Khalid crouched by the fork in the tunnels, leaning first into one, then into the other. He sniffed, like a cur on a trail. The left-hand tunnel had a subtle sting to the air, causing a slight burning in the nose. Smoke. He proceeded left, holding his lighter before him. He had been careful to twist the controls to set the flame at its lowest setting, creating only a feeble flicker, conserving the butane in his lighter. If it should run out, he would be blinded, unable to complete his mission. He had to pamper his tiny flame.

In the stygian darkness, even this small flame was enough to light the way for several meters. He marched steadily ahead, not wasting time to rest. There was no way of judging how much farther Linda and her group might be. But there were clues he was heading in the right direction: footprints in mud, a wrapper from a ration bar, a spot where someone had stopped to urinate, the ammonia odor still pungent. He was close.

His mind wandered as he raced along the monotonous tunnels, allowing his trained body to continue its pursuit, stepping around pitfalls, leaping crevices, climbing over boulder-strewn obstructions, hell-bent on narrowing the gap.

Linda pushed Jason farther back around the tunnel's curve, praying that Blakely knew what the heck he was doing. It was quite possible the entire tunnel system could collapse on them. Still, she knew they had to take the risk. To go back only invited disaster.

"I wanna watch," Jason said.

"No, honey. It's dangerous. Here, put in your ear-plugs." She handed him two cotton balls from their first-aid kit. "And when I tell you, cover your ears and open your mouth."

"Why?"

"The explosion is going to be dangerously loud. It can damage your eardrums."

Jason fidgeted. "I still want to watch."

Blakely suddenly appeared before them, slightly winded. "All set. I've shaped the charge to blow away from us. Are you ready?"

Linda nodded. "How good a shot are you?"

"Okay, but with this pressure . . ." He shrugged.

"You only have the one shot."

He raised the flare gun. "I know." The cherry bomb had been embedded in the plastic explosive, and the plan was to ignite it with the flare from a safe distance. He waved them back farther.

She nudged the boy behind her. "Good luck."

Blakely swiped his damp brow with the edge of his sleeve, then took a few steps down the tunnel to get a straight shot. She noticed his lips had a purple tinge to them. The stress and the foul air were worsening his heart condition. Watching as he plugged his ears with cotton, she admired his tenacity. He then gave her a thumbs-up sign and leveled the flare gun.

She pantomimed to Jason to cover his ears and open his mouth. He did as instructed but kept trying to peek around her to see where the doctor stood.

With her ears covered, she heard the pop of the flare gun, sounding like a toy, then saw Blakely lower his gun. Nothing happened.

He turned to her, shrugging, and opened his mouth to speak when the explosion occurred. The wind seemed to precede the noise. She watched as Blakely was suddenly blown backward by the concussion, flying off his feet, colliding with the wall.

Before she could move to help, she too was thrown down the tunnel, landing on top of Jason. The cracking roar washed over her like an invisible freight train barreling past, the noise so loud that her mind tried to turn it off. First the boom, then nothing but a dull ringing. Dust and smoke poured down the tunnel, choking her, leaving her and Jason isolated in a sphere of her helmet light. Walls of swirling dust swallowed them up.

She helped Jason to his feet. He held his elbow and winced, but otherwise he seemed unharmed. Dazed, she wasn't even sure which direction led back to Blakely. He could be hurt. She unhooked her hand lantern, hoping its additional light would penetrate the darkness better than just her helmet lamp. She swept the beam through the dusty air. Nothing.

Jason pointed with one hand, while pulling cotton out of his ears. "Over there. I think I see a light."

She now saw it too, a glow of light bouncing her way. She let out a relieved breath. She hurried over to check on Blakely, hoping that the way forward was now clear.

"Wait!" Jason suddenly yelled, pulling on her arm to halt her.

She glanced down at him. "What?" She then looked back as the figure penetrated the smoke, lunging into her sphere of light. It wasn't Blakely. She stumbled a step backward. No!

He held a lighter aloft in one hand and a pistol in the other, blood drizzling down his right cheek from a gash at his temple. "How appropriate that a thunderclap should precede my storm," Khalid said, then aimed the pistol at Linda's chest.

Blakely groaned, pain flaring red in his chest. His first thought was that it was his heart again, but he noticed that the pain worsened as he inhaled and retreated as he exhaled. Broken rib, he thought. He ran his hand over his right side. Just below his armpit, a lump of agony confirmed his suspicion. Definitely broken, but only one of them. Damn, like he didn't have enough problems already. He leaned his head back on the wall, closed his eyes, and pulled the damp handkerchief back over his nose. Although it stank of mucus and sweat, it was better than inhaling the air stirred by the blast.

He would wait for the dust to settle, then let Linda help wrap his chest before they continued forward. He sighed, meaning to relax, but a sudden fear opened his eyes again. What if the blast hadn't cleared enough of the rock to allow them passage, or worse yet, just collapsed the tunnel further? What if he had broken his rib for nothing? He needed to know.

Grimacing, teeth clenched against the pain, he reached to his waist for his flashlight. He popped it from his belt with a wince. Any motion felt like someone was jabbing him with a dull spear—and twisting it mercilessly! Struggling against the pain, he raised the light and clicked it on. The beam shot forward but was blocked by the eddying rock dust and smoke. He could not see beyond ten feet.

Maybe if he could move just a few yards forward he could examine the explosion site. What if he had screwed up in shaping the charge? No, he couldn't have. He had done just like Hans, the German demolition expert for Alpha Base, had shown him.

There was only one way to find out. He carefully pushed up to his feet; the pain flared worse but only to a point that raised tears in his eyes. He could stand it for a short time. He took a deep breath, girding himself for the painful journey forward. Just before he took his first step, he heard a raised voice echo from behind him. It was Linda. Good, at least she was okay. He pointed his light toward the voices. His lamp revealed only black smoke, and the dull ringing in his ears blocked out all but the loudest noises. He shook his head, swinging his light back toward the bomb site. They'd be joining him shortly.

He took a step forward, meaning to check the blast site before they returned. The increased motion burrowed the spear of pain deeper in his side. Cautiously he took shallow breaths, knowing that a broken shard of rib bone could slice into his lungs.

After taking two more steps, he stopped to rest, his brow now dripping with sweat. This wasn't good for his heart either, but desperation pushed him on. Besides, if he had screwed up in placing the charge, he wanted to be the first to know.

Following the trail of debris with his light, he saw the wall of rock that had blocked the way forward and smiled. A gaping maw large enough to pass a baby elephant through now opened the way ahead.

From behind him, a pistol shot suddenly echoed down the tunnel. Not thinking, Blakley jumped and twisted at the retort. A whiplash of searing fire ripped into his chest as he turned. His flashlight beam dimmed to a flicker as the pain blackened his field of vision, threatening to overwhelm him.

He took a step forward, his arms wrapped around his chest trying to squeeze back the pain. He coughed into the handkerchief over his face, triggering a spike of agony that sent him to his knees. Smelling his own blood in the sputum, he tore the handkerchief from his face in disgust. Pinpoints of lights cartwheeled across his vision as he fought oblivion.

A second shot rang out.

Linda winced as the bullet ricocheted off the rock over her head and zinged past her ear. Khalid stood coolly before her, punctuating his words with blasts from his pistol, pocking the walls with glancing shots. She placed a hand on Jason's head, trying to reassure him as he cowered behind her.

Khalid spoke slowly. "I had hoped that you would recognize the importance of my mission."

"Khalid," Linda began. Her words were sticking in her throat, but she had to try to reason with him. "You left me no choice. I couldn't let you abandon them, leaving them to die."

Quicker than she could react, Khalid lunged at her, shoving her aside, and grabbed Jason's arm, pulling him free of her. Set off balance, she slipped and fell to the floor, landing hard on her knee.

"Don't, Khalid!" she pleaded, tears welling in her eyes. "Please. I'll do anything."

For a moment, he seemed to hesitate, his pistol wavering. Then he clutched Jason tight to his chest, pressing the muzzle of his pistol to Jason's temple. The boy's eyes were wide with fear but dry, his lips pale. He squirmed, but Khalid knew how to restrain a hostage; even with Jason's frantic wiggling, the muzzle never shifted from his temple. She realized there was no hope.

Suddenly . . . "Leave the boy alone!" Blakely stumbled into view, startling Linda. Even Khalid jumped slightly, backing a step away.

Blakely leaned with one arm on the wall of the tunnel; the other held the flare gun pointed at Khalid. Linda knew it was an empty threat—the gun already spent—but Khalid didn't know. She allowed herself a small hope. She saw blood dribble from the doctor's lips, heard his labored breathing. The blow from the explosion must have hurt him badly. "I said," he wheezed, "leave the boy alone . . . Release him." The flare gun swung circles in his weakening grip.

Blakely stepped between Linda and Khalid. "Now!"

Khalid seemed to cower from the gun. Then, like a striking cobra, he burst forward, knocking the gun from Blakely's hand with a swipe of his pistol. "Empty threats are dangerous, Doctor. I watched you use the flare to blow the opening." Khalid nodded toward the blasted tunnel. "Thank you, by the way."

Blakely coughed and slumped against the wall, his lips narrowed and blue from pain and exhaustion. He turned to Linda, fresh blood flowed from his lips. "I'm sorry," he whispered.

She crossed to Blakely as Khalid backed away, clutching Jason with the pistol jammed to his temple again. She checked the doctor's pulse, weak and thready. He needed immediate medical attention. She turned to Khalid where he had backed about several feet away.

"Please, stop this," she begged. "We can all leave together. There's no reason anyone has to die. Let the boy go."

Staring at her, Khalid did the most amazing thing: He leaned down and placed his gun on the ground. For a moment, her heart soared. As he stood, however, he removed another small gun from a hidden holster above his boot. He pressed this new gun against Jason, whom he still held tight to his chest, the boy's arms pinned within the circle of Khalid's arm.

"You want the boy to live?" Khalid said, his eyes narrow. He kicked the gun toward Linda. "Kill the doctor."

She stared at the pistol as if it were something toxic, afraid to touch it. "What are you talking about?" she said, turning her eyes up to Khalid.

"We're carrying too much dead weight here. I'll take either the boy or the doctor with us. You choose. There's one bullet left. I want you to shoot Blakely, or I'll kill the boy."

"No!" she cried, backing away from the gun.

"Then the boy dies. It's your choice. I am only the instrument."

"Khalid . . . please," she said, tears flowing, "don't make me do this."

Blakely spoke up. "Pick up the gun." His words were so plain and calm that she found herself reaching for it before she realized it. She froze, her hand hovering over the grip.

"Do it!"

She snatched up the gun. It was still hot to the touch from the rounds already fired. She cradled it between her two hands, afraid to trust only one hand. She glanced up at Khalid.

As if reading her mind, Khalid warned, "You have a single shot, my dear. Even if you manage to hit me, the boy would be dead before you could squeeze the trigger."

Her shoulders slumped. "Why?" she asked in a small voice. "Why do this to me?"

"I need help. And I need obedience. I will teach you how to obey."

"I can't," she said. "I can't just kill someone like that."

"Listen," Blakely said, his voice hoarse and moist. "You've got to do this." Now in a whisper, "You need to buy some time. He's going to kill us all anyway."

"But . . ."

He coughed. Tears welled in his eyes; lines of pain etched his features. "Do it. I'm not going to make it anyway."

"I . . . I still can't," she whispered, her head falling to her chest.

Blakely reached to her, placing a hand on her head, whispering in her ear, "My wife died four years ago. My kids have grown up. I've bounced seven grand-kids on my knee. I've lived a full life. But Jason's is just starting." He lifted her head, then picked up her hands that held the gun. He placed the gun in one of her palms and raised her hand, positioning the muzzle against his forehead. "Be strong, Linda."

"No, please, no," she cried, tears flowing down her cheeks.

He closed his eyes, still holding up her hand with his own. Hidden from view, she felt his finger push hers off the trigger. "I know," he whispered. "I won't let the bastard win." His finger replaced hers on the trigger. She felt his finger twitch, and the blast and recoil jumped the gun from her hands. It clattered to the ground, smoke trailing from its muzzle.

Stunned, she froze in place, her hands still raised as if she held the gun. Blakely had slumped over to his side, staring blankly at the far wall, a hole the size of a dime in his forehead. The wound looked so small, like a simple bandage would fix it.

"No," she moaned, rocking back and forth, "no, no, no . . ."

Suddenly Jason ran up beside her, hugging her from behind. Khalid had released the boy. Jason held her silently, staring at Blakely's still form with wide eyes.

Linda turned to Khalid; his pistol was pointed at her. "You promised that you wouldn't harm the boy."

"I won't," he said. His words were cold, devoid of any concern for the dead man sprawled in the tunnel. "Unlike yours, my word is good. But it's now time for your next lesson."

"You can't keep me tied up for the whole trip," Linda protested. Her attempts to loosen the knots that bound her only tightened their cutting grip.

"You're clever, Linda," Khalid said, smirking at her effort to free herself. "And we still have a long way to go to reach Alpha Base. I won't lose you again." He grabbed Jason by the upper arm and manhandled him down the tunnel. "You can be sure of that."

Frightened that he intended some harm to Jason, she called after him, "What are . . . You promised not to hurt him."

"Don't worry. I'll keep my word." He disappeared around a bend.

She stared at the tunnel around her, her heart beating so hard in her throat she could hardly breathe. What did he have in mind now? She gave one final pull on the cords that gripped her.

She searched around her, the helmet lamp casting only a weak finger of light. At least the smoke had thinned, allowing them to breathe without masks, but there were still enough fumes to sting the eyes and nose.

Swinging her helmet the other way, she tried to see some sign of what Khalid was planning. She heard an occasional word or echo from where he and Jason had disappeared. What was he up to?

Almost two hours passed before she finally heard the scrape of boot on rock, signaling the return of Khalid and Jason. Exhausted, she had almost dozed off. It had to have been at least forty hours since she had last slept.

"Are you okay, Jason?" she asked.

He nodded but had a strange expression on his face.

Khalid crossed to her and loosened her bonds, freeing her hands. "I'll set up camp," he said. "We'll stay here for six hours, then continue."

Rubbing at her red wrists, she noticed Khalid did not have his gun. Strange, she had not seen him without a pistol clutched in his hand since Blakely's death. He turned his back on her and walked away, leaving her and Jason alone. His lack of concern jarred her. She could just grab Jason and run, but she knew better than to try; he would just track them down again. Still, this sudden lack of caution disconcerted her.

She knelt down by Jason. "Did he hurt you?"

"No, but . . . I couldn't stop him." Jason suddenly burst into tears.

She hugged him tight. "What is it, Jason? Tell me."

His sobbing subsided into spasms of quivering. "He . . . he . . . I don't wanna die!"

She just held him tight, allowing him to calm on his own. After several minutes, he sniffed back his final tears. "I'll get you out of here. I promise," she told him. She hoped it was a promise she could keep. "Now take a deep breath and tell me what happened."

He hung his head, then lifted up his shirt. She cringed a bit, expecting him to reveal some form of physical molestation by Khalid. But what Jason revealed was worse.

"My god!" Linda gasped. "What did he do to you?"

Jason cautiously fingered the black nylon belt strapped tight around his waist, cutting snug into his white belly. Bulges of gray plastic explosive dotted the belt, connected from one to the other by multicolored wires. She stared closer at the large belt buckle. A lighted LED panel with a small keyboard the size of a business card was attached to the clasp. A twisted bundle of colored wires converged into the device. Tiny red numbers counted backward on the display.

"Why?" Linda mumbled to herself.

"He said it was an obedience lesson," Jason answered. "Every two hours, Khalid has to punch in a secret code, or the bomb will go off. And if I try to take the belt off, it'll explode."

Linda's shoulders sank. "The bastard. So we're dependent on him. If we leave or something happens to Khalid, then . . ." She stopped.

"Then I'll explode," Jason finished. "He told me it wouldn't hurt."

"He explained all this to you! What sort of monster is he?"

Jason answered in a tiny voice, "A smart one."

TWENTY-SIX

Ashley tugged on Harry's sleeve, noticing how much like Major Michaelson he looked, especially when he wore a stern expression like now, his lips pinched, a deep trough between his eyebrows. "What the hell were they arguing about?" she asked.

Mo'amba had already followed the chief out of the chamber, and a good portion of the warriors had vanished in different directions. She glanced around her. A small cadre of spear-bearing tribesmen still surrounded them, their expressions wary.

"What sort of trouble are we in now?" she asked, turning her attention back to Harry.

He eyed the guards from between narrowed lids, then spoke. " 'Trouble' is too mild a word. They've decided that you two are still to die."

Ashley's eyes grew wide. "But why? What about you and Michaelson?"

"We've been adopted by the warrior sect. The group's got a strict honor code—*il'jann,* they call it. Not even the elders will mess with it. You two, on the other hand, are foreigners. Scapegoats."

Ashley glanced toward Ben. She should be terrified for her own life, but it was her son's fate that kept her chest tight and made breathing difficult. She couldn't die . . . not until she knew Jason was safe.

Ben kept watching the naked warriors around them, but she managed to catch his eye. He reached over and squeezed her arm. "I know, I know," he said, as if reading her mind. "We're going to get out of this, and we'll find Jason."

Ashley took a deep breath and turned to Harry. "What about Mo'amba?"

Harry shook his head. "The leader, Bo'rada, swayed the rest of the tribe against you. But you've gotta give it to the ol'guy. Mo'amba was able to get a full council hearing before the sentence is carried out—but just barely. It's scheduled for tomorrow morning."

Ben stepped up. "What if we make a break for it tonight?"

Shaking his head, Harry sighed. "You'd never make it. Too many snares, booby traps, and beasts out there.

Even if you managed to slip past unharmed, these little guys know this territory. Your throats would be slit before you heard 'em coming."

Ben rubbed his temples. "Well, bloody hell if they're getting my head without a fight. I'll—"

Ashley interrupted. "Harry, will we be given a chance to speak at this council hearing?"

"I suppose so."

"Can you translate for me?"

"Yeah, sure. It may be crude, but I'll do my best."

"Good. They've been acting hostile with us, but from the petroglyphs, they seem normally to be a be-nevolent society. Communal. Everyone sharing, the weak and lame supported, almost like a big family."

"They did take me in as one of their own," Harry agreed.

Ashley nodded. "Something's shaken them up and put them on edge. If we can discover what that is, maybe we can save our skins."

"And what if we can't?" Ben muttered.

Ashley's voice went cold. "Then we fight."

A gong suddenly sounded from somewhere deep in the village, almost vibrating the very rock. As if on cue, the group was shuffled by the armed guards through a warren of tunnels to another large chamber. Ben and Ashley were herded within, and several guards posted themselves at the portal, ensuring they did not wander back out.

Harry spoke to her from the doorway. "Dennis and I must spend the night in the warrior's den, but I'll make sure I'm here first thing in the morning. Maybe we can talk some sense into them."

"Make sure you're here," Ben said. "I was never good at charades."

Ashley watched as the brothers left. Then she turned to survey the room. Spread around the chamber were yard-wide pillows with folded blankets atop them, each in a different pattern of weave and hue. At the corners of the room, stone water basins dotted the floor.

"I guess this is our cell," Ben said, kicking one of the pillows.

Ashley nodded, her arms folded across her chest. After all the commotion of the day, she felt numb.

Ben put his arm around her. "We're gonna be fine," he said, his words so quiet and soft-spoken that she looked up at him, as if expecting someone other than Ben to be standing there. Where was his usual loud bravado? He squeezed her shoulder and stood quietly, supporting her.

"I'm so worried about Jason," she said, leaning into his embrace. "This not knowing is agony. What if—"

Ben laid a finger across her lips. "Shhh. Your boy's fine." Again his words were so firm and plain that she found herself believing him. She looked into his serious blue eyes; no longer were they the laughing eyes of the jester. It would be so easy to lose herself in him, just let those wide shoulders carry her burdens and worries for a time.

Old emotional wounds surfaced, willing her to protest, but before she could utter a word, Ben leaned over and replaced the finger brushing her lips with his own mouth, his lips pressing steadily, refusing to allow her to voice her misgivings. Only a small moan escaped her.

Then his lips slid down to her throat, his stubbled cheek brushing past her cheekbone as he sought the tender angle at the base of her neck. Losing herself in the gentle strength of his embrace, she arched her head back, offering her neck more fully to him.

For just a moment he paused, raising his eyes to look into hers, his ruddy cheeks flushed with passion. She knew this was her last chance. She could stop him now, his eyes said. For a frightened moment she froze, wary of releasing herself so fully to him, opening herself once again to the possibility of pain and abandonment.

Seeming to sense her fear, he pulled back slightly, the fire in his eyes dimming to a warm concern. Never had she encountered a man so passionate . . . yet at the same time so compassionate. She watched her own hand reach up and tangle itself in his thick hair. She pulled him to her, as if she were a drowning woman, struggling to fight to the surface.

Entwined in his arms, she allowed herself to be lifted and gently lowered to the pillowed floor.

Ben stared at the rocky ceiling, sleep still escaping him. Ashley lay curled at his side, an arm draped across his chest, a leg thrown over his belly. As she stirred in some dream, her tiny motions awakened a thickening heat. He had to resist rolling toward her and seeking once again to explore the depth of their passion. He knew she needed sleep. The next day would hold many challenges. Still . . . he couldn't resist reaching over and tracing a finger down the curve of her right breast. She moaned softly in her sleep.

Just as he reached to kiss her temple, a blackness suddenly slipped over him like a heavy blanket. He fell back into the darkness, away from the light and Ashley.

Then a voice startled him: "It's about time, Benny boy!"

The darkness flared into the image of his grandfather sitting cross-legged on a pillow only a few feet away. Groaning, Ben sat up. As he tried to focus on his granddad, the figure melted into the image of Mo'amba.

The old one nodded to him. "I've been waiting a bloody long time for you to hear my calling."

Clearing his throat, Ben looked down at his naked self, his body still prominently trumpeting his passion. He covered himself with his hands. "I've been busy."

Mo'amba cleared his throat. "I think three times is more than enough. It's time we talk."

Ben pulled a blanket over his lap. "You're right. I have a lot of questions for you. Like why in bloody hell does your leader want our heads?"

"He and the village are scared. Many have died. The *crak'an* have increased their forays into our territory, wiping out entire herds of our food animals, surprising our sentries with their sudden appearance deep in our territory, killing many of them."

"So what does that have to do with us?"

"For countless generations, our people and the *crak'an* have struggled. After the Scattering of our people, they became stranded here with us. When we first sought shelter here in the underworld to escape them and the cold, they followed us down. Eventually a great cataclysm shut off the upper world, trapping all of us down here together."

"How did you survive?"

"We adapted. Where you designed machines and iron tools to help your life, we designed living tools— plants and animals to help us. Through study, we learned to select those aspects of both that would best suit our needs, then propagated them. We learned to grow food." He pointed to the walls. "Even to grow light to guide us. We adapted. But the *crak'an* did not. They have haunted our periphery, living off the dregs of our work. But don't get me wrong, they are cunning. Constantly probing our defenses, trying to find a breach through to us."

"With all your smarts, why didn't you just make a concerted effort to wipe them out? Be done with them."

Mo'amba shook his head. "We must not. Just as they need us to survive, we need them. Their spoor contains a substance that we need to grow our food. Without it, the plants would die. And then we would die. We actually herd our aging milk animals, those no longer producing well, into the *crak'an*'s territory to feed them."

"You feed those monsters? No wonder there are so many of them."

"We must maintain their numbers to produce enough spoor. It is the main goal of our hunters to collect the spoor and bring it back here."

"Shit collectors," Ben said. "So much for the noble hunter image."

"They are noble. They risk much to venture into the realm of the *crak'an*. Especially now without the aid of a *heri'huti*'s sight." The old one looked meaningfully at him.

"Let's not bring up that argument again," Ben said, fearful that Mo'amba would again demand that he stay and help this village, a village that right now wanted him dead. "So you still haven't told me why this bloody death sentence hangs over our heads."

"I was getting to that. You see, we have for generations honed our tools to keep the *crak'an* in check, away from the center of our lives. One of our main defenses is the *tin'ai'fori*. It—"

Ben waved a hand. "Hold on a sec. What's that?"

Mo'amba pressed his lips together thoughtfully, his eyes narrowing. "You don't have a word for it." He reached behind him and scraped a sample of the glowing fungus from the wall. "It is a special type of this. But it kills. We have surrounded this central cavern with a thick perimeter of *tin'ai'fori*. It protects our village."

"So how come these monsters—um, *crak'an*— are now able to get through and attack you all of a sudden?"

"The answer is a secret known only to the warrior sect and the leaders." Mo'amba cleared his throat, his voice lowered slightly as if someone might be eavesdropping. "The *tin'ai'fori* is dying. Slowly now the edges of our defenses have blackened and fallen away, thinning the barrier between the *crak'an* and us. Eventually this barrier will crumble."

Ben imagined flocks of the beasts sweeping into the sheltered valley. Even though he had been given a death sentence by these people, he still shivered at the thought of the carnage. "So what has all this to do with us?"

"The *tin'ai'fori* began dying soon after the arrival of your people."

"What! How?"

"I don't know. A few of the warriors and I believe it is a sign. A portent that it is time for us to move back to the upper world. But many others believe you are demons meant to destroy us."

"And I suppose your chief is one of these believers?"

Mo'amba nodded. "As are most others."

"So how're we going to persuade him otherwise? I don't expect the word of a demon will mean much to him."

"No, it won't. So tomorrow you must follow my lead. Your companion, Harry, will help. Unknown to him, I have been teaching him the rudiments of our language during his dreamtime. Helping him learn our tongue. Listen to him."

"But what are you planning?"

Mo'amba's figure faded away as contact was broken, raising a hand in farewell. "*Tomorrow.*"

TWENTY-SEVEN

T he next morning, Ashley paced the floor of the room, still struggling with the information Ben had received from Mo'amba, their only ally among these people. How could they fight superstition? Like so many missionaries who had been killed by superstitious natives in hidden corners of the world, she found herself wondering how this could be happening.

Ben stepped close to her and hugged her from behind, nuzzling his chin next to hers. "You're gonna wear a track in the floor if you keep pacing like that," he said.

She sighed. He was right; there was nothing she could do now but wait. Her mind switched to another concern. "Listen, about last night."

"Hmmm?" He squeezed her closer to him.

"I was . . . well, I mean . . . just because we . . . I don't expect that you should . . . you know . . . it was just a moment."

"Listen, lady, don't try an' wiggle out of this. I'm no one-night stand. Do you think you can just use me up and toss me out?"

She smiled thinly and slipped out of his grip, suddenly uncomfortable with his intimacy. Was he as sincere as he sounded? How many other men had vowed perpetual commitment, only to vanish from her bed and disappear into the night? And what about her ex-husband? Scott had sworn devotion and love just as sincerely, and look what had become of that. She placed a hand on her belly, remembering the pain and her loss.

She stepped away from Ben, trying to ignore his wounded eyes. "We need to make a plan. Just in case we can't talk our way out. Michaelson still has his backpack of weapons. We should—"

A commotion at the entryway to the chamber interrupted her. Twisting around, she saw Harry push through the guards. Michaelson limped behind him, using one of the spears as a makeshift crutch. Ashley secretly sighed in relief at the interruption, glad to have others around to dilute the intimacy of the moment.

She cleared her throat. "Harry, have you heard anything?"

He nodded. "I've been up all night, prying information out of some of the local gossips. They've got this type of rotgut booze made from some type of mold—tastes like warm toothpaste. But hell, a buzz is a buzz."

"Get on with it," Ben prodded gruffly. "We don't have all bloody day."

Ashley glanced at him. It was unlike Ben to snap at people like that.

Harry blinked a few times, obviously tired, or maybe even a bit hungover. "Anyway, this little libation loosened a few tongues. It seems that everyone thinks you're killing their precious fungus."

Ashley nodded. "We know all about that."

His eyebrows shot up. "How the heck—"

"Never mind that now. What have you heard about the council meeting? Will we be given a chance to defend ourselves?"

Harry looked at her quizzically. "Rumor has it that Mo'amba will plead your case. Even though he's old, he's someone many don't want to cross. So we might have a pea-sized chance to dissuade them."

"But we still need a backup plan." She glanced over to Michaelson, noticing he still carried his holstered pistol. "How's our armament?"

He slapped his holster. "This, a stubbed AK-47, and my collapsible rifle back in Harry's room."

"What are the odds of shooting our way out of here?"

"I wouldn't bet a plugged nickel. I've seen the council chamber. It's deep in the village. It's doubtful we'll make it to the outside. And even if we should manage, we still have to find our way back up."

Ashley frowned. "Then we'd better be damned persuasive."

Drums began beating a slow cadence somewhere far off. The guards stirred at the door. One of them barked an order.

Harry turned to her. "It's showtime."

The first thing Ashley noticed about the council chamber was the floor. The rock had been polished to a mirrored sheen that gave it a slippery appearance, like black ice. The floor sloped to a small bowllike pit in the center of the chamber. Positioned in a circle around the room, like guards, were stone pillars, polished to the same silky smoothness. Ropes of fungus, some glowing red, some green, trailed in loops and spirals down the shafts of the pillars in delicate designs. Similar designs in phosphorus lines etched the walls.

Eight tufted pillows, each of a different color, ringed the central pit. Ashley raised an eyebrow at the scooped depression. This was the only nonpolished area of the chamber, looking as if it had been crudely chopped out of the rock. Her mind, even spinning with fears for Jason and trepidation for herself and Ben, was still that of an anthropologist. It kept gnawing at the many mysteries of these people. Like just what was the cultural significance of these pits? Almost every chamber, even those at Alpha Base, had one of these dugout spots. She had originally dismissed them as mere firepits, but after seeing how these creatures lived, she no longer believed this. She had yet to see even one flaming hearth. With the many boiling springs, the volcanic heat, and the scarcity of wood, she did not see the cultural necessity for so many firepits. So what the hell were they?

A hand, one of the guards', pushed her from behind. She stumbled into the chamber.

Ben nudged her. "Looks like we're the first to arrive."

Ashley moved aside to allow Harry to enter. Michaelson, with his injured ankle, had detoured back to the hunter's enclave to retrieve his weapons and ready them. The major's pistol dug into the small of her back where she had shoved it into her belt, hidden by her loose-hanging shirt. Just in case things went sour, they could use the gun to reach the hunters' area and join up with Michaelson . . . and his arsenal.

One of the tribe entered from another doorway, carrying an amethyst-tipped staff. Her pendulous breasts marked this one as female, and from the bulge in her belly, most likely pregnant. She crossed to kneel on one of the pillows, guards flanking her on either side. She ignored Ashley and her group, avoiding eye contact as she lowered to her pillow.

She did, however, acknowledge with a small nod the next creature to enter the chamber. He was difficult to look at, with a missing hand and a jagged scar ripping across his face. His left leg dragged slightly as he crossed to a purple pillow and collapsed with a loud sigh.

Harry stirred next to Ashley. "That's Tru'gula. He's the head of the warrior clan. He may look a mess, but he's a sharp one."

Harry's words, though merely whispered in her ear, apparently carried to Tru'gula. He gave them a stern heavy-browed look. Harry stepped away from Ashley, remaining silent as a procession of staffed figures eventually filled the remaining empty pillows. Soon, many armed guards lined the walls around them. Ashley shifted, trying to work the hidden gun into a comfortable position. Even though it dug into her back, there was a certain security in its pressure.

Mo'amba passed close by Ashley's side as he thumped over to his red-and-yellow-checkered pillow. He too ignored their presence.

The last to arrive was the village leader, Bo'rada. Harry had told her that Bo'rada was the son of the last chief. He had been bestowed the honor of chieftain out of respect for his famous father. Most of the other elders tolerated him, but he was not well respected. Too volatile, too quick to make decisions. The council liked to mull over decisions, sometimes taking years to decide on simple matters. The young chief, with his fidgeting and sudden anger, was an embarrassment to the older members.

Still, he did have his followers. Harry pointed out an exceptionally thin male tribesman whose eyes and ears kept darting in every direction. His hands tugged at the pillow under him as if struggling to find a comfortable position for his bony rear. "Sin'jari," Harry said. "An oily sycophant of Bo'rada. Beware of him. He's as sneaky as he is nervous."

"It looks as if a stiff wind could snap him in two," Ben said.

"Don't underestimate the creep. He's the one who convinced the leader that you two should be killed. He's a wheedling sort of guy. He knows how to play to people's fears. Work them into a frenzy."

The leader stamped his staff three times on the floor, then sat.

Harry stepped between Ben and Ashley, translating for them as the meeting opened.

Ashley had expected their fate would be the first item on the schedule, but she was sorely mistaken. The first item on the agenda seemed to deal with the harvesting of the fields. A lengthy dispute seemed to center on whether to proceed now or to allow the hoofed food animals another month of free grazing. After much arguing, during which Mo'amba seemed to be dozing, it was decided to harvest now.

Ashley straightened up, expecting their fate to be discussed next. She was wrong. The only female council member, Jus'siri, stood up next, assisted from her pillow by one of her guards due to the preponderance of her gravid belly.

Ashley shifted her feet. Now what? This interminable waiting was beginning to grate on her. Even Ben was beginning to grumble.

She watched Jus'siri waddle to the small dug-out pit at the center of the chamber. The other elders encircled her, many smiling in delight.

Ashley's jaw dropped at what happened next.

Ben curled his lip. "That's disgusting."

Jus'siri reached within her belly pouch, both hands disappearing within the fold. With a bit of a strained face, but with her eyes shining proudly, she pulled from her belly a brown-speckled egg, about the size of an ostrich egg. She held it aloft, her belly now sagging empty. The other elders began stamping their staffs and hooting. Jus'siri then carefully placed the egg within the small pit—not a pit, Ashley finally realized, but a nest! The proud mother stepped back.

"My god," Ashley blurted, stunned. "They're *not* marsupials! They're monotremes!"

"What?" Ben asked, his lips still curled in disgust.

"Linda and I discussed it. Monotremes. Just like the *crak'an*. Egg-laying mammals. Considered to be an evolutionary link between reptiles and mammals, sharing traits from both—egg-laying like reptiles, but fur-bearing and milk-producing like mammals. Supposedly an evolutionary dead end."

"Looks like this group took a detour," Ben said.

Ashley turned to Harry. "What're they doing?"

"It's a naming ceremony. Jus'siri is offering her child to the tribe."

Ashley watched as Mo'amba struggled up off his pillow and crossed to the egg. Kneeling down, he placed both hands gently on the egg.

"What's he doing?" Ashley asked.

Her question was directed at Harry, but Ben answered. "He's reading the egg and the child within."

Ashley raised an eyebrow toward Ben, but he just shook his head as if unsure himself how he knew this.

Mo'amba raised his head to the mother, still holding the egg. Smiling, he mumbled something to her.

"It's healthy," Harry translated.

Then Mo'amba suddenly jerked away, almost accidentally flipping the egg out of the nest.

Ben jumped beside her. "I felt it," he said. "Like a baby kicking."

"Felt what?" Ashley asked.

Ben just shook his head again.

Ashley watched as Mo'amba rested his hands back on the egg, even more tenderly this time, his hands trembling with more than just old age. He again turned to Jus'siri, who now wore a concerned look on her face. With tears in his eyes, he spoke to her.

The crowd erupted with cheers, staffs stamping jubilantly.

Ashley turned to Harry, impatient for his translation. "Well?"

Again Ben answered, "The child is *heri'huti*. It bears the trait of seeing and speaking with the mind." He turned to Ashley, wonder in his voice. "I actually felt the child stir."

Mo'amba stood up, his joy so powerful he didn't even use his crutch. He stamped his staff to quiet the crowd.

Once the commotion settled to a low murmur, he spoke again, punctuating his statement with two stamps.

"I name this child *Tu'shama*," Harry translated. "The One Who Sees Our Future."

The crowd erupted, the name Tu'shama chanted from many tongues.

"Well," Ben said, "at least they'll be in a good mood when it comes to deciding our fate."

Ashley nodded. "Hopefully, they won't simply delay the decision. I don't want to lose another day."

As if the scarred Tru'gula had understood her words, he stamped for attention and proposed that the decision on Ashley and Ben's fate be put off. In response, many heads nodded, even Bo'rada.

Then the bone-thin Sin'jari stamped to be heard. With Harry translating, his words chilled: "It truly is a time of joy, but we cannot forget that with joy there is also sorrow. How many widows now wail?"

His words sobered the audience.

"Here stand demons meant to destroy us." He pointed a long finger with thick knuckles at them. "Ever since they arrived and desecrated this world, we began to die. We have tried befriending them," he continued, nodding toward Harry, "but still we have continued to perish. I think it more than chance that when we finally decide to destroy the demons, a new *heri'huti* should suddenly appear. I say it's a sign from the gods. A sign that we must drive the demons from our world. Without delay!"

Now several heads nodded in agreement with Sin'jari's words.

Ashley reached behind her back and shoved her pistol deeper in her belt, securing it. She started eyeing the obstacles between her and the door.

Mo'amba stamped for attention.

Ben's nervous shifting calmed once he saw that Mo'amba was to speak in their defense. He reached over and squeezed Ashley's hand. "He'll make them see reason," he said.

Mo'amba waited for the noise of the crowd to subside before speaking. Sin'jari's eyes twitched, and his hands scrabbled on his staff; he was obviously worried. But as Mo'amba began speaking, a smile grew wider and wider on Sin'jari's gaunt face, revealing too many teeth.

Harry translated: "Sin'jari's correct that many of our protective barriers have fallen. That many of our people have died. I have given this much thought, spending many hours praying and seeking guidance from our ancestors. And have come to only one answer." Mo'amba pointed his staff toward Ben and Ashley. "Sin'jari is correct. They are to blame!"

TWENTY-EIGHT

Michaelson crouched over his arsenal, taking inventory of his weapons: One collapsible rifle, a snubnosed AK-47, two pistols, and four boxes of .34-caliber shells. Why hadn't he requisitioned a grenade launcher for this mission? He shook his head.

Frowning, he realized that they didn't have a chance in hell of getting out of here alive if a fight was necessary. He sat back on his haunches, wincing as his injured ankle protested.

Behind him a couple were copulating in full view of the other hunters, their grunting and moans interrupting the silence of the chamber. Having spent last night here with Harry, he had almost grown accustomed to their openness. During the night, the same open passion had been abundantly displayed. Still he kept his back to them and studied one of the warriors working in a corner.

The creature seemed old, graying at the temples, thin, but with piercing eyes. He clutched a crude diamond spearhead in his hand and smeared a gray paste over its surface. Even in the dim fungal light, a reddish glow could be seen developing in the spearhead. Clucking his tongue in satisfaction, he spread a thicker layer of paste to the edge of the rough blade. The edges now began glowing a deeper, fiery red.

Fascinated, Michaelson watched as the craftsman now used another tool to grind at the spearhead, filing the edge of the now-soft diamond. The paste seemed to have weakened the surface of the crystal into a malleable consistency. Though judging from the corded muscles of the creature's forearms, it was still stiff, resistant, almost like softened lead. Michaelson watched as he tooled the diamond into a wicked blade.

So that's how the fuckers did it, he thought. Sculpting chunks of diamond with the aid of some crystal-softening mold. As a final step, the old creature dipped his handiwork into a bowl of water. Removing the dripping spearhead, he tapped it with a bone tool. It rang like a struck goblet. Solid once again.

Awed, Michaelson stood up and stretched his legs. The passionate couple had finished their sexual dalliance and now lay napping in each other's arms. He worked the kinks out of his legs, but the low roof kept him from being able to straighten his back.

A sudden flurry of raised voices near the entrance to the hunter's warren of caves drew his attention. The garbled speech had a keening edge of panic in it. Thinking that the ruckus might be Ashley's group trying to beat a hurried retreat, Michaelson grabbed a loaded pistol. He elbowed his way through the small crowd to the center of the commotion. Shoving past the last onlooker, he froze as he saw the source of the agitation.

Four hunters carried the body in a rough woven sling. They laid the limp form at his feet, the SEAL's torn uniform bloodier than the last time he had seen him. From his cyanotic pallor and fixed glassy eyes, he knew there was no use checking for a pulse. "Villanueva," he said. "Goddamn it." Michaelson holstered his gun and knelt down. He picked up the limp hand of his friend. "Fuck," he spat out. He stared at the two bullet holes in the SEAL's forehead. Two. This was obviously no suicide. Someone murdered him. But who?

Ashley bit back a scream of frustration. It was bad enough that they had wasted a day in this council meeting. Now Mo'amba, their only ally, had betrayed them. She clenched her fists, and her shoulders trembled. Jason could be in danger right now. She closed her eyes. He has to be okay . . .

Ben spoke up beside her, poking a finger into Harry's chest. "You couldn't have heard Mo'amba correctly. He said he'd help."

"Shhh!" Harry said, waving Ben's hand away. "I'm trying to listen."

Mo'amba had started to talk again after his accusation. Probably cinching the noose tighter around our necks, Ashley thought. She studied the council chamber, eyeing the exits and counting the guards.

Harry began translating again, haltingly, but with gaining confidence as he concentrated.

Mo'amba spoke calmly, "These newcomers to our world caused the death of the *tin'ai'fori*. This I have read in the whispered words of our ancestors."

There was much stamping of staffs from Bo'roda's group of lackeys, echoing painfully across the chamber. Ashley noticed, however, that Sin'jari, the leader's right-hand man, refrained from stamping his approval but simply wore a thin smile of triumph.

Mo'amba held up a hand for silence before continuing. "But these newcomers are not demons. They are flesh and blood, tendon and bone. Like us. It is not their evil that is harming us. Only their *ignorance*."

Sin'jari, whose smile had deflated into a wary sneer, spoke up. "It does not matter. Our tribesmen die and the law is clear. The responsible must die. And even you agree that they are responsible. I say we vote."

Harry stopped his translating, licking his dry lips. He glanced over to Ashley. "I told you that guy's a bastard."

Ashley nodded, not taking her eyes from Mo'amba. The *heri'huti* wore a shadow of a grimace. He held up a hand. "Our esteemed Sin'jari states that our laws are clear in this matter. And again I must bow to the expertise of our colleague here. He is right. Those responsible for the death of another must die. It is the law." Mo'amba paused. When Sin'jari tried to speak again, Mo'amba frowned at him, silencing his outburst.

Mo'amba then leaned heavily on his staff, as if the meeting exhausted him. He spoke slowly, giving Harry plenty of time to translate: "The key word in our law is *responsible.* I did not say these newcomers were responsible. I said they were to *blame.* It was their ignorance of us and our ways that caused them to blunder and inadvertently harm us. We cannot hold someone responsible for actions they were not aware of."

Bo'rada spoke up this time. "These are just words. The result is the same."

"Words?" Mo'amba answered, focusing his eyes on the tribe's leader. "It was these words that kept your right hand attached to your wrist. I seem to remember a small boy who let a herd of *trefer'oshi* loose from their pens. They destroyed almost a tenth of that year's crop. The law states that a hand who harms the well-being of the tribe should be cut off."

"I was only a boy then," Bo'rada blurted. "I didn't know what I was doing. You couldn't hold me responsible for—"

Sin'jari reached over and clutched the leader's knee, stopping him from speaking anymore, attempting to limit the damage.

Mo'amba turned to the other village elders, leaning even harder on his staff now, his back bent. "I am an old man. Older by far than all of you. I have seen each and every one of you blunder while growing up. Yet all of you still have your hands, feet"—he pointed a finger at Sin'jari—"and noses. Blundering is a process of learning. These newcomers are learning too. We must teach them, not destroy them."

A murmur spread through the cavern. Sin'jari fidgeted in his seat. One of his underlings leaned down and whispered something in his ear. Sin'jari nodded, then cleared his throat.

Harry gave Ashley a glance that seemed to say, *Here we go again.* Harry translated Sin'jari's words as if they left a foul taste in his mouth: "Mo'amba is wise as always and has given us much to ponder. But how does he know the harm done to our protective *tin'ai'fori* was accidental? How did the newcomers cause this damage? How?"

Great, thought Ashley. How is the old man supposed to answer that?

Mo'amba spoke up. "I have prayed upon this matter for many days, and an answer has come to me. Through their blundering, they have created an imbalance between *ohna*, the female spirit, and *umbo*, the male spirit. An imbalance that is tearing apart the weaving of our world."

A hushed murmur spread throughout the room. Even Sin'jari remained silent.

Jus'siri pushed to her feet to speak. "How can this be stopped?"

"I must show you," Mo'amba said. "Then all will be clear. You will know why I have protected these foreigners. If we kill these newcomers, we destroy our only way to reverse this damage."

Sin'jari snorted. "This is preposterous. He's only trying to delay the vote. I say we vote now. Destroy them, before they destroy us."

Bo'rada placed a firm hand on Sin'jari's shoulder, silencing him. "I've been accused of being too rash before. But this time I will bow to the council. I say we hear Mo'amba out. The matter is too serious."

Sin'jari seemed to shrink with the leader's words.

"Show us, Mo'amba," Bo'rada continued. "Show us how this occurred, and how to stop it."

Mo'amba nodded and led the way to the exit of the council chamber; the other members fell in line behind him. Ashley and her group were ushered by guards behind the tribe's elders.

"I knew the old bloke wouldn't betray us," Ben said to Ashley.

"We're not out of here yet," she answered, but for the first time she felt hopeful. With the tribe's cooperation and their knowledge of the cavern system, she could be back at Alpha Base in a couple of days. She adjusted her pace to that of the village elders, repressing the urge to shove them from behind to get them to hurry.

After arcing through several tunnels and climbing a winding flight of carved rock stairs, the council filed into a cavern barely large enough to contain the group. Ashley had to squeeze between Tru'gula, whose fur reeked like a wet dog, and the rock wall to get a view of the proceedings.

She whispered to Harry, "Where are we?"

Harry shrugged, bumping Tru'gula with his shoulder. The leader of the hunters grunted something angrily at him. Wincing, Harry leaned toward Ashley. "Don't ask me to translate *that*."

"You've never been to this chamber before?" Ashley asked.

"No, this section of the village belongs to the religious sect. A very closemouthed lot. I usually stuck to the hunters' group."

Ashley wiggled, trying to get a better view of Mo'amba. All eyes were on him.

Something flashed brightly at the old man's feet, but she could not see the source. She waved to Ben. "Give me a boost."

Ben helped her place a foot on his bent knee, holding her steady with a firm grip. She pulled up, balancing on one foot, using a hand on Ben's shoulder and the wall to maintain her precarious perch. Her head was now far enough above the crowd to see Mo'amba's entire figure.

He began speaking as Harry translated. "I have brought you all here because you know the significance of this chamber. This is the home of *umbo*, the male spirit." He then stepped aside and pointed with his staff.

There on a stone pedestal Ashley saw a familiar object flashing brightly in the meager light. It seemed to collect the light in the room and radiate it out in bursts of sparking darts. A crystal idol about fifteen inches high. Diamond. Similar to the one

Blakely presented to her months ago, but this one had a definite and prominent protrusion below its naked waist. Male. This figure was the masculine twin of the other.

"Here stands *umbo*," Mo'amba declared. "As he should. Protecting our world. But he can't protect alone. He is only half of the whole. His other half, *ohna*, the female spirit, is missing."

"Yes," Sin'jari spoke up. "The newcomers stole her."

"Not stole. Our original village stood empty. They could not have known she was the connection to our distant past. She who was left to help guide our ancestors back to us in our new village. Now she is gone. The balance of *umbo* and *ohna* was destroyed by those unfamiliar with our ways. It is this imbalance that has disturbed the warp and weave that holds the fabric of our world together. It must be corrected."

"It can be," Sin'jari stated. "By destroying the invaders!" He looked around but was only met with worried murmuring.

"No," said Mo'amba. "The balance can only be achieved by returning *ohna* to her proper place."

The old man's logic seemed faultless, even to Ashley, who didn't believe a word of it. The elders around her, even their leader, were nodding their heads in agreement. Except for one.

Sin'jari strode to the center of the chamber, his bony limbs twitching in agitation. "Mo'amba has proven his wisdom." He turned to face the crowd. "It is clear we must kill the stragglers left from the attack of the *crak'an* and reclaim *ohna* for ourselves. Return her to her rightful place!"

A firm murmur of agreement followed his words, but no stamping of staffs. This seemed to rankle him. He rattled his staff on the rock floor, almost begging others to start stamping their own staffs.

Mo'amba, however, did not allow the crowd's murmur to grow. Harry continued to translate his words: "Our esteemed Sin'jari's wrath seems to have blinded him to an important law of the tribe." Mo'amba turned to the thick-chested leader. "Bo'rada, tell us what happened after you let loose the *trefer'oshi* from their pens to wreak havoc on our crops."

"Father and I rebuilt the pen and reseeded the trampled fields. It took us three days without sleeping to accomplish it."

"Exactly. You were given a chance to right your wrong. The newcomers deserve the same chance. Let them correct their own error."

Again the crowd murmured their assent. Even Tru'gula stamped his staff in agreement.

Sin'jari, though, was not ready to give up his battle. "The newcomers are not of our tribe. Our laws don't apply to them. What's to stop them from running off with *ohna* and letting our world die?"

"They *are* different," Mo'amba agreed. "One only has to look to see that. But the difference is minor." Mo'amba pointed his staff at Ashley, Harry, and Ben. "Come here. Join me."

Now what? Ashley thought. If things should go sour—and with Sin'jari's pitbull-like persistence, it was a good possibility—they would have the entire council and its entourage between them and the only exit.

Ben helped Ashley off his knee, rubbing at his thigh after she stepped down. "At least you weren't wearing high heels," he complained.

"Ben, we're putting our backs against the wall if we go out there."

"Trust him," he said. "He'll get us out of this mess." Ben squeezed through the narrow opening afforded him by the crowd, pausing only to reach back and pull Ashley after him. Harry trailed behind them.

Once they were congregated before the wall of staring eyes, Mo'amba stepped between her and Ben, then continued, with Harry translating: "These new-comers may look strange and even slightly offensive to some, but another villager might find Tru'gula with his scars strange and even unsettling, but he is still one of us. What matters is the spirit." He tapped his chest with his staff. "Here we are not so different."

He paused to level his staff at Harry. "Here, a newcomer has proven the bravery of his people, proven that they are worthy of *il'jann*, like any other tribesman." Next he swung the staff toward Ben. "Here is a newcomer with the powers of a *heri'huti*, a gift from the gods. Why would our spirits bestow such a gift unless they thought him worthy?"

Finally, he pointed the staff at Ashley. "The gods have given us another clue to their worthiness. The newcomer's *heri'huti* planted his seed in her during the last sleep cycle." He placed a hand on Ashley's belly. "It has taken root, and the gods have blessed her with a child. A child conceived here in our village. A new child of the tribe."

Ashley blinked a few times, staring at the hand on her belly. He had to be kidding! She looked up at Ben. His mouth hung open.

"If the gods have blessed them with a child, the spirits have judged them worthy. Who are we to judge them any less so?"

Sin'jari struck a rock with his staff. "We have only your word that this . . . this . . . this invader is a *heri'huti*," he spat.

Mo'amba, eyes thin with anger, opened his mouth to speak but was interrupted by the stamping of a spear. All eyes turned to Bo'rada, who stamped his stick a final time.

Bo'rada spoke. "Enough, Sin'jari. To accuse Mo'amba, who has served our tribe for generations, of falsehoods is a rudeness that can't be tolerated. I shun you from further discussion in this matter." Bo'rada waved the ruby tip of his staff across his lips.

The crowd gasped. Ashley looked questioningly at Harry, who leaned closer toward her. "This is a rare act. This society is very open to free expression. A shunning is a major punishment."

"Just as long as it keeps Sin'jari shut up," she muttered, fidgeting in place. Where did the council now lean? she wondered. Death or acquittal? Had Mo'amba convinced them? She glanced at her belly, swallowing hard. He could be very convincing.

Bo'rada had not finished speaking. "I believe Mo'amba. The newcomers deserve a chance to correct their mistake." He then pointed his staff at Ben. Harry translated. "Do you know where *ohna* is kept?"

Ben nodded.

"Will you return her?"

"I will try my bloody best," Ben said as they translated. "That's all I can promise."

"Then I cast my vote that we stay their execution depending on the successful completion of this mission. But, because I harbor reservations similar to those expressed by Sin'jari, I will require some reassurance . . . The female stays here until the mission is completed. If it's not accomplished within one day, then she dies." He stamped his staff.

His words caused all the elders to stamp their staffs in agreement. Except two: Sin'jari, who was shunned from voicing an opinion, and Mo'amba. The old *heri'huti* just stared, first at Ben then at Ashley. She could see the sorrow in his eyes as he finally raised his staff and stamped it three times on the ground— agreement.

TWENTY-NINE

I can't just leave her," Ben said to Mo'amba. The other elders had already left *umbo*'s chamber, leaving only a cluster of armed guards around them. Ben stared at Ashley where she leaned over the tumescent image of *umbo*, studying the figurine. Always the anthropologist, he thought, always in command. Still, he noted the way her hand trembled as she coursed a finger down the figurine.

"I'm sorry." Mo'amba's words were translated by Harry. "It's the best I could do. You have today to prepare yourself and your team of hunters. Then you have one day to return *ohna*, or else Bo'rada will kill Ashley . . . and your unborn child."

Ben rubbed at his temples with the tips of his fingers. "You . . . you mean . . . she's really pregnant?"

The old man nodded.

"A father," he mumbled to himself, shaking his head. Things were happening too quickly. The winds were blowing in too many directions.

The old man leaned closer to Ben, whispered something guttural to him, too low for Harry to translate, then touched the center of Ben's forehead. With the touch, a sense of peace and calmness saturated Ben, like a cool shower after a hot day under the Aussie sun. Ben sighed. How does the bugger do that? Mo'amba stepped away.

Now calmer, Ben could think more rationally, rather than just relying on gut reactions. He needed to plan. At least the village elders had given him a day to work out a strategy. Still . . . he remembered the long journey down here. Even if supplied with a map, it would take longer than a day to reach Alpha Cavern.

Exasperated, Ben turned to Harry. "Are you sure you translated that correctly? They're giving us one day? Twenty-four hours?"

Harry nodded. "Almost. Their daily cycle, termed *cucuru*, is actually twenty-six hours."

"That's a lot of help. Two extra hours. I don't suppose you happen to know a quicker way up to Alpha Base?"

"I know of a route up, but it'll still take at least a day and a half. And that's if we hurry and don't get ambushed by any of the *crak'an*. I was eventually planning on taking the journey myself once my broken arm had healed and strengthened, but Dennis beat me down here."

"Shit."

Mo'amba suddenly stamped his staff, looking frustrated. He motioned them over to the wall. He struggled to speak a few words of English: "I show . . . Fast. Up." He seemed to have understood the gist of their discussion.

Mo'amba crossed to the far wall and pressed the butt of his staff against a rocky outcropping. As he pressed, the outcropping receded into the wall, and a section of what looked like solid rock swung inward.

"It's a secret door!" Ben leaned down and stared into the revealed tunnel. "Leading to another of those goddamn wormholes." He waved Ashley over.

Mo'amba hobbled to the side with Harry in tow, the two already conversing animatedly.

Ashley knelt next to Ben. "I should have suspected," she whispered, a trace of tension in her voice. "The holy places of many cultures have hidden chambers and passages." Ashley sat back on her heels, seemingly despondent at missing a key anthropologic connection. Then suddenly she sprang up. "Damn, I've been so stupid!"

"What?"

"This . . . this tunnel. I can guess where this leads."

Baffled, Ben raised a questioning eyebrow.

"This is the male spirit's chamber. I would bet the female spirit's chamber in Alpha Cavern has a similar hidden passage that we all missed. I would bet my life that this tunnel connects with her chamber. A symbolic vaginal canal linking male and female spirits."

"You mean . . ."

"It's a straight and safe shot right back up top."

Ben allowed himself a glimmer of hope. "But are you sure? If you're right," he whispered to her, "maybe we can make a break for it. Use this tunnel so all of us can escape."

Ashley knelt back down. "No. With their small physiques, they would be on top of us in seconds. We wouldn't have a chance. Besides, Mo'amba and his tribe are trying to accept us. This is a crucial test between our peoples. I won't betray their trust. As an anthropologist, I can't destroy this tentative bond that they are working to establish with us."

"But what if—"

"No," she said, but Ben could see the agony in her eyes. It was taking all her will not to rush into the tunnel and go seek out her son.

A few steps away, Harry and Mo'amba had finished their animated discussion. "Well, I'll be damned,"

Harry declared loudly, drawing their attention. He turned back to face them. "You're not going to believe this. This wormhole—"

"—leads to Alpha Base," Ashley finished for him, standing up.

Harry's brow furrowed with creases. "How did you know?"

"I finally remembered I'm an anthropologist," Ashley said sourly. "So what else did you learn from Mo'amba?"

"If I'm understanding correctly, it's about a thirty-mile long tunnel."

Ben eyed the tunnel. And about two miles up, he guessed. "It'll be a bloody long crawl. And'll probably eat up a good part of the day."

"Maybe not," said Harry cryptically. "Let's get out of here. Join up with Dennis. Plan your strategy."

Ben turned to Mo'amba. "Harry, ask him to help us plan. He knows these caverns."

Nodding, Harry blurted a few words to Mo'amba, gesticulating with his arms. The old man answered, shaking his head.

Harry translated: "He says he has much to prepare, and he'll talk to you later, but I don't know if I'm translating that correctly. It's a looser translation. It's almost like he said he'd be '*dreaming*' of you later."

Ben nodded with a sigh. "Let's be going. We have a lot to do before tomorrow." As they turned to leave, he stared back at Mo'amba, the old man's eyes drilling him. Should be an interesting night of dreams, he thought as he followed Ashley out the exit.

Back at the hunters' enclave, Ashley stared at the still form of Villanueva at her feet, too stunned to speak. She had almost forgotten about the others left in the diamond cavern, figuring they were safer where they were. Eyeing the bullet wounds in the SEAL's forehead, she realized there were more dangers here than the caverns and its denizens.

"It must have been Khalid," Michaelson said.

"What about Linda?" Ashley asked. "Did the hunters see her?"

"I don't know," the major answered. "I didn't have a translator." He nodded toward his brother, who was deep in conversation with a hunter named Tomar'su. "Hopefully, Harry can get an answer to what happened."

Ashley couldn't stare at the corpse-white face of Villanueva any longer. As she turned away, something caught her eye—in a ragged pile of collected loot stood a familiar fluorescent green plastic object. Her sled. She had thought it lost after she and Ben had crashed here. She noticed Ben's red sled had also been recovered.

Pretty efficient scavengers, she thought, but that made perfect sense considering the meager resources afforded them.

Suddenly the conversation between Harry and Tomar'su escalated in volume. Ashley glanced in their direction. Harry was holding up his fingers, apparently counting off some point. Finally, in exasperation, Harry clenched his fist and turned away, ending the conversation.

"What was that all about?" Ashley asked as he rejoined the group.

"He wasn't making any sense," Harry said. "He described what sounded like gunfire. The noise drew his hunters to the diamond cavern. By the time they got there, they only found this . . . this dead soldier."

"Villanueva," Ashley corrected. "He was a friend."

Harry nodded, his brow furrowed in concern. "When I asked him about the other two, he said his team followed their trail to a cavern with a waterfall and observed them camping."

"So Linda is alive?"

"Well, that's the weird part. When I asked them how many were there, he said there were four of them."

"Four?" Ben said.

"I know." Harry ran a hand through his hair. "I kept asking him over and over again. He was adamant. Four." Harry held up four fingers.

"Seems as soon as we solve one mystery another crops up," Ben said.

The news gnawed at Ashley. Even with the recent events, she had to know . . . "Where are these four now?"

"Tomar'su says they went into a tunnel that smelled like death, and his hunters balked at following them."

"Smelled like *death*?"

Harry shrugged. "That's what he said."

They all stood silent for a long moment. Ashley finally spoke up. "To hell with it. We aren't going to solve this now. Let's concentrate on the situation at hand. Harry, you mentioned you might have a quicker way to traverse the wormhole."

Harry brightened at her words. "Yeah, maybe. If I can get it to work. Come see." He led her and the others to a neighboring cavern, almost a cubicle. "Not much," he said, ushering them in, "but it's home."

In a corner, thick green pillows huddled under a rumpled blanket. The remainder of Harry's cubicle consisted of an odd assortment of crude tools, spear-heads, and a long tarp-wrapped object. Ashley curled her nose at the strong smell of gasoline. Gasoline?

Harry followed them inside, squeezing past her. "All the others at Alpha Base are electric—whining little put-puts—but I jury-rigged my own with a combustion engine. I wanted power." He bent over and grabbed the edge of the tarp. "After I was attacked, my fellow hunters retrieved it from our last camp. It was pretty beat up, but I've been tinkering with it."

He yanked the tarp free, revealing a transport sled. One of the big ones. "I built it out of aluminum to be lightweight. Blakely let me bring it since we didn't think we'd need heavy ammunition for our explorations." He sniffed in derision. "I brought one fucking pistol with me. Stupid!"

"Does the sled still work?" Ashley said, trying to keep the conversation on course.

"Mostly. It used to collapse down to a compact size for carrying, but it's jammed open. Still, this is just a straight trip up. So that shouldn't be a problem." Harry patted the sled. "The engine's sound, but I only have a single tank of gasoline, so I've been leery of running the engine for a long time. Probably needs a bit of tuning still."

"Is there enough gas to get all the way up?" Ben knelt down and cocked his head from side to side, studying it.

"Should be plenty."

"Harry used to race dirt bikes," Michaelson said. "He knows his way around an engine. If he thinks it'll work, it will."

Ben nodded, seemingly satisfied. "This'll buy me several hours."

"There's only one problem," Harry said. "The front axle's bent. If I *can* fix it, it'll be an all-nighter. So you might want to have a Plan B . . . just in case."

"Right," Ashley said, "then let's get a few things settled. Since I'm the only one being held hostage here, I suggest everyone else accompany Ben on his mission. Put as few at risk as possible down here."

"No, ma'am!" Ben argued. "I'm going alone. A solo mission."

"You're gonna need firepower," Ashley said. "There's no telling how many of those *crak'an* are still hovering around Alpha Base."

"She's right," Harry said. "The council has allowed a small team of hunters to go with you. Since we're officially blood-bonded hunters, my brother and I can accompany you. Trust me, you'll need the backup. I can tie those cheap plastic sleds of yours to mine and form a train to drag everyone quickly up top."

Ben's face reddened with determination. "I won't leave Ashley here alone. She's—"

"I'll stay with Ashley," Michaelson interrupted. "My ankle's crap. I'll only slow you all down anyway. Maybe Ashley and I can come up with a contingency plan . . . if it comes to that."

Ben seemed as if he was going to argue further, but their arguments seemed to be wearing him thin. "All right! Harry can come. But, Michaelson, whatever it takes, I expect to see the mother of my child again."

"You will, Ben."

Ben nodded, but Ashley's mind was whirling. Mother? She had succeeded in pushing that fact from her mind, but Ben's words had dredged it back up. She placed a hand on her belly. Mother? She didn't even begin to know how to feel about that revelation. But one point of motherhood she was damned sure of . . . "Ben, you've got to find Jason. Even if it means scrubbing this mission. Promise me."

"I'll try," Ben said. "You know I will."

"Don't just try. *Do it.*"

Ben reached to her and folded her in his arms. In his embrace, the tears she had been holding back finally flowed. She sank deeper in his arms.

THIRTY

Ben lay awake in his cell. He knew he needed to rest. But after a day of planning, plotting, divvying up arms, and choosing the *mimi'swee* hunters to accompany them, his mind still ground on details of the mission. What if he didn't succeed? He rolled hard onto his left side, burrowing into his pile of pillows and twisting the thin blanket tight around his feet. Ashley's face kept flashing across his mind's eye.

Earlier, she had been led to a separate cell for the night. Guarded. A hostage. They were not even allowed a final night together.

He rolled onto his back and sighed loudly. This worrying was getting him nowhere. Maybe stretching his legs a bit would help. Besides, he should check on

Harry's progress. Slipping from his pillows, he crossed to the exit.

Within a few minutes, he had made his way back to the section of hunters' caves. Harry was bent over the disassembled sled, pieces strewn across the rocky floor. Michaelson leaned over his shoulder. A loud snap cracked across the cavern. "Shit!" Harry jumped back from the sled.

"What's wrong?" Ben asked, stepping up behind them.

Harry held up two pieces of aluminum rod. "Not good. I pushed too hard and snapped the axle."

Ben's heart clenched in his chest. "Can you fix it?"

"I don't think so. I was softening the aluminum with heat and trying to straighten the bend when it snapped. I should have waited until it was softer, but was afraid of weakening the metal." Harry threw the pieces to the floor. "Sorry, Ben. I screwed up."

Michaelson laid a hand on Harry's shoulder. "You did your best."

"Fuck that. I blew it." Harry shrugged off his brother's hand.

"Don't beat yourself up," Ben said. "So we use the plastic sleds and push our way up. It'll slow us down somewhat, but we'll manage." At least he prayed so. What if this delay made the difference between succeeding and failing in their mission?

"Listen," Michaelson said to Harry. "I may have an idea."

"What?" Ben said.

Michaelson, his eyes tired and irritated, glanced back over his shoulder and pointed to the exit. "Ben, just go to bed. Let my brother and I work this out. It's a long shot anyway, so get yourself some rest."

Ben only stared, glassy-eyed. He knew the major was right.

"We'll see you in the morning," Michaelson said, turning his attention back to Harry and the sled, dismissing him.

During Ben's journey back to bed, his mind spun with the ramifications of Harry's bad news. Even if it took them eight hours to crawl the thirty miles, surely the remaining day would leave them plenty of time to accomplish their goal. It would have to, he thought adamantly.

Suddenly he realized the twists and turns in the tunnels didn't look familiar. He turned and looked back the way he had come. Should have taken that last turn . . . or maybe angled left back by the big boulder.

A scraping noise behind him drew his attention. In the dim light, he could see a skeletally thin apparition approaching him from down the tunnel. He froze, startled by the otherworldliness of the figure, bathed in the greenish fungal glow like some netherworld phantom.

But as it approached, he recognized the gnarled and bony countenance. Sin'jari, the creature who had so stubbornly insisted on their deaths.

As the tribe's elder closed the space between them, Ben noticed the two brutish guards following Sin'jari. Butt-ugly fellows. Where most of the *mimi'swee* were small and sinewy, these two looked like scarred bull-dogs, hunched and menacing. Sin'jari stepped before Ben, raising his staff to block the way forward, then barked something angrily to his flanking guards.

The two burly creatures advanced toward him.

Though physically drained, Ashley still found sleep escaping her. Her head pounded and a bruise on her hip throbbed. She found herself recalling Ben's arms as he held her, the scent of his hair, his fingers on her back and neck. She had gone too far the night before, in a moment of horrible weakness, and misled him badly as to her true feelings. She clutched the blanket around her shoulders, afraid of an even more frightening reality. Had she *really* misled him?

She glanced at the glowing dial of her watch. Two hours until the clock began ticking toward her death sentence. Too many worries battled within her, bottled up in her chest: What had happened to Jason? And Linda too, for that matter? What about Ben? Would he die trying to save her? Could he save her? And worst of all, if he should fail, would she then die never knowing what had happened to her son?

She clutched the blanket to her face, her tears finally overwhelming her control. Time was running out.

Ben took a step back from the lumbering creatures, who now leered at him in a threatening way. They were unarmed, but somehow Ben knew this was small comfort. He backed another step, debating what to do. He could try making a dash, but they would be at him like dingos on a wallaby. He'd best take his chances where he stood.

"Okay, you bastards," he grumbled, more to center himself than to intimidate his combatants. "Let's see how bloody easily those long necks of yours break."

Ben dug a heel into a rut in the floor to gain some leverage for a punch. He was readying himself when something suddenly grabbed his shoulder from behind. Wound tight, he instinctively swung a roundhouse blow toward the unseen attacker. He halted his punch just in time.

It was Mo'amba.

The old man released Ben's shoulder, staring for just a heartbeat at Ben's upraised fist. Mo'amba then glanced away to stare down the two guards, who were frozen where they stood. He barked something that made the pet dogs of Sin'jari bow their heads and slink back.

Their master, though, stood his ground, his staff still raised across the passage, barring the way forward. Sin'jari hissed something at Mo'amba. The old man merely shrugged, which caused Sin'jari to rattle his staff and quiver with rage.

Mo'amba tapped Ben on the shoulder and indicated he should follow. Acting as a guide, Mo'amba led the way back, away from Sin'jari. But the elder's howls echoed behind them as Ben followed Mo'amba.

After much twisting and turning, Ben found himself back in a familiar chamber. He glanced with a sigh at the red gourd-shaped mushrooms hanging from the pillars. Why do I always end up here?

As he followed Mo'amba deeper into the chamber, weaving among the mushrooms, he noticed something strange about the pillars of stone. The first time through here, with Ashley, he had been so fixated on the red fungal pods that he had assumed the pillars were just natural rocky colonnades, but now on closer inspection, he realized he was wrong. He traced a finger down the coarse, grooved surface of one of the pillars. Bloody hell, it was a petrified tree trunk. He glanced around him, his mouth agape. The whole chamber contained a grove of petrified trees.

A grunt of impatience drew his attention back to Mo'amba. He waved for Ben to sit at the edge of the circle of painted glyphs. Ben found a comfortable spot on the rocky floor, and the old man slowly sat across from him. Once settled, Ben knew what Mo'amba wanted. He closed his eyes and let his body relax, starting at his toes and working up from there. Still, his mind spun with so many thoughts and worries, he could not focus. He tried again to relax, but stray concerns kept him edgy.

Just before he was about to give up, a calming sense of tranquillity washed over him. He knew it was some sort of sending from Mo'amba and allowed the sense of peace to quiet his worried thoughts.

The blackness behind his eyelids blossomed into full color. Again, for just a moment, the image of his dead grandfather was superimposed over Mo'amba's face. The familiar visage further calmed his heart, like a favorite old song heard in the background.

Mo'amba's image solidified. "You must be more careful, Ben," he admonished. "Wandering alone in the village. There are still factions here that would see you fail or wish you dead. Sin'jari is not one to give up easily."

"How'd you know I was in trouble anyway?"

"It's the job of a *heri'huti*. To see what no one else sees."

"Thanks. I owe you. I was about to get my butt kicked."

"No. You were about to be killed. Those two are part of Sin'jari's clan. They are *silaris*, the poisoned ones."

A shiver passed through Ben, disturbing his mental connection like a pebble dropped in a still pond. "What about Ashley? When I leave tomorrow, will she be safe?"

"Yes. She is guarded by Tru'gula's men. He'll protect her. No one, not even Sin'jari, will bother his circle."

"Are you sure?"

"I'll watch over her myself. Trust us. We will guard your mate until you return."

"She's not my . . . oh, never mind, I don't even know what she is. Please . . . just keep her safe until I'm back. And I *will* be back."

"You will fail, Ben."

Ben, stunned, was sure he must have heard wrong. "What?"

"I can see down narrow paths of time. If you go as you are now, you'll fail."

"What does that mean?"

"You are *heri'huti*, but you don't believe it here." Mo'amba pointed to his naked chest. "You must accept your heritage or you and many others will perish."

"But I don't see how—"

Mo'amba's image swirled into the image of his dead grandfather. "Your mind's eye chose this memory to represent me when first I called you. Yet you rejected your grandfather's heritage. It shamed you. For you to succeed, you must learn to embrace your blood, cherish its memory as much as you cherish this image. Only then will you have a chance."

"How am I to succeed, then?"

The old man held both fists to his chest. "Listen to your blood."

"But what do you mean by—" The images dissolved away, leaving Ben in blackness. Only the words echoed back to him: Listen to your blood.

He blinked his eyes and stared at the mute figure of Mo'amba, so many questions still on his tongue. But Mo'amba pulled himself up with his staff.

"Wait!" Ben crossed to Mo'amba. "I need to know what you meant."

"Y-you," he garbled at Ben gutturally, "you sleep." He turned his back on Ben, obviously believing he had said enough.

Sleep? Ben wondered. Like that's bloody likely.

Ashley woke with a start, surprised she had fallen into real sleep. A female member of the tribe bowed her way into her chamber, laden with clattering platters of colorful fruit and some type of steaming meat. She shuffled to a flat stone about knee-high and spread out the meal.

Ashley's heart sank as she realized where she was. She wanted to retreat back to her dreamland. She had dreamt that she was back in her tiny trailer in the New Mexico desert. Jason and Ben were playing catch in the dusty yard, their feet trampling her feeble attempt at growing a succulent garden. She should have known it was a dream because all her garden grew were those weird red mushroom pods. The oddest part, though, was how easily she accepted Ben in a fathering light. She glanced at her belly. Ben as a father?

A gentle snoring drew her attention to the mound of pillows beside her. She sat up straighter as she recognized the tangle of blond hair peeking from under the blanket nearby. Ben! What was he doing here?

As she reached to nudge him, his snoring tumbled on a loud snort. He jerked awake, startling her. He rubbed at his eyes. "What time is it?"

She ignored his question. "How did you get past the guards?"

He pushed up on an elbow, his eyes bloodshot and a rusty stubble on his cheeks. "Even down here, it's who you know. Mo'amba bullied the guards into letting me pass. I just needed to know you were okay."

"Why didn't you wake me?"

"And ruin your beauty sleep? Not a chance!" Ben crinkled up his nose. "What's that smell?"

The sizzling meat on the platter had filled the cavern with smells that tantalized the tongue. Her stomach growled in anticipation. "Breakfast," she said hungrily.

He sat up in his pillows, finally noticing the naked server. "Not exactly a modest group, are they?" Ben slipped out of his covers and, with his back shyly turned to the server, slipped into his trousers.

Ashley also used the moment to get dressed.

Both of them descended on the meal like locusts. Finally, Ashley pushed her stone platter away from her. "Phew, I think I've had enough. For a last supper that wasn't too bad."

Her words seemed to have a devastating effect on Ben. "This won't be your last meal, Ash. I promise you. We are getting out of here!"

She smiled at him, realizing he had misinterpreted her words. "I meant this was your last supper here before you left. Not mine."

"Oh." Ben's face was sullen.

She laughed at his serious expression.

"I just thought—"

"I know." She took a deep breath, sobering herself. She reached a hand out and took his fingers in hers. "I know, Ben. It's sweet."

"Sweet?" Her word seemed to wound him. He glanced at her fingers entwined in his. He spoke without raising his eyes. "Ash, you've got to know how I feel about you. I want to be more than something *sweet*."

She tried to pull back her hand, but he held her tight. "Ben . . ." She didn't know what to say. A part of her wanted to cry out that she loved him, but another part was frightened to give in. After Scott, after the miscarriage, that part refused to be hurt again or to trust again. She had barely survived it the first time. Jason had kept her going, and now her son was missing. Too many emotions warred within her to think clearly. How could she put this all into words?

She didn't have to. He released her hand and pulled away. His words were a strained whisper. "I guess we'd better get going, then. I'm sure Harry and the others are waiting."

He turned away, his shoulders slumped. She opened her mouth to say something, anything, to console him. To tell him not to give up on her. But was that fair? She closed her mouth.

As Ashley entered *umbo*'s chamber, she saw Harry huddled with the three other hunters who would be joining Ben's team. He seemed amazingly bright and chipper for someone who'd been working all night. The room was crowded with other members of the tribe. Mo'amba stood in conversation with Tru'gula. No other village elders were present, not even Sin'jari, and for that, Ashley was thankful.

"We did it!" Harry said, beaming as he crossed to join them.

"You fixed the axle?" Ben asked, excitement in his voice.

"Come see. You're not gonna believe it." He waved them over to where Michaelson was hunched beside one of the plastic sleds.

Ashley noticed there were now four fluorescent sleds hooked to the aluminum transport. The scavengers had retrieved all the stray sleds, even Villanueva's. She looked at her dead friend's yellow sled, and a chill passed through her. It seemed like a bad omen.

She studied Michaelson's work. With a final tug on a rope, he secured the last of the boards in place. Just like a little train.

Harry said, "It was Dennis's idea." He lifted the large sled up, careful of the motor. "Look. This little alteration makes this the most valuable vehicle on the planet."

Ben whistled his appreciation. "Fine piece of work."

Ashley squeezed up to see. She glanced at the front axle. It glittered in the feeble light. "Is that what I think it is?"

"You bet," said Harry. "A pure diamond axle."

"Will it hold?" Ben asked, eyeing it dubiously.

Harry shrugged. "I ran the axle through some stress tests. It seemed okay. Besides, what other choice do we have? We use it or we drag our way along on the plastic sleds."

Ben fingered the diamond. "All right, mate, we travel in style."

Ashley stepped back as Harry lowered the sled. "So . . . so you're all ready to go, then." For some reason, this bothered her. She had been anticipating this, but suddenly to be faced with the reality that Ben would be leaving her, and possibly killed, seemed too much. Tears threatened to well.

Sensing her anxiety, Ben stepped to her and held her close. "I guess we shouldn't wait. Every minute may matter."

Ashley just nodded, afraid to speak, fearful she would break down.

Harry called the other tribesmen to him and barked final orders, waving his hands and pointing at the various sleds. It seemed he would take the lead, being the most familiar with the motorized sled. Ben would take up the caboose, helping to steady the three nervous hunters, who were not accustomed to the concept of transportation.

Ashley stepped out of the way, trying not to get underfoot, as packs were stowed and instructions explained. Mo'amba stepped next to her and placed a hand on her shoulder. She glanced at him, and he gave her a reassuring squeeze.

Once everything was ready, Ben returned to her. He seemed rejuvenated by the activity, but there was still a sadness in his blue eyes. "I promise I'll find out about Jason. And I *will* be back."

With Mo'amba's hand on her shoulder steadying her, she felt capable of speaking. "I know you will, Ben. I trust you." And for the first time, she realized she did. Trusted him with her life. Trusted him with her son's safety. Tears welled up and rolled down her face.

He leaned over and kissed her on the cheek, then turned and crossed to his sled.

Ashley took a step forward. She could not let him leave without knowing how she truly felt. She called to him, her words catching in her throat: "Ben! I . . . I . . ."

Drowned out by the roaring of the ignited sled's motor, her words were lost. Harry revved the engine, and the sled slid smoothly into the wormhole, dragging the train of riders behind it.

She watched Ben disappear into the tunnel, riding Villanueva's yellow sled. Ashley clutched her arms around her chest, a coldness creeping into her stomach. "I love you, Ben," she whispered.

BOOK FIVE

Return to Alpha

THIRTY-ONE

Linda crawled between the boulder and the floor, too tired to acknowledge her nagging claustrophobic unease in such a tight space. The miles of stone above her were of less concern at the moment than her stinging eyes, sore muscles, and miserable situation.

This was the second day since she and Jason had been captured by Khalid, and the pace he set was exhausting: minimal rest stops, no lunch break, just a brief breakfast, and a cold dinner of ration bars. It was up to her and Jason to keep pace with him. He had warned her that he wasn't going to stop and wait for them. If he was to punch in the code on Jason's belt of explosives every two hours, then they had better keep up. So the entire day was spent trying to keep abreast of Khalid.

With a final heave, Linda cleared the boulder and pushed to her feet. The tunnel here was wider. The choking smoke had by now faded to a mild annoyance, which made breathing easier. Yet it was this continuing dispersal of the smoke that drove Khalid's savage pace. If the smoke should dissipate completely before they had tracked their way home, then they truly would be lost.

There was another reason to race the smoke. So far, not a single predator had blocked their trail upward. Linda had voiced her opinion that the acrid fumes were probably acting as a repellent. Khalid had merely nodded at her assessment, and with an oddly worried expression, he had set an even harder pace.

As Linda stretched her back and adjusted her handkerchief over her nose, her headlamp speared the darkness ahead. Khalid had halted several yards down the tunnel, leaning over something on the floor. Jason's upper arm was clutched in his grip. What now?

Jason turned to her. "Come look."

Squeezing next to Jason, she saw what had attracted Khalid. A half-yard-tall metal canister stood in the center of the tunnel, with thick cables leading from it and trailing forward into the darkness. A meshed dish, like a miniature satellite receiver, topped the canister.

"What is it?" she asked.

"It's one of those special radio things of Dr. . . . Dr. Blakely's." Jason stammered over the dead man's name. "The cables should lead us to the base."

"Then we did it," Linda said. "We made it."

Khalid continued down the tunnel, following the cables.

"Linda," Jason spoke up from beside her, taking her hand as they followed Khalid, "I don't think he's gonna let me go free."

She squeezed his hand. "Jason. He will. Once you're no longer needed as a hostage, he'll let you go."

The boy remained silent a moment, then spoke. "When we reach the base, when we get there . . ." His voice trailed off.

"What is it, Jason?"

"If you get a chance to escape, take it. Leave me behind."

She stopped, pulling him to a halt. "I'm not going to leave you with him. We'll find a way out of this mess."

"He's gonna kill me anyway. I can tell."

"Jason . . . honey, I won't let—"

"It's in his eyes," he interrupted. "He looks . . . looks at me as if I'm not really here. Like I'm already dead."

Linda knelt and cupped his face in her hands. "I promise you. We'll get through this. Together."

Jason shook his head, dislodging her hands. "He's gonna let me die." He then turned and marched down the tunnel.

She watched his back disappear around a bend. Like hell, she thought. Pushing to her feet, she followed him, determined to keep that animal from harming Jason. She caught up with the boy and put an arm around his shoulder. They both remained silent as they continued through the tunnel, following Khalid and the snaking cable.

After thirty minutes of hiking, the tunnel seemed to be brightening around them. Jason glanced up at her. She clicked off her helmet lamp, no longer needing the illumination. As they passed around a corner in the tunnel, lamps could be seen attached to the walls.

They were still lit! That meant the generators were still active. From Jason's account, she figured the base would have been demolished and sunk in darkness. Maybe there was a chance that the base had been retaken already. Maybe reinforcements had arrived.

As she passed down the illuminated passageway, she could see where Khalid had stopped at the mouth of the tunnel. "Alpha Base," he said to her without looking back.

She hurried beside him, holding her breath, hoping. She glanced out, and her heart sank. The tunnel exited out the west wall of the cavern, atop a slight rise. The view of Alpha Cavern was spread out below, the base a mere mile away.

Or what was left of the base. The place was a ruin. Lights still flickered here and there, but poles were toppled throughout the camp. Every building still standing was scarred by fires or explosions, and several smoldering red glows suggested some fires were still active. A haze of smudged clouds hovered over the base, as if trying to mask the damage. Even from here, bodies, looking like tossed rag dolls, could be seen dotting the empty alleys between collapsed buildings. Worst of all, nothing, absolutely nothing moved. The base was dead.

Linda tried to keep Jason from seeing, but he wiggled free and just stared silently at the carnage below.

"The elevator's still intact," Khalid said. "We can proceed."

Jason tugged at Linda's arm. She glanced down at him, having to tear her eyes away from the devastation. He had lifted up his shirt and pointed to the LED readout on his belt. The number thirty glowed on the panel. Thirty minutes until the plastique would be triggered.

She nodded. "Khalid, it's time to reset Jason's timer."

He glanced at her, his eyes cold. "Later."

She looked at Jason. He just stared back at her in resignation.

Bringing up the rear behind the roaring transport sled, all Ben could see ahead of him was the hairy bottom of the *mimi'swee* hunter on the next sled.

The exposed hunter went by the name of Nob'cobi. Harry had introduced the tiny warrior as Dennis's blood brother. The hunter had insisted on accompanying the party, since Dennis could not come. Nob'cobi would lose serious *il'jann* points if he should be denied a place in the party. It was an obligation of blood brothers.

Still, from the way Nob'cobi clutched his sled and shook with every bump, he was probably wishing, *il'jann* or no *il'jann*, that he had stayed behind. The other two hunters ahead of him didn't seem to be faring any better.

Ben reached a hand forward and gave Nob'cobi's leg a pat of reassurance. But his touch caused the hunter to squeak in panic and almost lose his grip. "Easy there, buddy," he shouted over the noise of the engine, trying to sound as calm as possible, which is difficult when yelling. "You're doing great. Just a little longer."

Ben glanced at his watch. They had been traveling for just shy of an hour. If he was estimating their speed correctly, that meant another three hours. They should be topside by midday. Not bad.

Ben laid his forehead on his arm, closing his eyes, letting the rocking motion and the persistent thrum of the engine lull him. If only the *mimi'swee* hunters could relax. He thought about Nob'cobi, who got suckered into this raw deal.

Without even opening his eyes, Ben could picture the hunter clutching his sled like a drowning man bobbing in the surf. The Nob'cobi he pictured then turned to him and spoke: "I can go just as fast on my own. This . . . this is . . . mad."

"Well, *we* can't," he thought in answer. "We're not built as compact as you."

"I hate this!"

"Oh, quit your whining," Ben thought.

Suddenly Nob'cobi's eyes grew so large, they looked almost entirely white. "You really are a *heri'huti.*"

Another voice suddenly intruded on his conversation. A familiar voice. "Very good, Benny boy. You're learning." Mo'amba's voice faded away.

"Wait . . . what did . . . ?" Ben opened his eyes to find Nob'cobi staring back at him, his eyes wide.

"*Heri'huti,*" he said, then turned forward.

Ben pondered the implications. He had done it. Just like Mo'amba had contacted him, he had contacted Nob'cobi. Even his head throbbed with the familiar ache from a mental conversation. So how come he had done it so easily? He had never been able to do anything like that before.

Mo'amba's disembodied voice again spoke to him. "The hunters are accustomed to the suggestions of the *heri'huti*. Their minds are trained to accept our contact. Your own people are not so trained." Mo'amba's voice faded away again.

Bloody hell, thought Ben. Enough of this bullshit. This Vulcan mind-meld crap wasn't going to get that statue out of Blakely's safe.

Just then the timbre of the engine changed again. Harry was slowing down. "What's up?" he yelled.

Harry answered, "We're reaching the halfway point."

Ben checked his watch. Another hour had passed. "So why stop?"

"The engine needs to cool. It's red-hot. I built this baby for speed, not to haul cargo. This is like pulling a U-haul with an Indy racer."

Suddenly the train dragged out of the wormhole and into a chamber the size of a two-car garage. A second wormhole opening was on the far wall.

"What's this?" Ben asked, rolling free of his sled. He groaned as he stood, shrugging out of his pack.

Harry stood a few feet away, rolling his head from side to side. "Mo'amba told me there was a resting place halfway up for religious travelers. I thought it would be a good spot to stretch our legs, drain our lizards, and let the engine cool."

Nob'cobi and the other two hunters were already off their sleds and standing as far from the plastic train as possible. The three were deep in animated conversation. The gestures they made toward the contraption, even without translation, were obviously foul.

Ben crossed to Harry. "So how's the gas supply?"

"Just fine. Quit worrying."

"How long till the engine cools?"

Harry shrugged. "I don't know. Half an hour. An hour."

Ben nodded, but his hands kept clenching and unclenching. He paced the narrow space. As long as they were moving, it wasn't so bad. This stop was agonizing.

"Relax!" Harry finally said. "We're making good time."

"I know, I know." Ben searched for something to distract him, but the chamber was a monotonous uniform room. He stared at the trio of hunters. "What are they talking about?"

"Mostly bitching." Harry took a diamond knife from a hide scabbard at his waist and picked at his nails. "They're also telling some old folk tales about the great exodus from their original dwellings above, down to their present village."

"Yeah, so why did they leave?"

"From what I can tell, there was some sort of earthquake and the cavern flooded. Lots of them died. I guess there's some holy site up above that Nob'cobi wants to visit. Something about ancient warriors who died in a flash flood. Their heads are buried in clear stone. I don't get that part."

"I think I do." Ben pictured the cave pearls that his team had discovered with the embedded skulls in the center.

Harry looked at him as if he were nuts. "Yeah, whatever. Anyway, after they left, the *crak'an* took over their cavern. The bastards use it as some sort of mating ground. Apparently there are several pods of these creatures. And once every decade, they converge in the big cavern and duke it out for mates."

"Something tells me this was the tenth year." Ben tried to picture herds of those bloody monsters, hyped up with territorial and mating aggression. Alpha Base never had a chance.

Harry nodded soberly. "I'd better check the sled."

Finally, after tinkering with the engine for twenty agonizing minutes, Harry gave the thumbs-up sign.

After much fidgeting, the group of *mimi'swee* climbed astride their sleds, and they were under way again.

The remainder of the trip was uneventful. No stalls, no problems. Still, it took forever, During the trip, Ben checked his watch at least sixty times.

At long last, Harry cut the engine. "End of the line, folks."

One of the hunters clambered over Harry to get to the stone door ahead. He manipulated something to the right of the door, and the wall of rock swung out into *ohna*'s chamber. Harry followed the hunter into the small cave, hauling the train behind him.

Once in the chamber, Ben rolled off his sled and crossed in a crouch to the chamber's threshold. He quickly scanned the immediate environment, expecting to see herds of mating beasts. But nothing was out there, just the still lake gently lapping at the rocky shore below.

He glanced across the cavern. Miles away, he could see the flickering lights of the distant camp. Alpha Base. From here it appeared okay, but on closer inspection he realized there were not enough lights. The base was partly extinguished.

The air, once so clear, now stung his nostrils. Reeking of old smoke and burning oil, it smelled like trouble.

THIRTY-TWO

The first thing that struck Jason as they got close to the base was the odor. The stench penetrated past the perpetual odor of oily soot. Jason pinched his nose and concentrated on breathing through his mouth but still felt like he was going to gag.

Linda patted him on the back but wore a sour expression too. "Khalid," she called. "We're close enough to the base, and Jason's timer is down to seven minutes."

"Then increase your pace. I won't reset it until we reach the camp."

"It's not safe to rush like this. There could still be more of those monsters around. We should go slowly."

"By now the smoky air has probably driven them out of the cavern, but it won't last forever. We need to strike now before the smoke clears."

Linda took quicker steps. "Jason, we'd better hurry."

Jason glanced down at the belt of explosives. He watched the number blink from six down to five. No kidding.

As they approached the edge of the base, the source of the odor became apparent, and they all slowed down. "Don't look, Jason," Linda said, trying to shelter him.

Ignoring her warning, Jason watched while Khalid gave the carcass of the dead beast a wide berth as he crept around it. Linda followed, pulling Jason along. As they rounded its bulk, the cause of death became apparent. Its stomach had been blown open by some explosive. Bits of metal and clotted intestines were strewn several yards across the floor. Jason swallowed hard, fighting back the urge to retch. He didn't know which was worse, the sight or the smell.

As they hurried around the reeking beast, Linda suddenly gasped and turned Jason's head to her chest. But not before he glimpsed the headless torso of one of the base personnel still caught in its dead jaws. This time he didn't fight to be free of her embrace.

Once past the remains, Linda released him, patting him on the back. He saw Khalid had stopped ahead, visibly shaken, his face blanched.

Linda crossed to him. "I don't want Jason to see any more of this."

Khalid actually nodded. "We're almost where I need to go. It's down this way." He turned and led the way. "Move quietly."

Leading the way, Khalid traced a path between two collapsed wooden buildings. As they followed, Jason noticed the booted legs of a soldier sticking out from under a jumbled pile of wooden beams and glass. He looked away.

The base was silent around them, their footsteps the only noise.

Khalid paused for a moment, glancing around him as if to get his bearings, then proceeded north across the edge of the base. In less than a minute, they had reached one of the yard-thick natural pillars that connected the distant ceiling to the floor.

Khalid pulled off his pack and opened it. He removed a length of climbing rope and tossed it to Linda. "Tie the boy here."

"What?" She dropped the rope, refusing.

"He has three minutes left on the timer. I'll reset it once he's secure."

"But why—"

"You're running out of time. Do it now!"

Linda glanced at Jason's timer, then bent down and picked up the rope. "I'm sorry," she said as she positioned his back against the stone column.

"Tie his hands behind his back first."

Jason saw the worried look in her eyes as she knotted the rope around his wrists. He could tell she was on the verge of tears. This bothered Jason more than being tied up. "It's okay," he whispered to her.

She secured his waist to the column with the rope.

"Make it tight. You'll use up precious seconds if I have to redo it."

Linda pulled the rope snug and tied a rapid knot. "I'm done." She sat back, her head hanging down. "There," she said, anger sharpening her voice. "Now reset the timer!"

Khalid checked the knots and the tautness of the ropes. He then bent down and tapped at the credit-card-sized keyboard below the LED readout. The number now flashed 120. Jason had another two hours.

"Why are you doing this?" Linda asked.

"Two reasons. First, the boy is slowing us down. And I have fifteen charges still to set. With your help, I can be done in less than two hours. The second reason is motivation. I won't return to reset his timer again until all fifteen charges are placed. This way you'll be encouraged to cooperate with the utmost speed."

"I'll help you. I told you I would. There's no need for this."

His next words were acid: "Your word is shit."

She remained silent.

Jason saw Khalid grab two handkerchiefs and come toward him. He tried to shy away, but the ropes held him tight. Khalid shoved the heel of his hand into Jason's forehead, pinning the back of his skull to the rock column. He then balled up one of the handkerchiefs and forced it into Jason's mouth. Before Jason could try to spit it out, he secured the gag with the second handkerchief.

By now, Linda was grabbing at Khalid's arm. "Leave him alone!"

Khalid elbowed her away, finishing his knot. "I don't want this brat screaming as soon as we leave. It could draw those creatures back." He pointed at Jason's belt. It now read 116. "We're wasting time."

Linda knelt by Jason. He tried to remain calm. She touched his cheek. "I'll be back. I promise."

He nodded, forcing back the tears that threatened.

She hugged him tight until Khalid pulled at her shoulder. "Now!"

Linda stood, and with a final squeeze on Jason's shoulder, she turned and followed Khalid. Jason watched them disappear out of sight behind him, then listened as their footsteps faded into the darkness. He was alone.

. . .

With his helmet lamp slicing a path forward into the blackness, Ben led the way across the empty cavern floor, heading for the lights of Alpha Base. He was careful to stop frequently and listen. Even though he could not see them, he knew the three *mimi'swee* hunters, armed with knives and spears, had fanned out to either side, watching for any signs of the *crak'an*. They moved without lights and were as silent as phantoms. The only thing Ben could hear was the scrape of Harry's boots on the rock behind him.

Ben switched his pistol to his other hand and wiped his palm on his trousers leg. The fires had heated up the cavern and the pall of smoke made it difficult to breathe. He licked at his cracked lips and removed his canteen, flipping the top with his thumb. Careful to no more than wet his mouth, he took a quick swig, then whispered to Harry, "I expected lots of those monsters to be still around."

"Maybe the heat and the smoke are keeping them away."

"I don't like it. This is just too damned easy. One thing I've learned when things look fine—shit happens!"

Harry shrugged. "Be careful what you wish for, buddy."

A noise to the right drew their attention. "It's Nob'cobi," Harry said. "C'mon. He's found something."

Ben followed Harry's bouncing lantern across the uneven floor. Nob'cobi was crouched by a steaming pile of dung. He had a fistful of it in front of his nose. He turned to Harry and spoke in hushed tones.

Harry translated. "He says it's fresh."

"Well, that's good." Ben crinkled his nose at the odor. "I'd hate to think it had spoiled."

"He estimates it's less than an hour old. There's other spoor too. He's guessing that it's a group of at least five of them. Two of them male."

"He can tell all that from sniffing shit?"

"It's their job."

"What should we do, then? Circle away from them?"

Harry knelt and conversed in whispers with Nob'cobi. The other two hunters stood yards away, scanning the periphery, ears twitching forward and back. Finally Harry stood and returned to Ben. "The plan is to follow the group. They seem to be aiming for the base. The *crak'an* travel in tight pods. As they march, any stragglers they encounter will either join the pod or be killed by them. So the wake of this pod should be relatively free of stray beasts."

"Yeah," Ben mumbled, kicking at the pile of damp spoor, "but if they turn back this way, we become *crak'an* shit ourselves."

Khalid watched Linda closely, making sure she set the wires correctly. Good. She was learning. This was the ninth charge. She had set the last three after he demonstrated with the first two. This time, her hands hardly shook.

As he finished his charge, he watched as she furtively glanced at her watch. He knew it was still another hour before Jason's timer ran out, and with only six more charges to set, they were making good time. "Now push the yellow button on the transceiver," he said to her, pointing over her shoulder. "Good, now it's activated and awaiting my signal."

As they neared the base, Ben could see the pod of *crak'an* through the darkness, their triangular heads and bristled crests outlined by the lights of the camp, now just yards away.

The pod totaled seven—two more had joined the group during the hour of travel to the base. Led by the larger of the two males, the pod of females traveled in a loose array, or "harem," as Harry described it. The smaller male, nicknamed "Tiny Tim," trailed them. He seemed to be guarding the pod's backside and frequently turned and ventured a ways behind the pod. He seemed to sense that something was amiss, frequently whirling back, scenting the air behind the group.

"Edgy son of a bitch," Harry whispered in Ben's ear as he crouched behind a boulder next to him.

Ben nodded, wary of even speaking, fearful of attracting the beast's attention. The journey had been tense. During the trek, the pod had encountered a solitary belligerent male. It was attacked by the group in a sharklike frenzy and torn to meaty ribbons.

Remembering the sight, Ben shivered. Out here in the middle of the open cavern floor, there were few places to hide. If they should attract the pod's attention . . . He shook his head, forcing the image from his mind.

He peeked around the boulder. He could see that the pod was just now entering the periphery of the base, fading into the shadows of the remaining buildings.

"It's clear," Harry said softly, waving to the trio of *mimi'swee* hunters. "Let's go."

Ben stood from his crouch and stepped to follow Harry. As he rounded the boulder, his foot slipped in an unseen hole and he fell. As his pistol struck the rocky floor, he saw the flash of muzzle fire from its barrel, and an explosive shot rang out across the cavern.

Christ, Ben thought, so much for a quiet entrance.

He watched as a reptilian snout reemerged from the shadows of the base ahead, darting back and forth, searching. Tiny Tim stepped back out into the light.

Jason squirmed in his ropes as the gunshot echoed across the cavern. He chewed at his gag, but he couldn't even move his tongue, and breathing through his mouth was all but impossible. He pulled deeply through his nose, panicked that he couldn't get enough air. Around him, shadows danced in the flickering light.

His first thought was that Khalid had shot Linda, and his heart pounded in his chest. Then a volley of gunfire from an automatic weapon echoed across the cavern. It wasn't Khalid! He struggled again with his gag. Maybe he could work free of it, call to whoever it was for help.

More gunfire erupted.

Was it coming closer? He listened. Blood thundered in his ears, making it hard to judge.

More blasts.

Yes! He struggled more frantically. Then a thought occurred to him and he froze.

What were they firing at?

Ben slammed into the entryway of one of the few concrete buildings still standing. Nob'cobi pounced in behind him, breathing hard. A quick scan revealed the building to be a dormitory—cots lined both walls. But Ben ignored the room and took a quick peek back out the entryway. He saw the tail of one of the *crak'an* disappear around the far corner.

Good. Luckily, it had been one of the slower females that had pursued them. A few quick moves and they had lost her. But what about Harry? Had he made it to the base?

Volleys of automatic fire flared to the south.

Ben clenched a fist. Okay, at least he was still alive and fighting. He considered his options, rubbing at his forehead. He could try to make it to Harry, but it would be damned difficult to find him. Or he could try to get to Blakely's office and retrieve the statue. That was the wisest plan, but he hated leaving Harry and the other hunters on their own.

Still, what could he do? His one pistol would be little help. No, he'd just have to hope Harry and the others could manage. Besides, Harry knew the base well and knew where Ben would be heading.

He pushed open the door of the building, leaned out, and took a moment to get his bearings. Spotting the elevator shaft off to the left, and the lake just past a set of trampled tents, he centered himself. Okay, he knew roughly where he was. Blakely's office was less than half a mile away. That's if the bridge spanning the gorge that split the camp was still intact. If he had to circle around the huge crevice, then it would be more like two miles. And with those bloody *crak'an* creeping around, he wanted the shortest route possible.

Taking a deep breath, he waved Nob'cobi to follow. The small hunter, clenching a spear longer than his own body, followed. Ben led the way, sticking close to shadows and ducking from hiding place to hiding place.

As Ben inched across the base, he heard periodic bursts of gunfire. He stopped and listened, biting his lower lip. The shots were getting farther and farther away. With all the hiding places available, Harry should have been able to lose the bastards by now.

He glanced at Nob'cobi. The hunter leaned casually on his spear shaft, his lids half-closed, scratching at his bare backside. Why was he so freakin' calm?

Again five shots rang out—even farther away now.

Then it dawned on Ben. Harry was purposefully firing off rounds, drawing the beasts away, leaving the way open for Ben to get to the office.

He looked at Nob'cobi. He nudged the *mimi'swee* hunter. "You knew that, didn't ya, bub? C'mon." He increased the pace, counting on Harry to lure the *crak'an* astray.

Now moving quicker, Ben reached the gorge in two minutes, but stopped when he saw the bridge. Or at least where the bridge used to be.

"Goddamn it," he muttered. "Can't anything go right?" All that was left of the bridge was a couple of broken spars jutting a few feet across the gorge, leaving a black gap of empty space. He eyed the span. At least thirty feet. Much too far to jump. They would have to walk—

He jumped at a loud crash behind him. Whirling around, he turned to see one of the *crak'an* lunge from between two buildings into the cleared area in front of the gorge. It was Tiny Tim, and he blocked the only way back to the maze of buildings and tents. The creature hissed and stalked forward.

"So, you little bastard," Ben said, backing away as he raised his gun, "you weren't fooled by Harry." He pointed his pistol and fired.

The creature shied away from the noise and pawed slightly at its neck. Ben could see the trail of blood oozing from the wound. He had hit the target, but the bullet hardly seemed to faze the thick-skinned beast. It stalked toward him.

Nob'cobi darted behind Ben as he fired. The shot went wild, but the noise stopped it. The *crak'an* paused warily, eyeing its prey.

Damn, you could almost see the bastard plotting. Ben backed another step. The edge of the gorge was now only a few feet behind him. He turned to tell Nob'cobi to make a run for it while he distracted the beast, but no one was behind him. Nob'cobi was already gone. Then he saw the small hunter balancing on the spar of the bridge a few yards away, tying a rope to the remains of a lamppost. What was he doing?

Ben turned his attention back to his adversary. The beast just cocked its head back and forth, staring at the pistol as if weighing its danger.

Ben's foot skidded on the slippery rock as he backed another step. He risked a quick glance over his shoulder. Nob'cobi had backed off the bridge and stood an arm's length away from Ben. "What are you—"

Before Ben could finish, Nob'cobi ran toward the damaged bridge. My god, thought Ben, he's gonna try to jump it. It was bloody suicide. He watched as Nob'cobi raced down the single thin spar as if he were running on solid ground. At the last moment, the small hunter brought his long spear forward and jammed the blunt end into the spar and vaulted upward, flying across the empty air. He landed in a roll on the far side of the gorge.

Ben noticed for the first time the loop of rope wrapped around Nob'cobi's waist. The length of climbing rope now trailed across the gorge to where the tiny hunter had secured it to the lamppost.

A roar drew his attention back around. Tiny Tim stared across the gorge at his escaped prey, obviously angered at his loss. Now those black eyes fixed back on Ben. He could almost see the smile spread on its lips, exposing the full length of its yellowed teeth. It stepped toward him.

Ben, whose gun was still vaguely pointing at the beast's head, realized his chances of a head shot were poor, a kill shot beyond his skill. He lowered his aim toward an easier target, its belly. If he had guessed Nob'cobi's intentions correctly, Ben needed only a few seconds of breathing room.

He pulled the trigger. The shot dug into Tiny Tim's flank, causing the beast to back up a few steps.

Ben didn't wait. He swung around and ran toward the damaged bridge. Just as he had anticipated, Nob'cobi had pulled up the slack in the rope and had secured his end around a post on the far side. Ben now had a rope bridge across the gorge.

Behind him, he heard a roar. It was coming! His feet almost slipped as the traction changed from rock to wood as he reached the broken bridge. His arms out for balance, he darted down the spar and leaped off the end.

He dove for the rope, stretching his arms out as far as he could.

Grimacing, he caught the rope with one hand, wrenching his shoulder as his weight swung down. He flailed for a second, his grip slipping slightly. Then he swung a second hand on the rope. He hung there a second, breathing heavily, shaken.

The rope jerked in Ben's grip. What the hell? He craned his neck around. Tiny Tim rammed the lamppost to which Nob'cobi had secured the rope. If the post went, so would that end of his rope bridge.

Ben glanced down at the black pit below him. He scrambled hand over hand across the bridge, but the jostling of the rope made his progress jerky and slow.

He wasn't going to make it.

And as the rope went limp in his grip, he realized for once in his life he was right.

THIRTY-THREE

Linda realized two things as she crouched in the semi-demolished latrine. First, there was no way that she and Khalid could complete all the explosive charges before Jason's time ran out. With only twenty minutes left, they still had three more charges to set. Second, she had also come to realize that Khalid had never intended to free Jason anyway.

She stared at the cold figure of Khalid as he peered out the broken door of the building. The stench of pine disinfectant was thick in the narrow space. Since the gunfire began, he had made no move to complete the charges; instead, he sought the nearest shelter and decided to lay low.

She slid next to Khalid. "Jason's timer is running out."

He nodded. "I know, but the gunfire is between us and the boy. A small pocket of resistance obviously withstood the initial onslaught. And whatever they're shooting at, I'd just as soon avoid."

Right, you bastard, she thought. A convenient excuse. The asshole never planned to return for Jason. By now, she had recognized a pattern to Khalid's charges. He was circling the camp, setting charges at the base of the largest colonnades that ran from floor to ceiling. He meant to blow up a majority of them and bring the roof down. Drop the volcano on top of the caverns.

She also noted that his route was circuitous, ending near the elevator. He obviously meant to complete the series of charges, then hop on the elevator and escape. Leaving Jason to be a human bomb.

Of course, the gunfire had put a crimp in his fine-tuned plans.

Suddenly a roar of rage erupted from across the base. One of those creatures. It sounded pissed. She noticed Khalid flinch with each roar. These things seemed to unnerve him in more ways than simple fear. Even now, he mumbled something low in Arabic. It sounded like a prayer.

Even though she enjoyed seeing the icy Khalid finally shaken up, it had left him paralyzed, afraid to leave this hiding place. And time was running out.

"We need to get going," Linda said firmly.

Khalid whirled on her, his eyes dark.

Before he could curse her, she spoke up. "The gunfire is heading this way, Khalid. Listen." She pointed out the door. "Whatever they're firing at is being driven this way. Toward us."

He clenched his fists, not in anger, but with fear and frustration. "We need to keep moving." Fear cracked his normally steady voice.

"Then let's go!"

A loud snap echoed across the gorge as Tiny Tim rammed loose the mooring of the rope bridge. As Ben began to plummet, he tightened his grip on the limp rope. He prayed Nob'cobi had the remaining mooring securely rigged. Wincing, he watched the far wall race toward him. This was going to hurt, but he had to hold his grip. If the collision should jar him loose from the rope, he would be nothing more than a messy splat on the floor of the gorge.

He twisted around to catch the brunt of the collision with his legs, but it was little use. When he hit, it felt like he had jumped off a ten-story building. His left hip smashed into the wall, almost blinding him with pain, but he ignored it, concentrating on one thing: keeping his grip on the rope, willing his ten fingers to clench tight.

He bounced off the wall and swung back. This time his legs did bear the brunt of the impact, and he came to a stop, hanging fifteen feet from the lip of the gorge.

Across the chasm, Tiny Tim bellowed its rage at him. It stalked back and forth by the damaged bridge, searching for a way across.

Ben squinted at its piercing cries of rage. "Shut the fuck up!" he screamed back at it.

Tiny Tim tensed at his outburst and crouched low just across the gorge. Ben knew it could see him. For a moment, he thought the *crak'an* might suicidally leap at him, but instead it hissed a final time and darted back into the maze of buildings. Good riddance.

Sighing in relief, Ben hung there, resting. He could feel blood running down the inside of his pants leg as he clutched the rope. He needed to finish the climb before he weakened any further.

Twisting a leg in the rope, he risked freeing a hand to snap the rope into the rappelling harness around his waist. With a modicum of a safety net now, he made a steady ascent to the lip.

Once there, Nob'cobi helped him over the edge. Ben rolled to his back on the hard floor, his breathing raspy. The hunter fingered Ben's blood-soaked trousers leg. He said something in his guttural language, his voice sounding concerned.

"It's just a gash. I'll live." He pushed himself up. "By the way, mate, thanks for the rescue. I was sure we were gonna be monster chow."

Nob'cobi wrinkled his brow in confusion.

"Oh, never mind." Ben tried to stand, but his injured hip protested. It wasn't broken, but it still hurt like hell. Hopping, he headed away from the gorge. "C'mon. We still need to get to that safe."

Nob'cobi followed, but after a few yards, he grabbed Ben's arm and pointed to the droplets of blood from his gash that dripped as he walked.

"I told you it's nothing. Blakely has a first-aid kit in his office." Ben turned to leave, but the little hunter persisted, pulling him back. He pantomimed sniffing at the bloody trail, then imitated a fair approximation of a *crak'an*'s throaty growl.

"You think I'm leaving a trail?" Ben studied the line of droplets. "You're right. I guess it's best if we don't leave such an obvious invitation."

Ben stripped out of his bloody trousers and wrung them out. Standing in his shorts, he examined his wound. A jagged slash across his upper thigh. It would leave an ugly scar but nothing worse. Frowning, he used the last dregs of his canteen to wash the wound, then secured a handkerchief around his upper thigh to stanch the flow of blood.

"There," Ben said, slipping back into his trousers. "Are you happy?"

The hunter had that bored look on his face again, apparently content.

"Fine. Let's go." Ben led the way, sneaking from shadow to shadow. He had enough of those stinking *crak'an* and didn't want to run into any others.

The way was clear. Within five minutes, he found himself at the door to Blakely's office. The glass door to the administration office was smashed, but otherwise the concrete-block building was intact. Stepping gingerly across the threshold, careful of the glass, Ben entered the reception area. Something large had trashed the room. A thick yellow substance reeking of ammonia smeared the walls.

"Looks like some bloody alley cat sprayed the place," Ben muttered as he examined the wreckage of desk and files. Pushing through the debris, he reached the undamaged metal door that led to the offices. He tried the knob. Locked.

"Goddamn it!" He struck the door, bruising his fist. He rattled the doorknob.

A voice called from behind the door, "Hello! Is someone out there?"

By god, someone was alive! He pounded on the door. "Open up. It's Ben Brust from the exploration team."

A pause, then meekly, "Is it safe?"

"For the moment. Now open up."

He heard the deadbolt releasing. The door pulled open from within. A small blond woman with straggly hair stood before him. A smart business suit was in shambles on her thin form.

"Sandy?" Ben recognized Blakely's secretary. "Are you all right?"

She ran to him and hugged him. "Thank god you're here!"

Nob'cobi stepped up to Ben and mumbled something, pointing back out the door.

Sandy stared at the small naked hunter, her eyes wide, her fingers digging into Ben's arm. She gave a small whimper and backed away.

Ben waved Nob'cobi outside so as not to scare her any further. He pushed Sandy down the hallway toward Blakely's office.

Once inside, he crossed to the safe where Blakely stored the diamond figurine, the *ohna* idol of the *mimi'swee*. He didn't know the combination, but there were enough blasting caps and explosives on the base that it shouldn't be hard to open. Harry knew where those supplies were and how to use them. So where was Harry now?

Sandy huddled on a sofa. "What . . . what was that . . . creature?"

"He's a friend. One of the cliff dwellers."

"How . . . I mean . . . when . . . ?"

He sat down next to her. "It's a long story, but trust me, he's a friend. He won't harm you."

She hugged her arms around her chest and shivered.

"How did you get left behind?" he asked. "Why didn't you evacuate with the others?"

She stared at him as if he were crazy. "There was no evacuation. They attacked so suddenly. There was no time. Everyone's dead."

"What? But what about reinforcements from above?"

"We lost radio communications almost immediately. On the day following the attack, I heard the elevator motor and took a chance and ran to look." Her face paled as she related the story.

"The elevator was packed with soldiers. But they didn't know." She turned to him, her eyes tearing up. "*They didn't know.* The noise drew those creatures. Scores of them. When the elevator opened, the men were overwhelmed, torn to pieces." She placed her face in her hands. "Since then, no one's tried to come down."

Ben nodded. "With McMurdo on the backass side of the world, it's no wonder. It'll probably take them at least a week to stage a full-scale assault. Until then we're on our own."

Sandy's sobbing worsened.

He patted her hand. "We'll make it until then."

With her voice full of tears, she said, "They all ran out. I was all alone. I couldn't do anything."

"What about Blakely?"

She shook her head. "The last time I saw him, he was running out of here with that boy Jason."

Ben's heart skipped a beat. "Do you know if they made it to safety?"

"I don't know what happened. I locked myself in here. But the screaming . . . the screaming went on for days. Then nothing. Nothing at all. That was the worst. The silence." She looked up at him, shaking. "I thought I was the last one left."

"Well, you're not." He stood up. What was he going to tell Ashley? He paced the floor and glanced at his watch. Fourteen hours had elapsed. He still had to blow the safe and return to the *mimi'swee* village. That didn't leave him room to thoroughly search the entire base with those beasts around. He stopped in front of the safe and clenched his fist. Where in bloody hell was Harry? He turned to Sandy. "I don't suppose you happen to know the combination to Blakely's safe?"

She nodded and told him.

Finally, maybe his luck was turning. He twirled the dial as she instructed and swung open the heavy door.

For a moment he didn't think it was in there, until he realized the statue had been wrapped in brown paper and twine. He picked it up and ripped the paper off, holding it up to the filtered light. Ben ran a finger across the statue's thick belly. Hopefully, she would bring him luck.

Just then Nob'cobi came rushing in, a panicked look on his face.

Somehow Ben knew his luck had just run short again.

Tears of frustration ran down Jason's face. He still couldn't believe it. At first he had thought he had imagined it, but the accent was clear. Ben! He had heard him talking to someone, followed by a loud knocking. From only a little distance away! He couldn't make out the words clearly, but it had to be Ben. Jason had tried to call to him, but the gag stifled all but a soft moan that barely reached his own ears.

Finally, he had heard a door slam shut, followed by silence. He strained to listen for any evidence that Ben was still around. Nothing. He must have gone into the building.

Jason struggled with his bonds. If only he could free a hand and pull the gag off. He had to find some way to call to Ben when he exited the building. If he should fail . . . He glanced at the LED readout on his belt. The number 11 glowed on the screen, and as he watched, it dissolved into the number 10.

He needed help . . . fast. He struggled again with the ropes, but it was no use. He slumped against the restraints. He needed another plan.

As he hung from the pillar, an idea suddenly struck him. Maybe . . .

He shifted his hips. If he could reach his left hand to his jacket pocket . . . He squeezed his eyes closed as he stretched and contorted his body, straining in his bonds. He felt his fingers close on the familiar plastic box. Careful not to drop it, he struggled to free it from his pocket, but it caught in the fabric. He stopped and took a deep breath. Don't rush! With more concentration, he slowly worked it free of his jacket, sighing in relief. It had been the only thing that Khalid had let him keep from his gym bag.

He prayed the batteries still worked as he flipped on his Nintendo Game Boy. A familiar jingle bounced from the toy. He twisted the volume control to its highest. The music was not particularly loud, but with luck, the oddity of the sound would attract Ben when he left the building.

He waited. Please, Ben, hurry. What if the batteries should die out too soon? What if he was wrong and Ben had already left? What if the timer on his belt reached zero before Ben heard him? His mind spun with awful misgivings.

But one worry he had not considered until he saw the black snout angle around the corner to his right. What if the noise attracted something other than Ben? Jason watched as it hissed softly at him, its nostrils flaring open and closed. He thumbed off his Nintendo and froze. The creature stalked fully into view. Bloody wounds oozed from its belly and neck, but it seemed unaffected by the injuries as it slowly slunk in his direction.

THIRTY-FOUR

Ashley was sure her son was fine. He had to be. She put down her pen. All day she had been working in *umbo*'s chamber, trying to keep her hands busy and her mind distracted. Cataloging, measuring, recording notes in her logbook.

She glanced at her watch. It was already late evening. Ben should be heading back by now. What if he didn't have any word of Jason? Or worse, what if he never came back? How much longer could she wait before this tension drove her mad?

Sighing, she sat back and stared across the chamber at the dozing figure of Mo'amba, seated with his eyes closed. He was her only guard. The others had been sent away. His word was obeyed without question.

She eyed the black wormhole through which Ben had disappeared. She could make a break for it. If Mo'amba was truly napping, then perhaps . . . She shook her head. It was a long crawl. They would surely catch her. Besides, she couldn't abandon Michaelson. Even if by some miracle she did manage to escape, he'd be killed in her place.

Suddenly, Mo'amba's eyes snapped open and he stared at her. He struggled to his feet, but his hours of sitting seemed to cramp him. Ashley crossed over and helped him up.

He eyed the opening to the chamber that led to the village.

"What is it?" she asked.

He placed a hand over her mouth for silence, then waved for her to follow. Using his staff as a crutch, he hobbled through the entrance and pulled her into a shadowed alcove just across the tunnel.

What was going on? But she did not have long to wait. The soft scrape of leather on stone could be heard approaching down the tunnel. Someone was coming. But who?

She squinted down the feebly lit tunnel until Mo'amba pulled her back into the shadows. She waited, holding her breath. From the sound of the approaching footsteps, more than one person approached.

Pressing farther back into the dark alcove, the party slipped past her hiding place and entered *umbo*'s chamber. She swallowed back a hiss as she recognized the bony physique of one of them. It was Sin'jari.

The other two were the exact opposite of Sin'jari. Where he was tall and bony, they were hunched and thick with muscle. But there was no question who was the boss here. A mere frown from Sin'jari would cause the offending party to cringe. And there was a lot of cringing. From the gesturing and sharp commands, it was apparent Sin'jari was giving orders that were only reluctantly being obeyed.

Finally, with a bark from their boss, the two bull-necked brutes ducked their heads and crept into the wormhole that led to Alpha Cavern.

What was going on? Ashley could not understand a word that was being spoken, but Mo'amba apparently did. She could feel him tensing beside her, actually quivering with suppressed emotion. His tension was contagious. She found herself clenching her fists. Sin'jari was up to something nefarious, something meant to harm her group.

Suddenly, Mo'amba burst from the alcove, startling her. She darted after him as he hobbled into *umbo*'s chamber. Sin'jari swung around with his mouth open, stunned and wide-eyed.

Mo'amba crossed to stand almost toe-to-toe with Sin'jari. He stamped his staff so hard splinters flew from its tip. Sin'jari took a step back, obviously flabbergasted by the sudden appearance of his nemesis.

Ashley stood to the side as heated words flowed from Mo'amba. Now it was Sin'jari's turn to cringe. He seemed to fold himself inward as Mo'amba's words assailed him. But where Sin'jari's lackeys had fear in their eyes, Sin'jari's pupils were slitted with menace. From Ashley's vantage, she could see his hand edging toward the knife at his belt.

She opened her mouth to warn Mo'amba, but words caught in her throat. How could she warn him? She couldn't speak a word of their language. She watched as Sin'jari's fingers closed on the knife. Mo'amba was a prominent leader. Surely, Sin'jari wouldn't dare . . .

Without warning, Sin'jari lashed out, driving the long diamond dagger into Mo'amba's chest. The knife cut Mo'amba's angry tirade. The old *mimi'swee* looked down at the hilt protruding from his chest as if analyzing an intriguing bug. He coughed once, a dribble of blood appearing on his lips.

Ashley, frozen with shock, finally screamed as Sin'jari yanked the dagger free, then plunged it a second time into Mo'amba's chest. The old man stumbled backward, pulling himself off the blade.

Sin'jari raised the dagger again, meaning to strike at Mo'amba's throat, but by now Ashley was upon him. She snapped a boot heel into the attacker's ribs, knocking him aside. As he stumbled to catch his balance, she positioned herself in front of Mo'amba. The old man had by now slumped to the floor. Blood flowed from between his fingers as he clutched his chest.

Sin'jari turned to her.

"Get the fuck away, you bastard!" she screamed.

He rubbed his bruised rib with one hand while toying with the blade with the other. His smile was all teeth and no warmth. He had the blade, she didn't.

She eyed the fallen staff that Mo'amba had dropped.

Sin'jari didn't give her a chance to formulate a plan. He lunged at her. But years of karate training and four older brothers had honed her reflexes. She twisted to the side, grabbing Sin'jari's wrist as his lunge missed her. Pivoting on her foot, she used her hip and Sin'jari's momentum to flip the bastard to the floor. The snap of cracking bone brought a smile to her lips. His knife skittered uselessly across the rock.

In two steps, she had the dagger in hand. Now let's see what the bastard thinks with the tables turned, she thought. Sin'jari had already scrabbled away, cradling his left arm. He backed from her to the other side of the chamber, obviously giving up the fight.

While keeping a wary eye on Sin'jari, she crossed to Mo'amba, who now lay sprawled on his back, his chest heaving in gurgling breaths. He seemed to be staring blindly at the ceiling. In shock.

He needed immediate help. But how?

She jumped as Sin'jari suddenly stood up. She pointed the knife at him, but he didn't approach. He slinked, instead, toward the wormhole. With a final sneer at her, he darted into the wormhole and disappeared.

Just as he vanished, she heard the sound of many feet approaching down the tunnel. Thank god help was coming.

She turned just as the first of the warriors burst into the chamber, spears pointing forward. A keening wail arose from them as they spotted the bloody figure of Mo'amba sprawled across the floor. Almost in unison, the angry and accusing eyes of the hunters turned on her.

She looked down at the bloody dagger still in her hand. Damn.

"Calm down," Ben said as he grabbed Nob'cobi's waving hands. He had been trying to make sense of Nob'cobi's frantic gestures and guttural words but was making no headway. His efforts had only succeeded in frustrating both of them.

Ben glanced toward Sandy. She had backed away into a far corner of Blakely's office, cringing. No help there.

He released Nob'cobi's hands. If only Harry would come . . . he knew their language.

Suddenly Nob'cobi reached over and touched Ben's forehead with a single finger, then touched his own. Ben stared at him blankly. The tiny hunter repeated the gesture, irritation starting to crinkle his eyes.

In another moment, Ben understood. Nob'cobi wanted him to communicate with his *heri'huti* skills. The hunter couldn't initiate the contact himself since he wasn't of the proper blood, but Ben could. Like back in the wormhole.

Ben nodded his understanding and gestured for Nob'cobi to sit on the couch. Nob'cobi eyed the leather sofa suspiciously and instead just sat cross-legged on the floor. Ben shrugged and did the same, facing the *mimi'swee* hunter.

Closing his eyes, Ben willed his breathing to slow, striving to calm his agitated mind. He pictured relaxing on the back porch of his father's sheep station with a warm beer and a lazy day ahead.

Suddenly Sandy burst out, "What are you doing?"

Frowning, Ben held up a hand but kept his eyes closed. "It's okay, Sandy. I need you to be quiet for a minute."

"But—"

"Shhh. Just relax." His words, dreamy, were directed at both her and himself. Relax.

He could hear her grumble under her breath, but he ignored her and sipped his tepid Foster's from a dusty bottle while tipping back his chair in the corner of the porch. He thought of Nob'cobi, picturing the little fellow's flat-nosed face and spindly neck. Suddenly, the hunter appeared next to Ben, seated on another chair.

Nob'cobi stared slack-jawed around him. He stood up and leaned on the porch railing, gawking up at the wide sky, not a cloud from horizon to horizon. He seemed to cower a bit, then turned his back on the view to face Ben. "It's . . . it's so big." He shuddered.

Ben felt a little sorry thrusting the poor man into such a foreign landscape, but Mo'amba had done the same with him. Besides, he missed the ranch. "Don't worry, Nob'cobi. It's not the size that counts."

"What?"

"Never mind. Bad joke." Ben took another swig of his beer. Hell if it didn't taste bloody real. "Now, what were you trying to tell me?"

Nob'cobi took a nervous swallow, one eye darting behind him. "I heard a strange noise in the cave. Like nothing I had heard before."

"What did it sound like?"

Nob'cobi scrunched up his face and repeated the sound he heard. It sounded like a tune or something. And it sounded familiar.

"Do that again." Ben concentrated as he listened, eyes closed. Where had he heard that? His eyes sprang open, and he sat up straight. Christ, it's that damned jingle from Jason's Nintendo game! He'd heard the infuriating thing a thousand times during the trek here.

"Where did you hear that?" Ben blurted.

"I went to look. To see what was making that sound. But I almost ran into that *crak'an* that's been hounding us. The smart one. He was following the sound too."

"Blast!" Ben pushed out of the dream, scattering it into colored shreds, until he was facing Nob'cobi again in Blakely's office. He shoved to his feet. Nob'cobi followed.

"Sandy, stay here," Ben said, as he slammed another clip in his gun. "Lock the door. If we come knocking, open the door in a hurry."

She nodded and followed him down the hall. "What's going on?"

"I don't have time to explain." He pushed through the door to the reception area. "Lock it and be quiet."

He heard the door slam behind him and a deadbolt click. He turned to Nob'cobi. "Now show me where that sound was coming from."

The hunter stared at him blankly. Hell, this was not the time for another communication gap. Ben imitated the tune and pretended to look around, then shrugged.

Nob'cobi nodded and pointed out the door, taking the lead.

Ben clenched his pistol in a white-knuckled grip and followed. If he was too late? He shook his head. He wouldn't be.

He followed Nob'cobi back outside. Just as they turned the corner, Harry suddenly appeared before them. Startled, Ben came within a hair of plugging the man with a bullet.

"You made it," Harry said, winded and sweating through his tattered fatigues. "Let's get the statue and get out of here. The other hunters are still leading that pod of *crak'an* on a wild-goose chase, but they can't keep it up much longer. We need to—"

Ben held up a hand. "I got it already."

"Great!"

"But we've got a new problem. We need to hurry." Ben motioned Nob'cobi ahead as he gave Harry a thumbnail account of the situation.

Harry followed. "So you think that's Ashley's kid?"

Ben nodded.

"Shit. Bad time to be playing a video game."

Nob'cobi signaled them to be quiet and waved Harry next to him. He whispered something in his ear. Harry grimaced and backed next to Ben. In a hushed voice, he translated. "This is where Nob'cobi spotted Tiny Tim. The music came from just around the next collapsed building."

Ben nodded. This time he made sure he placed each foot on solid rock before proceeding. He didn't want to repeat the previous blunder that had attracted the pod's attention. The group crept silently, edging past a demolished mess tent, its pots and pans strewn across the rocky floor.

After a minute of creeping, the now-familiar sound of claw on rock and snuffling of something large could be heard from up ahead. Nob'cobi, who was a few yards in front of Ben and Harry, peered around the edge of a pile of shredded lumber into the clearing beyond. Suddenly, he popped back, flattening himself against the corner. He signaled them to freeze.

Ben watched as the beast's thick tail swung into view ahead, sweeping aside a few stray pots. Their clattering was painfully loud in the silence of the dead camp. The tail then disappeared from view.

Nob'cobi waved them slowly forward. Ben crept up first and inched just enough around the corner to peer into the clearing ahead.

Its back was to him, tail slashing back and forth. He could see its head flicking from left to right as it examined something in front of it, snorting loudly. Then it shuffled to the side to get another vantage in which to examine its prey.

Ben suppressed a gasp. As the large creature moved, it revealed its intended target. Jason was roped to one of the columns, the boy's eyes wide with terror. But the *crak'an* just circled around the column, snorting and snuffling, obviously baffled as to why its prey wasn't running. Like a cat, Ben thought, it wasn't used to a meal just sitting there.

Ben slipped back around and allowed Harry a peek before speaking. He whispered in Harry's ear. "I need you to lure the bastard away. Like you did the others. Give me a chance to free Jason and get him to safety. We'll meet back at Blakely's office."

Harry nodded.

"But be careful," Ben warned. "This bastard's a tricky one."

Harry huddled a moment with Nob'cobi. Then the two slipped away to circle east a bit, to draw its attention away from Ben's hiding place.

Ben waited as they maneuvered into position, holding his breath, praying that he wouldn't all of a sudden hear a scream from Jason. The creature wouldn't wait forever. Eventually the novelty would wear thin and it would attack.

Tensed, muscles quivering with anticipation, Ben jumped at the sudden eruption of clanking pots and pans from just east of his position. Harry and Nob'cobi. It was about time. He risked peeking around the corner to see the commotion's effect on the *crak'an*.

It stood there frozen, its ears cocked back to listen, then slowly swung its head in the direction of the noise. It took a few steps toward the sound, then stopped and glanced back at Jason strapped to the pillar. It wasn't going to take the bait. At least not before nailing its easy prey. It took a step back toward Jason.

Goddamn you! Ben raised his pistol. Before Ben could shoot, Harry jumped into the clearing with two dented pots in his hands.

He hollered at it. "Hey there, big fellow, how about a little action?" To punctuate his statement, he slammed the pots together.

The voice and clank got its attention. With a roar, it swung back in Harry's direction. The quickness of the beast seemed to catch Harry off guard. He stumbled a step backward, almost falling. Ben clenched his teeth. Move it, soldier! Harry seemed to hear his silent command and dashed back into the alley.

The fleeing man was too much temptation for the monster. It scrabbled after Harry, disappearing down the alley.

Ben didn't wait. As soon as the tip of its tail vanished, he dashed into the clearing. Toward the boy.

Tears trailed down Jason's soot-blackened features. The boy still stared in the direction of the disappearing beast. Thank god he seemed otherwise unharmed.

Ben ran toward him. The scuffing of Ben's boots on rock drew Jason's attention. A fleeting look of terror crossed his features before he seemed to recognize Ben. Then fresh tears flowed.

Ben reached him in seconds. He hugged him hard in the ropes, pulling the gag free, wondering who the hell had bound and gagged the boy. But now wasn't the time for questions. Jason shook with sobs. "You're okay now, son. You're safe."

But Jason kept on sobbing, trying to get words out between choking sobs. "I . . . tried to . . . tried to call you . . . with my game." He dropped the toy still held in his hands, and it clattered to the stone.

"You did good." Ben crouched down, pulled out a knife, and attacked the ropes.

"My . . . my mom . . . is she okay?"

"She's fine. She's somewhere safe."

Suddenly, Jason jerked in the loosening ropes. Ben could barely get the boy's hands untied with him squirming so much. He finally succeeded.

"Stay still for a sec. Let me get that last rope from around you."

"I need to see!" Jason seemed frantic.

"What?"

Jason lifted up his untucked shirt. For the first time, Ben noticed the glowing LED readout on Jason's belt buckle. The number 6 glowed back at him.

Jason looked down, then moaned.

"What's that?"

"It's a bomb," he said, a desperate look in his eyes.

"What the hell are you talking about?"

Jason pointed out the gray squares of plastique hooked to the belt. "Khalid put it on me. To control Linda. It's set to go off in six minutes."

"Then let's get it off you." He reached for the boy with the knife.

Jason backed away. "If it's removed, it'll go off. Only the secret code will release it."

"Who knows the code?"

"Khalid . . . and he's out there somewhere setting other bombs."

The goddamn bastard. If I get my hands on him . . . "Well, there's got to be a way to disarm it.

Maybe Harry . . . he's a demolitions expert." Ben covered his face with his hands. Bloody hell. How was he going to get him back here in time? They weren't supposed to rendezvous back at Blakely's office for another half hour. He clenched his fists and pressed them against his temple. Goddamn it man, *think*!

Ben stared as the LED number dissolved from a 6 to a 5.

Ashley plopped down on the pillow in her small cave. Once again she was confined to her cell. Three guards stood at the threshold, diamond blades glinting in the fungal glow. She had tried through both pantomime and repeating Sin'jari's name to communicate her innocence in the attack on Mo'amba, but it was futile. Her only witness, Mo'amba, was near death.

A commotion at the entrance to her cell drew her attention. She watched as Michaelson was shoved past the guards. He stumbled on his weak ankle but caught his balance.

"Fuckers took my guns," he said as he crossed over to her. "All of them. What's going on?"

"Sorry, it was my fault," she said, standing up, her muscles still tense with frustration. "I was at the wrong place at the wrong time." She told him the story of Sin'jari's attack on Mo'amba, and the result of her interference. "I was caught with a smoking gun, so to speak. Mo'amba was found stabbed in the chest with me standing over him, the murder weapon in my hand. Can you blame them?"

"What's going to happen?"

She shrugged. "I don't know. I think everyone's more concerned about Mo'amba at the moment."

"Do you think the old guy has any chance of surviving?"

Ashley shook her head. "Doubtful. He lost a lot of blood. And with his mental abilities, if he was able, he'd be blowing the whistle on Sin'jari himself—telepathically on all wavelengths. For him to be remaining so silent, he's got to be nearly brain-dead. And if he dies, I don't think either one of us has much chance of living, regardless of whether or not Ben makes the deadline."

Michaelson glanced at his watch. "Ben has less than eight hours."

Sighing, she said, "Now I'm hoping he doesn't return. As angry as those tribesmen are, I think even if he returns with the statue, they'll just execute him along with us. It'd be best if he just stays away."

"He won't."

"I know." She sat back down on a pillow and waved Michaelson to do the same. "If only there was a way to warn him. To tell Harry and Ben not to come back."

"There's no way. Come hell or high water, Ben will return for you."

She smacked her knee with a fist. "Then I've got to find some way to let the village know about Sin'jari. Some way to communicate. But they won't even try to listen. Their judgment is too clouded with anger."

"Maybe Harry will return with Ben before Mo'amba dies. He could translate your story."

"Even if he did, do you think they'd believe us? Sin'jari is one of their elders. It would be his word against mine."

"Then we'll need evidence. What do you think the bastard was up to anyway?"

"No good, that's for sure. I think he means to interfere with Ben's mission. Thwart it in some way."

"If we could prove that, then that would go a long way to support your claim."

"But how?" she asked, exasperated.

"Catch him red-handed when he returns. The only easy route back to the village from Alpha Cavern is through that wormhole. If he went up that way, he'll sneak back that way."

"And how do you propose to catch him locked up in this cell?"

He shrugged. "Hey, I don't have all the answers."

She shook her head at the uselessness of their reverie. "Still, this all depends on Mo'amba surviving until Ben and Harry return. If he should—"

A keening wail erupted from the guards at the door. A cry that also echoed from the village around them, piercing the stone walls like paper, the pitch so high it caused the hairs to stand on Ashley's arms.

Michaelson covered his ears, eyes squinting at the noise.

As suddenly as it started, the wailing ceased. The sudden silence felt huge and empty, as if something vital had been removed from the air.

Ashley saw one of the guards look in her direction. Under his bony brow, tears were in his eyes, and something else too—hatred.

"What was that all about?" Michaelson asked.

"We just ran out of time. Mo'amba's dead."

Ben was just starting to stand when it hit. Like an explosion between his ears. He stumbled back to his knees. At first, he thought some bomb must have detonated, like the one attached to Jason's waist, but when he pried his eyes open, Jason was just staring at him with a quizzical look.

"Are you okay?" the boy asked, seemingly unaware of what had just transpired.

Ben nodded. "I think so . . ." Then the world went black.

What the hell? He struggled but seemed to be floating in a space without stars, nothing to push against, nothing to fight. He was not unconscious, just surrounded by an infinite blackness. Then a single dull ember appeared, glowing in the darkness ahead. As he concentrated on this landmark, like some distant beacon, the glow intensified to a bright flame. It spoke, vibrating with each word, in his grandfather's voice. ". . . Ben . . . Ben . . . you must . . . hurry . . ."

By now, Ben could recognize one of Mo'amba's callings. But now was not the time. "What is it? What's wrong? Is Ashley okay?"

". . . weak . . . tired . . ." The flame died again to only a feeble flicker. ". . . must hurry . . ." It flickered bright for a heartbeat. "Danger . . ." Then it faded, first back to a dull glow, then to nothing. And in the darkness, Ben felt an emptiness. Somehow he knew that Mo'amba had not just broken contact but was gone. Gone for good. As the world reappeared around him, he found tears trailing down his cheek.

"Ben, what's wrong?" Jason was shaking his shoulder.

He pushed off the stone floor where he had collapsed. Mo'amba was dead. He knew this as sure as he knew his father's name. "I'm okay," he answered the boy.

"You fainted."

"Don't worry, I'm fine." He patted the boy's knee, while pondering the meaning of Mo'amba's final urgent message. He had wanted Ben to return immediately. Not to waste any more time. But what was the hurry? Ben still had seven hours before his deadline. Something must be up. A new danger.

Jason looked at him with concern but didn't speak.

Ben glanced at the timer on the boy's belt. The number five still glowed on the panel. Hurry, Mo'amba had urged. No kidding. He needed a plan. A way to contact Harry. Get him back here to defuse the bomb.

Then it dawned on him . . . Hell, why didn't he think of this earlier?

He *did* have a means of contacting Harry. Well, at least Nob'cobi, who could then tell Harry to get his butt back here. Mo'amba's calling reminded him. He could do the same. He had never tried it at such a distance . . . and it was doubtful that Nob'cobi was in a relaxed trance state, susceptible to his calling, but it was possible. Mo'amba had done it to him before. He had to try.

"Jason, I know this is gonna seem bloody bonkers, but I'm gonna need to concentrate. I need you to stay quiet."

"Okay, but what—"

"Shhh. Later." Ben sat down cross-legged, closing his eyes and breathing deeply. He again pictured his childhood home outside Perth. The orange dust. The 'roos in the distance. Home.

He sat in a creaking chair on the porch again, not bothering with a beer this time. Instead he concentrated fiercely on Nob'cobi's image, visualizing the hunter sitting next to him. He filled in the details of the hunter's features. The scar across his cheek, the graying patch of fur at the top of his head. As he concentrated, the image flickered into reality for a heartbeat. Nob'cobi's surprised face turned to him, then winked back out.

Damn it! Ben concentrated again. C'mon, Nob'cobi, you saw me there for a second. You know what I want. He pressed forward again. C'mon, listen to me. Nothing. He persisted for what seemed like several wasted minutes. Minutes he didn't have.

Just before he was ready to scream in frustration and give up, Nob'cobi appeared. He seemed winded. "What do you want?" he growled at Ben. "I almost tripped and fell with that first call. You're supposed to—"

"Enough! I need Harry back here. Now!"

"Well, we're heading back that way. That *crak'an* must have it in for you. It gave up chasing us and turned back your way. Are you cleared out of there yet?"

"No. We've got a problem. I need Harry and you to forget about Tiny Tim and meet me back at the office. Run as fast as you can."

"You better do the same. That *crak'an* is coming your way fast."

"Hurry." But Nob'cobi had already vanished.

Ben pushed back out of his dream state and found Jason staring at him.

"What are you doing?"

"It's a long story," he said scrambling up. "We've got company coming." With a relieved sigh, he noticed Jason's LED readout showed a 4. Time moved oddly in the dreaming place. It seemed like he was there a lot longer than a mere moment. "Can you run?"

Jason shifted from foot to foot, obviously full of nervous energy. "Oh, yeah."

"Then come on." Ben grabbed his hand and hurried away, just as he made out the sound of Tiny Tim scrabbling toward them from the other direction. He increased the pace to a vigorous run. The office was barely a hundred yards away. He reached it with Jason in tow in less than a minute. The readout on the belt changed from 4 to 3 just as he pushed through into the trashed reception area. Now just bloody hurry, Harry.

Ben crossed to the door leading to the building's offices and knocked. "It's Ben," he called. He heard the deadbolt being released; the door swung open.

Sandy's worried face peered out. She spotted Jason and her eyes widened. "You found the boy!" She rushed out and scooped him up in a hug as if he were some sort of life preserver.

Then a voice behind him. "So what's the big rush?" Harry stumbled into the reception area. Nob'cobi stepped carefully in behind him.

Ben noticed Jason's eyes widen with surprise at his first glimpse of the *mimi'swee*.

Ben grabbed Harry's shoulder and pulled him forward. "Jason's rigged with explosives. We only have a couple minutes before it blows. I need you to defuse it."

"What the hell?" Harry said, crossing to Jason. "Let me see."

At Ben's words, Sandy had released Jason as if he carried the plague and backed away into the hallway.

Jason pointed to the belt, but kept looking over Harry's shoulder at Nob'cobi as Harry knelt down beside him. The number 2 glowed red. Gingerly, Harry fingered the device, having Jason spin around so he could examine the entire belt. "Hmmm," was all he said.

"Well?" Ben asked.

"I've seen this work before. All ready-made. The triggering device is housed in this little tin box. Even if we had time and tools, I can't get to it without significant risk. Without the code, this baby is gonna blow."

"Goddamn it!" Ben blurted. "Then we're screwed."

Harry shrugged and reached up for the clasp of the belt, triggering an alarmed "Don't!" from Jason. Harry ignored him and yanked it open. The belt merely parted and fell free from his waist. Harry stood up, holding the belt away from him as if it were some snake.

Jason tumbled away. "It was supposed to explode if you took it off."

"Who told you that?" Harry asked.

"Khalid."

"He was lying. There's no circuit around the belt."

Jason stood there trembling. "Then I . . . I could have taken that off . . . anytime." Ben noticed the boy seemed more disturbed by this fact than by the fact that he had been about to be blown up.

Harry nodded. "Yep. Now if you don't mind"—he pointed at the number 1 glowing on the belt—"this thing's still going to explode."

Ben snatched the belt from Harry. "Everyone to the back of the building. I'm gonna toss this baby as far as I can. Then run like hell."

Harry herded everyone into the hall as Ben headed for the door. From behind him, Harry called, "Don't throw like a girl. There's a shitload of plastic hooked to that belt."

"Just get everyone to the far side of the building!" Ben dashed out the door. He sprinted several feet away from the building to get a clear path to lob the belt. As he raised his arm, the beast pounced at him.

From a mere ten feet away, the wounded *crak'an* leaped in front of him, head low, hissing with cold menace. It blocked the entire way forward.

Ben scrambled for his pistol, but his hand came back empty. He had left the gun in the building. Ben backed up a few steps.

Tiny Tim opened its jaws wide and howled at him in triumph.

"Fuck you!" Ben whipped the belt toward the open maw, then spun on his heel and ran for the safety of the building. He risked a glance over his shoulder and saw the beast paw at its mouth, trying to dislodge the belt.

Bastard, you just bit off more than you can chew.

Ben flew through the demolished front door and dived for the hallway. Just as he reached the threshold, the explosion ripped the world apart behind him. The force of the explosion grabbed him and threw him down the hall.

He did his best to roll when he hit, but something snapped as he collided with the hallway floor. Debris rained upon him as he lay sprawled in the hallway. A choking smoke quickly followed.

Jason appeared at his side. "Ben, are you okay?"

In answer, he just groaned.

Harry knelt down. "Let me take a look at him."

Ben pushed to his hands and knees, coughing smoke from his throat. Pain flared at the base of his neck. His shoulder felt dislocated, but he'd live.

Ben glanced up to Jason's concerned face. "When we get out of this, I'm buying you a pair of suspenders. No more belts."

When the explosion occurred, Khalid saw Linda's spirit die. It was in her eyes. She had been fumbling with the last timer, obviously trying not to look at her watch constantly as Jason's time ran low. In her hurry, she had crossed two wires wrong and almost mistakenly activated the detonator. He had been correcting her mistake when the explosion roared from across the base.

As the echo faded around them, Linda just looked at Khalid.

"There just wasn't enough time," Khalid said, though truthfully he'd never intended to rescue the boy. Khalid studied her, expecting her to rage against him, to cry and scream. But no. She just stared at him, a cold deadness in her eyes. A woman who had given up.

Good. He didn't need her to fall apart on him now. She was learning. Expediency. The desert sun burned those who moved slowly. He shook his head. "Let's finish up here."

She turned and stared across the base to the cloud of smoke from the explosion. "It didn't work," she said dully.

He put down the tiny screwdriver. "What?"

She pointed, her arm leaden. "The column . . . Jason was tied to. It's still intact."

He straightened up and stared. She was right. It seemed totally undamaged. How was that possible?

He studied the drifting smoke. Something was wrong. The explosion had occurred slightly west of the column. "The boy must have gotten free of the ropes. Moved away from the column."

His words seemed to ignite a moment of hope in her bearing, but then she sagged, seeming to realize that, free of the column or not, the explosion had occurred.

"Let's go," Khalid ordered.

She didn't argue as she was led away.

THIRTY-FIVE

Ben sat on the leather sofa in Blakely's office, nursing his aching shoulder. He needed to keep moving. This sitting around was making his shoulder throb. Harry had painfully yanked it back in place earlier.

Jason sat next to him now, kicking the sofa with his heel, still tense. The boy had been through a hell of a lot. He had finally related the events that led to Ben's discovery of him.

Sandy sat on a chair behind Blakely's desk, twirling a strand of hair between her fingers. Dark circles were etched beneath her eyes. "Poor Dr. Blakely," she mumbled.

Ben nodded. He regretted all the foul thoughts he had harbored for the leader of this bloody mission. He didn't deserve to die like that.

Harry finally reappeared at the office door. "I've got everything ready, Ben. Let's get movin'."

It was about time. Mo'amba's message of danger still burned fiercely in Ben's mind. This waiting was agonizing, but Harry had insisted that Ben rest for a few minutes while he organized a quicker way for Ben to get back to Ashley. Pushing off the sofa, Ben felt a twinge of protest from his shoulder. "Show me what you're talking about," Ben said, wincing.

"It's just outside the office. C'mon." Harry led the way.

After telling Jason to stay put, Ben followed Harry down the scorched hall. The entrance was demolished, the door hanging askew on its hinges.

Harry waved to the two *mimi'swee* hunters who had led the *crak'an* on a wild-goose chase. They had returned, not even looking tired from the hours of cat-and-mousing. Harry patted his fellow hunters on the shoulders, then proceeded outside.

"I'll leave with the boy just as soon as you take off," Harry said. "We'll take the elevator to safety, but you need to hurry."

"I know. Watch your back, though, and protect that boy. There's still a madman setting other bombs around here, and I don't want Jason falling within his clutches again." Ben saw the shallow crater from the explosion for the first time. Almost two yards in diameter. The surface rock looked burned. He noticed there was no carcass of Tiny Tim. Ben smiled grimly. The beast had probably been blown to tiny pieces. He turned to Harry. "Now what are you hiding up your sleeve?"

Harry wore a shit-eating grin. "Come see." Harry led the way to the side of the building. He pointed proudly. "My masterpiece."

Leaning on the wall was a black motorcycle, trimmed in chrome. Ben whistled in appreciation.

"I retrieved it from my dormitory after reconnoitering the area. Figured it would be a quick way back to the wormhole. This baby will outrace any damned crak'an."

"Bloody grand idea." Ben patted the seat. "Is it gassed and ready?"

"Yep."

"Then let's get the show on the road. I don't know where that damned Khalid is, or what he's planning next, but I don't think we should wait."

"What about the woman he's holding hostage? The biologist?" Harry asked. "Should we look for her?"

Ben closed his eyes and clenched his fists. He pictured Linda's nervous smile. He hated his next words. "No, he said, his voice strained, "it's too risky. For all we know, she may be dead already. Just get that boy to the elevator and out of here."

Harry nodded. "Then let's move."

Within minutes, Harry had everything ready. Ben straddled the bike, a pilfered rifle strapped under his left thigh. His backpack was cleared of everything but the paper-wrapped statue of *ohna*.

One of the *mimi'swee* hunters—Ben couldn't remember his name—reluctantly climbed behind him on the bike.

Sighing, Ben called to Harry and pointed to the tiny hunter. "I can return the statue on my own."

"It's not safe to travel alone. There's sure to be other pods. Now go!"

Jason stood by the side of the bike, obviously nervous about seeing Ben leave.

Ben winked at him. "I'll be back. And it'll be your mom on the back of this hog the next time you see me."

This generated a small smile, but his eyes still had a worried look to them. "Be careful, Ben."

"Always." Ben engaged the throttle, and the bike roared, raising an involuntary smile to his lips. The smile turned to a grimace as the grip of his passenger tightened to the point of cutting off circulation to his lower half. Ben patted the squeezing arm. "Easy there, buddy." The grip loosened . . . but only slightly.

With a final wave, Ben slipped the bike forward, proceeding at a moderate pace. There was too much scattered debris to proceed faster than a man could run. But after a few minutes, getting accustomed to the cycle's handling, he increased his speed, a wide grin on his face. He flew past a field of flattened tents, heading east to detour around the chasm since the bridge was out. He tried his best to ignore some of the human debris on the path. Like roadkill, he thought dourly. His smile faded to a grim line.

Thankfully, within a few minutes he had cleared the base and sped toward the north wall. He breathed deeply the cleaner air, appreciating the abating stench of smoke and rotting flesh.

As he raced toward the distant dwellings, following the rough man-made track, he searched for any sign of the *crak'an* ahead. Nothing. But he was well aware that the darkness beyond his headlamp could hold herds of those monsters.

He held his breath as he sped along, his palms sweaty on the bike's handles. He kept searching, straining to pierce the black curtain around the bike. Something howled from a distance away, but otherwise no sign of the beasts ever appeared. Thankfully, he reached the north wall without encountering a single *crak'an*. Almost too easy.

He cut the engine.

The small hunter was off the bike in a heartbeat, backing away as if from some foul creature. Using his flashlight, Ben grabbed his rifle and followed his agile partner up the levels of dwellings to *ohna's* chamber. The little hunter was first to the chamber, practically flying into its security. Ben followed close behind.

As he reached the entrance to the dwelling, the hunter, just steps ahead of him, suddenly fell back into Ben's arms. What the hell? The hilt of a dagger protruded from his small chest. The hunter stiffened in his arms, then jerked into a violent convulsion. Ben couldn't hold him any longer and dropped him to the ground.

Poison.

Ben flashed his light forward. Two hunched *mimi'swee* tribesmen stood before him, thick with muscle and damned familiar. The *silaris*, the poisoned ones.

Ben backed a step away from the threshold, giving himself room to raise his rifle. Just as he shouldered the weapon, something slammed into the back of his head. He collapsed to his knees, a spray of lights dancing across his vision. He fell forward across the entryway, his rifle falling from limp fingers.

Pain squeezed his vision to a tiny dot. But it was enough to see the scrawny physique of Sin'jari step over him. He wiped Ben's blood from his staff, leaned over, and stared into Ben's eyes. He smiled in triumph as Ben's world faded to black.

"**I'm telling** you," Ashley said, pacing the dimensions of the cell, "that damned Sin'jari meant for everything to happen the way it did. He plotted the whole thing."

Michaelson studied the guards at the threshold to their prison cell. "From the way those guys keep eye-balling us, I don't think they're gonna be in any mood to listen to reason, even if we could speak their tongue."

Ashley glanced over to the four *mimi'swee* guards. "You know what the worst thing about this situation is? It's that these people will always view us as murderers. And I'm to blame. I've been an anthropologist for close to a decade, and this is how I handle first contact with a new tribe."

"Ashley, quit kicking yourself. The situation's extraordinary. And it was Sin'jari that screwed it up. Not you."

Ashley spoke between gritted teeth. "If only there was some damned way to correct it. If we could—"

The sudden prattling of the guards interrupted Ashley's words. She took a step forward to see who the guards were addressing and recognized the scarred face of Tru'gula, the leader of the hunters and a good friend of Mo'amba's. This didn't bode well.

Tru'gula snapped at the guards, his fellow hunters. They moved aside for their elder. He stalked into the chamber, his knuckles white on his staff. Stopping in front of Ashley, he just stared at her, his eyes wounded. He seemed to be weighing her, judging her.

Ashley knew she should not waste this moment. Maybe Tru'gula would listen. She turned to Michaelson and grabbed his shoulders.

"What the—" Michaelson began.

"Hush," she said to him. "I'm gonna try to make him understand. This may be our last chance to win an ally." She turned Michaelson so he faced her. Then she craned her head toward Tru'gula. She pointed to the Major. "Mo'amba." She again grabbed Michaelson's shoulders and repeated, "Mo'amba."

Then she took a step back and pointed to herself. "Sin'jari." She pantomimed his mincing gait and pointed to herself again. "Sin'jari."

Tru'gula just stared blankly at her.

Ashley rolled her eyes but proceeded to imitate Sin'jari. Stepping in front of Michaelson, she pretended to remove a knife from an imaginary scabbard, then pantomimed plunging the knife into Michaelson's chest twice. Then she stepped back and fingered her chest. "Sin'jari!" she said fiercely.

Tru'gula's eyes narrowed, his wounded face tightening with rage.

Ashley stepped away. Did he understand? If he did, did he believe her? She had just accused one of his fellow elders.

"Sin'jari," Tru'gula hissed. "Sin'jari!" He stepped toward Ashley.

She resisted the urge to step away, knowing instinctively that she needed to stand her ground, to proclaim the truth. She stared him in the eyes, never flinching, as he stopped toe-to-toe with her.

He stared for what seemed like several minutes, then spoke, obviously struggling with his words. He pointed to his head. "Mo'amba . . . wise." He grabbed Ashley's shoulder. "Mo'amba . . . trust . . . you."

She nodded, encouraging him.

"Harry's obviously been working with him," Michaelson mumbled.

The leader of the hunters turned to the Major. "Blood brother." He clenched his arms around his chest. "Trust." He then turned back to Ashley. "Tru'gula . . . Tru'gula . . . trust . . . you."

Did she hear right? Understand correctly? He believed her! In her relief, she reached over and hugged Tru'gula, tears coming to her eyes.

Tru'gula broke free of her embrace. "Dan . . . ger. Here. Go! Now!" Tru'gula tried to tug her toward the entrance.

"Wait." She resisted, pulling her arm free of his grip. "If you trust us, then you could tell the others. There's no need to run."

He just stared back at her in confusion. He didn't understand. He glanced at the doorway, then back at her. He sighed in frustration. "Tru'gula . . . trust you." He waved as if to encompass the entire village around them. "No trust."

Ashley realized he meant to help them escape from here. To run from her accusers. He didn't believe her innocence would be accepted by his people. The villagers were too suspicious of the strangers.

"Go. Now." Tru'gula repeated.

Ashley stood still. "No."

Michaelson stepped next to her. "I think we'd better accept his help."

"If I run, it'll be as good as admitting my guilt. I can't leave these people thinking we're just cold-blooded murderers."

"But Ashley. The risk."

She shook her head. "You mentioned a plan earlier. A way to prove my innocence. I thought it was a pipe dream. But with Tru'gula's help it might work."

"Might? Those are long odds when you're gambling with all our lives."

She stared him in the eyes. "I have to try."

Linda's legs felt heavy. She stumbled after Khalid, on autopilot, one leg following the other. She stared at Khalid's back as he weaved his way toward the distant elevator. She knew she should hate him, despise him.

But she was numb.

She had failed Jason. She had promised him she'd be back. She pictured his eyes as she bound him to the column. He had known he was going to die. Somehow she should have been able to stop it, but her fear had broken her. Fear of Khalid. Fear of death. Through her own inaction, she had sealed his fate.

A single tear rolled down her cheek.

Fear had always ruled her life. Whether it was her cloying claustrophobia or some other anxiety, fear had been her constant companion. Finally, her crippling weakness had resulted in the death of a boy.

With Jason's death, her fear was vanquished. Now all she had left was her guilt.

Khalid had stopped ahead. "Listen. Do you hear something?"

Linda heard nothing. She didn't answer him, finding words too difficult to form.

Khalid pointed. "There!"

Linda looked to where he pointed. Across the length of a football field, spotlights still speared the darkness above, highlighting the towering elevator shaft. Something moved up there. It was an elevator cage, descending toward the floor. Someone was coming.

As she watched, she could make out rifles and other weapons bristling through the bars of the cage, like some armed porcupine. Reinforcements were arriving.

Khalid's eyes narrowed to black slits. "So damn close. Just a few more minutes."

Linda allowed a smile to come to her lips, enjoying Khalid's consternation. "I guess you're not leaving that way."

Khalid glared at her, slipped out of his backpack, and began rummaging through it. He removed a transmitter from his pack. It was different from the one that controlled the bombs she had helped set.

"What're you doing?"

"Get down." He raised the transmitter and pressed the button. A green light flashed on the device. Khalid grabbed her in his arms and leaped behind a partially collapsed building. An explosion rocketed from ahead of them, blowing debris and smoke their way.

After the worst of the smoke billowed past them, Khalid climbed off of her and checked his handiwork. She followed to see what he had done.

A smoldering crater now existed where the supports for the elevator had stood. She stared up. Only one spotlight was still intact, illuminating the ghastly scene. In slow motion, she saw the remainder of the tower start to collapse. The cage hurtled toward the cavern floor, uncontrolled. Even with her ears echoing with the blast, she could hear the screaming.

She swung back behind the damaged wall, closing her eyes. For what seemed like years, she waited. Then she heard it. The booming crash as the cage hit the floor. She listened. The screaming had stopped.

Khalid stepped next to her. He lit a cigarette, his hand trembling slightly. "I'm glad I set those explosives the night before the team set out. I knew from the start this mission might end this way. But I thought with planning . . . ." He shrugged.

"What are we going to do now? We can't leave."

He puffed a cloud of smoke toward the distant roof. "I must try to contact my superiors, apprise them of the situation. We can try Blakely's communications center. See if I can raise anyone."

"Then what?"

He shrugged. "Then we die."

THIRTY-SIX

That bloody Sin'jari! It all came back in a flood. Ben pushed himself up, wincing. The back of his head throbbed with every movement. The echoes of the explosion that jarred him back to consciousness still reverberated across the cavern.

Groaning, Ben stood shakily. He peered back toward the distant glowing base. What happened? But he knew the answer: Khalid.

Should he head back to the base? Harry and the others could be in trouble. Fingering the tender spot at the back of his head, he glanced at his watch. Time was running out. He had been knocked out for almost an hour. He needed to get to Ashley. Free her.

First, though, he had to know what was going on. He sat on the floor of the cave and closed his eyes, letting his mind drift. He pictured Nob'cobi and called to him.

The answer was almost immediate. Nob'cobi's image coalesced out of the darkness. His facial whiskers were burned.

"What happened?" Ben said. "Is Jason okay?"

Nob'cobi nodded, out of breath. "Cage thing destroyed. Harry and my brother went to look for your enemy, to try to stop him. I took the boy and woman to the office place. They're safe. I'll guard them. Harry says you must hurry."

"I know."

"Bring help!"

Ben broke contact and pushed to his feet. He needed to get that statue back before . . . Bloody hell! He realized something was missing. His rifle still lay on the floor where he had dropped it. He patted his back and searched the tiny chamber. His pack was gone. And so was the statue it contained.

Sin'jari!

The bastard hadn't finished him off because he'd found what he needed to thwart the mission. Without the statue, Ashley would die.

Sneaky little bugger. Ben stared around the chamber, his eye settling on the aluminum transport sled with the diamond axle. He grabbed a knife from his belt and sliced the train of plastic sleds still attached to the gas-powered sled. Maybe . . . ?

Ashley could tell Tru'gula was perturbed by her demands, but he had finally acquiesced and agreed to bring her and Michaelson to *umbo*'s chamber. To reach the chamber, Tru'gula had to elbow the other hunters out of his way, several of whom gave their leader a look as if he had gone mad. He managed through bullying and what sounded like threats to gain them access.

Michaelson paced the room, eyeing the male statue of *umbo* with a mild look of distaste on his features. "It's only a guess," he said. "I don't like that you're putting your life in jeopardy based on my supposition."

"Your reasoning's sound. Sin'jari will surely try to make it back to the village through here. We just need to wait for him. Confront him."

"What if he's already back?"

She sighed. "I don't think he is. He would've made himself known. His voice would be raised loudly against us by now." Ashley glanced around the small chamber. It seemed crowded with the six *mimi'swee* guards and Tru'gula. Other hunters guarded the way here, but eventually word would spread and others would come and investigate. She just hoped they could capture Sin'jari before a circus erupted. A crowd could get ugly before she could prove her innocence.

As if confirming her thoughts, a commotion could be heard brewing out in the tunnel. Voices were raised. Suddenly an explosion of bodies burst into the chamber. Several figures, still wrestling, rolled into the room.

Michaelson yanked her behind him. Even Tru'gula stepped in front of her, blocking the way to her.

She watched as the hunters tangled with other, puglike *mimi'swee,* but the few hunters were quickly overwhelmed by the score of attackers. And to make matters worse, a single jab by an attacker's spear or dagger sent the mildly injured into convulsions.

Soon only she, Michaelson, and Tru'gula were still standing. At least ten of the short, muscular attackers surrounded them.

"Silaris!" Tru'gula said, and spat in their direction.

The offenders made no move toward them, seeming nervous about attacking one of the elders.

A noise behind them drew everyone's attention to the wormhole. As she watched, Sin'jari slipped out of the tunnel, followed by two ugly *mimi'swee.* Ashley recognized them as the two who were with Sin'jari before. She also recognized the resemblance between them and the attackers blocking the exit. They were Sin'jari's men, his clan.

Sin'jari smiled, showing all his teeth. He didn't have to say a word. He just fingered a dagger and stepped toward Ashley.

Groaning, Ashley realized she'd led them all into a trap.

Ben willed Harry's sled to faster speeds, the rock walls a blur around him. Going downhill with the throttle fully open had increased the speed to fifty miles an hour. On turns, he banked to the ceiling.

He squinted forward, needing to pay close attention, ready to brake as soon as he saw the exit. To fly out of the wormhole at this speed was certain death. He shifted the rifle from under his hip where it chafed.

C'mon, the exit shouldn't be too far ahead, he thought. Maybe if he concentrated, used his *heri'huti* powers, he'd get an inkling of how far he had to go.

He relaxed his eyes and willed his heart to slow. Even before he'd achieved the proper state, someone reached him. *Someone was calling to him.* An image coalesced in front of him, superimposed over the sight ahead like some wispy ghost. A scarred face. Tru'gula.

The figure blinked a few times, then spoke. "Hurry!"

"I know. I got that message already," Ben said.

"Then see with my eyes."

For just a few seconds, the tunnel vanished and he was in *umbo*'s chamber. He saw. Gasping, his heart clenched, and the link shattered.

Ben prayed for more speed, rage fueling him forward.

Michaelson tried to block Sin'jari's approach toward Ashley, but a quick flip of the elder's wrist had five of the *silaris* dragging him back.

Ashley glanced over to Tru'gula. He struggled futilely in the clutches of two of the *silaris*. No aid there either.

Sin'jari stepped toward her. "He no help. He weak."

Ashley was flabbergasted at his words. "You speak English."

He nodded. "I learn my enemy. Best way—" He scrunched his brows together, pondering his next words.

"To know them," she offered.

He smiled at her as if she were a small child. "No. To kill them."

Raising the dagger to her chin, he leered at her. "Poison. That right word?" He motioned toward the dead hunters.

She nodded.

He pricked his own finger. Then waved as if it were nothing. "I lead *silaris*. Poison not kill us. We strong. We lead."

"What about Bo'rada? I thought he was your leader."

"Bo'rada?" He made a foul sound with his mouth. "No smart. I lead Bo'rada."

Ashley realized that this coup had been in the works long before her team appeared. Their arrival had almost screwed up Sin'jari's plan, but he'd turned it to his own ends.

"Now I lead. I say kill all you. And any others come here."

Ashley shook her head. "You won't win this. Tru'gula's hunters won't allow it."

A sly look came to his eyes. He pointed to Tru'gula. "Bad. He help you others kill Mo'amba." He then tapped his chest with the dagger. "I find out." He slashed the dagger through the air. "I stop."

So Tru'gula was going to be pinned as an accessory to the crime, a coconspirator. Dead men tell no tales. She glanced at him, but his eyes were half closed.

Sin'jari noticed it too. He poked the wounded hunter with a finger, getting his attention. They spoke back and forth for a few minutes. Angry words. Finally, Sin'jari turned his back on him and faced Ashley again.

He pointed a thumb toward Tru'gula. "No smart. He call help. But nobody there. Mo'amba dead." He sneered at her. "Now you."

He raised the poisoned dagger and stepped toward her. She tried to back away but was blocked by the *silaris* behind her.

Just as Sin'jari grabbed Ashley's throat with a bony hand, a noise erupted from the wormhole. Sin'jari twisted his neck around to look.

Ashley jumped as the transport sled blasted out of the wormhole and flew across the chamber, colliding into several of the *silaris,* knocking them off their feet.

The distraction was enough to allow Ben to crawl from the wormhole. He was standing before anyone was even aware he had appeared. He raised the rifle to his shoulder and pointed it at Sin'jari. "Mate, I suggest you let the lady go."

Sin'jari hissed at him and plunged the dagger toward her chest.

Ben fired.

Ashley saw the left side of Sin'jari's head fly away. His body stood there for half a second, dagger still poised, then crumpled to the floor.

A couple *silaris* rushed toward Ben. He swung his rifle, and in two shots, two bodies lay on the floor. "Any others?"

Suddenly, from behind the group of *silaris*, as if by magic, a troop of hunters appeared, bristling with long spears.

"Meet a few of my friends," Ben said with a smile. "I placed a quick call before arriving. This bloody *heri'huti* means of communication could put the phone company out of business."

The *silaris*, without their leader, put up little fight and were roughly herded away.

Ashley rushed over to Ben and wrapped him in her arms. "You're okay. I didn't know . . . didn't know what Sin'jari had done up there." She squeezed him and, muffled against his chest, said the words she had held so long in her chest. "I love you."

"Ay? What was that?" he said, pulling back to look her square in the face.

"I . . . I love you."

He slipped back into her embrace. "Oh, that. I knew you did. I was just wondering when you'd figure it out."

"Shut up." She reached up and kissed him.

Ben then moved his lips to her ear. "You know, there's someone up top who's waiting for a big hug and kiss too."

She pulled back from him, her hands clenched on his shoulders. "Do you mean—"

He nodded. "Jason's fine. Just a bit shook up like the rest of us."

Tears blurred her vision as Ben smiled down at her. He then pulled her into a tight embrace. In his arms, she felt the strength of family she'd never experienced before.

Still in his arms, Ashley watched Bo'rada stalk into the chamber, confusion evident on his features. Crossing to the scarred figure, he spoke heatedly to Tru'gula, who answered with repeated gestures. Bo'rada's eyes grew wide.

"I leave you for a second," Ben whispered, "and see how much trouble you get into."

Once Tru'gula finished, the leader stared with disgust at Sin'jari's body, then turned to Ashley and Ben. He bent his head solemnly in their direction. As apology or thanks, she wasn't sure.

Ben broke free of her embrace. "I forgot." He crossed to Sin'jari's body and fingered open the pouch on the dead man's belt. He reached inside and pulled out the diamond statue.

"*Ohna!*" Ben held the figure up for all to see, then crossed over and placed the female statue on the pedestal next to the male figure. "They make a nice couple, don't you think?"

THIRTY-SEVEN

Jason sat on a soiled chair in the demolished reception room of Blakely's office. He had his cracked Nintendo Game Boy in his lap and was trying to tape it together. Harry and his companion creatures were outside somewhere, patrolling, keeping an eye on things. Ever since the explosion of the elevator, Harry wanted the area watched closely.

Jason knew he was supposed to stay with Sandy back in Blakely's office, but she was giving him the creeps. All she did was stare off into space, fiddling with her hair. She didn't even say a word when he got up.

He thought about how Ben had saved him, and hoped desperately that he would return soon with his mom.

Then a soft *scritch-scritch*ing noise from outside froze him in the chair. It was probably Harry or one of the others. Wasn't it? The noise came again. It sounded like a bunch of boards was being shifted around.

He quietly stood up and took a step toward the hallway, toward safety. When he heard the noise once more, his curiosity got the better of him. He took a step toward the decimated entrance to the building.

He'd just take a peek. It might be important, or nothing at all.

Holding his breath to avoid any detection of his position, he snuck around an overturned desk to get a clear view out the building.

He stared, waiting for the sound to repeat so he could tell where it was coming from, afraid even to blink in case he should miss something. Nothing was out there besides the crater from the explosion and piles of debris strewn around the edge by the blast. Nothing moved.

He started to straighten from where he crouched. Probably just—

Then he heard and saw it at the same time. A muzzle, protruding from under a pile of tumbled lumber and bricks, about twenty yards away. It was easy to miss, camouflaged well with the black rock and scorched debris. If it hadn't moved, he'd have overlooked it.

It moved again, shifting the debris until a black eye swung clear. It seemed to be staring straight at him. Jason knew it was the beast who'd been sniffing him when he was tied up. The one Ben called Tiny Tim. Jason froze, afraid to draw its attention further.

He watched as it dropped its head back to the floor, obviously still dazed, groggy, recovering from the explosion. Jason needed to warn someone that it had survived.

Then a new sound intruded.

A voice. A familiar voice. Female. Crying.

He watched as Linda ran into view, her eyes glued to the crater. Her face was smudged, her hair in stringy tangles. Tears swelled in her eyes.

Khalid stepped into view behind her, smoking a cigarette. "It's done," he heard Khalid say. "The boy's gone."

Linda stumbled to the crater's far edge and began walking around it. Jason realized she was going to cross within a yard of the buried monster.

Jason dashed from the building and ran to the crater's edge. He called across the hole to her. "Linda! Get back! Run!"

Linda jumped at the sight of him, her hands fluttering around her cheeks like scared birds. "Jason?" His words and sudden appearance seemed to shock her. Her foot slipped, and she tripped into the crater.

"Watch out!"

With a roar, the beast reacted, erupting from the pile of debris like some bloody jack-in-the-box. It reared up. A white bone protruded from its side where its arm had been. Its entire flank was charred. It lunged at Linda, who cowered on the crater floor.

"No!" Jason screamed.

Khalid reacted first, in panic, firing madly at the beast. The beast swung toward Khalid, drawn by the noise of the gun. Yelling, Khalid pawed at his pocket, his eyes so wide they bulged. He barely seemed to react when the monster snatched him up. Only a weak groan escaped his lips as he was yanked upward, his waist trapped in the beast's jaws.

The man's weight, however, proved too much for the beast in its weakened state. It collapsed back into the pile of debris with a crash, still clutching Khalid in its jaws.

Linda scuttled on her hands and knees to the far side of the crater, her face a mask of horror as the beast crept away, dragging the Egyptian with it.

Khalid thrashed in its teeth, his arms still free. He had the pistol in his hand but wasn't using it. Instead he was trying to free something from his pocket.

With a fierce yank and a yell of triumph, blood flowing from his lips, he pulled his hand free. Jason recognized the object. Khalid had showed it to him before. A radio transmitter for setting off bombs.

Linda spotted it too. "Don't!" she screamed.

Khalid smiled painfully. Blood flowed freely from his lips. He raised his hand.

"No!" Linda screamed.

Before Khalid could press the detonator, the monster spasmed, jarring Khalid and knocking the transmitter from his hands. It bounced a few feet away.

Khalid scrabbled for the device; it was just out of reach. Jason watched as the creature, weakening, went limp. Khalid's eyes squinted in agony as he struggled to inch himself from the clenched jaws and reach the transmitter. His fingers brushed the edge of the device on his second attempt.

Jason did not wait. He dashed forward.

Linda called. "Get back!"

He ignored her and snatched the transmitter seconds before Khalid's hand reached the same spot. Khalid swore at him, bloody spittle flying from his mouth. Jason danced back.

"Give it to me, boy!"

"No." Jason backed another step away, out of Khalid's reach.

"Then die." Khalid raised his other hand, the pistol still in his grip. Almost point-blank range.

The last thing Jason saw was the flash of muzzle fire.

Ashley stood and stretched her legs in *ohna*'s chamber. She gave Harry's aluminum transport a kick with her toe. Four hours riding piggyback on top of Ben from the *mimi'swee* village! She worked a kink out of her lower back with a knuckle. Damn!

"C'mon," Ben called from outside. "It's clear. Let's go."

Ashley crawled from the tiny chamber into Alpha Cavern. She had wondered if she would ever see this place again. Bone-tired, she smiled. Finally!

However, when she spotted the means of transport from here, her smile sank. "A motorcycle?" Ashley clambered down the cliff to Ben.

"I have to hand it to Harry," he said. "He builds mean machines."

She nodded, climbing behind Ben on the cycle. It was unfortunate that Harry's brother, Dennis, had to be left back with the *mimi'swee*, but his injured ankle compromised their speed. He was coming up with the band of *mimi'swee* hunters, on foot. "I don't care if we have to get there by mule," she said. "I need to see Jason."

"I know. It's bugging me that I can't reach Nob'cobi. Hang on." Within moments, they were racing through darkness toward the distant glow of the base.

Ashley pressed herself against Ben's back, leaning her cheek on his shoulder. She hugged him tighter. She could almost hear his heartbeat.

"Keep an eye out for any of those *crak'an*," Ben yelled above the engine noise. "Those nasties are creeping all over the cavern."

"You just keep this bike aiming straight toward the base. I don't care what gets in the way. Run over it."

She watched the surroundings for any flash of movement as they traveled. Nothing but darkness. Soon the blackness faded to a dusky twilight as they approached the base. As night was beaten back by the camp lights, a growing stench filled the air.

She crinkled her nose. "My god."

"You'll get used to it."

She prayed she never would. When Ashley saw the devastation and destruction, she closed her eyes. How did Jason survive this?

"Almost there," Ben shouted.

Suddenly, to the right, a reptilian head sprang up behind an overturned car, its muzzle bloody. Ben saw it and gunned the bike. The cycle shot forward, leaving the beast bellowing far behind.

"Over there," Ben said finally, pointing.

She had already recognized it. Though scarred with burns, Blakely's office still stood intact. Ben slowed the bike to a crawl and edged around a corner of the building.

The sight that came into view stopped Ashley's heart cold.

No! She flew off the cycle. The hulking carcass of one of the predators lay sprawled just yards from the building. Khalid lay limp in its jaws, his pallor pale, his eyes staring blindly upward.

This was not the sight that had panicked her. Harry was hunched over a small figure that lay twisted on the rock.

No, she prayed, not after so much.

Ben caught up to her, pulling her back. "Wait," he said.

She resisted his restraint, pushing his arm away. She crossed over to Harry. Standing up, he moved aside for her. Ben stood next to her.

"It's not Jason, Ash," Ben said, placing a hand on her shoulder. "That's what I was trying to tell you. I knew from your face what you were thinking."

She stared down at the dead *mimi'swee* hunter, a bullet hole in his chest. "Who is it?"

Ben knelt down next to the dead man, placing his hand on his shoulder. "No wonder I couldn't reach him. It's Nob'cobi." Ben lifted his eyes to Harry. "What happened?"

With tears threatening, Harry explained, "I'd gone to check for survivors from the elevator explosion. The *mimi'swee* were left to guard the building. While I was away, Khalid and Linda returned." He continued to relate how the *crak'an* attacked and how Khalid attempted to blow the place up as a final act before he died. "The hunters were watching, waiting for the best time to intervene. When Jason grabbed the transmitter, Khalid tried to kill him. But Nob'cobi knocked the boy to the side and took the bullet instead."

Ashley knelt next to Ben. "He saved my boy's life."

"Yes," Harry said. "Jason got a good knock on the head. Blacked out for a few seconds, but he's fine. Linda took him—"

"Mom!"

Ashley whirled to face the building. Jason stood in the blasted opening, a bandage wrapped over his forehead. "Jason!"

She stood up and ran to him. They collapsed into each other's arms. "Oh, honey, I'm so sorry." She hugged him hard to her chest.

"I love you, Mom."

She just held him, rocking him in her arms.

Ben pointed to the large carcass. "I thought I had killed that bloody beast."

"Apparently it had a hide as thick as yours," Harry said.

Linda then stepped through the doorway, a smile on her face. Jason saw her and wiggled out of Ashley's arms. He wiped at his nose and straightened his bandage, obviously embarrassed at such a childish display of motherly attention.

Ashley smiled. Was he already that old?

Harry suddenly called out, "Look!" He jabbed a finger toward the roof.

She stood up and joined the others, staring at where Harry pointed.

Lights, pirouetting downward.

In the feeble glow of a few remaining spotlights, ballooning parachutes drifted downward. As she watched, more and more chutes flared open from the top of the skeletal elevator shaft. The chutists each had a halogen light, which they waved to and fro as they descended. Within minutes there seemed to be hundreds of them, drifting in all directions to cover the entire base.

Like fireflies on a warm spring night.

"Who are they?" Jason asked.

"I believe that's the cavalry coming over the hill," Harry said.

Ben snorted. "About bloody time!"

Epilogue

Mount Erebus, Antarctica

Ben crawled into bed, sighing. What a day! He snuggled next to Ashley. She moaned in her sleep and rolled onto her side. He placed his hand on her belly. She was already showing. Four months along, and not a sign that she was ready to cut back on her cultural study of the *mimi'swee*. Knowing her, she would wait until her water broke before finally putting pen and paper down.

He smiled in the darkness and lay back with an arm propping his head, staring at the ceiling. Alpha Base had almost been put back together again. The sonic repellents that Linda had developed were succeeding in keeping the *crak'an* away. Her team of biologists had also made another discovery: The erosion of the *mimi'swee*'s ring of protective fungus had not been due to the imbalance of *umbo* and *ohna*, as Mo'amba had claimed, but rather to the introduction of and competition from a modern fungus, carried here by humans. So Sin'jari had been right after all—humans *were* to blame. At least indirectly.

Ben let out a rattling sigh and stretched, bone-tired. As *heri'huti*, his responsibilities with the tribe seemed endless. No wonder Mo'amba had wanted to pass the baton on to him. Still, in memory of the old man, he felt an obligation to carry on the position. At least until the tiny *mimi'swee* offspring gifted with *heri'huti* blood grew to maturity. Ben had overseen the hatching of the child, another of his duties. The child, who had been named Tu'shama by Mo'amba before his death, was a girl, the first female *heri'huti* of the tribe. Her gender had shocked the community, but Ben didn't care. Male or female, here was his replacement!

Ben wiggled deeper under the blankets. He really shouldn't complain. The job did have its perks. In his spare time, he could explore the vast trails of caverns. The hunters who traveled the dark paths showed him sights so wondrous that he sometimes thought he was dreaming.

Even if it was while collecting *crak'an* dung.

Ben closed his eyes. Morning would come too soon. He rolled onto his side and wrapped an arm around Ashley's waist.

As he drifted into slumber, something touched his dreams. Weak and tentative. Someone calling to him.

He opened himself up, inviting, but the contact faded. Only a passing connection, like a warm breeze wafting across a cold cheek.

Then nothing.

Who?

Under his hand, he felt the baby move in Ashley's belly. And Ben remembered Mo'amba's words: "Blood runs true."

THE NEW LUXURY IN READING

We hope you enjoyed reading
our new, comfortable print size and found it
an experience you would like to repeat.

Well – you're in luck!

HarperLuxe offers the finest in fiction and
nonfiction books in this same larger print size and
paperback format. Light and easy to read, HarperLuxe
paperbacks are for book lovers who want to see
what they are reading without the strain.

For a full listing of titles and
new releases to come, please visit our website:

www.HarperLuxe.com